ARMAGEDDON

The beast I am seeking seeks me out in turn. Huge, towering above its lesser kin, packed with unnatural muscle around its malformed bones and reeking of the fungal blood that fuels its foul heart. It launches itself onto the tank's hull, perhaps expecting some titanic duel to impress its tribe. A champion, perhaps. A chieftain. It matters not. The brutes' leaders rarely resist the chance to engage Imperial commanders in full view – they are loathsomely predictable.

There is no time for sport. My first strike is my last, hammering through its guard, shattering its crossed axes and pounding the aquila head of my crozius into its roaring face.

It topples from the Baneblade, all loose limbs and worthless armour, as pathetic in death as it had been in life.

WAR OF THE FANG
Includes the novel *Battle of the Fang* and the novella 'The Hunt for Magnus', featuring the Space Wolves
Chris Wraight

THE WORLD ENGINE
A novel featuring the Astral Knights
Ben Counter

DAMOCLES
Includes the novellas 'Blood Oath', 'Broken Sword', 'Black Leviathan' and 'Hunter's Snare', featuring the White Scars, Raven Guard and Ultramarines
Phil Kelly, Guy Haley, Ben Counter and Josh Reynolds

SONS OF WRATH
A novella featuring the Flesh Tearers
Andy Smillie

FLESH OF CRETACIA
A novella featuring the Flesh Tearers
Andy Smillie

PANDORAX
A novel featuring the Dark Angels and Grey Knights
C Z Dunn

THE WAR FOR RYNN'S WORLD
Includes the novel *Rynn's World* and the novella 'Traitor's Gorge', featuring the Crimson Fists
Steve Parker and *Mike Lee*

OVERFIEND
Includes the novellas 'Stormseer', 'Shadow Captain' and 'Forgemaster', featuring the White Scars, Raven Guard and Salamanders
David Annandale

CATECHISM OF HATE
A novella featuring the Ultramarines
Gav Thorpe

MALODRAX
A novel featuring the Imperial Fists
Ben Counter

VISIONS OF WAR
The Space Marine Battles artbook

A WARHAMMER 40,000 NOVEL

ARMAGEDDON

HELSREACH • BLOOD AND FIRE

AARON DEMBSKI-BOWDEN

BLACK LIBRARY

For my granddad – the apotheosis of all granddads – who died mere months before getting to see the book dedicated to him. This could be my fault for not writing fast enough, but we'll blame his fourth (!) heart attack instead.

I miss you, granddad. I hope the day comes when thinking about you makes me smile without the threat of tears.

A BLACK LIBRARY PUBLICATION

Helsreach copyright © 2010, Games Workshop Ltd.
Blood and Fire copyright © 2013, Games Workshop Ltd.

Hardback edition published 2013.
This edition published in Great Britain in 2015 by
Black Library,
Games Workshop Ltd.,
Willow Road,
Nottingham, NG7 2WS, UK.

10 9 8 7 6 5 4 3 2 1

Cover illustration by Kai Lim of Imaginary Friends Studios.
Internal artwork by Sam Lamont.

A CIP record for this book is available from the British Library.

UK ISBN 13: 978 1 84970 987 3
US ISBN 13: 978 1 84970 964 4

See Black Library on the internet at
blacklibrary.com

Find out more about Games Workshop
and the world of Warhammer 40,000 at
games-workshop.com

Printed and bound by CPI Group (UK) Ltd, Croydon, CR0 4YY

It is the 41st millennium. For more than a hundred centuries the Emperor has sat immobile on the Golden Throne of Earth. He is the master of mankind by the will of the gods, and master of a million worlds by the might of his inexhaustible armies. He is a rotting carcass writhing invisibly with power from the Dark Age of Technology. He is the Carrion Lord of the Imperium for whom a thousand souls are sacrificed every day, so that he may never truly die.

Yet even in his deathless state, the Emperor continues his eternal vigilance. Mighty battlefleets cross the daemon-infested miasma of the warp, the only route between distant stars, their way lit by the Astronomican, the psychic manifestation of the Emperor's will. Vast armies give battle in His name on uncounted worlds. Greatest amongst his soldiers are the Adeptus Astartes, the Space Marines, bio-engineered super-warriors. Their comrades in arms are legion: the Astra Militarium and countless planetary defence forces, the ever-vigilant Inquisition and the tech-priests of the Adeptus Mechanicus to name only a few. But for all their multitudes, they are barely enough to hold off the ever-present threat from aliens, heretics, mutants — and worse.

To be a man in such times is to be one amongst untold billions. It is to live in the cruellest and most bloody regime imaginable. These are the tales of those times. Forget the power of technology and science, for so much has been forgotten, never to be re-learned. Forget the promise of progress and understanding, for in the grim dark future there is only war. There is no peace amongst the stars, only an eternity of carnage and slaughter, and the laughter of thirsting gods.

But the universe is a big place and, whatever happens, you will not be missed...

CONTENTS

HELSREACH

PART ONE
THE EXILED KNIGHT

PROLOGUE
KNIGHT OF THE INNER CIRCLE

I WILL DIE on this world.

I cannot tell where this conviction comes from. Whatever birthed it is a mystery to me, and yet the thought clings like a virus, blooming behind my eyes and taking deep root within my mind. It almost feels real enough to spread corruption to the rest of my body, like a true sickness.

It will happen soon, within the coming nights of blood and fire. I will draw my last breath, and when my brothers return to the stars, my ashes will be scattered over the priceless earth of this accursed world.

Armageddon.

Even the name twists my blood until burning oil beats through my veins. I feel anger now, hot and heavy, flowing through my heart and filtering into my limbs like boiling poison.

When the sensation – and it is a physical sensation – reaches my fingertips, my hands curl into fists. I do not make them adopt this shape, it simply happens. Fury is as natural to me as breathing. I neither fear nor resent its influence on my actions.

I am strong, born only to slay for the Emperor and the Imperium. I am pure, wearing the blackest of the black, trained to serve as a spiritual guide as well as a warleader. I am wrath incarnate, living only to kill until finally killed.

I am a weapon in the Eternal Crusade to forge humanity's mastership of the stars.

Yet strength, purity and wrath will not be enough. I will die on this world. I will die on Armageddon.

Soon, my brothers will ask me to consecrate the war that will be my death.

The thought plagues me not because I fear death, but because a futile death is anathema to me.

But this is no night to think such things. My lords, masters and brothers have gathered to honour me.

I am not sure I deserve this, but as with my sick sense of foreboding, this is a thought I keep to myself. I wear the black, and glare from behind the skulled visage of the immortal Emperor. It is not for one such as I to show doubt, to show weakness, to show even the whispering edges of blasphemy.

In the holiest chamber of our ancient flagship, I lower myself to one knee and bow my head, because this is what is asked of me. The time has come after a century and a half, and I wish it had not.

My mentor – the warrior who was my brother, father, teacher and master – is dead. After one hundred and sixty-six years of his guidance, I am on the edge of inheriting his mantle.

These are my thoughts as I kneel before my commanders,

this bleak mesh of my master's death and my own yet to come. This is the blackness that festers unspoken.

At last, unaware of my secret torments, the High Marshal speaks my name.

'GRIMALDUS,' HIGH MARSHAL Helbrecht intoned. His voice was a guttural rumble, rendered harsh from yelling orders and battle cries in a hundred wars on a hundred worlds.

Grimaldus did not raise his head. The knight closed his disquietingly gentle eyes, as if this gesture could seal the doubts within his skull.

'Yes, my liege.'

'We have brought you here to honour you, just as you have honoured us for so many years.'

Grimaldus said nothing, sensing it was not his time to speak. He knew why they were honouring him now, of course, and the knowledge was bitter. Mordred – Grimaldus's mentor, a Reclusiarch of the Eternal Crusade – was dead.

After the ritual, Grimaldus would take his place.

It was an honour he had waited one hundred and sixty-six years to receive.

A century and a half of wrath, courage and pain since the Battle of Fire and Blood, when he drew the eye of the revered Mordred – who was already ancient but unbowed, and who saw within the young Grimaldus a burning core of potential.

A century and a half since he was inducted into the lowest ranks of the Chaplain brotherhood, rising through the tiers in his master's shadow, knowing that he was being forged in war to replace his ageing guardian.

Over a century and a half of believing he would not deserve the title when it finally rested upon his shoulders.

Now the time had come, and his conviction had not changed.

'We have summoned you,' Helbrecht said, 'to be judged.'

'I have answered the summons,' Grimaldus said in the silence of the Reclusiam. 'I submit myself before your judgement, my liege.'

Helbrecht wore no armour, but his bulk was barely diminished. Clad in layered robes of bone-white and bearing his personal black heraldry, the High Marshal stood in the Temple of Dorn, his hands clutching an ornate helm with all due respect.

'Mordred is dead,' Helbrecht's voice was a deep murmur. 'Slain by the archenemy. You, Grimaldus, have lost a master. We have all of us lost a brother.'

The Temple of Dorn, a museum, a Reclusiam, a sanctuary of hanging banners from ten thousand years of crusading, briefly came alive as the knights in the shadows intoned their agreement with their liege lord's words.

Silence returned, and Grimaldus kept his gaze on the floor.

'We mourn his loss,' the High Marshal said, 'but honour his wisdom in this, his final order.'

It comes to this. Grimaldus tensed. *Show no weakness. Show no doubt.*

'Grimaldus, warrior-priest of the Eternal Crusade. It was the belief of Reclusiarch Mordred that upon his death, you would be worthiest of our Brother-Chaplains to stand in his stead. His final decree before the returning of his gene-seed to the Chapter was that you, of all your brethren, would be the one to rise to the rank of Reclusiarch.'

Grimaldus opened his eyes and licked lips that had suddenly turned dry. Slowly he raised his head, facing the High

Marshal, seeing Mordred's helm – a grinning steel skull – in the commander's scarred hands.

'Grimaldus,' Helbrecht spoke again, no hint of emotion colouring his voice. 'You are a veteran in your own right, and once stood as the youngest Sword Brother in the history of the Black Templars. As a Chaplain, your life has been without cowardice or shame, your ferocity and faith without equal. It is my belief, not merely the wish of your fallen master, that you should take the honour we offer you now.'

Grimaldus nodded, but uttered no words. His eyes, so deceptively soft in their gaze, did not waver from their stare. The helm's slanted eye lenses were the rich, deep red of arterial blood. The death mask was utterly familiar to him – the face of his master when the knights went to war, making it the face of his master for most of his life.

Its skullish visage smiled.

'Rise, if you would refuse this honour,' Helbrecht finished. 'Rise and walk from this sacred chamber, if you wish no place in the hierarchy of our most noble Chapter.'

HE TELLS ME to rise if I want to turn my back on the great honour being offered to me. Leave if I wish no place among the commanders of the Eternal Crusade.

I don't move. Despite my doubts, my muscles remain locked. The steel mask sneers, a dark leer that is soothing for its brutal familiarity. From beyond the grave, Mordred grins at me.

He believed I was worthy of this. That is all that matters. I had never known him to be wrong.

I feel the edge of a smile creeping across my own lips. It will not fade, no matter how I try to quell it. As I kneel in this hallowed hall, I know I'm smiling, but it's a private moment despite the dozens of fellow warriors watching from the banner-lined walls.

Perhaps they mistake my smile for confidence?

I will never ask, because I do not care.

Helbrecht approaches at last, and with the silken rasp of steel stroking steel, he draws the holiest blade in the Imperium of Man.

THE SWORD WAS as ancient as human relics could be, given form and purpose in the forges of Terra after the great Heresy. In those nights of saga and legend, it was carried into battle by Sigismund, the first Emperor's Champion, favoured son of the primarch Rogal Dorn.

The blade itself, as long as a mortal man is tall, was wrought from the broken remains of Lord Dorn's own sword. In this temple, where the Chapter's greatest artefacts are kept in reverently maintained stasis fields to ward off the corrosive touch of time, the High Marshal held the most sacred treasure in the Black Templars armoury.

'You will have your own rituals within the Chaplain brotherhood,' Helbrecht said, his voice solemn with respect. 'For now, I recognise you as the inheritor to your master's mantle.'

The blade's silver tip lowered, pointing directly at Grimaldus's throat. 'You have waged war at my side for two hundred years, Grimaldus. Will you stand at my side as Reclusiarch of the Eternal Crusade?'

'Yes, my liege.'

Helbrecht nodded, sheathing the blade. Grimaldus tensed again, turning his head and baring his cheek.

With the force of a hammer, the back of Helbrecht's fist crashed into the Chaplain's jaw. Grimaldus grunted, tasting the coppery vitality of his own blood – his primarch's blood – and he grinned up at his commander through blood-pinked teeth. Helbrecht spoke again.

'I dub thee Reclusiarch of the Eternal Crusade. You are now a leader of our blessed Chapter.' The High Marshal raised his hand, showing the flecks of Grimaldus's blood marking his curled fingers. 'As a knight of the inner circle, let that be the last blow you receive unanswered.'

Grimaldus nodded, unclenching his jaw, calming his hearts and fighting the sudden flood of his killing urge. Even expecting the ritual strike, his instincts cried at him to respond in kind.

'It… will be so, my liege.'

'As it should be,' said Helbrecht. 'Rise, Grimaldus, Reclusiarch of the Eternal Crusade.'

CHAPTER I

ARRIVAL

FOR SOME HOURS after his ritual entrance into the highest echelons of the Chapter, Grimaldus stood alone in the Temple of Dorn.

Without a breeze to breathe life into the austere chamber, the great banners hung unmoving, some faded with the years, others brightly woven, still others even bearing dried bloodstains. Grimaldus looked upon the heraldry of his brothers' crusades.

Lastrati, piles of skulls and burning braziers depicting the war of attrition on the surface of that accursed heretic world…

Apostasy, showing the aquila chained to the globe, when the Templars were recalled to Holy Terra for the first time in thousands of years, to shed the blood of the false High Lord Vandire…

And on into the more recent wars in which Grimaldus himself had played a part – *Vinculus*, with the sword impaling a daemon, where the knights had crashed against the tainted followers of the archenemy in the great Battle of Fire and Blood – when Grimaldus himself had been taken from the ranks of the Sword Brethren and begun his gruelling rise through the tiers of the Chaplain brotherhood.

Dozens of banners hung in the still air, descending from the ornately carved ceiling, telling the tales of the glories won and the lives lost in each single facet of the Eternal Crusade.

The only noise except for Grimaldus's own breathing was the crackling hum of stasis fields enclosing Templars relics. Grimaldus passed one, a blurry field of smoky blue force revealing through its milky surface a bolter that had once belonged to Castellan Duron two thousand years before. The kill-markings scratched into the firearm's surface, etched in the tiniest Gothic lettering, covered the entire weapon like holy scripture.

Grimaldus stood by the plinth displaying the bolter for some time, his fingers itching to enter the release code on the keypad built into the shield's column. Such secrets were the purview of the Chaplain brotherhood that maintained this shrine, and even before he had risen to his current rank, Grimaldus had honoured the machine-spirits of the chamber's relics through ritual blessings and reconsecrations.

There was great succour in bearing the weapons of champions, even if only to cleanse and purify them after a warp jump.

Only one of the plinths – and in the Temple of Dorn, there were over a hundred occupied displays – bore what Grimaldus had come for. He stood before the short column, reading the silver plaque beneath the pulsing stasis shield.

Mordred
Reclusiarch
'We are judged in life for the evil we destroy.'

Beneath the words was a keypad, each key bearing a Gothic sigil in gold leaf. Grimaldus entered the nineteen-digit code for this specific column, and the stasis field powered down with a grinding of ancient engines inside the stone plinth.

Upon the flat surface of the white stone column, a weapon rested, deactivated and silent, freed of the blue illumination that had protected it.

Without any ceremony at all, Grimaldus clutched the maul's haft and raised it in his sure grip. The head was a hammer of holy gold and blessed adamantium fashioned into the shape of eagle wings over a stylised Templar cross. The haft was darkened metal as long as the knight's own arm.

The weapon's ornate head caught the dim glow from the lume-globes ensconced in the walls, and was painted briefly in flashes of reflected light as he turned it in his hands.

The warrior-priest stood like this for some time.

'Brother,' came a voice from behind. Grimaldus turned, instinct bringing the weapon to bear.

Despite never holding the relic before, his scarred fingertips found the activation rune along its handle before his heart could even beat once. The eagle-winged hammerhead flared with threatening brightness, serpents of hissing electricity flickering over the gold and silver metal.

The figure smiled to be revealed in such stark illumination. In a face pockmarked and crevassed by decades of battle, Grimaldus saw the amusement in the younger knight's pale eyes.

'Reclusiarch,' the figure inclined his head in greeting. 'Artarion.'

'We draw near to our destination. Estimates put translation back into realspace within the hour. I took the liberty of readying the squad for planetfall.'

Artarion's grin, much like Artarion himself, was ugly to look upon. In contrast, Grimaldus finally returned the smile, but as with his eyes there was an unsuspected gentleness in the expression.

'This world will burn,' the warrior-priest said, not even a shadow of doubt creeping into his voice.

'It will not be the first.' Artarion's scratched lips parted to reveal steel teeth – implanted replacements due to a sniper shot fifteen years before. The rifle round had taken him in the side of the face, shattering his jaw. The mess of scar tissue webbing the flesh around the left side of his lips added to the thin, sneering image he projected when his helm was removed. 'It will not be the first,' he said again, 'nor the last.'

'Have you seen the projections? The fleet auguries, the number of vessels in the local systems already, the reports of those yet to arrive?'

'I lost interest when the numbers became too high for me to count on my fingers.' Artarion snorted at his own weak jest. 'We will fight and win, or fight and die. All that ever changes is the colour of the sky we fight under, and the shade of the blood on our blades.'

Grimaldus lowered the crozius hammer, as if only then realising he still held it at the ready. A rich darkness settled over their sight as the relic's crackling illumination faded. In the wake of the brightness, the sharp scent of ozone – that strange freshness after a storm – filled the air. The power cells within the maul's haft whined as they reluctantly cooled down. The weapon's spirit hungered for war.

'You speak with a soldier's heart, but you are wrong to be so dismissive. This campaign… This has the weight of history about it. It would be the gravest of errors to consider this merely another conflict to add to the honour rolls.'

The softness had left Grimaldus's voice now. When he spoke, it was with the bitter passion Artarion was all too familiar with, fierce and thick with anticipation – the growled challenge of a caged animal. 'The surface of this world will burn until all of mankind's great achievements upon it are naught but ash and memory.'

'I have never heard you claim we would lose before, brother.'

Grimaldus shook his head, his voice still low and fevered. 'The planet will burn regardless of our triumph or defeat. I speak of the coming crusade's underpinning truth.'

'You are so certain?'

'I feel it in my blood. Win or lose,' the Chaplain said, 'come the final day on Armageddon, those of us that still stand will realise no war has ever cost us so dearly.'

'Have you shared these concerns with the High Marshal?' Artarion scratched the back of his neck, his fingertips soothing the itching skin around a spinal socket.

Grimaldus chuckled, momentarily blindsided by his brother's naivety.

'You think he needs me to tell him?'

FEW SHIPS IN the Imperium of Man matched the lethal grandeur of *The Eternal Crusader*.

Some ships sailed the heavens like the seaborne vessels of ancient Terra, journeying between the stars with solemnity and a measured grace. *The Eternal Crusader* was not one of these. Like a spear hurled into the void by the hand of Rogal Dorn himself, the flagship of the Templars had been slicing through space for ten thousand years of war. Its engines raged, streaming plasma contrails in their wake as they powered the vessel from world to world in echo of the Emperor's Great Crusade.

And the *Crusader* was not alone.

At her back, the capital vessels *Night's Vigil* and *Majesty* burned their engines hard, striving to keep pace and fall into a lance formation with their flagship. In the wake of these heavy cruisers – a battle-barge and smaller strike cruiser respectively – a wing of support frigates formed the rest of the lance. Seven in total, each of these faster interceptor vessels powered forward with less of a struggle to maintain formation with the *Crusader.*

The ship burst back into reality, trailing discoloured warp-smog from its protesting Geller field, the brilliance of its plasma drives flaring with gaseous leakage that misted around the void shields of the vessels which slammed back into realspace just behind.

Ahead of them lay an ashen globe, darkened by unclean cloud cover, strangely at peace despite the turmoil surrounding it.

If one were to look into the void around the bitter, punished world of Armageddon, one would see a thriving subsector of Imperial space where even the most prosperous hive planets bore more than their fair share of slowly-healing wounds.

It was a region of space where the worlds themselves were scarred. War, and the fear of another colossal sector-wide conflict, hung over the trillions of loyal Imperial souls like the threat of a storm forever on the edge of breaking.

It was always said by some that the Imperium of Man was dying. These heretical voices spoke of mankind's endless wars against its manifold foes, and decreed that humanity's ultimate fate was being decided in the fires of a million, million battlefields across the countless stars within the God-Emperor's grip.

Nowhere were the words of these seers and prophets more evident than the ravaged – yet rebuilt – Armageddon subsector, named for its greatest world, a world responsible for production and consumption on an immense and unmatched level.

Armageddon itself stood as a bastion of Imperial strength, churning out regiments of tanks from manufactories that never ceased activity by day or night. Millions of men and women wore the ochre armour of Armageddon's Steel Legions, their features hidden behind the traditional respirator masks of this honoured and renowned division of the Imperial Guard.

The hives of this defiant planet reached into the pollution-rich cloud cover that wreathed the world in perpetual twilight. No wildlife howled on Armageddon. No beasts stalked their prey outside the ever-growing hive-cities. The call of the wild was the rattle and clank of ten thousand ammunition manufactories that never halted production. The stalking of animals was the grinding of tank treads across the world's rockcrete surfaces, awaiting transport into the sky to serve in a hundred and more distant conflicts.

It was a world devoted to war in every way imaginable, made bitter by the scars of the past, soured by the wounds gouged into its face by humanity's enemies. Armageddon always rebuilt after each devastation, but it was never permitted to forget.

The first and foremost reminder of the last war, the almighty Second War that saw billions dead, was a deep space installation named for one of the Emperor's Angels of Death.

Dante, they called it.

It was from there that the mortals of Armageddon stared into the blackness of space, watching, waiting, praying that nothing stared back.

For fifty-seven years, those prayers had been answered.

But no longer. Imperial tacticians already had reliable figures from early engagements that confirmed the greenskin fleet bearing down on Armageddon as the largest xenos invasion force in the history of the segmentum. As the alien fleets closed around the system, Imperial reinforcements raced to break the blockaded sectors and land their troops on Armageddon before the invasion fleet arrived in the heavens above the doomed world.

A battle-barge of no standard design, the *Crusader* was a princely fortress-monastery, charcoal-black and bristling with gothic cathedral spires like a beast's spines along its back. Weapons capable of pounding cities into dust – the claws of this night-stalking predator – aimed into the void. Along the ship's length and clustered across its prow, hundreds of weapons batteries and lance cannons stood with mouths open to the silent darkness of space.

Aboard the ship, a thousand warriors cast off the shackles of training, preparation and meditation. At last, after weeks of passage through the Sea of Souls, Armageddon, beating heart-world of the subsector, was finally in sight.

MY BROTHERS' NAMES are Artarion, Priamus, Cador, Nerovar and Bastilan.

These are the knights that have waged war beside me for decades.

I watch them, each in turn, as we make ready for planetfall. Our arming chamber is a cell devoid of decoration, bare of sentiment, alive now with the methodical movements of dead-minded servitors machining our armour into place. The chamber is thick with the scholarly scent of fresh vellum from our armour scrolls, coppery oils from our ritually-cleansed weapons, and the ever-present cloying salty reek of sweating servitors.

I flex my arm, feeling my war-plate's false muscles of cable and fibre buzz with smooth vibration at the cycle of motion. Papyrus scrolls are draped over the angles of my armour, their delicate runic lettering listing the details of battles I could never forget. This paper, of good quality by Imperial standards, is manufactured on board the *Crusader* by serfs who pass the technique down generation to generation. Every role on the ship is vital. Every duty has its own honour.

My tabard, the white of sun-bleached bone, offers a stark contrast to the blacker than black plate beneath. The heraldic cross stands proud on my chest, where Astartes of lesser Chapters wear the Emperor's aquila. We do not wear His symbol. We *are* His symbol.

My fingers twitch as my gauntlet locks into place. That was not intentional – a nerve-spasm, a pain response. An invasive but familiar coldness settles over my forearm as my gauntlet's neural linkage spike sinks into my wrist to bond with the bones and true muscles there.

I make a fist with my hand armoured in black ceramite, then release it. Each finger flexes in turn, as if pulling a trigger. Satisfied, its dead eyes flashing with an acknowledgement of a job complete, an arming servitor moves away to bring my second gauntlet.

My brothers go through the same rituals of checking and rechecking. A curious sense of unease descends upon me, but I refuse to give it voice. I watch them now because I believe this is the last time we will go through this ritual together.

I will not be the only one to die upon Armageddon.

Artarion, Priamus, Cador, Nerovar and Bastilan. We are the knights of Squad Grimaldus.

Within his veins, Cador carries the blessed blood of Rogal Dorn with what seems like weary honour. His face is shattered and his body tormented – now half-bionic due to untreatable wounds – but he remains defiant, even indefatigable. He is older than I, older by far. His decades within the Sword Brethren are behind him now; he was released with all honour when his advancing age and increasing bionics left him less than the exemplar he had been before.

Priamus is the rising sun to Cador's dusk. He is aware of his skills in the unsubtle and undignified way of many young warriors. Without even the ghost of humility, his roars of triumph on the battlefield sound like cries for attention, a braggart's declarations. A blademaster, he calls himself. Yet he is not mistaken.

Artarion is… Artarion. My shadow, just as I am his. It is rare among our number for any knight to lay aside personal glory, yet Artarion is the one who carries my banner into battle. He has joked more times than I care to remember that he does so only to provide the enemy with a target lock on my location. For all his great courage, he is not a man blessed with a skilful sense of humour. The mangling wound that fouled his face was a sniper shot meant for me. I carry that knowledge with me each time we go to war.

Nerovar is the newest among us. He holds the dubious honour of being the only knight I chose to stand with me, while all others were appointed to fight by my side. The squad required the presence of an Apothecary. In the trials, only Nerovar impressed the rest of us with his quiet endurance. He labours now over his arm-mounted narthecium, blue eyes narrowed as he tests the flickering snap of surgical blades and cutting lasers. A sickening *clack!* sounds as he fires his reductor. The giver of merciful death, the extractor of gene-seed – its impaling component snaps from its housing, then retracts with sinister slowness.

Bastilan is last. Bastilan, always the best and least of us all. A leader but not a commander – an inspiring presence, but not a strategist – forever a sergeant, never fated to rise as a castellan or marshal. He has always said his role as such is all he desires. I pray he speaks the truth, for if he is deceiving us, he hides the lie well behind his dark eyes.

He is the one who speaks to me now. What he says chills my blood.

'I have heard from Geraint and Lograine of the Sword Brethren,' he chooses his words carefully, 'that there is talk of the High Marshal nominating you to lead a crusade.'

And for a moment, everyone stops moving.

THE SKIES OVER Armageddon were rich and thick with a sick, greyish-yellow cast. Sulphurous cloud cover was nothing new to the population, with their hive walls treated and shielded against the storm season's downpours of acid rain.

Around each hive-city across the planet's surface, vast landing fields were cleared, either hurriedly paved with rockcrete or simply ground flat under the treads of hundreds of landscaper trucks. Around Hades Hive, rain scythed down onto the cleared areas and sparked off the dense heat-shimmer of the city's protective void shields. Across the world, the heavens were in turmoil, weather patterns ravaged by the atmospheric disturbance caused by countless ships breaking cloud cover every day.

Yet at Hades Hive, the storms were especially fierce. Hundreds of troop carriers, their paint already melted to reveal bare, dull metal in places, endured the rainfall as they rested on the landing fields. Some were disgorging columns of men into the hastily-erected campsites that were spreading across the wastelands between the hives, while others sat in silence, awaiting clearance to return to orbit.

Hades itself was little more than industrial scar tissue blighting Armageddon's face. Despite efforts to repair the city after the last war over half a century before, it still bore a ragged share of memories. Toppled spires, broken domes, shattered cathedrals – this was the skyline after the death of a hive.

A squadron of Thunderhawk gunships pierced the caul of cloud cover. To those manning the battlements of Hades, they were a flock of crows winging down from the darkening sky.

Mordechai Ryken scanned the gunships through his magnoculars. After several seconds of zoom-blur, green reticules locked on to the streaking avian hulls and transcribed an analysis in dim white text alongside the image.

Ryken lowered the viewfinder scope. It hung on a leather cord around his neck, resting on the ochre jacket he wore as part of his uniform. His breath was hot on his face, recycled and filtered through the cheap rebreather mask he wore over his mouth and nose.

The air still tasted like a latrine, though. And it didn't exactly smell any better. The joys of high sulphur content in the atmosphere. Ryken was still waiting for the day he would be used to it, and he'd been stuck on this rock so far for every day of his thirty-seven years of life.

A way down the battlements, working on getting an anti-air turret operational, a team of his men clustered with a robed tech-priest. The multi-barrelled monstrosity dwarfed the half a dozen soldiers standing in its shadow.

'Sir?' one of them voxed. Ryken knew who it was despite the shapeless overcoats they all wore. Only one of them was female.

'What is it, Vantine?'

'Those are Adeptus Astartes gunships, aren't they?'

'Good eyes.' And they were, at that. Vantine would've made sniper a long time ago if she could aim worth a damn. Alas, there was more to sniping than just seeing.

'Which ones?' she pressed.

'Does it matter? Adeptus Astartes are Adeptus Astartes. Reinforcements are reinforcements.'

'Yes, but which ones?'

'Black Templars.' Ryken took a breath, tonguing a sore cut on his lip as he watched the fleet of Thunderhawks touching down in the distance. 'Hundreds of them.'

AN IMPERIAL GUARD column rolled out from Hades to meet the newest arrivals. A command Chimera, flying no shortage of impressive flags, led six Leman Russ battle tanks, their collective passage chewing into the newly laid rockcrete.

Bulky troop landers were still setting down elsewhere on the landing field, the wash from their engines blasting wind and gritty dust in all directions, but General Kurov of the Armageddon Steel Legion did not make personal appearances to greet just anyone.

Despite his advancing age, Kurov cut a straight-backed figure in his grimy uniform of ochre fatigues and black webbing, with flak padding on the torso. No sign of his many medals, not a hint of gold, silver, ribbon, or the other trappings of pomp. Here was the man that had led the Council of Armageddon for decades, and earned the respect of his people by wading knee-deep in the sulphur marshes and bracken forests after the last war, hunting xenos survivors in the infamous ork hunter platoons.

He stomped down the ramp, setting his cap to guard his eyes against the heatless, yet annoyingly bright, afternoon sunlight. A team of Guardsmen, each as raggedly attired as their commanding officer, clanged down the ramp after the general. As they moved, misshapen skulls clacked and rattled together from where they hung on belts and bandoliers. Across their chests, they gripped lasguns that hadn't resembled standard-issue for some time – each bore its own display of modifications and accoutrements.

Kurov marched his ramshackle gang of bodyguards in decent parade order, yet without any conscious effort. He led them to the waiting Thunderhawks, each of which was still emitting a dull machine-whine as their boosters cycled into inactivity.

Eighteen gunships. Kurov knew that from the initial auspex report as the Templars had landed. They sat now in disorganised unmoving ranks, ramps withdrawn and bulkheads sealed. Their undersides, blunt noses and wing edges still showed a glimmer of cooling heat shields with the after-effects of planetfall.

Three Adeptus Astartes stood before the gunship fleet, still as statues, with no evidence of which vessels they'd disembarked from.

Only one wore a helm. It stared through ruby eye lenses, its faceplate a skull of steel.

'Are you Kurov?' one of the Adeptus Astartes demanded.

'I am,' the general replied. 'It is my h–'

In unison, the three inhuman warriors drew their weapons. Kurov took an involuntary step back, not out of fear but surprise. The knights' weapons went live in a humming chorus of wakening power cells. Lightning, controlled and rippling, coated the killing edges of the three artefacts.

The first was a giant clad in armour of bronze and gold against black, the surface of his war-plate inscribed with retellings of his deeds in miniscule Gothic runes, as well as trinkets, trophies and honour badges of red wax seals and papyrus strips. He clutched a two-handed sword, its blade longer than Kurov was tall, and drove its point into the ground. The knight's face was shaped by the wars he had fought – square-jawed, scarred, blunt-featured and expressionless.

The second Adeptus Astartes, clad in plainer black war-plate, wore a cloak of dark weave and scarlet lining. His sword in no way matched the grandeur of the first knight's relic, but the long blade of darkened iron was no less lethal for its simplicity. This knight's face lacked the expression-less ease of the first. He fought not to sneer as he drove his own sword tip into the ground.

And the last, the knight who still wore his helm, carried no blade. The rockcrete beneath their feet shivered slightly under the pounding of his war-mace thudding onto the ground. The mace's head, a stylised knightly cross atop Imperial eagle wings, flared in protest, lightning crackling as the metal kissed the ground.

The three knights knelt, heads lowered. All of this

happened at once, in the space of no more than three seconds since Kurov last spoke.

'We are the Emperor's knights,' the giant in bronze and gold intoned. 'We are the warriors of the Eternal Crusade, and the sons of Rogal Dorn. I am Helbrecht, High Marshal of the Black Templars. With me is Bayard, Emperor's Champion, and Grimaldus, Reclusiarch.'

At their names, both knights nodded in turn.

Helbrecht continued, his voice a growled drawl. 'Aboard our vessels in orbit are Marshals Ricard and Amalrich. We come to offer you our blades, our service, and the lives of over nine hundred warriors in the defence of your world.'

Kurov stood in silence. Nine hundred Adeptus Astartes... Entire star systems were conquered with a fraction of that. He had greeted a dozen Adeptus Astartes commanders in recent weeks, but few had brought such significant strength with them.

'High Marshal,' the general said at last. 'There is a war council forming tonight. You and your warriors are welcome there.'

'It will be done,' the High Marshal said.

'I'm glad to hear it,' Kurov replied. 'Welcome to Armageddon.'

CHAPTER II
THE ABANDONED CRUSADE

RYKEN WAS NOT smiling.

He'd been a lifelong believer in not shooting the messenger, but today that tradition was in danger of expiring. Behind him loomed an anti-air turret, blanketing them all in its shadow and shielding them from the dim glare of the morning sun. A squad of his men worked on this turret, as they had worked on countless others along the walls in the space of the last two months. It was almost operational. They weren't techs, by any means, but they knew the basic maintenance rites and calibration rituals.

'One minute to test fire,' Vantine said, her voice muffled by her rebreather mask.

And that was when the messenger showed up. It was also when Ryken stopped smiling, despite the fact the messenger was easy on the eyes, as over-starched, narrowed-eyed tactica types went.

'I want these orders rechecked,' he demanded – calmly, but a demand nevertheless.

'With all due respect, sir,' the messenger straightened her own ochre uniform, 'these orders come from the Old Man himself. He's reorganising the disposition of all our forces, and the Steel Legion are honoured to be first in that reappraisal.'

The words stole Ryken's desire to argue. So it was true, then. The Old Man was back.

'But Helsreach is half a continent away,' he tried. 'We've been working on the Hades wall-guns for months.'

'Thirty seconds to test fire,' Vantine called.

The messenger, whose name was Cyria Tyro, wasn't smiling either. In her position as adjutant quintus to General Kurov, grunts and plebeians were forever questioning the orders she relayed, as if she would ever dare alter a single word of the general's instructions. The other adjutants had no difficulties in this area, she was sure of it. For some unknown reason, these lowborn dregs just simply didn't take well to her. Perhaps they were jealous of her position? If so, then they were more foolish than she'd have given them credence for.

'I have long been entrusted with certain aspects of the general's plans,' Tyro lied, 'that frontliners such as yourself are only now being made aware of. I apologise if this is a surprise to you, major, but orders are orders. And these orders come with the highest mandate imaginable.'

'Are we not even going to defend the damn hive?'

At that moment, Vantine test-fired the turret. The floor beneath their feet shook as four cannon barrels blared their anger up at the empty sky. Ryken swore, though it was drowned out in the ear-ringing thunder of the gun's echo.

Tyro also swore, though unlike Ryken's general lament, hers was aimed at Vantine and the gun crew.

The major was close to yelling over the ache in his ears. It was fading, but not fast.

'I said, *are we not even going to defend the damn hive?*'

'*You* are not,' Tyro almost pouted, her mouth compressed in restrained irritation. '*You* are going to Helsreach with your regiment. Your transports leave tonight. All of the 101st Steel Legion is to be aboard and ready for transport by sunset in six point five hours.'

Ryken paused. Six and a half hours to get three thousand men and women into heavy lifter transports, gunships and land trains. It was the kind of bad news that made the major feel the need to be overwhelmingly honest.

'Colonel Sarren is going to be furious.'

'Colonel Sarren has dealt with this assignment with grace and solemn devotion to his duty, major. Your commanding officer still has much to teach you in that regard, I see.'

'Cute. Now tell me *why* it's us being sent all the way to Helsreach. I thought Insan and the 121st were kings of that shitpile.'

'Colonel Insan had a terminal failure of his augmetic heart infusers this morning. His second officer requested Sarren by name, and General Kurov agreed.'

'That old bastard's finally dead? That'll teach him to lay off the garage-brewed sauce. Ha! All those expensive augmetics he had done, and he keels over six months later. I like that. That's delicious.'

'Major! Some respect, if you please.'

Ryken frowned. 'I don't like you,' he told Tyro.

'How grievous,' the general's assistant replied, and there was no mistaking the dark, unamused scowl on her face.

'For you have been appointed a liaison to aid in dealings with the Adeptus Astartes and the conscripted militia.' She looked as if she'd eaten something sour and it was still wriggling on her tongue. 'So… I will be coming with you.'

A moment of curious kinship passed between them, almost going unspoken. They were being exiled to the same place, after all. Their eyes met in that moment, and the foundations of something like a reluctant friendship almost bloomed between them.

It was broken when Ryken walked away.

'I still don't like you.'

'HADES HIVE WILL not survive the first week.'

The man speaking is ancient, and he looks every hour of his age. What keeps him on his feet is a mixture of minimal rejuvenat chem-surgeries, crude bionics, and a faith in the Emperor founded in hatred for the enemies of man.

I liked him the moment my visor's targeting reticules locked on to him. Both piety and hate echo in his every word.

He should not hold rank here – not to the degree he does. He is merely a commissar in the Imperial Guard, and such a title does not tend to make generals, colonels, Adeptus Astartes captains and Chapter Masters remain in polite silence when it comes to tactical planning. Yet to the humans at this war council, and the citizens of Armageddon, he is the Old Man, a beloved hero of the Second War fifty-seven years ago.

Not just a hero. *The* hero.

His name is Sebastian Yarrick. Even we Adeptus Astartes must respect that name.

And when he tells us all that Hades Hive will be destroyed within a matter of days, a hundred Imperial commanders, human and Adeptus Astartes alike, hang on his every word.

I am one of them. This will be my first true command.

Commissar Sebastian Yarrick leans over the edge of a hololithic display table. With his remaining hand – the other arm is nothing but a stump – he keys in coordinates on the numeric datapad, and the hololith projection of Hades Hive widens with flickering impatience to display both of the planet's hemispheres in insignificant detail.

The Old Man, a gaunt and wizened human of sharp features and skeletally-obvious facial bones, gestures to the blip on the map that represents Hades Hive and its surrounding territories. Wastelands, in the main.

'Six decades ago,' he says, 'the Great Enemy met his defeat at Hades. Our defence here was what won us that war.'

There are general murmurs of assent. The commissar's voice carries around the expansive chamber through floating skull drones equipped with vox-speakers where their jaws had once been.

I am surrounded by the familiar hum of active power armour, though the scents and faces that meet my eyes are new to me. Standing to my left at a respectful distance, his face raggedly proud around extensive bionics, is Chapter Master Seth of the Flesh Tearers – known to his men as the Guardian of the Rage. He smells of sacred weapon oils, his primarch's potent blood running beneath his weathered skin, and the spicy, unwholesome reptilian scent of the lizard predator-kings that stalk the jungles of his home world. Seth is flanked by his own officers, all bareheaded and with faces as pitted and cracked as their master's. Whatever wars have occupied the Flesh Tearers in recent decades, the conflicts have not been kind to them.

To my left, my liege Helbrecht stands resplendent in his battle armour of black and bronze. Bayard, the Emperor's

Champion, is by his side. Both rest their helmets on the table's surface, the stern helms distorting the edge of the hololithic display, and give their full attention to the ancient commissar.

I cross my arms over my chest and do the same.

'Why?' someone asks. Their voice is low, too low to be human, and carries over the chamber without the need of vox-amplification. A hundred heads turn to regard an Adeptus Astartes in the bright red-orange of a lesser Chapter, one unknown to me. He steps forward, leaning his knuckles on the table, facing Yarrick from almost twenty metres distance.

'We recognise Brother-Captain Amaras,' an Imperial herald announces from his position at Yarrick's side, smoothing the formal blue robes of his office. He bangs the butt of his staff on the ground three times. 'Commander of the Angels of Fire.'

Amaras nods in thanks, and fixes Yarrick with his unblinking gaze.

'Why would the greenskin warlord simply annihilate the greatest battlefield of the last war? Surely our forces should muster at Hades and stand ready to defend against the largest assault.'

Murmurs of agreement ripple throughout the gathered commanders. Emboldened, Amaras smiles at Yarrick.

'We are the Emperor's Chosen, mortal. We are His Angels of Death. We have centuries of battle experience compared to these human commanders at your side.'

'No,' another voice replies. This one is distorted into a vox-borne snarl, filtered through a helm's speakers. I swallow as the herald bangs the staff another three times.

I had not realised I'd spoken out loud.

'We recognise Brother-Chaplain Grimaldus,' he calls out. 'Reclusiarch of the Black Templars.'

GRIMALDUS SHOOK HIS head at the gathered commanders. Over a hundred, human and Adeptus Astartes, all standing around the huge table in this converted auditorium once used for whatever dreary theatre performances occurred on a manufactory world. A riot of colours, heraldry, symbols of unity, varied uniforms, regimental designations and iconography. General Kurov stood at the commissar's shoulder, deferring to the Old Man in all things.

'The xenos do not think as we do,' Grimaldus said. 'The greenskins do not come to Armageddon for vengeance, or to seek to bleed us for the defeats they have suffered at Imperial hands in the past. They come for the pleasure of violence.'

Yarrick, a skeleton wreathed in pale flesh and a dark uniform, watched the knight in silence. Amaras pounded his fist onto the table and pointed at the Templar. For a moment of deathly calm, Grimaldus considered drawing his pistol and slaying him where he stood.

'That lends credence to *my* belief,' Amaras almost snarled.

'Not at all. Have you inspected what remains of Hades Hive? It is a ruin. There is nothing to fight over, nothing to defend. The Great Enemy knows this. He will be aware that Imperial forces will put up no more than a token resistance here, and fall back to defend hives that are still worth defending. It is likely the warlord will obliterate Hades from orbit, rather than seek to take it.'

'We cannot let this hive fall! It is a symbol of mankind's defiance! With respect, Chaplain–'

'Enough,' Yarrick said. 'Peace, Brother-Captain Amaras. Grimaldus speaks with wisdom.'

Grimaldus inclined his head in thanks.

'I will not be silenced by a mortal,' Amaras growled, but the fight was gone from him. Yarrick – the thin, ancient commissar – just stared at the Adeptus Astartes captain. After several moments, Amaras looked back to the hololithic topography around the hive. Yarrick turned back to the gathered officers, his one human eye stern and his augmetic one whirring in its socket as it refocused on the faces before him.

'Hades will not survive the first week,' he said again, this time shaking his head. 'We must abandon the hive and spread the forces here to other bastions of strength. This is not the Second War. What is coming in-system now far exceeds what has laid waste to the planet before. The other hives must be reinforced a thousand times over.' He took a moment to clear his throat, and a cough stole over him, dry and hoarse. When it subsided, the Old Man smiled without even the ghost of humour.

'Hades will burn. We must make our stand elsewhere.'

At this cue, General Kurov stepped forward with a data-slate.

'We come to the divisions of command.' He took a breath, and pressed on. 'The fleet that will besiege Armageddon is too vast to repel.'

A chorus of jeers rose. Kurov rode them out. Grimaldus, Helbrecht and Bayard were among those that remained absolutely silent.

'Hear me, friends and brothers,' Kurov sighed. 'And hear me well. Those of you who insist this war will be anything more than a conflict of bitter attrition are deceiving yourselves. At current estimates, we have over fifty thousand Adeptus Astartes in the Armageddon subsector, and thirty times the number of Imperial Guardsmen. And it will still not be enough to secure a clean victory. At our best esti-mations, Battlefleet Armageddon, the orbital defences, and the Adeptus Astartes fleets remaining in the void will be able to deny the enemy landing for nine days. These are our *best* estimates.'

'And the worst?' asked an Adeptus Astartes officer bedecked in white wolf furs, wearing the grey war-plate of the Space Wolves. His body language betrayed his impatience. He almost paced, like a canine in a cage.

'Four days,' the Old Man said through his grim smile.

Silence descended again. Kurov didn't waste it.

'Admiral Parol of Battlefleet Armageddon has outlined his plan and uploaded it to the tactical network for all commanders to review. Once the orbital war is lost, be it four days or nine, our fleets will break from the planet in a fighting withdrawal. From then on, Armageddon will be defenceless beyond what is already entrenched upon the surface. The orks will be free to land whatever and wher-ever they wish.

'Admiral Parol will lead the remaining Naval ships of the fleet in repeated guerrilla strikes against the invaders' ves-sels still in orbit.'

'Who will lead the Adeptus Astartes vessels?' Captain Amaras spoke up again.

There was another pause, before Commissar Yarrick nod-ded to a dark-armoured cluster of warriors across the table.

'Given his seniority and the expertise of his Chapter, High Marshal Helbrecht of the Black Templars will take overall command of the Adeptus Astartes fleets.'

And once more, there was uproar, several Adeptus Astartes commanders demanding that the glory be theirs. The knights ignored it.

'We are to remain in orbit?' Grimaldus leaned closer to his commander and voiced the question.

The High Marshal didn't take his eyes from Yarrick. 'We are the obvious choice to command the Adeptus Astartes elements in the orbital battles.'

The Chaplain looked across the chamber, at the various leaders and officers of a hundred different forces.

I was wrong, he thought. I will not die in futility on this world. Eagerness, hot and urgent, flushed through his system, as real and vital as a flood of adrenaline gushing through his two hearts.

'The *Crusader* will plunge like a lance into the core of their fleet. High Marshal, we can slaughter the greenskin tyrant before he even sets foot on the world below us.'

Helbrecht lifted his gaze from the ancient commissar as his Chaplain spoke. He turned to Grimaldus, his dark eyes piercing the other knight's skull mask with their intensity.

'I have already spoken with the other marshals, my brother. We must leave a contingent on the surface. I will lead the orbital crusade. Amalrich and Ricard will lead the forces in the Ash Wastes. All that remains is a single crusade, to defend one of the hive cities that yet remains ungarrisoned by Adeptus Astartes.'

Grimaldus shook his head. 'That is not our duty, my liege. Both Amalrich and Ricard have a host of honours inscribed upon their armour. Each has led greater crusades alone. Neither will relish an exile to a filthy manufactorum hive while a thousand of their brothers wage a glorious war in the heavens. You would shame them.'

'And yet,' Helbrecht was implacable, his features set in stone, 'a commander must remain.'

'Don't.' The knight's blood ran cold. 'Don't do this.'

'It is already done.'

'No,' he said, and meant it with every fibre of his being. '*No.*'

'This is not the time. The decision is made, Grimaldus. I know you, as I knew Mordred. You will not refuse this honour.'

'*No,*' Grimaldus said again, loud enough that other commanders began to stare.

Helbrecht said nothing. Grimaldus stepped closer to him.

'I would burst the Great Enemy's black heart in my hand, and cast his blasphemous flagship to the surface of Armageddon wreathed in holy fire. Do not leave me here, Helbrecht. Do not deny me this glory.'

'You will not refuse this honour,' the High Marshal said, his voice as stony as his face.

Grimaldus wanted no further part in the proceedings. Worse, he knew he was irrelevant here. As deliberations and tactics were discussed for the coming orbital defence, he turned from the hololithic display.

'Wait, brother.' Helbrecht's voice made it a request, not an order, and that made it easy to refuse.

Grimaldus stalked from the chamber without another word.

THEIR DESTINATION WAS called, with bleakness so typical of this world, Helsreach.

'Blood of Dorn,' Artarion swore with feeling. 'Now that's a sight.'

'This is… huge,' Nerovar whispered.

The four Thunderhawks tore across the sulphurous sky, parting sick yellow clouds that drifted apart in their wake. From the cockpit of the lead aircraft, six knights watched the expansive city below.

And *expansive* barely covered it.

The four gunships, boosters howling, veered in graceful unison around one of the tallest industrial spires. It was slate-grey, belching thick smoke into the dirty sky, merely one of hundreds.

A wing of escorts, small and manoeuvrable Lightning-pattern air superiority fighters, coasted alongside the Adeptus Astartes Thunderhawks. They were neither welcome nor unwelcome, merely ignored.

'We cannot be the only Adeptus Astartes strength sent to this city,' Nerovar removed his white helmet with a hiss of venting air pressure and stared with naked eyes at the metropolis flashing beneath. 'How can we hold this alone?'

'We will not be alone,' Sergeant Bastilan said. 'The Guard is with us. And militia forces.'

'Humans,' Priamus sneered.

'The Legio Invigilata has landed to the east of the city,' Bastilan said to the swordsman. 'Titans, my brother. I don't see you sneering at that.'

Priamus didn't answer. But nor did he agree.

'What is that?'

The knights leaned forward at their leader's words. Grimaldus gestured down at a vast stretch of rockcreted roadway, wide enough to accommodate the landing of a bulk cruiser or a wallowing Imperial Guard troop carrier.

'A highway, sir,' the pilot said. He checked his instruments. 'Hel's Highway.'

Grimaldus was silent for several moments, just watching the colossal road and the thousands upon thousands of conveyances making their way along it in both directions.

'This roadway splits the city like a spine. I see hundreds of capillary roads and byways leading from it.'

'So?' Priamus asked, his tone indicating just how little he cared about the answer.

'So,' Grimaldus turned back to the squad, 'whoever holds Hel's Highway holds the beating heart of the city in their hands. They will have unprecedented, unstoppable ability to manoeuvre troops and armour. Even Titans will move faster, at perhaps twice the speed than if they had to stalk through hive towers and city blocks.'

Nerovar shook his head. He was the only one without his helm covering his features. Insofar as it was possible for an Adeptus Astartes to look uncertain, he was doing so now.

'Reclusiarch.' He spoke Grimaldus's new title with hesitancy. 'How can we defend... all *this*? An endless road that leads into to a thousand others.'

'With blade and bolter,' said Bastilan. 'With faith and fire.'

Grimaldus recognised his own words spoken from the sergeant's mouth. He looked down in silence at the city below, at the insane stretch of road that left the entire hive open, accessible.

Vulnerable.

CHAPTER III
HIVE HELSREACH

THE THUNDERHAWKS TOUCHED down on a landing pad that was clearly designed for freight use. Cranes moved and servitors droned out of their way as the gunships came down in a hovering shower of engine wash and heat shimmer.

Ramps clanged onto the landing pad's surface and the four gunships disgorged their living cargo – one hundred knights in orderly ranks, marching into formation before their Thunderhawks.

Watching this display, and desperately trying not to show how impressed he felt, was Colonel Sarren of the Armageddon 101st Steel Legion. He stood with his hands clasped together, fingers interlaced, over his not inconsiderable stomach. Flanking him were a dozen men, some soldiers, some civilians, and all nervous – to varying degrees – about the hundred giants in black armour forming up before them.

He cleared his throat, checked the buttons on his ochre

greatcoat were fastened in correct order, and marched to the giants.

One of the giants, wearing a helm shaped into a grinning skull mask of shining silver and steel, stepped forward to meet the colonel. With him came five other knights, carrying swords and massive bolters, but for one who bore a towering standard. Upon the banner, which waved lazily in the dull breeze, a scene of red and black depicted the skull-helmed knight bathed in the golden purity of a flaming aquila overhead.

'I am Grimaldus,' the first knight said, his gem-like eye lenses staring down at the portly colonel. 'Reclusiarch of the Helsreach Crusade.'

The colonel drew breath to make his own greeting, when the hundred knights in formation cried out a chant in skin-crawling unity.

'Imperator Vult!'

Sarren glanced at the ranks of knights, formed up in five ranks of twenty warriors. None of them seemed to have moved, despite their cry in High Gothic: *The Emperor wills it.*

'I am Colonel Sarren of the 101st Steel Legion, and over-all commander of the Imperial Guard forces defending the hive.' He offered a hand to the towering knight, and turned the gesture quite smartly into a salute when it became clear the knight was not going to shake hands.

Muted clicks could be heard every few seconds from the helms of the knights standing closest to him. Sarren knew full well they were speaking with each other over a shared vox-channel. He didn't like it, not at all.

'Who are these others?' the first knight asked. With a war maul of brutal size and weight, he gestured to Sarren's staff arrayed in a loose crescent behind the colonel. 'I would meet every commander of this hive, if they are present.'

'They are present, sir,' Sarren said. 'Allow me to make introductions.'

'Reclusiarch,' Grimaldus growled. 'Not "sir".'

'As you wish, Reclusiarch. This is Cyria Tyro, adjutant quintus to General Kurov.' Grimaldus looked down at the slender, dark-haired female. She made no effort to salute. Instead, she spoke.

'I am to act as liaison between off-planet forces – such as yours, Reclusiarch, and the Titan Legion – and the soldiers of Hive Helsreach. Simply summon me if you require my aid,' she finished.

'I will,' Grimaldus said, knowing he would not.

'This is Commissar Falkov, of my command staff,' Colonel Sarren resumed.

The officer named clicked his heels together and made an immaculate sign of the aquila over his chest. The commissar's dark uniform singled him out with absolute clarity among the ochre-wearing Steel Legion officers.

'This is Major Mordechai Ryken, second officer of the 101st and XO of the city defence.'

Ryken made the aquila himself, and offered a cautious nod of greeting.

'Commander Korten Barasath,' Sarren introduced the next man, 'of the Imperial 5082nd Naval Wing.'

Korten, a lean figure still dressed in his grey flightsuit, saluted smartly.

'My men were in the Lightnings that guided you down, Reclusiarch. A pleasure to serve with the Black Templars again.'

Grimaldus narrowed his eyes behind his helm's false grin. 'You have served with the Knights of Dorn before?'

'I have personally – nine years ago on Dathax – and the Fifty-Eighty-Twos have on no fewer than four separate occasions. Sixteen of our fighters are marked with the heraldic cross, with permission given by Marshal Tarrison of the Dathax Crusade.'

Grimaldus inclined his head, his respect solemn and obvious, despite the helm.

'I am honoured, Barasath,' he said.

The squadron leader suppressed a pleased smile and saluted again.

And on it went, through the ranks of senior Steel Legion officers. At the end of the line stood two men, one in a clean and decorated uniform of azure blue, the shade of skies on worlds much cleaner than this one, and the other in oil-stained overalls.

Colonel Sarren gestured to the thin man in the immaculate uniform.

'The most honourable Moderati Primus Valian Carsomir of the Legio Invigilata, crewman of the blessed engine *Stormherald*.'

Grimaldus nodded, but made no other outward show of respect. The Titan pilot inclined his gaunt face in turn, utterly emotionless.

'Moderati,' the knight said. 'You speak with the voice of your Legion?'

'A full battle group,' the man replied. 'I am the voice of Princeps Majoris Zarha Mancion. The rest of Invigilata is committed to other engagements.'

'Fortune favours us that you still remain,' the knight said. The Titan pilot made the cog sign of the Mechanicus, his knuckles interlinked over his chest, and Sarren finished the final introduction.

'And here is Dockmaster Tomaz Maghernus, lead foreman of the Helsreach Dockers' Union.'

The knight hesitated, and nodded again, just as he had for the soldiers. 'We have much to discuss,' Grimaldus said to the colonel, who was sweating faintly in the stifling afternoon air.

'Indeed we do. This way, if you please.'

TOMAZ MAGHERNUS WASN'T sure what to think.

Back at the docks, as soon as he walked into the warehouse, his crew flocked around him, barraging him with questions. *How many Adeptus Astartes were there? How tall were they? What was it like to see one? Were all the stories true?*

Tomaz wasn't sure what to say. There had been little grandeur in the meeting. The towering warrior with his skull face had seemed more dismissive than anything else. The ranks of knights in their black armour were silent and inhuman, utterly separate from the hive's delegation and not interacting at all.

He answered the questions with a level of vagueness lessened by a convincing false smile.

An hour later, he was back in his crane's command cabin, strapped to the creaking leather seat and turning the axis wheel to bring the loading claw around again. Levers controlled the claw's vertical position and the grip of its magnetic talons. Tomaz slammed the claw onto the deck of the tanker ship closest to his station, and hauled a cargo crate into the air. The markings alongside the sturdy metal crate marked it as volatile. More promethium, he knew. The final imports of fuel for the Imperial Guard's tanks were arriving this week. Dried food rations and shipments of fuel were all they'd been unloading on the docks for months now.

He tried not to dwell on his meeting with the Adeptus

Astartes. He'd been expecting a rousing speech from a warrior armoured in gold. He'd expected plans and promises, oaths and oratory.

All in all, he decided, it had been a disappointing day.

A CITY.

I am in command of a *city*.

Preparations have been under way for months, but estimates pit the Great Enemy arriving in-system within a handful of days. My men, the precious few knights that remain with me on the surface of Armageddon, are spread across the sprawling hive. They are to serve as inspiration to the human soldiers when the fighting becomes thickest.

I recognise the tactical validity of this, yet lament their absence. This is not how a holy crusade should be fought.

The hours pass in a blur of statistical outlays, charts, hololithic projections and graphs.

The food supplies for the entire city. How long they will last once nothing can be brought in from outside the hive. Where the food is stored. The durability of these silos, buildings and granaries. What weapons they can withstand. How they appear from the air. Ration projections. Sustainable food ration planning. Unsustainable food ration planning, with appended lists of estimated sacrificial casualties. Where food riots are likely to break out once starvation is a reality.

Water filtration centres. How many are required to be fully operational in order to supply the entire population. Which ones are likely to be destroyed first, once the city walls fall. Underground bunkers where water is currently stored. Ancient wellsprings that might be tapped in times of great need.

Estimates of disease once the city is shelled and civilian

casualties are too heavy to be dealt with efficiently. Types of disease. Symptoms. Severity. Risk of contagion. Compatibility with the ork genus.

Lists of medical facilities. Endless, endless screeds of how each one is supplied as of the most recent stock reports, to the most minute detail. New stock-checks are constantly performed. Updated information cycles in all the while, even as we review the previous batch.

Militia numbers, conscripted and volunteer. Training regimes and training schedules. Weapon supplies. Ammunition supplies for the civilian population currently under arms. Projections for how long those supplies will last.

Hive Defence Forces, straddling the line between militia and Guard. Who leads the individual sector forces. Their weapons. Their ammunition. Their proximity to significant industrial targets.

Imperial Guard numbers. Throne, what numbers. Regiments, their officers, their live fire training accuracy records, their citations, their shames, their moments of greatest glory and ignominy on a host of distant worlds. Their insignia. Their weapon and ammunition supplies. Their access to armour units, ranging from light scout vehicles such as Sentinels and Chimeras, through to super-heavy Baneblades and Stormswords.

The Guard figures alone take two days to file through. And this, they say, is merely the overview.

Landing platforms come next. Hive Defence landing platforms, civilian sites already in use by the Guard, and civilian sites currently in use for the importation of essential supplies, either from Navy vessels, traders in orbit, or elsewhere on the planet. The access to and from these sites is critical, regarding reinforcements making it into the hive, refugees making their way out, and the enemy capturing them as bases when the siege begins.

Air superiority. The numbers of light fighters, heavy fighters, and bombers at our disposal. The records of every pilot and officer among the Imperial 5082nd Skyborne. These, I skip past. If they wear the Templar cross with permission of a marshal, then there is little need to review their acts of valour. It is already clear. The projections move on to simulated displays of how long our air forces can prevent enemy landings, and what situations would merit the use of bombers beyond the city walls. On and on, the simulations roll in flickering hololithic imagery. Barasath is relieved to go when it is complete, complaining of a dozen headaches at once. I smile, though I let none of the humans witness it.

Helsreach heavy defence emplacements. What anti-air turrets are stationed on the walls, and where they are. Their optimal firing arcs. The make and calibre of each barrel and shell. The number of crew appointed to man these positions. Estimated projections on damage they can inflict upon the enemy, run through countless scenarios of varying greenskin offensive strength. The teams resupplying their ammunition, and from where that ammunition comes. Freight routes from manufactories.

And the manufactories themselves. Industrial plants churning out legions of tanks, all of various classes. Other manufactories where shells are made and dispatched for use. Which industrial sites are the most valuable, the most profitable, the most reliable and the most likely to suffer assault in a protracted siege.

The Titan Legion, most noble and glorious Invigilata. What engines they have on the Ash Wastes outside the city.

Which ones will walk in the defence of Helsreach, and which ones are promised to reinforce the hordes of Cadian Shock and our brother Adeptus Astartes, the Salamanders, out in the wilds of Armageddon.

Invigilata keeps its internal records from our sight, but we are fed enough information to thread into yet more holo-lithic charts and simulations, adding the might of Titans – of various grades and sizes – to the potential carnage.

The docks. The Helsreach Docks, greatest port on the planet. Coastal defences – walls and turrets and anti-air towers – and trade requirements and union complaints and petitions arguing over docking rights and warehouses appropriated as barracks for soldiers and complaints from merchants and dock-officers and...

And I endure this for nine days.

Nine. Days.

On the tenth day, I rise from my chair in Sarren's command centre. Around me in the colonel's armoured fortress at the heart of the city, three hundred servitors and junior officers work at stations: calculating, collating, transmitting, receiving, talking, shouting, and sometimes quietly panicking, begging for aid from those around them.

Sarren and several of his officers and aides watch me. Their necks crane up as they follow my movement. It is the first time I have moved in seven hours. Indeed, the first time I have moved since I sat down this morning at dawn.

'Is something wrong?' Sarren asks me.

I look at the sweating, porcine commander; this man unable to shape his body into a warrior's fitness, confined as he is – and totally at home – with this relentless trial of a million, million numbers.

What kind of question is that? Are they blind? I am one of

the Emperor's Chosen. I am a knight of Dorn's blood, and a warrior-priest of the Black Templars. *Is something wrong?*

'Yes,' I say to him, to them all. 'Something is wrong.'

'But... what?'

I do not answer that question. Instead, I move to walk from the room, not caring that uniformed humans scatter before me like frightened vermin.

With a volume that would put a peal of overhead thunder to shame, a siren starts to wail.

I turn back to the table.

'What is that?'

They flinch at the rough bark from my helm's vocaliser. The siren keeps whining.

'Throne of the God-Emperor,' Sarren whispers.

HIVE HELSREACH DID not have city walls. It had battlements.

When the citywide siren began to ring, Artarion was standing in the shadow of a towering cannon, its linked barrels aiming into the sick sky. Several metres away, the human crew worked at its base, performing the daily rituals of maintenance. They hesitated at the sound of the siren, and talked among themselves.

Artarion briefly looked back in the direction of the tower fortress in the city's centre, blocked as it was from view by distance and the forest-like mess of hive spires between here and there.

He felt the humans casting occasional glances his way. Knowing he was distracting them from their necessary mechanical rites, he moved away, walking further down the wall. His gaze fell, as it did almost every hour since coming to the hive a week before, on the endless expanse of wasteland that reached to the horizon and beyond.

Blink-clicking a communication rune on his visor display, he opened a vox-channel. The siren rang on. Artarion knew what it signalled.

'About time.'

FROM VOX-TOWERS ACROSS the city, an announcement was spoken in deceptively colourless tones. Colonel Sarren, not wishing to incite the populace to unrest, had tasked a lobotomised servitor to speak the words to the people.

'**People of Hive Helsreach. Across the planet, the first sirens are sounding. Do not be alarmed. Do not be alarmed. The enemy fleet has translated in-system. The might of Battlefleet Armageddon and the greatest Adeptus Astartes fleet in Imperial history stands between our world and the foe's forces. Do not be alarmed. Maintain your daily rites of faith. Trust in the God-Emperor of Mankind. That is all.**'

In the control centre, Grimaldus turned to the closest human officer sat at a vox-station.

'You. Hail the Black Templars flagship *Eternal Crusader*, immediately.'

The man swallowed, his skin paling at being spoken to so directly and with such force by an Adeptus Astartes.

'I... My lord, I am coordinating the–'

The knight's black fist pounded into the table. '*Do it now.*'

'Y-yes, my lord. A moment, please.'

The human officers of Sarren's staff shared a worried look. Grimaldus paid no attention at all. The seconds passed with sickening slowness.

'The *Eternal Crusader* is making ready to engage the enemy fleet,' the officer replied. 'I can send a message, but their two-way communications are in lockdown without the proper command codes. D-do you have the codes, my lord?'

Grimaldus did indeed have the codes. He looked at the frightened human, then back at the worried faces of the command staff as they sat at the table.

I am being a fool. My fury is blinding me to my sworn duty. What did he expect, truly? That Helbrecht would send down a Thunderhawk and allow him to take part in the glorious orbital war above? No. He was consigned here, to Helsreach, and there would be no other fate beyond this.

I will die on this world, he thought once more.

'I have the codes,' the knight replied, 'but this is not an emergency. Simply send the following message to their incoming logs, with no need for a reply: "Fight well, brothers."'

'Sent, lord.'

Grimaldus nodded. 'My thanks.' He turned to the gathered officers, and leaned over the hololithic display, his gauntleted knuckles on the table's surface.

'Forgive me a moment's choler. We have a war to plan,' the knight said, and breathed out the most difficult words he had ever spoken. 'And a city to defend.'

UNTIL THEIR DYING nights, the warriors of the Helsreach Crusade bore their lamentations and rage with all the dignity that could be expected of them. But it was no easy feat. No easy feat to be consigned to a city of several million frightened souls while above the stained clouds, hundreds upon hundreds of their battle-brothers were carving their glory from the steel and flesh of an ancient and hated foe. The Black Templars across the city looked skywards, as if their helms' red eye lenses could pierce the wretched clouds and see the holy war above.

Grimaldus's own anger was a physical ache. It burned

behind his eyes, and beat acid through his veins. But he mastered it, as was his duty. He sat at the table with the human planners, and agreed with them, disagreed, nodded and argued.

At one point, a whisper made its way through the room. It was a serpentine thing, as if it threaded its way from human mouths to human ears seeking to avoid enraging the black-clad Adeptus Astartes knight. When Colonel Sarren cleared his throat and announced that the two fleets had engaged, Grimaldus simply nodded. He'd heard the very first whispers thirty seconds before, of crackled voices coming over the vox-headsets of those at the communication stations.

It was beginning.

'We should give the order,' Sarren said quietly, to murmured agreement among the officer cadre.

Grimaldus turned to the vox-officer he had spoken to before. This time, he glanced at the man's rank badge. The officer saw the silver skull helm nod once in his direction.

'Lieutenant,' the knight said.

'Yes, Reclusiarch?'

'Give the order to Imperial forces throughout Helsreach. Martial law is in immediate effect.' He felt his throat dry at the gravity of what he was saying.

'Seal the city.'

FOUR THOUSAND ANTI-AIR turrets along the hive's towering walls primed and aimed their multiple barrels into the sky.

Atop countless spires and manufactory rooftops, secondary defence lasers did the same. Hangars and warehouses converted for use by the Naval air squadrons readied the short rockcrete runways necessary for STOL fighters. Grey-uniformed Naval armsmen patrolled their bases' perimeters, keeping their sites enclosed and operating almost independently of the rest of the hive.

Across the city, recently-established makeshift roadway checkpoints became barricades and outposts of defence in readiness for the walls falling to the enemy. Thousands of buildings that had been serving as barracks for the Imperial Guard and militia forces sealed themselves with flakboard-reinforced doors and windows.

Announcements from vox-towers ordered the citizens of the hive who weren't engaged in vital industrial duty to remain in their homes until summoned by Guard squads and escorted to the underground shelters.

Hel's Highway, lifeline of the hive, was strangled by Guard checkpoints clearing the way of civilian traffic, making room for processions of tanks and Sentinel walkers, a rattling, grinding parade stretching over a kilometre. Clusters of the war machines veered off as they dispersed across the hive.

Helsreach was locked down, and its defenders clutched their weapons as they stared into the bleak sky.

Unseen by any of the humans within the city, one hundred knights – separated by distance but united by the blood of a demigod in their veins – knelt in silent prayer.

Eighteen minutes after the sirens started to wail, the first serious problem with force deployment began. Representatives of Legio Invigilata demanded to speak with the hive's commanders.

Forty-two minutes later, born entirely of panic, the first civilian riot broke out.

I ASK SARREN a reasonable question, and he responds with the very answer I have no wish to hear.

'Three days,' he says.

Invigilata needs three days. Three days to finish the fitting and arming of their Titans out in the wastelands before they can be deployed within the city. Three days before they can walk through the immense gates in the hive's impenetrable walls, and station themselves within the city limits according to the agreed upon plan.

And then Sarren makes it worse.

'In three days, they will decide if they are to come to our aid, or deploy along the Hemlock River with the rest of their Legio.'

I quench the rush of fury through a moment's significant effort. 'There is a chance they will not even walk in our defence?'

'So it seems,' Sarren nods.

'Projections have the enemy breaching the orbital defences in four to nine days,' one of the other Steel Legion colonels – his name is Hargus – speaks from across the table. 'So we have time to allow them the largesse they require.'

None of us are seated now. The siren's drone has been lowered to less inconvenient levels, and speech is a realistic possibility for the unenhanced human officers once again.

'I am going to the view-tower,' I inform them. 'I wish to look upon this problem with my own eyes. Is the moderati primus still within the hive?'

'Yes, Reclusiarch.'

'Tell him meet to me there.' I pause as I stride from the room, and look back over my shoulder. 'Be polite, but do not ask. Tell him.'

CHAPTER IV
INVIGILATA

MODERATI PRIMUS VALIAN Carsomir scratched at the greying stubble that darkened his jawline. His time was limited, and he had made that clear.

'You are not alone in that position,' Grimaldus pointed out.

Carsomir smiled darkly, though not without empathy. 'The difference, Reclusiarch, is that I do not intend to die here. My princeps majoris is still in doubt if Invigilata will walk for Helsreach.'

The knight moved to the railing, his armour joints humming with the gentle motions. The viewing platform was a modest space atop the central spire of the command fortress, but Grimaldus had spent much of his time up here each night, staring over the hive as it made ready for war.

In the faded distance, over the city walls, his gene-enhanced sight could make out the skeletal details of Titans on the horizon. There, in the wastelands, Invigilata's engines also made ready. Fat-hulled landers made the wallowing journey back into orbit as part of the final phase of Imperial deployment. Soon, within a matter of days, there would be no hope of landing anything more on the planet's surface.

'This is the greatest of Armageddon's port cities. We are about to be assaulted by the largest greenskin-breed xenos invasion ever endured by the Imperium of Man.' The Adeptus Astartes did not turn to the Titan pilot. He watched the gigantic war machines, blurred by the sandy mist of distant dust storms. 'We must have Titans, Carsomir.'

The officer stepped alongside the Adeptus Astartes, his bionic eyes – both with lenses of multifaceted jade set in bronze mountings – clicking and whirring as he followed the knight's gaze over the city and beyond.

'I am aware of your need.'

'*My* need? It is the hive's need. Armageddon's need.'

'As you say, the hive's need. But I am not the princeps majoris. I report on the hive's defences to her, and the decision is hers to make. Invigilata has received strong petitions from other cities, and other forces.'

Grimaldus closed his eyes in thought. Unblinking, his skulled helm continued to stare at the distant Titans.

'I must speak with her.'

'I am her eyes, ears and voice, Reclusiarch. What I know, she knows; what I say, she has bid me speak. If you wish, I could – perhaps – arrange a conversation over the vox. But I am here – a man of not inconsiderable station myself – to show that Invigilata is earnest in its dealings with you.'

Grimaldus said nothing for several seconds.

'I appreciate that. I am not blind to your rank. Tell me, moderati, is it permissible to speak with your princeps majoris in person?'

'No, Reclusiarch. That would be a violation of Invigilata tradition.'

Grimaldus's brown eyes opened once more, drinking in the scarce detail of the war machines on the horizon.

'Your objection is noted,' the knight said, 'and duly ignored.'

'What?' the Titan pilot said, not sure he heard correctly.

Grimaldus didn't answer. He was already speaking into the vox.

'Artarion, ready the Land Raider. We're going out into the wastelands.'

FOUR HOURS LATER, Grimaldus and his brothers stood in the shadows cast by giants.

A light dust storm sent grit rattling against their war-plate, which they ignored as easily as Grimaldus had ignored Carsomir's offended protests about the nature of this mission.

Crews of servitors laboured at the ground level, and while they were mind-wiped never to process or acknowledge physical discomfort, the abrasive wasteland grit was rubbing their exposed skin raw, and crudely sandblasting mechanical parts.

The Titans themselves stood watch over the wastelands in austere vigil – nineteen of them in total, ranging from the smaller twelve-crew Warhound-classes, to the larger Reaver- and Warlord-classes. Godlike, immune to the elements, the Titans were bedecked in the crawling forms of tech-adepts and maintenance drones performing the rites of awakening.

Despite their slumber, it was anything but silent. The grinding, deafening machine-whine of internal plasma reactors trying to start was a sound from primordial nightmare, ripped right from worlds where humans feared gigantic reptilian predators and their ground-shaking roars.

It was all too easy to imagine hundreds of robed tech-priests within the fleet of Titans, chanting and praying to their Machine-God and the spirits of these slumbering war-giants. As Grimaldus and his brothers walked in the shade cast by one Warlord, the relentless grind of metal on metal became a full-throated thunderclap that broke the air like a sonic boom. Heated air blasted outwards from the Titan's hull, and around the site, thousands of men instantly fell to their knees in the sand, facing the Titan and murmuring their reverence in the aftershock of its rebirth.

The Titan's birth cry rang out through its warning sirens. The sound was somewhere between pure mechanical noise and organic exultation; as loud as a hundred manufactories with a full workforce, and as terrible as the wrath of a newborn god.

It moved. Not with speed, but with the halting, unsure strides of a man that has not used his muscles in many months. One splayed claw of a foot, easily huge enough to crush a Land Raider, rose several metres off the ground. It crashed back to earth a moment later, blasting dust in all directions.

'Sacrosanct awakens!' came the cry from hundreds of vox-altered voices. 'Sacrosanct walks!'

The Titan answered the worshipful cries of its cult below. It roared again, the cry blaring from its speaker horns and echoing across the wastelands.

As impressive as the sight was, it was not why Grimaldus had led his men out here. Their goal was larger still, dwarfing even these mighty Warlords, paying them no heed as they stood or walked around at the height of its weapon-arms.

It was called *Stormherald*.

The battle-class Titans were walking weapons platforms, capable of levelling hive blocks. *Stormherald* was a walking fortress. Its weapons could level cities. Its legs, capable of supporting the weight of this colossal sixty-metre war machine, were bastions – barracks – with turrets and arched windows for the troops transported within to fire at the foe even as their Titan crushed them underfoot. Upon its hunched back, *Stormherald* carried crenellated battlements and the seven spires of a sacred, armoured cathedral devoted to the Emperor in His aspect as the Machine-God. Gargoyles clung to the edges of the architecture, carved around defence turrets and stained glass windows, their hideous mouths open as they wailed silently at the enemy from their holy castle above the ground.

Banners hung from its cannon arms and the battlements themselves, listing the names of enemy war machines it had slain in the millennia since its birth. As the birth cry of *Sacrosanct* faded, the knights could hear the sound of religious communion in the fortress-cathedral on *Stormherald*'s giant shoulders, as pious souls no doubt beseeched their ethereal master for the blessing of the greatest god-machine waking once more.

The Titan's clawed feet were tiered stairs leading into the armoured chambers of its lower legs. With the immense structure still unmoving, Grimaldus made his way through scores of scurrying menial tech-priests and servitors. As his booted foot thudded down on the first stair layer, the resistant welcome he was expecting finally made itself known.

'Hold,' he said to his brothers. Troops, their features covered, filed from the archways into the Titan's limb-innards. The knights' attempted entrance was blocked by Mechanicus minions.

The soldiers facing them were called skitarii. These were the elite of the Adeptus Mechanicus infantry forces – a fusion of integrated weapon augmetics and the human form. Grimaldus, like many Adeptus Astartes, regarded their unsubtle flesh-manipulation and the crude surgeries bestowing weapons upon their limbs as making them little more than glorified servitors, and equally wretched in their own way.

Twelve of these bionic creatures, their skin robed against the wind, levelled thrumming plasma weapons at the five knights.

'I am Grimaldus, Reclusiarch of the Black Tem–'

–*Your identity is known to us*– they all spoke at once. There was little unity in the chorus of voices, with some sounding unnaturally deep, others inhuman and mechanical, still others perfectly human.

'The next time I am interrupted,' the knight warned, 'I will kill one of you.'

–*We are not to be threatened*– all twelve said, still in unison, still in a chorus of unmatching voices.

'Neither are you to be addressed. You are nothing; slaves, all of you, barely above servitors. Now move aside. I have business with your mistress.'

–*We are not to be ordered into submission. We are to remain as duty demands*–

A human would have missed the division within their unified speech, but Grimaldus's senses could trace the minute deviations in the way they spoke. Four of them started and finished words a fraction of a second later than the others. Whatever mind-link bound the twelve warriors, it was more efficient in some than others. While his experience with the servants of the Machine-God was limited, he found this a curious flaw.

'I will speak with the princeps majoris of Invigilata, even if I have to shout up to the cathedral itself.'

They had no orders pertaining to such an action, and lacked the cognition to make an assessment of how it would matter to their superiors, so they remained silent.

'Reclusiarch...' Priamus voxed. 'Must we bear this foolish indignity?'

'No.' The skull helm scanned the skitarii each in turn, its red eyes unblinking. 'Kill them.'

SHE FLOATED, AS she had floated for seventy-nine years, in a coffin-like tank of milky amniotic fluid. The metallic, chemical tang of the watery, oxygen-rich ooze had been the only constant in almost a century of life, and its taste, its feel, its intrusion into her lungs and its replacement of air in her respiration had never ceased to feel somewhat alien.

That was not to say she found it uncomfortable. Quite the opposite. It was forever unsettling, but not unnatural.

In moments of battle, which always seemed too few and far between, Princeps Majoris Zarha believed with cold certainty that this was what gestation within the womb must have felt like. The cooling fluid supporting her would become warm in sympathy with the plasma reactor at *Stormherald*'s core. The pounding, world-shaking tread echoed around her, magnified like the beat of a mighty heart.

A feeling of absolute power coupled with being utterly protected. It was all she needed to focus on to remain herself in those frantic, bladed moments when *Stormherald*'s broken, violent mind knifed into her consciousness with sudden strength, seeking to overpower her.

She knew that there would come a day when her assistants unplugged her for the last time – when she would be denied a return to the machine's soul, for fear its ingrained temperament and personality would swallow her weaker, too-human sense of identity.

But that was not now. Not today.

No, Zarha focused on her simulated regression to the womb, and it was all she ever needed to push aside the clinging insistency of *Stormherald*'s blunt and primal advances.

Voices from the outside always reached her with a muffled dullness, despite the vox-receivers implanted where the cartilage of her inner ears once were, and the receptors built into the sides of her confinement tank.

They spoke, those voices, of intrusion.

Princeps Majoris Zarha did not share their appraisal of the situation. She turned in her milky fluid, as graceful as a sea-nymph from the tales of the impious Ancient Terra, though the augmented, wrinkled, hairless creature within the spacious coffin was anything but lovely. Her feet had been removed, for she would never need them again. Her bones were weak and soft, and her body curled and hunched.

She replied to them, to her minions and brothers and sisters, with a stab of thought.

I wish to speak with the intruders.

'I wish to speak with the intruders,' the vox-emitters on her coffin droned in a toneless echo of her silent words.

One of them came closer to the clear walls of her amniotic chamber, looking in at the floating husk with great respect.

'My princeps,' it was Lonn speaking, and though she liked Lonn, he was not her favourite.

Hello, Lonn. Where is Valian?

'Hello, Lonn. Where is Valian?'

'Moderati Carsomir is returning from the hive, my princeps. We thought you would still sleep for some time.'

76

With all this noise? What was left of her face turned into a smile.

'With all this noise?'

'My princeps, Adeptus Astartes are seeking to gain entrance.'

I heard.

'I heard.'

I know.

'I know.'

'Your orders, my princeps?'

She twisted in the water again, in her own way as graceful as a seaborne mammal, despite the cables, wires and cords running from the coffin's mechanical generators into her spine, skull and limbs. She was an ancient, withered marionette in the water, serene and smiling.

Access granted.

'Access granted.'

–ACCESS GRANTED– SAID twelve voices at once.

The crackling edge of the maul remained motionless, no more than a finger's thickness above the lead skitarii's skull. A small spark of electrical force snapped at the soldier's face from the armed power weapon, forcing him to recoil.

–*Access granted*– they all intoned a second time.

Grimaldus deactivated his crozius hammer and shoved the augmented human soldiers aside.

'That is what I thought you would say.'

THE JOURNEY WAS short and uneventful, through narrow corridors and ascending in elevator shafts, until they stood outside the sealed bulkhead doors of the bridge. The process of reaching the control deck involved a great deal of silently staring tech-adepts, their green-lens replacement eyes rotating and refocusing, either scanning or in some eerie mimicry of human facial expressions.

The interior of the Titan was dark, too dark for unaugmented humans to work by, lit by the kind of emergency-red lighting the knights had only seen before in bunkers and ships at war. Their gene-enhanced eyes would have pierced the gloom with ease, even without the vision filters of their helm's visors.

No guards stood outside the large double bulkhead leading onto the command deck, and the doors themselves slid open on clunking rails as the knights waited.

Artarion gripped Grimaldus's scroll-draped pauldron.

'Make this count, brother.'

The Chaplain looked at the bearer of his war banner through the silver face of his slain master.

'Trust me.'

THE COMMAND DECK was a circular bay, with a raised dais in the centre surrounded by five ornate and heavily-cabled thrones. At the edges of the chamber, robed tech-adepts worked at consoles filled with a dizzying array of levers, dials and buttons.

Two vast windows offered a grand view across the harsh landscape. With a shiver of realisation, Grimaldus knew he was looking out from the god-machine's eyes.

Upon the dais itself, a huge, clear-glass tank stood supported by humming machinery. Within its milky depths floated a naked crone, ravaged by her years and the bionics necessary to sustain her life under such conditions. She stared through bug-eyed augmetic replacements where her human eyes once were.

'**Greetings, Adeptus Astartes,**' the vox-speakers built into her coffin spoke.

'Princeps Majoris,' Grimaldus nodded to the swimming husk. 'An honour to stand in your presence.'

There was a distinct pause before she replied, though her gaze never left him. **'You are keen to speak with me. Waste no time on pleasantries.** *Stormherald* **wakes, and soon I must walk. Speak.'**

'I am told by one of this Titan's pilots, as an ambassador to Helsreach, that Invigilata may not walk in our defence.'

Again, the pause.

'This is so. I command one-third of this Legio. The rest already walks in defence of the Hemlock region, many with your brothers, the Salamanders. Do you come to petition me for my portion of mighty Invigilata?'

'I do not beg, princeps. I came to see you with my own eyes and ask you, face to face, to fight and die with us.'

The withered woman smiled, the expression both maternal and amused.

'But you have not yet completed your intended duty, Adeptus Astartes.'

'Is that so?'

This time, the pause was longer. The old woman laughed within her bubbling tank. **'We are not face to face.'**

The knight reached up to his armoured collar, disengaging the seals there.

WITHOUT MY HELM, the scent of sacred oils and the chemical-rich tang of her amniotic tank are much stronger. The first thing she says to me is something I am not sure how to respond to.

'You have very kind eyes.'

Her own eyes are long-removed from her skull, the sockets covered by these bulbous lenses that twist as she watches me. I cannot return the comment she made, and I do not know what else I could say.

So I say nothing.

'What is your name?'

'Grimaldus of the Black Templars.'

'Now we are face to face, Grimaldus of the Black Templars. You have been bold enough to come here, and honour me with your face. I am no fool. I know how rare it is for a Chaplain to reveal his human features to one not of his brotherhood. Ask what you came to ask, and I will answer.'

I step closer and press my palm against the casket's surface. The vibration is twinned with that of my armour. I can feel the eyes of the Mechanicus minions upon me, upon my dark ceramite, their reverent gazes showing their longing to touch the perfection of the machinesmith's craft represented by Adeptus Astartes war-plate.

And I look into the mechanical eyes of the princeps as she floats in the milky waters.

'Princeps Zarha. Helsreach calls for you. Will you walk?'

She smiles again, a blind grandmother with rotten teeth, as she presses her own palm against mine. Only the reinforced glass separates us.

'Invigilata will walk.'

SEVEN HOURS LATER, the people of the city heard a distant mechanical howl from the wastelands, eclipsing the cries of the lesser Titans. It echoed through the streets and around the spiretops, chilling the blood of every soul in the hive. Street dogs barked in response, as if sensing a larger predator nearby.

Colonel Sarren shivered, though he smiled at the others

in his command meeting. Through bloodshot eyes, heavy with sleeplessness, he regarded them all.

'*Stormherald* has awoken,' he said.

THREE DAYS, JUST as promised, and the city shook with the tread of the god-machines.

Invigilata's engines walked, and the great gates in the northern wall rumbled open to welcome them. Grimaldus and the hive's command staff watched from atop the viewing platform. The knight blink-clicked a rune on his retinal display, accessing a coded channel.

'Good morning, princeps,' he said softly. 'Welcome to Helsreach.'

In the distance, a walking cathedral-fortress pounded its slow, stately way through the first city blocks.

'**Hail, Chaplain.**' The crone's voice was laden with barely-contained energy. '**I was born in a hive like this, you know.**'

'It is fitting then, that you'll be dying here, Zarha.'

'**Do you say so, sir knight? Have you seen me today?**'

Grimaldus watched the distant form of *Stormherald*, as tall as the towers surrounding it.

'It is impossible not to see you, princeps.'

'**It's impossible to kill me, as well. Remember that, Grimaldus.**'

No human had ever dared use his name so informally before. The knight smiled for the first time in days.

The city was finally sealed. Helsreach was ready.

And as night fell, the sky caught fire.

CHAPTER V

FIRE IN THE SKY

Its name had been, in nobler years, *The Purest Intent*.

A strike cruiser, constructed on the minor forge world Shevilar and granted to the Shadow Wolves Chapter of the Adeptus Astartes. It had been lost with all hands, captured by xenos raiders, thirty-two years before the Third War for Armageddon.

When a huge and shapeless amalgamation of scrap and flame came burning through the cloud cover above the fortified city, warning sirens sounded once more across the hive. The squadron of fighters in the air – commanded by Korten Barasath – voxed their inability to engage. The hulk was burning up already, and far out of their capability to damage with their Lightnings' lascannons and long-barrelled autocannons.

The wing of fighters broke away as the hulk burned through the sky.

Thousands of soldiers manning the immense walls

watched as the wreckage blazed its way overhead. The air itself shook with its passage, a palpable tremor from the thrum of overworked, dying engines.

Exactly eighteen seconds after it cleared the city walls, *The Purest Intent* ended its spaceborne life as it ploughed a new scar into Armageddon's war-torn face. All of Helsreach shook to its foundations as the massive cruiser hammered into the ground and carved a blackened canyon in its wake.

It took a further two minutes for the crippling damage inflicted by the impact to kill the immense, howling engines. Several booster rings still roared gaseous plasma and fire as they tried to propel the vessel through the stars, unaware it was half-buried in the stinging sulphuric sands that would be its grave.

But the engines failed.

The flames cooled.

At last, there was silence.

The Purest Intent was dead, its bones strewn across the wastelands of Armageddon.

'THE SHIP REGISTERS as *The Purest Intent*,' Colonel Sarren read out from the data-slate to the crowded war room. 'An Adeptus Astartes vessel, strike cruiser-class, belonging to the–'

'Shadow Wolves,' Grimaldus cut him off. The knight's vox-voice was harsh and mechanical, betraying no emotion. 'The Black Templars were with them at the end.'

'The end?' asked Cyria Tyro.

'They fell at the Battle of Varadon eleven years ago. Their last companies were annihilated by the tyranid-breed xenos.'

Grimaldus closed his eyes and relished the momentary drift of focus into memory. *Varadon*. Blood of Dorn, it had been beautiful. No purer war had ever been fought.

The enemy was endless, soulless, merciless... utterly alien, utterly hated, utterly without right to exist.

The knights had tried to fight their way to join up with the last of their brother Chapter, but the enemy tide was unrelenting in its ferocity. The aliens were viciously cunning, their swarming tides of claws and flesh-hooked appendages smashing into the two Adeptus Astartes forces and keeping them isolated from each other. The Wolves were there in full force. Varadon was their home world. Distress calls had been screamed into the warp by astropaths weeks before, when their fortress-monastery fell to the enemy.

Grimaldus had been there at the very end. The last handful of Wolves, their blades broken and their bolters empty, had intoned the Litanies of Hate into the vox-channel they shared with the Black Templars. Such a death! They chanted their bitter fury at the foes even as they were slain. Grimaldus would never, *could* never, forget the Chapter's final moment. A lone warrior, a mere battle-brother, horrendously wounded and on his knees beneath the Chapter's standard, keeping the banner proud and upright even as the xenos creatures tore into him.

The war banner would never be allowed to fall while one of the Wolves yet lived.

Such a moment. Such honour. Such *glory*, to inspire warriors to remember your deeds for the rest of their own lives, and to fight harder in the hopes of matching such a beautiful death.

Grimaldus breathed out, restoring his senses to the present with irritated reluctance. How filthy this war would be by comparison.

Sarren continued. 'The latest report from the fleet lists thirty-seven enemy ships have breached the blockade.

Thirty-one were annihilated by the orbital defence array. Six have crashed onto the surface.'

'What is the status of Battlefleet Armageddon?' the knight asked.

'Holding. But we have a greater comprehension of enemy numbers now. The four to nine day estimate has been abandoned, as of thirty minutes ago. This is the greatest greenskin fleet ever to face the Imperium. The fleet's casualties are approaching a million souls. One or two more days, at best.'

'Throne of the Emperor,' one of the militia colonels swore in a whisper.

'Focus,' Grimaldus warned. 'The crashed ship.'

Here, the colonel paused and gestured to Grimaldus. 'I suggest we hold, Reclusiarch. A handful of greenskin survivors cannot hope to survive an assault against the walls. They would be insane – even for orks – to try.'

'We are comfortable letting these survivors add their numbers to their brethren when the enemy's main forces make planetfall?' This, from Cyria Tyro.

'A handful of additional foes will make no difference,' Sarren pointed out. 'We all saw the *Intent* hit. Not many of its crew are walking away from that.'

'I have fought the greenskins before, sir,' Major Ryken put in. 'They're tougher than a marsh lizard's hide. Almost unbreakable. There'll be plenty who survived that crash, I promise you.'

'Send a Titan,' Commissar Falkov smiled without any humour whatsoever, and the room fell quiet. 'I am not making a jest. Send a Titan to obliterate the wreckage. Inspire the men. Give them an overwhelming victory before the true battle is even joined. Morale among the Steel Legion is mediocre at best. It is lower still among the volunteer militia, and barely existent among the conscripts. So send a Titan. We need first blood in this war.'

'At least get Barasath's fighters to scan for life readings,' Tyro added, 'before we commit to sending any troops outside the city.'

Throughout all of this, Grimaldus had remained silent. It was his silence that eventually killed all talk, and had faces turning towards him.

The knight rose to his feet. Despite the slowness of his movement, his armour's joints emitted a low snarl.

'The commissar is correct,' he said. 'Helsreach needs an overwhelming victory. The benefit to morale among the human forces would be considerable.'

Sarren swallowed. No one around the table enjoyed Grimaldus pointing out the difference in species between the humans and the genetically-forged Adeptus Astartes.

'It is time my knights took to the field,' the Reclusiarch said, his deep, soft voice coming out from his skull helm as a machine-growl. 'The humans may need first blood, but my knights hunger for it. We will give you your victory.'

'How many of your Adeptus Astartes will you take?' Sarren asked after a moment's thought.

'All of them.'

The colonel paled. 'But surely you don't need–'

'Of course not. But this is for appearances. You wanted an overwhelming display of Imperial force. I am giving you that.'

'We can make this even better,' Cyria said. 'If you can have your men stand in formation before they move out of the city, long enough for us to arrange live pict-feeds to all visual terminals across Helsreach...' She trailed off, a pleased smile brightening her features.

Falkov slammed a fist on the table. 'Let's get started. The first charge of the black knights!' He smiled a thin, nasty grin. 'If that doesn't light a fire in the heart of every man breathing, nothing will.'

PRIAMUS TWISTED THE blade, widening the wound before wrenching the sword clear. Stinking blood gushed from the creature's chest, and the alien died with its filthy claws scratching at the knight's armour.

Within the crashed ship, stalking from room to room, corridor by corridor, the Templars hunted mongrels in the name of purification.

'This is bad comedy,' he breathed into the vox.

The reply he received was punctuated by the dull clang of weapons clashing together. Artarion, some way behind. 'Fall back, damn it.'

Priamus sensed another lecture about vainglory in his future. He walked on, his precious blade held at the ready, moving deeper into the darkness that his red visor pierced with consummate ease.

Like vermin, the orks scrambled through the tunnels of the wrecked ship, springing ambushes with their crude weapons and snorting their piggish war cries. Priamus's contempt burned hot on his tongue. They were above this. They were Black Templars, and the morale of the puling humans was none of their concern.

Grimaldus was spending too much time among the mortals. The Reclusiarch was beginning to think like them. It had galled Priamus to stand in ranked formation for the pict-drones to hover around and capture the knights' images, just as it galled him now to hunt the scarce survivors of this wreck. It was beneath him, beneath them all. This was work for the Imperial Guard. Perhaps even the militia.

'We will draw first blood,' Grimaldus had said to them all, as if it were something to care about – as if it would affect the final battle in any way at all. 'Join me, brothers. Join me as I shake off this disgust at the stasis gripping my bones, and slake my bloodthirst in holy slaughter.'

The others, as they stood in their foolish ranks for the benefit of the mortals, had cheered. They had *cheered*.

Priamus remained silent, swallowing the rise of bile in his throat. He had known in that moment, with clarity sharper than ever before, that he was unlike his brothers. They *cared* about shedding blood now, as if this pathetic gesture mattered.

These warriors who called him vainglorious were blind to the truth: there was nothing vain in glory. He was not rash, he merely trusted in his skills to carry him through any challenge, just as the great Sigismund, First High Marshal of the Black Templars, had trusted his skills to do the same. Was that a weakness? Was it a flaw to exemplify the fury of the Chapter's founder and the favoured son of Rogal Dorn? How could it be considered so, when Priamus's deeds and glories were already rising to eclipse those of his brothers?

Movement ahead.

Priamus narrowed his eyes, his pupils flicking across his field of vision to lock targeting reticules on the brutish shapes swarming in the darkness of the wide, lightless corridor.

Three greenskins, their xenos flesh exuding a greasy, fungal scent that reached the knight from a dozen metres away. They lay waiting in a puerile ambush, believing themselves hidden by fallen gantries and a half-destroyed bulkhead door.

Priamus heard them grunting to one another in what passed for whispers in their foul tongue.

This was the best they could do. *This* was their cunning ambush against warriors made in the Emperor's image. The knight swore under his breath, the curse never leaving his helm, and charged.

Artarion licks his steel teeth. I hear him doing it, even though he wears his helm.

'Priamus?' he asks. The vox answers with silence.

Unlike the swordsman, I am not alone. I walk with Artarion, the two of us slaying our way through the enginarium decks. Resistance is light. Most of our venture so far has consisted of kicking xenos corpses out of our path, or butchering lone stragglers.

Most of the Templars were sent across the wastelands in their Rhinos and Land Raiders, chasing down the crash survivors who sought to hide in the wilderness. I have given them their head, and let them hunt. Better the greenskins die now, rather than allow them to lie in wait and rejoin their bestial kin in the true invasion. I took only a handful of warriors into the downed cruiser to purge whatever remains.

'Leave him be,' I say to Artarion. 'Let him hunt. He needs to stand alone for now.'

Artarion pauses before answering. I know him well enough to know he is scowling. 'He needs discipline.'

'He needs our trust.' My tone brooks no further argument.

The ship is in pieces. The floor is uneven, torn and wrenched from the crash. We turn a corner, our boots clinging to the sloping decking as we head into a plasma generator's coolant chamber. As huge as a cathedral's prayer chamber, the expansive room is largely taken up by the cylindrical metal housing that encases the temperamental and arcane technology used for cooling the ship's engines.

I see nothing alive. I hear nothing alive. And yet…

'I smell fresh blood,' I vox to Artarion. 'A survivor, still bleeding.' I gesture to the vast coolant tower with my crozius. The mace flashes with lightning as I squeeze the trigger rune. 'The alien lurks beneath there.'

The survivor is barely deserving of the description. It lies pinned under metal debris, impaled through the stomach and pinned to the floor. As we approach, it barks in its rudimentary command of the Gothic tongue. Judging from the pool of cooling blood spreading from its sundered form, the alien's life will end in mere minutes. Feral red eyes glare at us. Its porcine face is curled in a rictus of anger.

Artarion raises his chainsword, gunning the motor. The saw-teeth whine as they cut through the air.

'No.'

Artarion freezes. At first, my brother knight isn't sure what he'd heard. His glance flicks to me.

'What did you say?'

'I said,' I'm stepping closer to the dying alien even as I speak, looking down through my skulled mask, '…no.'

Artarion lowers his sword. Its teeth stutter to a halt.

'They always seem so immune to pain,' I tell him, and I feel my voice fall to a whisper. I place a boot upon the creature's bleeding chest. The ork snaps its jaws at me, choking on the blood that runs into its burst lungs.

Artarion must surely hear the smile in my voice. 'But no. Look into its eyes, brother.'

Artarion complies. I can tell from his hesitation that he does not see what I see. He looks down and sees nothing but impotent rage.

'I see fury,' he tells me. 'Frustration. Not even hatred. Just wrath.'

'Then look harder.' I press down with my boot. Ribs crunch with the sound of dry twigs snapping, one after the other, as the weight descends harder. The ork bellows, drooling and snarling.

'Do you see?' I ask, knowing the smile is still evident in my voice.

'No, brother,' Artarion grunts. 'If there is a lesson in this, I am blind to it.'

I lift the boot, letting the ork cough its lifeblood through its blood-streaked maw.

'I see it in the creature's eyes. Defeat is pain. Its nerves may be dead to torment, but whatever passes for its soul knows how to suffer. To be at an enemy's mercy... Look at its face, brother. See how it dies in agony because we are here to watch such a shameful end.'

Artarion watches, and I think perhaps he sees it, as well. However, it does not fascinate him the way it does me. 'Let me end it,' he says. 'Its existence offends me.'

I shake my head. That would not do at all.

'No. Its life's span is measured in moments.' I feel the dying alien's gaze lock with my red eye lenses. 'Let it die in this pain.'

NEROVAR HESITATED.

'Nero?' Cador called over his shoulder. 'Do you see something?'

The Apothecary blink-clicked several visualiser runes on his retinal display.

'Yes. Something.'

The two of them were searching the ruined enginarium

chambers on the level beneath Grimaldus and Artarion. Nerovar frowned at what the digital readouts across his eye lenses were telling him. He looked to the bulky narthecium unit built into his left bracer.

'So enlighten me,' Cador said, his voice as gruff as always.

Nerovar tapped a code into the multicoloured buttons next to the display screen on his armoured forearm. Runic text scrolled in a blur.

'It's Priamus.'

Cador grunted in agreement. Nothing but trouble, that one. 'Isn't it always?'

'I've lost his life signs.'

'That cannot be,' Cador laughed. 'Here? Among this rabble?'

'I do not make mistakes,' Nerovar replied. He activated the squad's shared channel. 'Reclusiarch?'

'Speak.' The Chaplain sounded distracted, and faintly amused. 'What is it?'

'I've lost Priamus's life signs, sir. No heightened returns, just an immediate severance.'

'Confirm at once.'

'Confirmed, Reclusiarch. I verified it before contacting you.'

'Brothers,' the Chaplain said, his voice suddenly ice. 'Maintain search and destroy orders.'

'What?' Artarion drew breath to object. 'We need–'

'Be silent. *I* will find Priamus.'

HE WASN'T SURE what they hit him with.

The greenskins had melted from their hiding places in the darkness, one of them carrying a weighty amalgamation of scrap that only loosely resembled a weapon. Priamus had slain one, laughing at its porcine snorting as it fell to the deck, and launched at the next.

The scrap-weapon bucked in the greenskin's hands. A claw of charged, crackling metal fired from the alien device and crunched into the knight's chest. There was a moment of stinging pain as his suit's interface tendrils, the connection spikes lodged in his muscles and bones, crackled with an overload of power.

Then his vision went black. His armour fell silent, and became heavier on his shoulders and limbs. Out of power. They'd deactivated his armour.

'Dorn's blood...'

Priamus tore his helm clear just in time to see the alien racking his scrap-weapon like a primitive solid-slug launcher. The claw embedded in his chest armour, defiling the Templar cross there, was still connected to the device by a cable of chains and wires. Priamus raised his blade to sever the bond even as the alien laughed and pulled a second trigger.

This time, the channelled force didn't just overload his armour's electrical systems. It burned through the neural connections and muscle interfaces, blasting agony through the swordsman's body.

Priamus, gene-forged like all Adeptus Astartes to tolerate any pain the enemies of mankind could inflict upon him, would have screamed if he could. His muscles locked, his teeth clamped together, and his attempt to cry out left his clenched jaw as an ululating, shuddering 'Hnn-hnn-hnn'.

Priamus crashed to the ground fourteen seconds later, when the agony finally ceased.

* * *

THE GREENSKINS HUNCH over his prone form.

Now they have managed to bring him down, they seem to have no idea what to do with their prize. One of them turns my brother's black helm over in its fat-knuckled hands. If it means to turn Priamus's armour into a trophy, it is about to pay for such blasphemy.

As I walk down the darkened corridor, I drag my mace along the wall – the ornate head clangs against the steel arches. I have no wish to be subtle.

'Greetings.' I breathe the word from my skulled face.

They raise their hideous alien faces, their jaws slack and filled with rows of grinding teeth. One of them hefts a heavy composite of detritus and debris that apparently serves as a weapon.

It fires… something… at me. I do not care what. It's smashed from the air with a single swing of my inactive maul. The clang of metal on metal echoes throughout the corridor, and I thumb the trigger rune on the haft of my crozius. The mace flares into crackling life as I aim it at the aliens.

'You dare exist in humanity's domain? You dare spread your cancerous touch to our worlds?'

They do not answer this challenge with words. Instead, they come at me in a lumbering run, raising cleaver swords; primitive weapons to suit primitive beings.

I am laughing when they reach me.

GRIMALDUS SWUNG HIS mace two-handed, pounding the first alien back. The sparking force field around the weapon's head flashed as it reacted with opposing kinetic force, and amplified the already inhuman strike to insane levels of strength. The greenskin was already dead, its skull obliterated, as it flew twenty metres back down the corridor to smash into a damaged bulkhead.

The second tried to flee. It turned its back and ran, hunched and ape-like, back in the direction it had come.

Grimaldus was faster. He caught the creature in a handful of heartbeats, hooked his gauntleted fingers in the ork's armoured collar to halt its flight, and smashed it against the corridor wall.

The alien grunted a stream of curses in Gothic as it struggled in the knight's grip.

Grimaldus clutched at the creature's throat, black gauntlets squeezing, choking, crunching bone beneath his grip.

'You *dare* defile the language of the pure race...' He slammed the alien back, breaking its head open on the steel wall behind. Foetid breath steamed across Grimaldus's faceplate as the ork's attempt to roar came out as a panicked whine. The Adeptus Astartes would not be appeased. His grip tightened.

'You dare desecrate our tongue?'

Again, he bashed the greenskin back, the alien's head splitting wide as it struck a girder.

The ork's struggles died immediately. Grimaldus let the creature fall to the metal decking, where it hit and folded with a muffled thud.

Priamus.

The fury was fading now. Reality asserted itself with cold, unwanted clarity. Priamus lay on the deck, head to the side, bleeding from his ears and open mouth. Grimaldus came to his side, kneeling there in the darkness.

'Nero,' he said quietly.

'Reclusiarch,' the younger knight returned.

'I have found Priamus. Aft, deck four, tertiary spine corridor.'

'On my way. Assessment?'

Grimaldus's targeting reticule flicked over his brother's prone body, then locked on to the scrap-weapon carried by the orks he'd killed.

'Some kind of force-discharging weapon. His armour is powered down, but he's still breathing. Both his hearts are beating.' This last part was the most serious aspect of the downed knight's condition. If his reserve heart had begun to beat, there must have been significant trauma done to Priamus's body.

'Three minutes, Reclusiarch.' There was the dampened suggestion of bolter fire.

'Resistance, Cador?' Grimaldus asked.

'Nothing of consequence.'

'Stragglers,' Nerovar clarified. 'Three minutes, Reclusiarch. No more than that.'

IT WAS CLOSER to two minutes. When Nerovar and Cador arrived at a run, they smelled of the chemical combat stimulants in their blood and the acrid tang of discharged bolters.

The Apothecary knelt by Priamus, scanning his fallen brother with the medical auspex bio-scanner built into his arm-mounted narthecium.

Grimaldus looked at Cador. The oldest member of the squad was reloading his bolt pistol, and muttering into the vox.

'Speak,' the Chaplain said. 'I would hear your thoughts.'

'Nothing, sir.'

Grimaldus felt his eyes narrow and teeth grind together. He almost repeated his words as an order. What held him back was not tact, but discipline. His rage still boiled beneath the surface. He was no mere knight, to give in to his emotion and remain flooded by it. As a Chaplain, he held himself to a higher standard. Putting the chill of normality into his voice, he said simply:

'We will speak of this later. I am not blind to your tensions of late.'

'As you wish, Reclusiarch,' Cador replied.

Priamus opened his eyes, and did two things at once. He reached for his sword – still chained to his wrist – and he said through tight lips, 'Those whoresons. They shot me.'

'Some kind of nerve weapon.' Nerovar was still scanning him. 'It attacked your nervous system through the interface feeds from your armour.'

'Get away from me,' the swordsman said, rising to his feet. Nerovar offered a hand, which Priamus knocked aside. 'I said *get away*.'

Grimaldus handed the knight his helm.

'If you are finished with your lone reconnaissance, perhaps you can stay with Nero and Cador this time.'

The pause that followed the Chaplain's words was pregnant with Priamus's bitterness.

'As you wish. My lord.'

WHEN WE EMERGE from the wrecked ship, the weak sun is rising, spreading its worthlessly dim light across the clouded heavens.

The rest of my force, the hundred knights of the Helsreach Crusade, is assembling in the wastelands around the broken ship's metal bones.

Three Land Raiders, six Rhinos, the air around them all thrumming with the chuckle of idling engines. I think, for a strange moment, that even our tanks are amused at the pathetic hunting on offer last night.

Kill-totals scroll across my visor display as squad leaders report the success of their hunts. A paltry night's work, all in all, but the mortals behind the city walls have the first blood they so ardently desired.

'You're not cheering,' Artarion voxes to me, and only me.

'Little was cleansed. Little was purified.'

'Duty is not always glorious,' he says, and I wonder if he refers to our exile on the planet's surface with those words.

'I presume that is a barbed reference for my benefit?'

'Perhaps.' He clambers aboard our Land Raider, still speaking from within. 'Brother, you have changed since inheriting Mordred's mantle.'

'You are speaking foolishness.'

'No. Hear me. We have spoken: Cador, Nero, Bastilan, Priamus and myself. And we have listened to the talk among the others. We must all deal with these changes, and we must all face this duty. Your darkness is spreading to the entire Crusade. One hundred warriors all fearing that the fire in your heart is naught but embers now.'

And for a moment, his words ring true. My blood runs cold. My heart chills in my chest.

'Reclusiarch,' a voice crackles over the vox. I do not immediately recognise it – Artarion's words have stolen my thoughts.

'Grimaldus. Speak.'

'Reclusiarch. Throne of the God-Emperor… It's truly beginning.' Colonel Sarren sounds awed, almost eager.

'Elaborate,' I tell him.

'Battlefleet Armageddon is in full retreat. The Adeptus Astartes fleet is withdrawing alongside them.' The colonel's voice breaks up in a storm of vox-feedback, only to return a moment later. '…breaking against the orbital defence array. Breaking *through*, already. It's beginning.'

'We are returning to the city at once. Has there been any communication from *The Eternal Crusader*?'

'Yes. The planetary vox-network is struggling to cope with the influx. Shall I have the message relayed to you?'

'At once, colonel.'

I embark and slam the Land Raider's side hatch closed. Within the tank, all is suffused in the muted darkness of emergency lighting. I stand with my squad, gripping the overhead rail as the tank starts with a lurch.

At last, after the vox-clicking of several channels being linked together, I hear the words of High Marshal Helbrecht, the brother I have fought beside for so many decades. His voice, even on a low-quality recording, is filled with his presence.

'Helsreach, this is the *Crusader*. We are breaking from the planet. The orbital war is lost. Repeat: the orbital war is lost. Grimaldus… Once you hear these words, stand ready. You are Mordred's heir, and my trust rides with you. Hell is coming, brother. The Great Enemy's fleet is without number, but faith and fury will see your duty done.'

I curse him, without giving voice to my spite. A silent oath that I will never forgive him for this exile… For damning me to die in futility.

Behind his words, I hear the cacophony of a ship enduring colossal assault. Dull explosions, horrendous and thunderous shaking – *The Eternal Crusader*'s shields were down when he sent me this message. I cannot conceive of any enemy in history that has managed to inflict such damage to our flagship.

'Grimaldus,' he says my name with cold, raw solemnity, and his final words knife into me like a bitter blade.

'Die well.'

CHAPTER VI
PLANETFALL

GRIMALDUS WATCHED HELSREACH erupting in fury.

They came through the morning clouds, fat-bellied troop landers that streaked with fire from atmospheric entry and the damage they had sustained breaking through the orbital defences.

Burning hulks juddered as their boosters fired, slowing them before they ploughed into the ground. They came from the horizon, or descended from stretches of cloud cover far from the city. Those few that sailed overhead, close enough for the city's defence platforms to reach, were subjected to horrendous battery fire, destroyed with such swift force that flaming wreckage rained upon the city below.

He stood with his command squad, fists resting on the edge of the battlements, watching the bulk landers coming down in the northern wastelands. Imperial fighters of all classes and designs flitted between the sedate troop ships, unleashing their payloads to minimal effect. The ships were too big for fighter-scale weapons to make any significant difference. As more alien scrapships broke the poison-yellow cloud cover, xenos fighter craft descended with their motherships. Barasath and his Lightning squadrons engaged these, punching them out of the air like buzzing insects.

Across the city, almost drowned out by the booming rage of the battlement guns, a siren wailed between automated announcements that demanded every soul take up arms and man their appointed positions.

The walls.

During the opening phase, Helsreach's defenders would stand upon the city's walls and be ready to repel an archaic siege. Hundreds of thousands of soldiers and militia, standing vigil on walls that were as tall as a Titan.

Several bold ork drop-ships sought to land within the city. Spiretop platforms, wall guns and cannon batteries mounted upon the tops of towers annihilated those that made the attempt. The luckier failures managed to climb with enough altitude to escape the city's reach and crash on the wastelands. Most were torn asunder by unrelenting weapons fire, pulled apart and cast to the ground in flames.

Guard units stationed throughout the hive and pre-selected for the duty moved in on the downed hulks, slaughtering any alien survivors. Across the city, fire containment teams worked to put out blazes that spread from the crashing junkers.

Grimaldus looked along the walls to either side, where thousands of uniformed men stood in loose groups, every one clad in the ochre of the Armageddon Steel Legion. These were not Sarren's own 101st. The colonel's regiment remained at the command centre, as well as being spread across the city in platoons to defend key areas.

Artarion's words still burned behind the Chaplain's eyes.

'Brothers,' he spoke into the vox. 'To me.'

The knights drew closer – Nerovar watching the distant landings without a word; Priamus, his blade already in his hands, resting on one pauldron; Cador, projecting a sense of implacable patience; Bastilan, grim and silent; and Artarion, holding Grimaldus's banner, the only one of them without his helmet. He seemed to enjoy the uncomfortable glances he received from the human soldiers as they saw his shattered face. Occasionally, he'd grin at them, baring his metal teeth.

'Helm on,' Grimaldus said, the words emerging from his vocaliser as a low growl. Artarion complied with a chuckle.

'We must speak,' Grimaldus said.

'You have chosen a curious moment to realise that,' Artarion said. The wall shivered beneath their feet again as the turrets unleashed another volley at an alien scrap-cruiser shaking the sky overhead.

'The city has awoken to its duty,' Grimaldus intoned. 'It is time I did the same.'

The knights stood and watched as xenos landers touched down on the plains several kilometres from the city. Even from this distance, the Templars could make out hordes of greenskins spilling from the grounded ships, mustering on the wastelands.

Reports clashed with each other over the vox, telling of similar landings being made to the east and west of the city.

'Speak,' Grimaldus demanded in the face of his brothers' silence.

'What would you have us say, Reclusiarch?' asked Bastilan.

'The truth. Your perceptions of this doomed crusade, and the way it is being led.'

The ork ship that had passed overhead minutes before now came down in the wasteland with slow, grinding, earth-shaking force. It ploughed into the dusty ground, throwing up a trail of dust in its wake, and Helsreach shook to its foundations.

A cheer went up along the wall – thousands of soldiers crying out at the sight.

'We hold the largest city on the planet, with hundreds of thousands of soldiers,' Cador said, 'as well as countless experienced Guard and militia officers. And we have Invigilata.'

'Your point?' Grimaldus asked, watching the crashed ship burn. 'Do you think that will be even half of what we would need to repel the siege that we'll soon suffer?'

'No,' Cador replied. 'We are going to die here, but that is not my point. My point, brother, is that the city has a command structure already in place.'

Bastilan pitched in. 'You are not a general, Grimaldus. And you were not sent here to be one.'

Grimaldus nodded, his mind flashing back from the fire on the wastelands, snapping into recollections of the endless command staff meetings when the mortals had requested his presence.

He had thought it was his duty to be present, to grasp the full situation facing the hive. When he said these words to his brothers, he was answered with curses and smiles.

The Chaplain watched the greenskin swarm growing in size as more landers came down. The alien vessels darkened the sky, such was their number. Like steel beetles, they infested the wastelands in every direction, disgorging hosts of xenos warriors.

'It *was* my duty to study every soul, every weapon, every

metre of this hive. But I have erred, brothers. The High Marshal did not send me here to command.'

'We know,' Artarion said softly, his skin tingling at the change in Grimaldus's tone. He sounded almost himself again.

'Until this moment, until I looked upon the enemy myself, I had not resigned myself to dying here. I was... enraged... with Helbrecht for damning me to this exile.'

'As were we all,' Priamus said, his voice rich with the sneer he wore on his face. 'But we will carve a legend here, Reclusiarch. We will make the High Marshal remember the day he sent us here to die.'

Good words, Grimaldus thought. Fine words.

'He will always recall that day. It is not he who must be forced to remember the Helsreach Crusade.' The Chaplain nodded out to the massing army. 'It is them.'

Grimaldus looked to his left, then his right. The Steel Legion stood in organised ranks, watching the mass of enemies coming together on the plains. When his own gaze returned to the foe, he couldn't help a smile creeping its way across his features.

'This is Grimaldus of the Black Templars,' he voxed. 'Colonel Sarren, answer me.'

'I am here, Reclusiarch. Commander Barasath reports–'

'Later, colonel. Later. I am looking at the enemy, tens of thousands, with more landing each moment. They will not wait for their wreck-Titans to be landed. These beasts are hungry for bloodshed. The first strike will come at the north wall, within the next two hours.'

'With respect, Reclusiarch, how will they reach the wall without Titans to breach it?'

'Propulsion packs to gain the battlements. Ladders to climb.

Artillery to pound holes in the walls. They will do whatever they can, and as soon as they are able. These creatures have been imprisoned on bulk ships for weeks, and in some cases, months. Do not expect sense. Expect madness and rage.'

'Understood. I will have Barasath's squadrons ready for bombing runs on enemy artillery.'

'I would have suggested the same, colonel. The gates, Sarren. We must watch the gates. A wall is only as strong as its weakest point, and they will come at the north gate with everything they have.'

'Reinforcements are already being rerouted to–'

'No.'

'Pardon me?'

'You heard me. I will not require reinforcement. I have fifteen of my knights with me, and an entire Steel Legion regiment. I will provide updates as the situation evolves.' Grimaldus killed the vox-link before Sarren could argue more.

The Templar watched the enemy massing in the distance for several more minutes, listening to the chatter of the Guard soldiers nearby. The men around him wore the insignia of the 273rd Steel Legion. Their shoulder badges showed a black carrion bird, clutching the Imperial aquila in its claws.

The Reclusiarch closed his eyes, recalling the personnel data meetings he'd endured. The 273rd. The Desert Vultures. Their commanding officer was Colonel F. Nathett. His second officers were Major K. Johan, and Major V. Oros.

In the distance, a great cry was raised. It barely reached the defenders' ears over the powerful refrain of wall-guns firing, but it was there nevertheless. Thousands upon thousands of orks bellowing their racial war cry.

They were charging.

Charging alongside grumbling, rickety vehicles: troop-carriers stolen from the Imperium and subsequently junked in the spirit of alien 'improvement'; growling tanks that already lobbed shells that fell far short of the city walls; even great beasts of burden, the size of scout-class Titans, with scrap-metal howdahs on their rocking backs, filled with howling orks.

'We have sixteen minutes before they reach the range of the wall-guns,' Nerovar said. 'Twenty-two before they reach the gates, if their rate of advance remains unaltered.'

Grimaldus opened his eyes, and took a breath. The humans were muttering amongst themselves, and even though they were trained veterans, Grimaldus's gene-enhanced senses could scent the reek of sudden sweat and fear-soured breath through their respirators. No mortal could fail to be moved by the horde of devastation rumbling their way. Even without their greater war machines, the first ork assault was vast.

The city was ready. The enemy was coming. It was time to face up to why he was exiled here.

Grimaldus took a step up onto the battlements.

The wind was strong – an atmospheric disturbance from so many heavy craft making planetfall – but despite the powerful gale that whipped the greatcoats of the human soldiers, Grimaldus remained steady.

He walked along the edge of the wall, his weapons drawn and activated. The generator coils on the back of his plasma pistol burned with fierce light, and his crozius maul sparked with lethal force. As he moved, the eyes of the soldiers followed him. The wind tore at his tabard and the parchment scrolls fastened to his armour. He paid no heed to the anger of the elements.

'Do you see that?' he asked quietly.

At first, only silence followed. Hesitantly, the Guard soldiers began to cast glances to each other, uncomfortable with the Chaplain's presence and confused by his behaviour.

All eyes were on him now. Grimaldus aimed his mace out at the advancing hordes. Thousands. Tens of thousands. And only the very beginning.

'*Do you see that?*' he roared at the humans. The closest ranks flinched back from the mechanical bark that issued almost deafeningly loud from his skull helm.

'*Answer me!*'

He received several trembling nods. 'Yes, sir...' uttered a handful of them, the speakers faceless within the masses behind their rebreather masks.

Grimaldus turned back to the wasteland, already dark with the teeming, chaotic ranks of the enemy. At first, his helm emitted a low, vox-distorted chuckle. Within a few seconds, he was laughing, laughing up at the burning sky while aiming his crozius hammer at the enemy.

'Are you all as insulted as I am? *This* is what they send against us?'

He turned back to the men, the laughter fading, but amused contempt filling his voice even through the inhumanising vocalisers of his helm.

'This is what they send? This *rabble*? We hold one of the mightiest cities on the face of the planet. The fury of its guns sends all skyborne enemies to the ground in flames. We stand united in our thousands – our weapons without number, our purity without question, and our hearts beating courage through our blood. And *this* is how they attack us?

'Brothers and sisters... A legion of beggars and alien dregs wheezes its way across the plains. Forgive me when the moment comes that they whine and weep against our walls. Forgive me that I must order you to waste ammunition upon their worthless bodies.'

Grimaldus paused, lowering his weapon at last, turning his back on the invaders as if bored by their very existence. His entire attention was focused upon the soldiers below him.

'I have heard many souls speak my name in whispers since I came to Helsreach. I ask you now: Do you know me?'

'Yes,' several voices replied, several among the hundreds.

'*Do you know me?*' he bellowed at them over the firing of the wall-guns.

'*Yes!*' a chorus answered now.

'*I am Grimaldus of the Black Templars! A brother to the Steel Legions of this defiant world!*'

A muted cheer greeted his words. It wasn't enough, not even close.

'*Never again in life will your actions carry such consequence. Never again will you serve as you serve now. No duty will matter as much, and no glory will taste as true. We are the defenders of Helsreach. On this day, we carve our legend in the flesh of every alien we slay. Will you stand with me?*'

Now the cheers came in truth. They thundered in the air around him.

'*Will you stand with me?*'

Again, a roar.

'*Sons and daughters of the Imperium! Our blood is the blood of heroes and martyrs! The xenos dare defile our city? They dare tread the sacred soil of our world? We will throw their bodies from these walls when the final day dawns!*'

A wave of noise crashed against his armour as they

cheered. Grimaldus raised his war maul, aiming it to the embattled heavens.

'This is *our* city! This is *our* world! Say it! *Say it! Cry it out so the bastards in orbit will hear our fury! Our city! Our world!'*

'OUR CITY! OUR WORLD!'

Laughing again, Grimaldus turned to face the oncoming horde. *'Run, alien dogs! Come to me! Come to us all! Come and die in blood and fire!'*

'BLOOD AND FIRE!'

The Reclusiarch cut the air with his crozius, as if ordering his men forward. *'For the Templars! For the Steel Legion! For Helsreach!'*

'FOR HELSREACH!'

'Louder!'

'FOR HELSREACH!'

'They cannot hear you, brothers!'

'FOR HELSREACH!'

'Hurl yourselves at these walls, inhuman filth! Die on our blades! I am Grimaldus of the Black Templars, and I will cast your carcasses from these holy walls!'

'GRIMALDUS! GRIMALDUS! GRIMALDUS!'

Grimaldus nodded, still staring out over the wastelands, letting the cheering chant mix with the howling wind, knowing it would carry to the advancing enemy.

A vox-voice pulled him from his reverie. 'That is the first time since we landed,' said Artarion, 'that you have sounded like yourself.'

'We have a war to fight,' the Chaplain replied. 'The past is done with. Nero, how long?'

The Apothecary tilted his head, watching the horde for several moments.

'Six minutes until they are within range of the wall-guns.'

Grimaldus stepped down from the edge of the wall, standing among the Guard. They backed away from him, even as they all still cheered his name.

'Vultures!' he called, 'I must speak with Colonel Nathett, and Majors Oros and Johan. Where are your officers?'

A GREAT DEAL can happen in six minutes, especially when one has the resources of a fortress-city to call upon.

Dozens of fighters in the gunmetal grey of the 5082nd Naval Skyborne streaked over the advancing horde, punishing them from above with strafing runs. Autocannons chattered, spitting into the tide of enemy flesh. Lascannons beamed with eye-aching brilliance, destroying dozens of the few heavy tanks present in this initial ork host.

Grimaldus stood upon the battlements, weapons in hands, watching Commander Barasath's Lightnings and Thunderbolts unleashing devastation from the sky. He was a veteran of two hundred years. He knew, with cold clarity, when something was wasted effort.

Every death counts, he thought, seeking to force himself to believe it as the immense sea of foes came crashing closer.

Priamus was similarly unmoved. 'Barasath's best attempt is no more than spitting into a tidal wave.'

'Every death counts,' Grimaldus growled. 'Every life lost out there is one less enemy assailing our walls.'

A great beast, some kind of stomping mammoth covered in scales, cried out as it went down, lanced through its legs and belly by a volley of lascannon fire. The orks fell from the howdah on its back, vanishing into the swarm of warriors. Grimaldus prayed they were crushed underfoot by their allies.

On his retinal display, a runic countdown began to flicker red.

He raised his crozius.

ALONG THE NORTH wall, hundreds of multi-barrelled turrets began their realignment. On grinding joints, they cycled down to aim at the wastelands, leaving the city vulnerable from above.

Around each turret, a cluster of soldiers stood ready – loaders, sighters, vox-officers, adjutants, all ready for the order.

'Wall-guns,' Nero voxed to Grimaldus. 'Wall-guns, now.'

Grimaldus sliced the air with his blazing maul, screaming a single word.

'*Fire!*'

CRATERS APPEARED IN the enemy horde. Huge explosions of dirt, scrap metal, bodies and gore erupted from the army. With the numbers facing them, the gunners on Helsreach's walls couldn't miss.

Thousands died in the first barrage. Thousands more came on.

'*Reload!*' a lone figure, armoured in black, shouted into the vox.

The walls themselves shook again, tremors pulsing through the rockcrete as the second volley fired. And the third. And the fourth. In a sane army, the annihilation inflicted upon them would be catastrophic. Entire legions would be breaking and running in fear.

The aliens, blood-maddened and howling their throaty war cries, didn't even slow down. They ignored their dead, trampled their wounded, and crashed against the towering walls like a peal of thunder.

With nothing capable of breaching the metres-thick sealed gates in the northern wall, the berserk aliens began to climb.

I HAVE ALWAYS believed there is something beautiful in the very first moments of a battle. Here are the moments of highest emotion; the fear of mortal men, the frustrated bloodlust and screaming overconfidence of mankind's enemies. In the moments when a battle is joined, the purity of the human species is first revealed to the foe.

In organised union, the hundreds of Steel Legion soldiers step forward. They move like different limbs of the same being. Like a reflection stretching into infinity, every man and woman down the line aims their lasguns over the wall, down at the greenskins howling and clambering. The aliens drag themselves up by their own claws; they climb on ladders and poles; they boost up on the whining thrusters of jump packs.

And all of it so delightfully futile.

The *crack!* of thousands of lasguns discharging in a chorus is a strangely evocative song. It sings of discipline, defiance, strength and courage. More than that, it's a furious response – the first time the defenders can vent their rage at the invaders. Every soldier in the line squeezes their triggers, letting their lasrifles shout for them, spitting death down at the foe. Las-bolts tear into green flesh, ripping orks open, throwing them to the ground far below to be pulped under the boots of their kin.

Barasath's fighters streak overhead, their weapons still stuttering into the massed horde. Their targets have changed – more often than not, they rain their viciousness upon the artillery tanks that were unloaded last from the landers, and are only now catching up to the back to the besieging army.

I watch as the first of our fighters is brought down. Anti-air fire rattles up from a junked Hydra, its two remaining turrets tracking a group of Lightnings. The explosion is almost ignorable – a crumpled pop of fuel tanks detonating, and the protests of engines as the fighter spirals down.

It impacts in a burning wreck, wings shorn off, spinning and crashing through the ranks of the enemy. Some might consider it tragic that the pilot likely killed more of the enemy with his death than he did in life. I care only that more of the invaders are dead.

The first of the enemy to gain the ramparts does so alone. A hundred metres and more down the wall, a lone ork crashes down with his back-mounted propulsion pack streaming smoky fire. The others that were with him are either dead or dying, falling from their ascent as their bodies and thruster fuel tanks are riddled with las-fire. The one alien that touches down on the wall lasts less than a heartbeat. The creature is bayoneted in the throat, the eye, the chest and both legs by half a dozen soldiers, and their rifles blast the beast back over the edge.

First blood to Helsreach.

THE MINUTES BECAME hours.

The orks hurled themselves against the walls, still lacking any ability to secure a hold there, clambering up the hulls of wrecked tanks, mounds of their own dead, and ladders of twisted metal in a vain effort to reach the battlements.

Word was filtering through the wall commanders now; the east and west walls were enduring similar sieges. In the wasteland around the city, more landers were making planetfall, unloading fresh warriors and legions of tanks. While plenty of these new forces committed themselves immediately to the first attack already in progress, many more remained far from the city, making camps, clearing more landing zones and organising for a far more coordinated assault in the future.

The hive's defenders could make out individual banners among the ork swarm – clans and tribes united under the Great Enemy – many of which were now holding back rather than hurling themselves into this first, doomed attack.

Grimaldus remained with the Steel Legion troops on the northern wall, his knights spread out among the Guard's ranks, the Adeptus Astartes' own squad unity suspended. Occasionally, greenskins would manage to reach the battlements rather than being slaughtered as they climbed. In those rare moments, Templar chainblades would shear through stinking alien flesh, before Guard-issue lasrifles would finish the job with precision beams of laser light.

At some point during the endless firing downward, Major Oros had voxed Grimaldus in bemusement.

'They're just lining up to die,' he'd laughed.

'These are the most foolish, and the least in control of themselves. They hunger to fight, no matter the odds or the war being waged. Look out onto the plains, major. Witness the gathering of our real enemies.'

'Understood, Reclusiarch.'

Grimaldus heard the Legion officers shouting to their men then, ordering another change of rank. The soldiers at the battlements fell back to reload, to clean their weapons and cool down overheating power-packs. The next line advanced to take their comrades' vacated positions, stepping up to the ramparts and immediately opening fire on the climbing orks.

The smell of the siege was drifting into the city now. Mountains of alien dead lay at the foot of the walls, their bodies ruptured and their tainted fluids leaking into the ashy soil. While the Templars and the Legionnaires were spared the worst of the stench by their helms and rebreathers, within the city itself, the civilians and militia forces were getting their first, foul taste of war against the ork-breed xenos. It was an unpleasant revelation.

Night was threatening to fall before the aliens finally fled.

Whether the mountain of their own dead had turned their fury to futility, or whether some cognition finally dawned over them all that the true battles were yet to come, the green tide retreated en masse. Horns sounded across the wasteland, hundreds of them, signalling a retreat that otherwise lacked even a hint of cohesion. Las-bolts flashed down from the walls as the Legion kept up a savage rate of fire, punishing the orks for their cowardice now just as they had punished them for their eager madness before. Hundreds more of the xenos collapsed to the ground, slain by the day's last, bitterest volley.

Soon, even the stragglers were out of range, limping their way behind the horde back to their landing sites.

Ork ships covered the wasteland now from horizon to horizon. The largest ships, almost as tall as hive spires themselves, were opening to release colossal, stomping scrap-Titans. Like hunched, fat-bellied aliens in shape, the junk-giants crashed across the plains, their pounding tread raising dust clouds in their wake.

These were the weapons that would bring the wall down. These were the foes that Invigilata had to destroy.

'That,' Artarion nodded at the sight as the knights remained on the wall, 'is a bleak picture.'

'The real battle begins tomorrow,' Cador grunted. 'At least we will not be bored.'

'I believe they will wait.' It was Grimaldus who spoke, his voice less bitter now the war cries and speeches were over. 'They will wait until they have overwhelming force with which to crush us, and they will strike like a hammer.'

The Chaplain paused, leaning on the battlements and staring at the army as sunset claimed the surrounded city.

'I requested we withdraw all Guard forces from the wasteland installations across all of southern Armageddon Secundus. The colonel agreed in principle.'

Bastilan joined the Reclusiarch at the wall. The sergeant disengaged his helm's seals and stood barefaced, ignoring the cool wind that prickled at his unshaven scalp.

'What's worth guarding out there?'

The Reclusiarch smiled, his expression hidden.

'The days and days of briefings were a necessary evil to answer questions like that. Munitions,' Grimaldus said. 'A great deal of munitions, to be used when the hive cities fall and need to be reclaimed. But that is not all. The Desert Vultures spoke of a curious legend. Something buried beneath the sands. A weapon.'

'We are involving ourselves in this world's mythology now?'

'Do not dismiss this. I heard something today that gave me hope.' He took a breath, narrowing his eyes as he watched the sea of enemy banners. 'And I have an idea. Where is Forgemaster Jurisian?'

CHAPTER VII
ANCIENT SECRETS

CYRIA TYRO LEANED back in her chair, closing her eyes to rid her vision of the numbers she'd been staring at.

Casualties from the first day's engagement were light, and damage to the wall was minimal. Flamer teams had been lowered to drag the alien dead away from the city walls and burn them in massive pyres. It was a volunteer-only duty, and one that came with an element of risk – if the orks decided to attack in the night, there was no guarantee the hundreds of pyre-lighters outside could be brought back in time.

The funeral fires burned now, an hour before dawn, and though there were far too many bodies to complete the duty in a single night, the mounds of xenos dead were at least reduced.

For now, she sighed.

The ammunition expended on the first day alone had been... Well, she'd seen the numbers and could scarcely believe her eyes. The city was a fortress and its weapon reserves had seemed inexhaustible, but on a day of relatively sporadic fighting with only three regiments engaged, the logistical nightmare soon to be facing them was all too apparent. Their ammunition stocks would last months, but supplying it to regiments scattered throughout the city, ensuring they were aware of boltholes, weapons caches and…

I'm tired, she thought with a dry smile. She'd not even fought today.

Tyro signed a few data-slates with her thumbprint, authorising the transferral of reports to Lord General Kurov and Commissar Yarrick, far off in distant hives, already engaged in their own sieges.

The door's proximity chime pulsed once.

'Enter,' she called out.

Major Ryken walked in. His greatcoat was unbuttoned, his rebreather mask was hanging from its cord around his neck, and his black hair was scruffy from the rain.

'It's hurling it down out there,' he grumbled. He'd come all the way from the east wall. 'You wouldn't believe what the orbital disturbance has done to the atmosphere. What did you want that couldn't be done over the vox?'

'I couldn't reach Colonel Sarren.'

'He'd not slept in over sixty hours. I think Falkov threatened to shoot him unless he got some rest.' Ryken narrowed his eyes. 'There are other colonels. Dozens of them.'

'True, but none of those are the city commander's executive officer.'

The major scratched the back of his neck. His skin was cold, itching and grimy with the faintly acidic rainwater.

'Miss Tyro,' he began.

'Actually, given my rank as adjutant quintus to the planetary leader, I'll settle for "ma'am" or "advisor". Not "Miss Tyro". This is not a society function, and if it were, I would not be spending it talking to a drowned rat like you, major.'

Ryken grinned. Tyro didn't.

'Very well, *ma'am*, how may this lowly rodent be of service? I have a storm to get back out into before dawn.'

She looked around her own cramped but warm office in the central command tower, hiding her guilty flush by faking a cough.

'We received these from Acheron Hive an hour ago.' She gestured at several printed sheets of paper featuring topographic images. Ryken picked them up from her messy desk, flipping through them.

'These are orbital picts,' he said.

'I know what they are.'

'I thought the enemy fleet had destroyed all our satellites.'

'They have. These were among the last images our orbital defence array was able to send. Acheron received them, and sent them on to the other cities.'

Ryken turned one of the images to face her. 'This one has a caffeine stain on it. Did Acheron send that?'

Tyro scowled at him. 'Grow up, major.'

He spent a few more moments regarding the printed picts. 'What am I looking for here?'

'These are picts of the Dead Lands to the south. *Far* to the south, across the ocean.'

'I paid attention in basic geography, thank you, ma'am.' Ryken went through the picts a second time, lingering over the images of massive ork planetfall discolouring the landscape. 'This makes no sense,' he said at last.

'I know.'

'There's nothing in the Dead Lands. Not a thing.'

'I know, major.'

'So do we have any idea why they landed a force there that looks large enough to take a city?'

'Tacticians suggest the enemy is establishing a spaceport there. Or a colony.'

Ryken snorted, letting the picts drop back onto her desk.

'The tacticians are drunk,' he said. 'Every man, woman and child knows why the xenos come here: to fight. To fight until either they're all dead, or we are. They don't raise the greatest armada in history just to pitch tents at the south pole and raise ugly alien babies.'

'The fact remains,' Tyro gestured to the prints, 'that the enemy is there. Their distance across the ocean puts them out of reach for air strikes. No flyers would reach us without needing to refuel several times. They could just as easily set up airstrips in the wastelands much nearer the hive cities. In fact, we can already see they're doing just that.'

'What about the oil platforms?' he asked.

'The platforms?' she shook her head, not sure where he was leading with this.

'You're kidding me,' Ryken said. 'The Valdez oil platforms. Didn't you study Helsreach before you were posted here? Where do you think half of the hive cities in Armageddon Secundus get their fuel from? They take it in here from the offshore platforms and cook it into promethium for the rest of the continent.'

Tyro already knew this. She let him have his moment of feigned indignity.

'I paid attention,' she smiled, 'in basic economics. The platforms are protected from these southernmost raiders by the same virtue we are. It's just too far to strike at them.'

'Then with all due respect, ma'am, why did you pull me off the wall? I have duties to perform.'

And here it was. She had to deal with this matter delicately.

'I... would appreciate your assistance. First, I must disseminate this information among the other officers.'

'You don't need my help for that. You need access to a vox-caster, and you're sitting in a building full of them. Why should they care, anyway? What does a potential colony of the enemy on the polar cap have to do with the defence of the hive?'

'High Command has informed me that the matter is to be considered Helsreach's problem. We are – relatively speaking – the closest city.'

Ryken laughed. 'Would they like us to invade? I'll get the men ready and tell them to wrap up warm and lay siege to the south pole. I hope the orks outside the city respect the fact we'll be absent for the rest of the siege. They look like sporting gentlemen. I'm sure they'll wait for us to return to the hive before attacking again.'

'*Major.*'

'Yes, ma'am.'

'High Command has informed me to spread the information and let all officers be aware of the concern. That is all. No invasions. And it is not what I require your aid with.'

'Then what is it?'

'Grimaldus,' she said.

'Is that a fact? Problems with the Emperor's finest?'

'This is a serious matter.' Tyro frowned.

'Fair enough. But talk from the Vultures said that he was finally getting involved. They apparently got one hell of a speech.'

'He performed his duties on the wall with great skill and

devotion.' She still wasn't smiling. 'That is not the problem at hand.'

Ryken let his raised eyebrow do the talking.

Tyro sighed. 'The problem is one of contact and mediation. He refuses to talk to me.' She paused, as if considering something for the first time. 'Perhaps because I'm female.'

'You're serious,' Ryken said. 'You truly believe that.'

'Well… He has bonded with the male officers, hasn't he?'

Ryken thought that was debatable. He'd heard that the only commander in the city Grimaldus had treated with anything more than disdainful impatience was the ancient woman that led the Legio Invigilata. And even that was just rumour.

'It's not because you're female,' the major said. 'It's because you're useless.'

The pause lasted several seconds, during which Cyria Tyro's face hardened with each passing moment.

'*Excuse me?*' she asked.

'Useless to them, shall we say. It's simple. You're the liaison between a High Command that is too busy to care what happens here, too distant to make much difference even if it did care, and off-world forces that have no need or interest in playing nice with the grunts of the Guard. Does the Crone of Invigilata need to pass orders through you? Does Grimaldus? No. Neither group cares.'

'The chain of command…' she started, but trailed off.

'The chain of command is a system both the Legio and the Templars are outside. And above, if they choose to be.'

'I feel useless,' she finally said. 'And not just to them.'

He could see how much that admission cost her. He could also see that she didn't seem such a haughty bitch when her defences were down. Just as Ryken drew breath to speak, and tell her a more polite version of his current thoughts, her desk vox-speaker buzzed.

'Adjutant Quintus Cyria Tyro?' asked a deep, resonant male voice.

'Yes. Who is this?'

'Reclusiarch Grimaldus of the Black Templars. I must speak with you.'

THE CRONE OF Invigilata floated in her fluid-filled coffin, appearing to listen to the muffled sounds outside.

In truth, she was paying little attention. The muted sounds of speech and movement belonged to a world of physicality that she barely remembered. Linked with *Stormherald*, the god-machine's ever-present rumbling anger infected her like a chemical injected into her mind. Even in moments of peace, it was difficult to focus on anything but wrath.

To share a mind with *Stormherald* was to dwell within a maze of memories that were not her own. *Stormherald* had looked upon countless battlefields for hundreds of years before Princeps Zarha was even born. She had only to shut down the imagefinders that now served as her eyes, and as the hazy image of her milky surroundings faded to nothing, she could remember deserts she had never seen, wars she had never fought, glories she had never won.

Stormherald's voice in her mind was an unrelenting murmur, a hum of quiet tension, like a low-burning fire. It challenged her, with wordless growls, to taste of the victories it had tasted for so long – to swim beneath the surface memories and surrender to them. Its spirit was a proud and indefatigable machine-soul, and it hungered not only for the fiery maelstrom of war, but also the cold exultation of triumph. It felt the banners of past wars that hung from its metal skin, and it knew fierce, unbreakable pride.

'My princeps,' came a muffled voice.

Zarha activated her photoreceptors. Borrowed memories faded and vision returned. Strange, how the former were so much clearer than the latter, these days.

Hello, Valian.

'Hello, Valian.'

'My princeps, the adepts of the soul are reporting discontent within *Stormherald*'s heart. We are getting anomalous readings of ill-temper from the reactor core.'

We are angry, moderati. We yearn to bring the thunder down upon our foes.

'We are angry, moderati. We yearn to bring the thunder down upon our foes.'

'That is understandable, my princeps. You are… operating at peak capacity? You are sanguine?'

Are you querying if I am at risk of being consumed by Stormherald's heart?

'Are you querying if I am at risk of be*kkrrrssshhhhh* **heart?'**

'Maintenance adept,' Valian Carsomir called to a robed tech-priest. 'Attend to the princeps's vocaliser unit.' He turned back to his commander. 'I trust you, my princeps. Forgive me for troubling you.'

There is nothing to forgive, Valian.

'There is noth*kkkrrrrrsssssssssh.'*

That would become annoying after a while, she thought, but did not pulse the sentiment to her vocaliser. *Your concern touches me, Valian.*

'Your concern touches me, Valian.'

But I am well.

'B*krsh* I am well.'

The tech-adept stood by the side of Zarha's amniotic tank. Mechanical arms slid from his robe and began to do their work.

Moderati Primus Valian Carsomir hesitated, before making the sign of the cog and returning to his station.

We will see battle soon, Valian. Grimaldus has promised it to us.

'We will see battle soon, Valian. Grimaldus has promised it to us.'

Valian didn't reply at first. If the enemy was going to amass its numbers first, shelling the foe from the safety of the city walls was hardly seeing battle, in his eyes.

'We are all ready, my princeps.'

TOMAZ COULDN'T SLEEP.

He sat up in bed, swallowing another stinging mouthful of amasec, the cheap, thin stuff that Heddon brewed in one of the back warehouses down at the docks. The stuff tasted more than a little of engine oil. It wouldn't have surprised Tomaz to learn that was one of the ingredients.

He swallowed another burning gulp that itched its way down his throat. There was, he realised, a more than good chance he was going to throw this stuff back up soon. It had a habit of not sitting too well on an empty stomach once it went down, but he didn't think he could manage another dry meal of preserved rations. Tomaz glanced at several packets of unopened, densely packed grain tablets on the table.

Maybe later.

He'd not been anywhere near the north and eastern walls. At the south docks, there was little difference between today and any other day. The grinding joints of his crane drowned out any of the distant sounds of the war, and he'd spent his twelve-hour shift unloading tankers and organising distribution from the warehouses in his district – just as he spent every shift.

The backlog of docked tankers, and those awaiting docking clearance, was beyond a joke. Half of Tomaz's crew was gone, conscripted into the militia reserves and sent across the city to play at being Guardsmen, kilometres away from where they were really needed. He was the elected representative of the Dockers' Union, and he knew every other foreman was suffering the same lack of manpower. It made a difficult job completely laughable, except none of them were smiling.

There had been talk of limiting the flow of crude coming in from the Valdez platforms once the orbital defences fell, under fears the orks would bombard the shipping lanes.

Necessity outweighed the risk of tanker crews dying, of course. Helsreach needed fuel. The flow continued. Even with the city sealed, the docks remained open.

And they were somehow busier than before, despite the fact there was only half the manpower on the crews. Teams of Steel Legionnaires and menial servitors manned the many anti-air turrets along the dockside and the warehouse rooftops. Hundreds upon hundreds of warehouses were now used to house tanks, converted into maintenance terminals and garages for war machine repair. Convoys of Leman Russ battle tanks shuddered through the docks, strangling thoroughfares with their slow processions.

Half-crewed and slowed by constant interference, the Helsreach docks were almost at a standstill.

And still the tankers arrived.

Tomaz checked his wrist chronometer. Just over two hours until dawn.

He resigned himself to not getting any sleep before his shift began, and took another drink from the bottle of disgusting amasec.

Heddon really should be shot for brewing this rat piss.

SHE STOOD IN the storm, her Steel Legion greatcoat heavy around her shoulders.

The lashing rainfall did little to clean the streets. The reek of sulphur rose from the wet buildings around her as the acidic rain mixed with the pollution coating the stonework and rockcrete across the city.

Not a good time to forget your rebreather, Cyria…

Major Ryken escorted her along the north wall. In the dim distance to the east, the sun was already bringing dawn's first glimmer to the sky. Cyria didn't want to look over the wall's edge, but couldn't help herself. The dim illumination revealed the enemy's army, a tide of darkness that reached from horizon to horizon.

'Throne of the God-Emperor,' she whispered.

'It could be worse,' Ryken said, guiding her onwards after she'd frozen at the sight.

'There must be millions of them out there.'

'Without a doubt.'

'Hundreds of tribes… You can make out their banners…'

'I try not to. Eyes ahead, ma'am.'

Cyria turned with reluctance. Ahead of her, fifty metres down the wall, a group of giant black statues stood in the rainfall, the deluge making the edges of their armour shine.

One of the giants moved, his boots thudding on the wall as he walked towards her. The harsh wind whipped the soaked scrolls tied to his armour, and drenched his tabard with its black cross upon the chest.

His face was a grinning silver skull, the eyes staring a soulless red, right through her.

'Cyria Tyro,' he said in a deep, vox-crackling voice, 'greetings.' The Adeptus Astartes made the sign of the aquila, his dark gauntlets banging against his chestplate as they formed the symbol. 'And Major Ryken of the 101st. Welcome to the north wall.'

Ryken returned the salute. 'I heard you gave the Vultures a speech earlier, Reclusiarch,' he said.

'They are fine warriors, all,' Grimaldus said. 'They needed none of my words, but it was a pleasure to share them, nevertheless.'

Ryken was caught momentarily off-guard. He'd not expected an answer, let alone this unnerving humility. Before he could reply, Cyria spoke up. She looked up at Grimaldus, shielding her eyes from the downpour. The hum of his armour made her gums itch. The sound seemed to be louder than before, as if reacting to the bad weather.

'How may I be of service, Reclusiarch?'

'That is the wrong question,' the knight said, his vox-voice a low growl. The rain scythed onto his armour, hissing as it hit the dark ceramite. 'The question is one you must answer, not one you must ask.'

'As you wish,' she said. His formality was making her uncomfortable. In fact, everything about him was making her uncomfortable.

'We have defensive positions in the wastelands, manned by the Steel Legion. Platoons of the Desert Vultures, among other regiments, have dug in to hold these against the enemy. Small towns, coastal depots, weapons caches, fuel dumps, listening stations.'

Tyro nodded. Most of these outposts, and their relative strategic value, had been covered in the command meetings.

'Yes,' she said, for want of anything else to say.

'Yes,' he repeated her reply, sounding amused. 'I was informed today exactly what is stored in the underground hangar of the D-16 West outpost, ninety-eight kilometres to the north-west of the city. None of our briefings mentioned it was a sealed Mechanicus facility.'

Tyro and Ryken exchanged a glance. The major shrugged a shoulder. Although most of his face was masked by his rebreather, his eyes showed he had no idea what the Chaplain was inferring. Cyria's glance fell back to the towering knight's crimson gaze.

'I've seen little data on D-16 West's storage consignments, Reclusiarch. All I know is that a deactivated relic from the era of the First War is stored in the sub-level compound. No Guard personnel are permitted access to the innards of the facility. It is considered sovereign Mechanicus territory.'

'I learned the same today. That does not intrigue you?' the Adeptus Astartes asked.

It was a fair question. In truth, no, it didn't interest her at all. The First War had been won almost six hundred years ago, and the planet's face was one of different cities and different armies now.

'Whether I find it fascinating or not is hardly of consequence,' she said. 'Whatever is stored there is impounded under orders of the Adeptus Mechanicus – I suspect for a damn good reason – and is a secret even from Planetary High Command. Even our Guard force there is a token battle group. They are not expected to survive the first month.'

'Do you know your history, Adjutant Tyro?' Grimaldus's voice was calm, low and composed. 'Before we made planetfall here, a great deal was committed to our memories. All lore is useful in the right hands. All information can be a weapon against the enemy.'

'I have studied several of the decisive battles of the First War,' she said. All Steel Legion officers had.

'Then you will know what Mechanicus weapon was designed and first deployed here.'

'Throne,' Ryken whispered. 'Holy Throne of Terra.'

'I… don't think you can be right…' Tyro told the Adeptus Astartes.

'Perhaps not,' Grimaldus conceded, 'but I intend to learn the truth for myself. One of our gunships will carry a small group to D-16 West in one hour.'

'But it's sealed!'

'It will not be sealed for long.'

'It's Mechanicus territory!'

'I do not care. If I am right in my suspicions, there is a weapon there. I want that weapon, Cyria Tyro. And I will have it.'

She pulled her greatcoat tighter around her body as the storm intensified.

'If it were something that would help with the war,' she said, 'the Mechanicus would have deployed it by now.'

'I do not believe that, and I am surprised that you do. The Mechanicus has committed a great deal in the defence of Armageddon. That does not mean they have the same stake in the war that we do. I have battled alongside the Cult of Mars many times. They breathe secrecy instead of air.'

'You can't leave the city before dawn. The enemy–'

'The enemy will not break the city walls in the first day.

And Bayard, Emperor's Champion of the Helsreach Crusade, will command the Templars in my absence.'

'I can't allow you to do this. It will enrage the Mechanicus.'

'I am not asking for your permission, adjutant.' Grimaldus paused, and she swore she could hear a smile in his next words. 'I am asking if you wish to come with us.'

'I... I...'

'You informed me upon my arrival that you were here to facilitate interaction between the off-world forces and those of Armageddon.'

'I know, but–'

'Mark my words, Cyria Tyro. If the Mechanicus has reasons for not deploying that weapon, they may not be reasons that other Imperial commanders will find acceptable. I do not care about those reasons. I care about winning this war.'

'I'll accompany you,' she almost choked on the words. Throne, what was she doing...

'I thought you would,' said Grimaldus. 'The sun is rising. Come, to the Thunderhawk. My brothers already wait.'

THE GUNSHIP SHUDDERED as its boosters lifted it from the landing platform.

The pilot, an Initiate knight with few honour markings on his armour, guided the ship skyward.

'Try not to get us shot down,' Artarion said to him, standing behind the pilot's throne in the cockpit. They were set to fly above the clouds anyway, and take a course over the ocean and the coast before veering inland once they were clear of the besieging army and its fighter support.

'Brother,' the Initiate said, watching the city falling below as he applied vertical thrust, 'does anyone ever laugh at your jokes?'

'Humans sometimes do.'

The pilot didn't reply to that. Artarion's answer said it all. The gunship gave a kick as its velocity boosters fired, and through the cockpit window, the toxic cloud cover began to slide past.

CHAPTER VIII

OBERON

DOMOSKA MUTTERED THE Litany of Focus as she looked through the sight of her lasrifle. She blinked behind her sunglare goggles, then raised them to look through the gunsight again without the tinted lenses darkening her vision.

'Uh, Andrej?' she called over her shoulder.

The two soldiers were at their modest camp on the perimeter of D-16's boundaries. Sat on the desert sands, cleaning their rifles, the fact they were away from the main base also set them apart from the other forty-eight Steel Legionnaires assigned to this pointless, suicidal duty.

Andrej didn't look up from his lap, where he was wiping laspistol power cell packs with an oily rag.

'What is it now, eh? I'm busy, okay?'

'Is that a gunship?'

'What are you talking about, eh?' Andrej was from Armageddon Prime, on the far side of the world. His accent always made Domoska grin. Almost everything he said sounded like a question.

'That,' she pointed into the sky, close to the horizon. Nothing was visible to the naked eye, and Andrej groped on the coat laid out on the ground, reaching for his detached gunsight.

'Listen, okay, I am trying to respect the spirit of my weapon, yes? What is this you want? I see no gunship.' He stared through his sight, squinting.

'A few degrees above the horizon.'

'Oh, hey, yes that is a gunship, okay? You must report it at once.'

'This is Domoska, at Boundary Three. Contact, contact, contact. Imperial gunship inbound.'

'That is the Black Templars, yes? They are from Helsreach. I know this. I listen to my briefings. I do not sleep, like you.'

'Be quiet,' she murmured, waiting for confirmation over the vox.

'I will be the one with so many medals, I think. You have nothing, eh?'

'Be quiet!'

'Acknowledged,' the reply finally came. Andrej took that as his cue to speak again.

'I hope they are saying we may return to the city, okay? That would be good news. High walls! Titans! We might even survive this war, eh?'

Neither of them had ever seen a Thunderhawk gunship before. As it came in on howling thrusters, slowing down and hovering over the almost abandoned facility of empty warehouses and storage bunkers, Domoska had a sinking sensation in her stomach.

'This can't be good.' She bit her lower lip.

'I do not agree, you know? This is Adeptus Astartes business. It will be good. Good for us, bad for the enemy.'

She just looked at him.

'What? It will be good. You will see, eh? I am always right.'

Storm trooper Captain Insa Rashevska glanced at the soldiers on either side of her as the gunship's front ramp lowered on hissing hydraulics.

One thought had been rattling around her mind in the five minutes since Domoska had voxed in the sighting, and that was a very simple, clear: *Why in the hells are the Adeptus Astartes here?*

She was about to get her answer.

'Should we... salute?' one of her men asked from his position at Rashevska's side. 'Is that what you're supposed to do?'

'I don't know,' she replied. 'Just stand at attention.'

The gang ramp clanged as boots descended. A human – from the Legion, no less – and two Templars.

Both Adeptus Astartes wore the black of their Chapter. One was draped in a tabard showing personal heraldry, and his helm showed an ornate death mask as the faceplate. The other wore much bulkier armour, with additional layers of ablative plating, and the war-plate whirred and clanked as its false-muscles moved.

'Captain,' the Legion officer said. 'I'm Adjutant Quintus Tyro, seconded to Hive Helsreach from the Lord General's command staff. With me are Reclusiarch Grimaldus and Master of the Forge Jurisian, of the Black Templars Chapter.'

Rashevska made the sign of the aquila, trying not to show her unease in the presence of the towering warriors. Four machine-arms, their servo-joints grinding, unlocked from

Jurisian's thrumming back-mounted power pack. Their metal claws clicked open and snapped closed while the arms themselves extended as if stretching.

'Greetings,' Jurisian rumbled.

'Captain,' Grimaldus said.

'We have come to enter the installation,' Cyria Tyro smiled.

Rashevska said nothing for almost ten seconds. When she did speak, it was with a stunned and disbelieving laugh.

'Forgive me, is this a joke?'

'Far from it,' Grimaldus said, striding past her.

On the surface, D-16 West wasn't a particularly grand site. Rising from the wasteland's sandy soil were a cluster of buildings, all of which were solidly built and armoured – almost bunker-like in their squat construction. All were empty, save for those now occupied by the small Steel Legion force stationed here. In those buildings, bedrolls and equipment were arranged in an order that spoke of discipline. Two expansive landing platforms, easily big enough for the bulky Mechanicus cruisers that could even carry Titans, were half buried in sand, as the desert slowly reclaimed the facility.

The only architecture of significant interest was a roadway over a hundred metres in width that led into the ground beneath the surface complex. Whatever colossal doors had once opened into the underground complex were long buried beneath the wasteland's shifting tides. It would only be a handful of decades before the last evidence of the roadway itself was covered over.

One of the bunker buildings contained nothing but a series of elevators. The bulkhead doors to each lift were sealed, and the machinery lining the walls and connected to the shafts was all powered down. Keypads with runic buttons of various colours were installed on the wall next to each closed door.

'There is no power here,' the Reclusiarch said as he looked around. 'They left this place entirely devoid of energy?' That would make reactivation – if this installation was even ever meant to be reactivated – an incredibly difficult operation.

Jurisian walked around the interior of the bunker, his thudding tread making the floor tremble.

'No,' he said, his vox-voice a slow, considering drawl. 'There is power. The installation sleeps, but does not lie dead. It is locked in hibernation. Power still beats through its veins. The resonance is low, the pulse is slow. I hear it, nevertheless.'

Grimaldus stroked his fingertips along the closest keypad, staring at the unknown sigils that marked each button. The language of the runes was not High Gothic.

'Can you open these doors?' he asked. 'Can you get us down into the complex?'

Jurisian's four machine-arms extended again, their claws articulating. Two of the servo-arms came over the Tech-marine's shoulders. The other two remained closely aligned with his true arms. The Master of the Forge approached one of the other elevator bulkheads, already reaching for his enhanced auspex scanner mag-locked to his belt. The arms reaching over his shoulders took Jurisian's bolter and blade, gripping them in claw clamps and leaving the knight's hands free.

'Jurisian? Can you do this?'

'It will necessitate a great deal of rerouting power from auxiliary sources, and those will be difficult to reach from a remote connection point here. A parasitic feed is required from–'

'Jurisian. Answer the question.'

'Forgive me, Reclusiarch. Yes. I will need one hour.'

Grimaldus waited, statue-still, watching Jurisian work. Cyria quickly grew bored, and wandered through the complex, speaking with the storm troopers on duty. Two were returning from their shift at a boundary post, and the adjutant waved them over as she stood in the avian shadow cast by the gunship.

'Ma'am,' the female trooper saluted. 'Welcome to D-16 West.'

'Now we have Helsreach brass coming to visit, okay?' said the other. He made the sign of the aquila a moment later. 'I told you it would be good.'

Cyria returned their salutes, not even a little off-guard at their nonchalance. Storm troopers were the best of the best, and their distance from regular troops often bred a little… uniqueness… into their attitudes.

'I'm Adjutant Quintus Tyro.'

'We know. We were told this on the vox. Digging for secrets in the sand, yes? That is not going to make the Mechanicus smile, I think.'

Whether the Mechanicus would be pleased or not evidently didn't matter to this man. He was smiling, either way.

'A big risk,' he added, nodding sagely as if this were some hidden truth he had worked out alone. 'It may bring much trouble, eh?' He still seemed entertained by the concept.

'With respect,' the female trooper – her stormcoat badge read DOMOSKA in flat black letters – said, looking uncomfortable, 'Will this not anger the Legio Invigilata?'

Tyro stroked a stray lock of her dark hair from her face, tucking it behind her ear. She repeated exactly what Grimaldus had said to her when she'd asked the same question during the Thunderhawk flight here.

'Perhaps,' she said, 'but it's not like they can leave the city in protest, is it?'

THE DOORS OPENED.

The motion was smooth, but the noise of resistant machine-innards was immense: a squealing, unlubricated whine that split the air. Inside the elevator, the spacious car had enough room for twenty humans. Its walls were a matt, gunmetal grey.

Jurisian stepped back from the control console.

'It was necessary to power down all other ascent/descent systems. This one shaft will function. The others are now soulless.'

Grimaldus nodded. 'Will we be able to return to the surface once we go down?'

'There is a thirty-three point eight per cent chance, given current system destabilisation, that a return ascent will require additional maintenance and reconfiguring. There is a further twenty-nine per cent chance that no reconfiguring will restore function without access to the primary installation power network.'

'The word you're looking for, brother,' Grimaldus stepped towards the open doors, 'is "maybe".'

THEY WANDERED DOWN there for hours.

The underground complex was a silent – and initially lightless – series of labyrinthine corridors and deserted chambers. Jurisian brought the installation's overhead lighting back online after several minutes at a wall console.

Cyria clicked her torch off. Grimaldus cancelled his helm's vision intensifier settings. With flickering reluctance, dull yellow lighting illuminated their surroundings.

'I have resuscitated the spirits of the illuminatory array,' Jurisian said. 'They are weak from slumber, but should hold.'

The bland greyness all around them soon grew uninspiring as they ventured deeper into the complex. Around corners, through silent chambers with inactive engines, motionless machinery and generators of unknowable purpose.

Jurisian would occasionally pause and examine some of the Mechanicus's abandoned technology.

'This is a magnetic field stabiliser housing,' he said at one point, walking around what looked to Cyria like an oversized tank engine as big as a Chimera.

'What does it do?' she made the mistake of asking.

'It houses the stabilisers for a magnetic field generator.'

Her fear of the Adeptus Astartes had dimmed some way by this point. She fought the urge to sigh, but failed.

'Do you mean,' Jurisian enquired, 'what application does this have in Imperial technology?'

'That's close to what I meant, yes. What is its purpose?'

'Magnetic fields of significant size and intensity are difficult to create and a struggle to maintain. Many of these units would be required to work in synchronicity, stabilising a powerful field of magnetic force. Such standard constructs as this housing are used in anti-gravitational technology, much of which is kept sealed by Mechanicus secrecy. More commonly, the Imperial Navy would use these units in the construction and maintenance of starship-sized magnetic accelerator rings. Plasma weapon technology, on a grand scale.'

'No,' Cyria shook her head. 'It can't be.'

'We shall see,' Jurisian rumbled. 'This is only the installation's first level. From the angle of the buried roadway, I would conjecture that the complex proceeds beneath the earth for at least a kilometre. From my knowledge of template patterns used in Mechanicus facility construction, it is more likely to be two or three kilometres deep.'

NINE HOURS AFTER Grimaldus, Jurisian and Cyria had entered the installation, they reached the fourth sublevel. The third level had taken almost six hours to traverse, with sealed doors requiring more and more intensive manipulation to coax open. At one point, Grimaldus had been certain they were thwarted. He hefted his crozius in both hands, triggering it live, ready to vent his anger on the unopening door.

'Don't,' Jurisian said, without looking up from the controls.

'Why not? You said this might be impossible, and time is not our ally down here.'

'Do not apply force to the doors. These are, as you have seen, each no less than four metres thick. While you will eventually hammer through to the other side, it will not be a rapid endeavour, and such violence is likely to activate the installation's significant defences.'

Grimaldus lowered his mace. 'I see no defences.'

'No. That is their strength, and the primary reason no living and augmetic guards are required.'

He still did not look away from his work as he spoke. Four of Jurisian's six arms all worked at the console: hitting buttons, pulling clusters of wires and cables, tying them, fusing them together, replacing them, tuning dead screens. His lower servo-arms were now coiled close to his back-mounted power pack, carrying his bolter and power sword.

'There are,' Jurisian continued, 'twelve hundred needle-thin holes in the walls, spaced ten centimetres apart, in this corridor alone.'

Grimaldus examined the walls. His visor locked on to one immediately, now he knew they were there.

'And these are…?'

'A defence. Part of one. The application of force, no matter how righteous, brother, will trigger the machinery behind these holes – and the same holes in many other corridors and chambers throughout the complex – to release a toxic gas. It is my estimation that the gas would attack the nervous system and respiration above all, making it especially lethal to fully biological intruders.'

The Master of the Forge nodded pointedly to Cyria.

Grimaldus's crozius went dead as he released the trigger. 'Have there been other defences that escaped our attention?'

'Yes,' Jurisian said. 'Many. From automated las-turrets to voidshield screens. Forgive me, Reclusiarch, this code manipulation requires my full attention.'

That had been three hours ago.

Finally, the doors opened to the fourth sublevel. To Cyria, the air was painfully cold, and she pulled her stormcoat tightly closed.

Grimaldus failed to notice her discomfort. Jurisian merely commented, 'The temperature is at a survivable level. You will not suffer lasting harm. This is common in Mechanicus facilities that are left on minimal power.'

She nodded, her teeth chattering.

Ahead of them, the corridor widened to end in a huge double doorway, sealed as every other door had been so far. On this one, etched into the dull, grey metal, was a single word in bold Gothic.

- OBERON -

This was why Grimaldus hadn't noticed Cyria's shivering. He could not take his eyes off the inscription, with each letter standing as tall as a Templar.

'I was right,' he breathed. 'This is it.'

Jurisian was already at the door. One of his human hands stroked the surface of the sealed portal, while the others accessed the wall terminal nearby. Its complexity was horrific compared to those stationed at the previous doors.

'It is so beautiful...' Jurisian sounded both hesitant and awed. 'It is magnificent. This would survive orbital bombardment. Even the use of cyclonic torpedoes against nearby hives would barely harm the protection around this chamber. It is void-shielded, armoured like no bunker I have ever seen... and sealed with... with a billion or more individual codes.'

'Can you do it?' Grimaldus asked, his gauntleted fingertips brushing the 'O' in the inscribed name.

'I have never witnessed anything so complex and incredible. It would be like mapping every particle within a star.'

Grimaldus withdrew his hand. He seemed not to have heard.

'Can you do it?'

'Yes, Reclusiarch. But it will take between nine and eleven days. And I would like my servitors sent to me as soon as you return. '

'It will be done.'

Cyria Tyro felt tears standing in her eyes as she stared at the name. 'I don't believe it. It can't be here.'

'It is,' Grimaldus said, taking a last look at the doors. 'This is where the Mechanicus hid the Ordinatus Armageddon after the First War. This is the tomb of *Oberon*.'

AS THEY RETURNED to the surface, Cyria's hand-vox crackled for her attention, and a signal rune pulsed on Grimaldus's retinal display.

'Tyro, here,' she said into her communicator.

'Grimaldus. Speak,' he said within his helm.

It was the same message, delivered by two different sources. Tyro had Colonel Sarren, his voice more of an exhausted sigh than anything else. Grimaldus heard the clipped, imperious tones of Champion Bayard.

'Reclusiarch,' the champion said. 'The Old Man's predictions were correct, as you suspected. The enemy is annihilating Hades Hive from orbit. It is crudely done. Standard bombardment, with mass drivers to hurl asteroids at a defenceless city. A dark day's work, brother. Will you return soon?'

'We are on our way back now,' he said, and killed the link.

Tyro lowered her communicator, her face pale.

'Yarrick was right,' she said. 'Hades is burning.'

CHAPTER IX

GAMBITS

THE ENEMY DID not come on the second day.

The defenders watched from the walls of Helsreach as the wastelands turned black with enemy vessels and clans of orks establishing their territory, making primitive camps and raising banners to the sky. More landers brought new floods of troops. Bulk cruisers disgorged fat-hulled wreck-Titans.

Upon the enemy banners, thousands of crudely painted symbols faced the city, each one depicting a bloodline, a tribe, a xenos war-clan that would soon be hurling itself into battle.

From the battlements, the Imperial soldiers marked these symbols, and responded in kind. Standards flew above the walls – one for every regiment serving inside the city. The Steel Legion banners flew in greatest number, ochre and orange and yellow and black.

After he returned from D-16 West, Grimaldus himself planted the banner of the Black Templars among those already standing on the north wall. The Desert Vultures gathered to watch the knight ram the banner pole into the rockcrete, and swear an oath that Helsreach would never fall while one defender still lived.

'Hades may burn,' he called to the gathered soldiers, 'but it burns because the enemy fears us. It burns to hide the enemy's shame, so they need never look upon the place where they lost the last war. While the walls of Helsreach stand, so stands this banner. While one defender draws breath, the city will never be lost.'

In echo of his gesture, Cyria Tyro persuaded a moderati to plant the banner of the Legio Invigilata nearby. Lacking a banner suitable for handling by humans rather than the huge standards that were borne by the god-machines, one of the weapon-arm pennants from the Warhound Titan *Executor* was used in absentia – mounted on a pole and driven into the wall between two Steel Legion banners.

The soldiers on the wall cheered. Unused to such attention outside the cockpit of his beloved Warhound, the moderati seemed awkwardly pleased by the reaction. He made the sign of the cog to the officers present, and made the sign of the aquila a moment later, as if anxiously covering a mistake.

At night, the winds blew harder and colder. It almost cleared the air of the sulphuric stench that was forever present and, at its strongest, it dragged the standard of the 91st Steel Legion from the battlements of the west wall. Preachers attached to the regiment warned that it was an omen – that the 91st would be the first to fall if they did not stand defiant when the true storm struck.

As the sun was setting, Helsreach shook with thunder to match the maelstrom taking place on the wastelands. *Stormherald* was leading several of its metal kin to the walls, where the largest – the battle-class Titans – could fire over the battlements once the enemy came in range.

The Guard were ordered to abandon the walls for hundreds of metres around the god-machines. The sound of their weapons discharging would be deafening to anyone too close, and even being near the gigantic guns could be lethal, with the amount of energy they unleashed as they fired.

No one in Helsreach would be sleeping tonight.

HE OPENED HIS eyes.

'Brother,' a voice called to him. 'The Crone of Invigilata requests your presence.'

Grimaldus had returned to the city hours ago. He had been expecting this summons.

'I am in prayer,' he said into the vox.

'I know, Reclusiarch.' It was not like Artarion to be so formal.

'Did she *request* my presence, Artarion?'

'No, Reclusiarch. She, ah, "demanded" it.'

'Inform Invigilata I will attend Princeps Zarha within the hour, once my ritual observations are complete.'

'I do not believe she is in the mood to be kept waiting, Grimaldus.'

'Nevertheless, waiting is what she will do.'

The Chaplain closed his eyes again as he kneeled on the floor of the small, empty chamber in the command spire, and once more let his mouth form the whispered words of reverence.

I APPROACH THE amniotic tank.

My weapons are not in my hands, and this time, in the close confines of the Titan's busy cockpit chamber, the tension from before is distilled into something altogether more fierce. The crewmen, the pilots, the tech-priests... They stare with unconcealed hostility. Several hands rest on belts close to sheathed blades or holstered firearms.

I refrain from laughing at this display, though it is no easy feat. They command the greatest war machine in the entire city, yet they concern themselves with ceremonial daggers and autopistols.

Zarha, the Crone of Invigilata, floats before me. Her lined, matronly face is twisted by emotion. Her limbs twitch in gentle spasm every few moments – feedback from the link with *Stormherald*'s soul.

'You requested my presence?' I say to her.

The old woman suspended in the fluid licks her metallic teeth. **'No. I summoned you.'**

'And that was your first mistake, princeps,' I tell her. 'You are granted permission to make only two more before this conversation is over.'

She snarls, her face hideous in the milky fluids. **'Enough of your posturing, Adeptus Astartes. You should be slain where you stand.'**

I look around the cockpit, at the nine souls in here with me. My targeting reticule locks on to all visible weapons, before returning to focus on the Crone's withered features.

'That would be an unwise solution,' I tell her. 'No one in this room is capable of wounding me. Should you call the eight skitarii waiting outside the doors, I would still leave this chamber a charnel house. And you, princeps, would be the last to die. Could you run from me? I think not. I would tear you from your artificial womb, and as you choked in the air, I would hurl you from the eye-windows of your precious Titan, to die naked and alone on the cold ground of the city you were too proud to defend. Now, if you are quite finished with the exchange of threats, I would ask you to move on to more important matters.'

She smiles, but the hatred curling her lips is all I see. It is, in its own way, beautiful. Nothing is purer than hatred. With hatred, humanity was forged. Through hatred, we have brought the galaxy to its knees.

'**I see you do not show your face this time, knight. You see me revealed, yet you hide behind the death mask of your Emperor.**'

'*Our* Emperor,' I remind her. 'You have just made your second mistake, Zarha.'

I disengage my helm's collar seals and lift the mask clear. The air smells of sweat, oil, fear and chemical-rich fluids. I ignore the others, ignore all but her. Despite the bitterness around me that deepens with each moment, it is comfortable to stand without my senses enclosed by my helm. Since planetfall, the only time I have removed my helm in the company of others has been on the two occasions I have spoken with the Crone.

'**I said when last we met,**' she watches me carefully, '**that you had kind eyes.**'

'I remember.'

'**It is true. But I regret it. I regret ever speaking a fair word to you, blasphemer.**'

For a moment, I am not sure how to respond to that.

'You stand on difficult ground, Zarha. I am a Chaplain of the Adeptus Astartes, sworn into my position with the grace of the Ecclesiarchy of Terra. In my presence, you have just expressed the notion that the Emperor of Mankind is not your god, as He is for the entire glorious Imperium. While I am not blind to the... separatist... elements within the

Mechanicus, the fact remains that you are speaking heresy before a Reclusiarch of the Emperor's Chosen.

'You are speaking heresy, and I am charged with the responsibility of ending any heresy I encounter in the Eternal Crusade. So let us tread carefully, you and I. You will not insult me with false accusations of blasphemy, and I will answer the questions you have regarding D-16 West. This is not a request. Agree, or I will execute you for heresy before your crew can even soil themselves in fear.'

I see her swallow, and despite herself, her smile shows her amusement.

'It is entertaining to be spoken to in this manner,' she says, almost thoughtful.

'I can imagine that your perceptions offer a much grander view than mine,' I meet her optic augments with my own gaze. 'But the time for misunderstandings is over. Speak, Zarha. I will answer what you ask. This must be resolved, for the good of Helsreach.'

She turns in her tank, swimming slowly in the fluid-filled coffin before eventually coming back to face me.

'Tell me why,' she says. **'Tell me why you have done this.'**

I had not expected such a base question. 'It is the Ordinatus Armageddon. It is one of the greatest weapons ever wielded by man. This is a war, Zarha. I need weapons to win it.'

She shakes her head. **'Necessity is not enough. You may not harness** Oberon **on a whim, Grimaldus.'** She floats closer, pressing her forehead to the glass. Throne, she looks tired. Withered, tired and without hope. **'It is sealed now because it must be sealed. It is not used now because it cannot be used.'**

'The Master of the Forge will determine that for himself,' I tell her.

'No. Grimaldus, please stop this. You will tear the Mechanicus forces on the world apart. It is a matter of the greatest import to the servants of the Machine-God. Oberon cannot be reactivated. It would be blasphemy to use it in battle.'

'I will not lose this war because of Martian tradition. When Jurisian accesses the final chamber, he will examine the Ordinatus Armageddon and evaluate the trials ahead in awakening the spirit within the machine. *Help us*, Zarha. We do not have to die here in futility. Throne of the Emperor, *Oberon* would win us this war. Are you too blind to see that?'

She twists in the fluid again, seeming lost in thought.

'No,' she says at last. 'It cannot, and will not, be reawakened.'

'It grieves me to ignore your wishes, princeps. But I will not have Jurisian cease his ministrations. Perhaps *Oberon*'s reactivation is far beyond his skills. I am prepared to die with that as an acceptable truth. But I will not die here until I have done all in my power to save this city.'

'Grimaldus.' She smiles again, looking much as she did at our first meeting. 'I am ordered by my superiors to see you dead before you continue this course of action. This can only end one way. I ask you now, before the final threats must be spoken. Please do not do this. The insult to the Mechanicus would be infinite.'

I reach to my armoured collar and trigger the vox-link there. A single pulse answers – an acknowledgement signal.

'You have made your third mistake by threatening me, Zarha. I am leaving.'

From the pilots' thrones, voices begin to chatter. 'My princeps?' one calls.

'Yes, Valian.'

'We're getting auspex returns. Four heat signatures inbound. From directly above. The city's wall-guns are not tracking them.'

'No,' I say, without taking my eyes from Zarha. 'The city defences wouldn't shoot down four of my Thunderhawks.'

'Grimaldus... No...'

'My princeps!' Valian Carsomir screams. '*Forget him!* We demand orders at once!'

It is too late. Already, the chamber starts to shake. The noise from outside is muted by the Titan's immense armour plating, but remains nevertheless: four gunships on hover, their boosters roaring, black hulls eclipsing the moonlight that had beamed in through the eye-windows.

I look over my shoulder, seeing the four gunships align their heavy bolter turrets and wing-mounted missiles.

'Raise shields!'

'Don't,' I say softly. 'If you try to raise the shields and prevent my attempt to leave, I will order my gunships to open fire on this bridge. Your void shields will never rise in time.'

'You would kill yourself.'

'I would. And you. And your Titan.'

'Keep the shields down,' she says, the bitterness returning to her visage. Her bridge crew comply, reluctance evident in their every movement and whispered word. '**You do not understand. It would be blasphemy for** Oberon **to enter battle. The sacred war platforms must be blessed by the Lord of the Centurio Ordinatus. Their machine-spirits would be enraged without this appeasement.** Oberon **will never function. Do you not see?'**

I see.

But what I see is a compromise.

'The only reason the Mechanicus is not committing one of its greatest weapons to the war to save this world is because it remains unblessed?'

'Yes. The soul of the machine will rebel. If it even awakens, it will be wrathful.'

Within these words, I see the way through our stalemate. If their rites require a blessing that is impossible to give, then we must alter our demands to the most basic, viable needs.

'I understand, Zarha. Jurisian will not reactivate the Ordinatus Armageddon and bring it to Helsreach,' I tell her. She watches me closely, her visual receptors clicking and whirring in poor mimicry of human expression.

'He will not?'

'No.' The pause lasts several heartbeats, until I say, 'We will remove the nova cannon and bring it to Helsreach. It is all we needed, anyway.'

'You are not permitted to defile Oberon's body. To remove the cannon would be to sever its head or remove its heart.'

'Consider this, Zarha, for I am finished with standing here and posturing over Mechanicus banalities. The Master of the Forge was trained on Mars, under the guidance of the Machine Cult and in accordance with the most ancient oath between the Adeptus Astartes and the Mechanicus. He reveres this weapon, and counts his role in its reawakening as the greatest honour of his life.'

'If he were true to our principles, he would not do this.'

'And if you were true to the Imperium, you would. Think on that, Zarha. We need this weapon.'

'The Lord of the Centurio Ordinatus is en route from Terra. If he arrives in time, and if his vessel can break

the blockade, then there is a chance Helsreach will see Oberon **deployed. I can give you no more support than that.'**

'For now, that is all I need.'

I thought that would end it. Not end it *well*, by any means. But end it nevertheless.

Yet as I walk away, she calls me back.

'**Stop for a moment. Answer me this one question: Why are you here, Grimaldus?'**

I face her once more, this twisted, ancient creature in her coffin of fluids, watching me with machine-eyes.

'Clarify the question, Zarha. I do not believe you speak of this moment.'

She smiles. '**No. I do not. Why are you here, at Helsreach?'**

Strange to be asked such a thing, and I see no reason to lie. Not to her.

'I am here because one who was brother to my dead master has sent me to die on this world. High Marshal Helbrecht demanded that one Templars commander stay to inspire the defence. He chose me.'

'**Why you? Have you not asked yourself that question? Why did he choose you?'**

'I do not know. All I know for certain, princeps, is that I am taking that cannon.'

'I FIND IT difficult to countenance,' Artarion said, 'that your plan actually worked.' The knights stood together on the wall, watching the enemy. The aliens were massing, forming into clusters and chaotic regiments. It still resembled a swarm of vermin more than anything else, Grimaldus thought, but he could make out distinct clan markings and the unity of tribal groups standing apart from others.

It would be dawn soon. Whether or not that was the signal the xenos were waiting for didn't matter. The flow of landers had fallen to a trickle, no more than one every hour now. The wastelands were already home to millions of orks. The attack would come today. The overwhelming force they needed to take the city was here.

'It has not worked yet,' Grimaldus replied. 'Ultimately, it comes down to what they will allow. We need their cooperation.' The Chaplain nodded to the gathering horde. 'If we do not have Mechanicus aid in reactivating the cannon, these alien dogs will already be gnawing on our bones within a handful of months.'

A cry went up from further down the wall. Few Guardsmen remained posted on the battlements, and those that were served mainly as sentries. Two more of them shouted, and the call was taken up along the entire northern wall. The general vox-channel came alive with eager voices. The city's siren once more began to wail.

Grimaldus said nothing at first. He watched the horde sweeping closer like a slow tide. What little order had been evident within the enemy's ranks was broken now, and in the sea of jagged metal and green flesh, scrap-tanks and wreck-Titans powered forward – the former dense with aliens clinging to their sides and howling, the latter shaking the wastelands with their waddling tread.

'I have heard it said,' Artarion noted, 'that the greenskins raise their Titans as idols to their strange, piggish gods.'

Priamus grunted. 'That would explain why they are so hideous. Look at that one. How can that be a god?'

He had a point. The wreck-Titan was an iron effigy of a

corpulent alien, its distended belly used to house the arming chambers for the proliferation of cannons thrusting from its gut.

'I would laugh,' Nero said, 'if there weren't so many of them. They outnumber Invigilata's engines at a ratio of six-to-one. '

'I see bombers,' Cador noted, neither interested nor disinterested, merely stating a fact. A wing of ugly aircraft, over forty of them, rose from landing platforms hidden behind the landers of the main force. Grimaldus could hear their engines from here, labouring like a sick elder ascending the stairs.

'We should abandon the walls, brothers.' Nero turned to watch the last Guardsmen making their way down the ramps and ladders leading from the battlements. 'The Titans will be firing soon.'

'So will theirs,' Priamus smiled within his helm. 'And these mighty walls will be reduced to so much powder.'

At that moment, a squadron of fighters soared overheard – the sleek metal hulls of Barasath's Lightnings turned silver by the reflections of the rising sun.

'Now that is courage,' said Cador.

COMMANDER BARASATH HAD argued long and hard for permission to make his first attack run. This was principally because anyone with even a vague grasp of tactics could see full well it would almost definitely be not only his first attack run, but also his last.

Colonel Sarren had been against it. Adjutant Tyro had been against it. Even the Emperor-damned dockmaster had been against it. Barasath was a patient man; he prided himself on tact and the willingness to deliberate being among his chief virtues, but to have to sit there and listen to a *civilian* complaining and questioning his tactical expertise was beyond galling.

'Won't we need your planes to protect the tankers still coming from the Valdez platforms?' the dockmaster, Maghernus, had asked. Barasath gave the man a feigned smile and a nod of acknowledgement.

'It is unlikely the orks have the presence of mind to seek to cut our supplies of fuel, and even if they have, they would need to take the long route around the city, and risk running out of fuel themselves long before they reached our shipping lanes over the ocean.'

'It is still not worth the risk,' Sarren said, shaking his head and seeking to conclude the matter.

'With all due respect,' he said, none of his inner turmoil showing through to his demeanour, 'This attack run offers us too much to merely dismiss out of hand.'

'The risks are too great,' Tyro said, and Barasath was fast coming to hate her. A petulant little princess from the Lord General's staff – she should go back to her clerical duties and leave war to the men and women who were trained to deal with it.

'War,' Barasath mastered his temper, 'is nothing but risk. If I take three-quarters of my squadron, we can destroy the enemy's first waves of bombers and fighter support. They will never even reach the city.'

'That is exactly why this is a fool's errand,' Tyro argued. She was less skilled at controlling her agitation. 'The city's defences will annihilate any aerial attack. We don't even need to risk a single one of our fighters.'

My fighters, Barasath said silently.

'Adjutant, I would ask you to consider the practicalities.'

'I have,' she scoffed.

Uppity bitch, he added to the previous thought.

'This is a two-bladed attack that I suggest.' Barasath looked at his fellow commanders gathered here in the briefing room. While the chamber itself was a bustling hive of activity, with staff and servitors manning vox-consoles, scanner decks and tactical displays, the main table that had once seated the entire city's command section was almost deserted. Almost every regimental leader was with his or her soldiers now, standing ready.

'I'm listening,' Colonel Sarren said.

'If we engage the enemy above the city, a great deal of burning wreckage will fall to the streets and spires below. Add to that the fact we will be under fire from our own defensive guns. Anti-air turrets on spires will be firing up at the sky battle, and have a significant chance of hitting my pilots with their flak-bursts. But if we take the fight to them, their precious junk-fighters will rain down upon their own troops in flames. Once my first wave has pierced their formation, send a second and a third. We can cut overhead to perform strafing runs on their airstrips.'

Silence met this statement. Barasath capitalised on it. 'Their aerial capabilities will be butchered *in a single hour*. You cannot tell me, colonel, that such a victory isn't worth the risk. This is how we must strike.'

He could tell the colonel wasn't convinced. Tempted, yes, but not convinced. Tyro shook her head slightly, half in thought, half already preparing her advised refusal.

'I have spoken with the Reclusiarch,' Barasath said suddenly.

'What?' from both Sarren and Tyro.

'This plan. I have discussed it with the Reclusiarch. He

commended me on it, and assured me that city command would allow it.'

Of course, Barasath had done no such thing. The last he'd heard of the knight leader was that Grimaldus was evidently involved in some sort of difficult negotiation with the Crone of Invigilata. But it turned Tyro's head, and that was all he needed. A wedge of doubt. A sliver of her interest.

'If Grimaldus advises this…' she said.

'Grimaldus?' Sarren arched an eyebrow. His jowly face was caught between amusement and alarm. 'A trifle familiar of you to use his name like that.'

'The Reclusiarch,' she swallowed. 'If he believes this is a sound plan, perhaps we should take that into consideration.'

Barasath was adept at hiding all emotion, not just the negative ones. He battled down the urge to grin now.

'Colonel,' he said, 'and Adjutant Tyro. I can see why you wish to hold as much of our forces in reserve as is tactically viable. This is a defensive war, and aggressive attacks will play little part in it. But my pilots and I are useless once the walls are breached and the enemy floods the city. Even the hololithic simulations made that clear, did they not?'

Sarren sighed as he linked his fingers over his belly.

'Do it,' he'd said. And Barasath had. His squadron was airborne an hour later, tearing over the city streets below before powering low over the wastelands.

In the tight confines of his Lightning's cockpit, he was more than just comfortable. He was home. Both control sticks in his hands were extensions of his own body. They said infantry felt the same about their rifles, but by the Holy Throne, there was no comparison. A rifle to a Lightning was like a spear to an angel of iron and steel.

The mass of the alien invasion darkened the ground beneath them.

'Need I remind anyone,' he said over the squadron's vox, 'that bailing out over this mess is extremely ill-advised?'

A volley of 'No sirs' was his answer.

'If you're hit – and by the Throne, some of us will be – then bring your bird down into one of their fat-arsed god-walkers. Take as many of the bastards with you as you can.'

'Gargants, sir.' That was Helika's voice. 'The orks call their Titans "gargants"'.

'Duly noted, Helika. Fifty-Eighty-Twos, on my mark, you will break formation and open fire. The Emperor is with us, boys and girls. And the Templars are watching. Let's show them how we earned the knights' crosses painted on our hulls.

'For Armageddon,' he narrowed his eyes, breathing in a lungful of the recycled oxygen offered by his facemask, 'and Helsreach.'

CHAPTER X

SIEGE

WHEN THE WALL is first breached, it dies in an avalanche of pulverised rockcrete.

Dark powdery dust blasts into the air, thicker than smoke and expanding like a stormcloud, blinding in its density.

I watch this from hundreds of metres away, standing with my brothers and the soldiers of the Desert Vultures. At the end of the street, the wall is no more. Our defences are broken, and behind the dust cloud, the breach gapes wide.

The true siege has begun. On every rooftop, in every alley, on every street and from every window – for kilometres around – Imperial guns stand ready, clutched in loyal hands, ready to slay the invaders.

Road by road, home by home. This was always how the Battle of Helsreach would be fought, and it is what every soul in the city stands ready for.

The great figures of the Titans begin to withdraw. Their first duty is done; they stood at the walls and pounded the enemy forces with their immense artillery. Invigilata's engines fall back now, not in defeat, nor even willingly – but because they must reload for the true battle. The Crone updated the commanders' shared tactical grid with the locations of the Mechanicus landers within the city limits that serve as Invigilata's rearming stations. Her Titans trudge back to the closest ones now, their tread shaking the city around them. They are tall enough to darken the rising sun as they pass, even though they walk through distant streets.

Reports filter in from across the vox-network. The wall is falling to pieces, crumbling under the insane firepower of so many tanks and wreck-Titans. Around me, the smell of fear rises from the human soldiers. It is a foul musk; the sourness of breath, the tangy reek of liquid waste, and the rich, stinging scent of cold sweat. This fear-smell emanates from several of them, and while I do not hold them to the standards of Adeptus Astartes, while I acknowledge the fact the human body will always react in this way even with the bravest of souls inhabiting it, it is still hard to stand in their presence. Their fear disgusts me.

Above the dust cloud, the head and shoulders of a wreck-Titan emerge, its bulbous head of scrap metal shaped into a roaring alien maw. Throne of the Emperor, it would have towered above the wall even if our insignificant barricade were still there. Glass shatters in every window along the street as its slow march brings it closer.

A moment later, the street thunders beneath our feet. Every one of the human soldiers with us falls to the ground, their curses lost amid the noise. I maintain my balance only because of my armour's joint stabilisers compensating for the tremors. With the brightness of a flaring sun, the wreck-Titan's head detonates, showering debris into the dust cloud below.

The cheer that rises around me is the loudest sound yet.

'**Engine kill,**' comes Zarha's voice over the vox, sounding amused despite the interference. '**You owe me for that, Grimaldus.**'

I do not answer. The shot must have been a truly difficult challenge, but I do not care where *Stormherald* is, nor that it is retreating. My focus is here and now. Tension burns through my body like superheated blood. I feel it in my brothers, as well. Twenty of us, our breathing fast, our hands clutching weapons that are ritually chained to our armour. Chainswords complain as they rev, cutting only air. Last-minute oaths are whispered, or sworn to the sky.

Emerging from the dust cloud, snorting their porcine war cries, come the hunched silhouettes of the enemy.

Hundreds of them, flooding into the street.

'Fire at will!' calls one of the Steel Legion officers.

'*Hold your fire!*' I scream, my helm's vocalisers piercing the surrounding noise.

'They're in range!' the officer, Major Oros, yells back.

'*Hold your fire!*'

I am already running, sprinting, my armour joints snarling as I leave the humans behind. Proximity runes, my brothers' life-markers, flicker on my retinal display, but I have no need for them. I know who follows me.

'*Sons of Dorn! Knights of the Emperor! Charge!*'

The first of the aliens runs from the dust, its green skin plastered grey from the cloud. It raises a junk weapon in its brutish fists, and dies with my crozius annihilating its malformed face a moment later.

The two battle lines meet with a discordant crunch of

weapon against weapon and flesh against armour. The sick, fungal stench of ork blood fills the air. Chainswords chew through xenos flesh. Bolters discharge their lethal loads – the crashing bangs of release followed by the muffled thumps of shells detonating within bodies.

The creatures howl and laugh as they die.

My knights remain silent as they slaughter.

Perception fades, as it always does in war, to flickering images that come moment to moment. Concentration is impossible, anathema to the holy rage that fills my senses. I grip my master's relic weapon in both hands, and swing at three aliens before me. They are hurled back from the mace's crackling power field, all three slain by the impact with their chests shattered, each of them tumbling across the road to end in limp, lifeless heaps.

I kill, and kill, and kill. It does not concern me that there is no end to this horde. The enemy fall before us, thrown to the floor by the righteous arcs of sacred weapons, and all that matters is how much blood flows before we are forced to retreat.

Over the vox, I hear Oros and the men cheering. It is an easy sound to ignore.

Artarion suffers more than the rest of us. He sacrifices one hand to hold my banner aloft, his chainblade held in his other. The standard draws the enemy to him. *They want our banner. They always do.* Without even a grunt of effort, he hacks left and right, parries clumsy strikes and lashes back with vicious ripostes.

Priamus saw the danger first. I see one of the aliens behind Artarion fall in two pieces, the young knight's sword splitting the creature in twain through the torso. He kicks the biological wreckage from his blade and cleaves his way to fight side by side with Artarion.

'Reclusiarch,' Nerovar is still with me, tearing his sword free from the belly of a disembowelled greenskin. His boots crush the viscous, stinking ropes of intestine that spill to the road. 'We are being overwhelmed.'

A spear crashes against my helm, reducing my visor display to static for a moment. I swing back at the creature that hurled it, and my sight flickers back online to see the beast's skull demolished beneath my crozius. More discoloured blood spatters over my armour in a light rainfall.

Two more orks fall, one to Nero's chainsword ripping across its throat, the other to my maul, hammered into its chest and sending it flying against the wall of a nearby building. Blood of Dorn, Mordred's weapon is an incredible gift. It slays with effortless ease.

I can feel its charge and release with each alien that dies. There is a split second before every impact as the energy field around the head pulses in a low growl, conflicted by the closeness of other material, before it unleashes its force in a snapping burst of kinetic power.

The enemy have encircled us, but that is little worry. Fighting our way free will be no effort.

'Oros,' I breathe into the vox. 'We are preparing to fall back to you.'

'Give me the mark,' he says. 'We're itching for a turn ourselves.'

WITH THE TRUE siege under way, the Imperial forces fell into their prepared defensive strategies.

Every road had a barricade, where Steel Legion soldiers arrayed in ranks would unleash las-fire at the swarming foe. Snipers worked their deadly duties from rooftops. Battle tanks of every pattern and class ground their way down streets, shelling the first waves of enemy infantry pouring into the outlying sectors of the city.

Every road and building had its assigned piece to play in the battle. Every section had its orders to hold and inflict as much punishment upon the advancing foe as possible, before falling back to the next barricade.

Rearmed Titans stood as vigilant sentinels over entire city blocks, their weapons reaping life from the creatures that swarmed around their feet. The enemy gargants were still engaged in pulling down and breaking through the wall. In these first hours, Invigilata was unrivalled in its destruction.

The invaders spilled into Helsreach, and died in their thousands. Every metre they took was bought with foul alien blood.

Colonel Sarren watched the battle unfolding on the hololithic table. Stuttering images relayed the position of Imperial forces at the very edges of the city, inexorably withdrawing from the walls. Larger locator runes showed the position of Invigilata's engines, or battalions of Steel Legion tanks. He had formulated this endless, relentless fighting withdrawal over the course of the past weeks, and by the Emperor, it was a fine thing to see it in action.

In this first phase, it was imperative that casualties be kept to a minimum. The grind of army against army would come in time. For now, losses must be kept light and the death toll suffered by the enemy must be kept high. Let the invaders claim the outlying city sectors. Let them purchase these abandoned, worthless zones with their lives. It was all part of the plan.

The wave would break soon.

Sarren watched the flickering icons depicting his forces across the immense map. It would come soon, that perfect moment in the shifting winds of battle when the enemy's first push would falter and slow as the advance elements outpaced their slower support units. The initial hordes of infantry would crash against Steel Legion resistance in the outer city streets that they could never break without support from their tanks and wreck-Titans.

And at that moment, the wave would break like the tide against the shore. With the ferocious momentum of the first attack lost, the defence would begin in earnest.

Counterattacks would be mounted in some streets, especially those close to Invigilata's engines or Legion armour units. In other zones, the Guard would stand fast, unable to take ground back but entrenched well enough to hold it.

All that mattered was keeping the enemy from reaching Hel's Highway.

At the last meeting, when the commanders had gathered in their battle armour, Sarren had outlined once more the necessity to holding the highway.

'It is the key to the siege,' he'd said. 'Once they reach Hel's Highway, the city becomes twice as difficult to defend. They will have access to the entire hive. Think of it as an artery, ladies and gentlemen. *The* artery. Once it is severed, the body will bleed out. Once the enemy takes the highway, the city is lost.'

Grave expressions had answered this statement.

The colonel hunched over the table now, his squinting eyes taking the scene in, road by road, building by building, unit by unit.

He watched the war in silence, waiting for the wave to break.

BARASATH HAD HIT the ground hard.

He'd seen Helika fall from the sky – and heard her, too. That'd been difficult to deal with. The night they'd spent together sharing a bunk had been almost three years ago now, when they'd both pretended to be drunker than they were, but Korten had never forgotten it, nor had he wished it to be the only one. Hearing her die had chilled his blood, and he had to fight not to deactivate his vox as she screamed on the way down, her engine trailing fire.

Her Lightning, with its white-painted wings, had ploughed into the chest of an alien god-walker. The Titan had shuddered for a moment, then vented flames and wreckage from its spine as Helika's bird – now nothing more than spinning debris – burst through its back.

The gargant kept walking as if unharmed, even with a hole blown clear through it.

That had been in the first run. Helika didn't even get time to fire.

A wicked, weaving scrap of a battle through the alien fighters saw most of them spiralling groundwards on dying engines. He'd taken cannon-fire along his hull, but a lucky shot saw him bleeding fuel instead of turned into a fireball in the sky. With the way clear and only a handful of his flyers down, Barasath's second and third waves were inbound.

That's when things had gotten really nasty.

The enemy god-walkers weren't marching idly. Turrets on their shoulders and heads aimed up into the sky spat both laser fire and solid shells at the Imperial fighters. Dodging these alone would have been a chore. Dodging these when they were joined by more ork scrap-flyers and anti-air fire from the tanks below turned the situation into the nightmare that Colonel Sarren had promised.

Barasath's first wave scattered, boosting towards the primitive landing strips the enemy had formed in the desert.

Hundreds of ork fighters still waited on the ground,

unable to take off yet, consigned to waiting their turn on the scraped-flat runways. A more pessimistic man might have noted there was little he could do to such a massive, grounded force when he led the remaining birds of an air superiority squadron. A more pessimistic man might also have circled the enemy airbase and waited for his Thunderbolt bombers in the second wave.

Korten Barasath was not a pessimistic man, and his patience took a backseat when it came to necessity. In graceful arcing dives and strafing runs, he unloaded his autocannons and drained his lascannon power packs, hurling everything he could down at the grounded fighters below. Dozens sought to take to the skies in panicked defence – most of these crashed during their ill-attempted takeoffs as their landing gear became fouled in the sandy wasteland soil. Those few that managed to get airborne were easy prey for Imperial cannons.

His second wave arrived, unleashing their payloads. Thunderbolts, much larger and heavier armed than the Lightnings, sent great plumes of smoke and dust rising from the wasteland's surface as their incendiaries impacted.

'Bomb this place to ashes,' Barasath voxed, and watched his pilots do exactly that.

Fire ripped across the wastelands in hungry trails, consuming the ragged airstrips that would never be allowed to take shape after this. Grounded junk-fighters exploded in succession.

Of course, the site wasn't completely defenceless, even with most of it in flames. A few tanks fired gamely up at the strafing Imperial flyers, with all the grace and accuracy of old men trying to swat flies.

He'd taken fire on his last banking swoop over the airbase.

A lucky – or unlucky, as Barasath saw it – shot sheared off the best part of his left wing. There would be no climbing from this death-dive. No aiming for a wreck-Titan as Helika and a handful of others had done.

He pulled the cockpit release as the fighter started to spin, ditching above the burning site. There was a moment of disorientation, the push of the wind, the world coming into focus after the twisting plunge of the falling fighter... And then he was falling into black smoke and dust clouds.

Darkness embraced him. His respirator saved him having to breathe the choking smog, but his flight goggles were unenhanced and couldn't pierce the smoke. Barasath pulled his cord, feeling himself jerked upwards as his grav-chute opened.

With no idea where the ground was, he was lucky to hit the earth without breaking both of his legs. His ankle flared up in protest, but he considered that to be getting off lightly.

Cautiously, aware of the fact that the smoke hid him as much as it hid the enemy, he pulled his laspistol and moved through the blinding darkness. It was hot, a savage heat all around him that spoke of burning planes and landers nearby, yet not enough light to offer direction.

When he finally broke through the black cloud, pistol in his sure grip, he blinked once at what stood before him, and started to fire.

'Oh Throne,' he said with surprising politeness, right before the orks lumbering ahead shot him through the chest.

STORMHERALD HUNGERED.

It ached with each pounding step, its roiling plasma core burning in its chest as it reluctantly turned its back on the enemy and marched through the streets.

Its way was clear, its path already set. Buildings had been demolished earlier in the week – their foundations blown up and the hab-blocks themselves fallen to rubble – to make way for its passage.

The need to turn around and pour its hatred into the enemy was fierce, a hunter's urge, almost strong enough to overwhelm the Crone's whispers in its mind.

The Crone. Her presence was a savage irritant. Again, *Stormherald* leaned as it walked, seeking to turn with its ponderous, striding slowness. And again, the Crone's claws in its mind forced its body to comply with her intent.

We move, she whispered, *to fight a greater battle soon.*

Stormherald's rage faded at her voice. There was something new in her words, something its predator's mind clutched and recognised immediately. A fear. A doubt. A plea.

The Crone was weaker now than she ever had been before.

Stormherald knew nothing of pleasure or amusement. Its soul was forged in ancient rites of fire, molten metal, and plasmic energy that churned with the ferocity of a caged sun. The closest it came to an emotion approximating pleasure was the rush of awareness and the dimming of its painful anger as enemies died under its guns.

It felt a ghost of that sensation now. It complied with her urgings now, still bound to her control.

But the Crone was weaker.

Soon, she would be his.

NIGHTFALL FOUND DOMOSKA with her storm trooper platoon holed up in the ruins of what had once been a hab-block.

Greenskin heavy armour had rolled through and changed all that. Now it was a tumbledown ruin of rock-crete and flakboard, and Domoska crouched behind a low wall, clutching her hellgun to her chest. Strapped to her back, her power pack hummed. The cable-feeds between her hellgun's intake port and the backpack were vibrating and hot.

She was glad the skull-faced Adeptus Astartes and that prissy adjutant quintus had ordered them back to the city. She didn't want to admit it, but travelling in an Adeptus Astartes gunship – even just in the bay with the racked jump packs and attack bikes – had been a thrill.

She was less delighted with her platoon's assigned position in the urban war, but she was a storm trooper, the Legion's finest, and she prided herself on her devotion to duty without raising a complaint.

With the bulk of Imperial forces in slow, fighting withdrawals and protracted holding actions, units across the city were tasked with lying in wait as the orks advanced, or stalking past undetected to take positions behind the enemy.

Across Helsreach, it was almost uniformly veteran outfits and storm trooper squads tasked with these movements. Colonel Sarren was using his best soldiers to achieve the most difficult operations.

And it was working.

Domoska would have preferred to be safely crouched behind a barricade, with Leman Russ tanks in support, but such was life.

'Hey,' Andrej whispered as he ducked next to her. 'This is better than sitting on our arses in the desert, yes? Yes, it is, that's what I think.'

'Be quiet,' she whispered back. Her auspex returns were coming back clear. No enemy heat signatures or movement nearby. Still, Andrej was being annoying.

'The last one I gutted with my bayonet, eh? I am tempted

to go back for his skull. Sand it down, wear it on my belt like a trophy. That would get me much attention, I think.'

'It would get you shot first, most likely.'

'Hm. Not the right kind of attention. You are too negative, okay? Yes, I said it. It is true.'

'And I said to be quiet.'

Miraculously, he was. The two of them moved on, keeping crouched and low, moving from cover to cover. Sounds of battle were coming from the adjacent street – Domoska could hear the guttural roars and piggish snorts of embattled orks.

'This is Domoska,' she whispered into her hand-vox. 'Contact ahead. Most likely the second group that passed us an hour ago.'

'Acknowledged, Scout Team Three. Proceed as instructed, with all due caution.'

'Yes, captain.' Domoska clicked her vox off. 'Ready, Andrej?'

Andrej nodded, crouched next to her once again. 'I have three det-packs left, okay? Three more tanks must die. Then I get that caffeine the captain promised.'

THE HOLOGRAPHIC TABLE told its tale with reassuring accuracy. Sarren could not look away, despite how staring at the flickering light-images stung the eyes after a while.

The wave was breaking.

His bulwark units were digging in and holding their ground. Already, the pincer platoons were moving into position behind the first horde of invaders, ready to drive them forward and crush them between the hammer and anvil.

Sarren smiled. It had been a fine day.

JURISIAN HAD NOT moved from his position in almost twenty-four hours.

He had said he would need over a week, and closer to two. He no longer believed this. This would take weeks, months… Perhaps even years.

The codes that kept the impenetrable bunker doors sealed were beautiful in their artistry – clearly the work of many masters of the Mechanicus. Jurisian feared no living being, and had slain in the name of the Emperor for twenty-three decades. This was the first time he had loathed his duty.

'I need more time, Grimaldus,' he had spoken into the vox several hours before.

'You ask for the one thing I cannot give,' the Reclusiarch had answered.

'This might take me months. Perhaps years. As the code evolves, it breeds sub-ciphers that – in turn – require dedicated cracking. It breeds like an ecology, always changing, reacting to my intrusions by evolving into more complex systems.'

The pause had been laden with bitten-back anger. 'I want that cannon, Jurisian. *Bring it to me.*'

'As you will, Reclusiarch.'

Gone was the thrill of hoping to look upon *Oberon*, and being the soul to reawaken the great Ordinatus Armageddon. In its place was cold efficiency and undeniable disgust. This sealing code was one of the most complex creations humanity had pieced together from its various spheres of knowledge. Destroying it afflicted him with a pain akin to that which an artist would feel in destroying a priceless painting.

Runes spilled across his retinal display in green lettering. He solved six of the scrolling codes in the space of a single breath. The final five involved additional calculations based on the parameters established by the previous ones.

The code evolved. It reacted to his interference like a living thing, its ancient spirit fighting against his manipulations. So, so beautiful, Jurisian thought as he worked. Damn Grimaldus for asking this of him.

His servitors stood behind him, slack-jawed, dull-eyed and slowly starving to death.

Jurisian paid no heed.

He had a masterpiece to slay.

CHAPTER XI
THE FIRST DAY

THE SHAKING NO longer bothered Asavan Tortellius.

His presence was an honour, and one he thanked the Mechanicus for in his daily prayers. In his eleven years of service, he'd quickly grown used to the shaking, the lurching tread, and even the rattling of weapons fire against the walls of his monastery. What Tortellius had never grown used to was the Shield.

In many ways, the Shield replaced the sky. He had been born on Jirrian – an unremarkable world in an unremarkable subsector a middling distance from Holy Terra. If Jirrian could be said to possess any attribute of note, it was its weather in the equatorial regions. The sky over the city of Handra-Lai was the deep, rich blue that poets spent so much time trying to capture in words, and imagists spent so much time trying to capture in picts. In a world of tedious tradition and the greyness of infinite societal equality – where everyone was just as poverty-stricken as everyone else – the skies above the slum hive Handra-Lai were the one aspect of his early life worth remembering.

The Shield had stolen that from him. He still had the memories, of course. But every year, they became duller, as if the Shield's overreaching presence caused all else to fade.

It wasn't that the Shield had any particular colour, because it didn't. And it wasn't that the Shield was brazenly oppressive, because it wasn't.

Most of the time it wasn't even visible, and at the best of times, it wasn't even *there*.

And yet, in a way, it always was. It was oppressive. It was always there. It did discolour the sky. Its existence was betrayed by the abrasive electrical fizz in the air. Static would crackle between fingertips and metal surfaces. After a while, one's teeth began to ache. It was most irritating.

And to think that it could be raised any moment. Looking up at alien skies held no pleasure at all, and it was all because of the Shield. It severed any real enjoyment of the heavens. Even when deactivated, there was forever the risk of it slamming up into life without notice, cutting Tortellius off from the outside world once more.

In moments of battle, the Shield was more beautiful than threatening. It would ripple like breaking waves, the colours of oil on water cascading across the sky. The smell of the Shield as it suffered attack was a heady clash of ozone and copper that, if one stood outside on the monastery's battlements, would actually begin to make you feel lightheaded after a time. Tortellius made a point of standing outside when the Shield was under siege, not for the stimulant effects of the Shield's electrical charge, but because it was a dark pleasure to see his prison's limits, rather than fear the invisible oppression.

Sometimes he would wonder if he was watching it in the secret hope it would fail. If the Shield came down... then what? Did he truly desire such a thing? No. No, of course not.

Still. He did wonder.

As he leaned on the battlements of the monastery, watching the city below, Tortellius reflected on the loathsomeness of this particular breed of xenos. The greenskins were filthy and bestial, their intelligence generously described as rudimentary, and more accurately as feral.

The mighty *Stormherald*, instrument of the God-Emperor's divine will, had come to a halt. Tortellius noticed only because of the relative silence in the wake of its crashing tread.

His monastery, only part of the cathedral of spires and battlements adorning the Titan's hunched shoulders, remained silent. Fifty metres below, he could hear the rattling of the leg turrets killing the aliens in the street. But the domed weapon mounts – each one bristling with granite gargoyles and stone representations of the angelic primarchs, those blessed slain sons of the God-Emperor – merely moved in their set alignments, their cannons ready.

Tortellius scratched his thinning hair (a curse he blamed entirely on the harsh electro-static charge of the Shield), and summoned his servo-skull. It hovered along the battlements towards him, its miniature suspension technology purring as it stayed aloft. The skull itself was human, sanded smooth and modified after it was removed from a corpse, now showing augmetic pict-takers and a voice-activated data-slate for recording sermons.

'Hello, Tharvon,' said Tortellius. The skull had once belonged to Tharvon Ushan, his favoured servant. How noble a fate, to serve the Ecclesiarchy even in death. How blessed Tharvon's spirit must be, in the eternal light of the Golden Throne.

The skull probe said nothing. Its gravity suspensors hummed as it bobbed in the air.

'Dictation,' said Tortellius. The skull emitted an acknowledgement chime as its data-slate – no larger than a human palm and built into its augmented forehead – blinked active.

What little breeze penetrated the Shield wasn't enough to cool his sweating face. The Armageddon sun might have been weak compared to the star that burned down on equatorial Jirrian, but it was stifling enough. Tortellius mopped his dark-skinned brow with a scented kerchief.

'On this, the first day of the Siege of Hive Helsreach, the invaders have spilled into the city in unprecedented numbers. No, hold. Command word: Pause. Delete "unprecedented". Replace with "overwhelming". Command word: Unpause. The skies are clogged with pollution from the world's industry, flak hanging in the clouds from the hive's defences, and smoke from the outlying fires that ravage the outermost districts where the invaders have already conquered ground.

'It is my belief that few chronicles of this immense war will survive to be interred in Imperial archives. I make this record now not out of a desire to spread my name in pomposity, but to accurately detail the holy bloodshed of this vast crusade.'

Here he hesitated. Tortellius struggled for the words, and as he chewed his lower lip, musing over dramatic description, the monastery shook beneath his feet again.

The Titan was moving.

* * *

STORMHERALD STRODE THROUGH the city, its passage unopposed.

Three enemy engines – the scrap-walkers that the aliens called gargants – had already died to its guns. In her prison of fluid, Zarha felt the stump at the end of her arm aching with a dull heat.

Once, she thought with an ugly smile, I had hands.

She aimed her next thought with care. *The annihilator is overheating.*

'The annihilator is overheating.'

'Understood, my princeps,' replied Carsomir. He twitched in his restraint throne, accessing the status of the weapon through his hardwired link to the Titan's heart-systems. 'Confirmed. Chambers three through sixteen show rising temperature pressure.'

Zarha turned in her milky coffin, feeling instinctively what every other soul on board needed to perceive through calculations on monitors or slower hardwire links. She watched Carsomir twitch again, feeling the orders pulsing from his mind through willpower alone, reaching into the cognitive receptors at the Titan's core. 'Coolant flush, moderate intensity,' he said. 'Commencing in eight seconds.'

Zarha moved her right arm in the ooze, feeling pain in fingers that no longer existed.

'Flushing coolant,' said a nearby adept, hunched over his wall-mounted control panel.

The relief was immediate and blissful, like a sunburned hand plunged into a bucket of ice. She cancelled the vision feed from her photoreceptors, immersing herself in blackness as relief washed through her arm.

Thank you, Valian.

'Thank you, Valian.'

Her vision flickered back into existence as she reactivated her optical implants. It was the work of a moment to readjust her perceptions, filtering out the immediacy of her surroundings. She took a breath, and stared out across the city with a god's eyes.

The enemy, ant-like and amusing, swarmed in the street around her ankles. Zarha lifted her foot, feeling both the rush of air on her metallic skin and the swirling of fluid around her footless limb. The aliens fled from her crushing tread. A tank died, pounded into scrap.

Incidental fire from *Stormherald*'s leg battlements spilled into the road, cutting the orks down in droves.

'My princeps,' Moderati Secundus Lonn was twitching in his throne as he spoke, his muscles spasming in response to the flood of pulses from his connection to the Titan.

Speak, Lonn.

'**Speak, Lonn.**'

'We are venturing ahead of our skitarii support.'

Zarha was not blind to this. She hunched her shoulders, wasted muscles tensed and trembling, striding forward through the street.

I know. I sense… something.

'**I know. I sense something.**'

The hab-towers on either side of the marching Titan were abandoned – this sector was one of the few lucky enough to be within easy range of the city's scarce subterranean communal bunker complexes.

Inform Colonel Sarren I am pressing ahead with phase two.

'**Inform Colonel Sarren I am pressing ahead with phase two.**'

'Yes, my princeps.'

This sector, Omega-south-nineteen, had been one of the

first to fall when the walls came down the day before. The aliens had been crawling through the area for many hours, but significant scrap-Titan strength was – as yet – unseen. It represented the perfect opportunity to slaughter legions of the enemy while their gargant groups were engaged elsewhere.

A feeling grew in the back of her head – something invasive and sharp, blooming through the webbing of veins in her brain. It was something she had not heard in many, many decades.

Someone was weeping.

Zarha felt her face locked in a rictus as the feeling blossomed and grew fangs. The sharpness was jagged now, an acidic pulse through her skull.

'My princeps?'

She didn't hear at first.

'My princeps?'

Yes, Valian.

'Yes, Valian.'

'We're receiving word from *Draconian*. He's dying, my princeps.'

I know… I feel him…

A moment later, Zarha felt the full shock grasp at her senses. The mortis-cry slashed through her cognitive link like a hurricane, shrieking at a soundless pitch of pain. *Draconian* was down. The princeps aboard her, Jacen Veragon, was screaming as the aliens scuttled over his corpse, pulling at his armoured metal skin as he lay prone.

How had he fallen?

And there it was. In the screaming cry was the memory she sought. The lurching of vision as the Reaver-class engine was dragged to its knees. The sense of infuriating immobility.

He was a god… How could this happen… Why would his limbs no longer function…

Everywhere around was rubble and smoke. It was impossible to see clearly.

The scream was fading now. *Draconian*'s reactor-heart, a boiling cauldron of plasmic fusion, was growing cold and still.

'We've lost contact,' said Valian, a second after Zarha sensed it herself. She was weeping, though the saltwater secreted from her tear ducts was immediately dissolved in the fluid entombing her.

Lonn had his eyes closed, accessing an internal hololithic display within the cognitive link. '*Draconian* was in Omega-west-five.' His dark eyes flicked open. 'Reports show the site is the same as here: evacuated habitation towers, minimal engine resistance.'

The adept manning the scanning console, his mouth replaced by a scarab-like vocaliser, blurted a screed of machine code across the cockpit.

'Confirmed,' Carsomir said. 'We're getting an auspex return to the south. Significant heat signature. Almost definitely an enemy engine.'

Zarha heard almost none of this. Images of *Draconian*'s death played out behind her false eyes like scenes from a play, coloured by the stinking taint of black emotion beneath. She sobbed once, her heart aching like it would burst. Hearing only that an enemy was nearby, she walked in the fluid, her limbs moving.

The Titan shook as it took another step.

'My princeps?' both moderati said at once.

I will have vengeance. Even in her own mind, she could barely hear herself in the words. A mechanical overtone twinned with her thoughts – and it was protective in its overwhelming rage. *I will have vengeance.*

'We will have vengeance.'

Tower blocks passed by its shoulders as the Titan strode on.

'My princeps,' began Carsomir, 'I recommend we hold here and wait for the skitarii to scout ahead.'

No. I will avenge Jacen.

'No,' the vox-voice was harsh. **'We will avenge** Draconian.'

Blind to the disparity between her thoughts and the emerging voice, Zarha pushed onwards. Voices assailed her, but these she cast aside with a brush of willpower. Never before had she felt it so easy to disregard the chattering, needy voices of her lesser kin. Valian's voice, coming from the cockpit chamber rather than the cognitive link, was another matter.

'My princeps, we are receiving requests for Communion.'

There will be no Communion. I hunt. Communion with the Legio can come tonight.

'There will be no Communion. We hunt. Communion with the Legio can come tonight.'

With effort, Valian turned around in his restraint throne. The cables snaking from his skull's implant sockets turned with him, like a beast's many tails.

'My princeps, Princeps Veragon is dead and the Legio demands Communion.' In his voice was the edge of concern, but never panic, nor fear. The rest of the battle group desired the momentary sharing of focus and purpose – the unity of princeps and the souls of their engines – that was tradition in the aftermath of loss.

The Legio will wait. I hunger.

'The Legio will wait. We hunger.'

Forwards. Ready main weapons. I smell the xenos from here.

Her voice emerged as a crackle of static, but *Stormherald* marched on.

While Carsomir was not a man prone to extremes of emotion, something cold and uncomfortable crawled through his thoughts as he turned back to watch the cityscape through the Titan's huge eye lenses.

He may not have been as connected to *Stormherald*'s burning heart as the princeps was, but his own bonds with the god-walker were not devoid of intimate familiarity. Through his weaker tie to the engine's semi-sentient core, he felt a depth of fury that was almost addictive in its all-encompassing purity. The passion transferred through his empathic link into grim irritability, and he had to resist the urge to curse the inefficiency of those around him as he guided the Titan onwards. Knowing the cause of his distracted irritation was no balm for it.

The Titan's right foot came down on a street corner, pulverising a cargo conveyer truck into flat scrap. *Stormherald* turned with a majestic lack of speed, and hull-mounted pict-takers panned to show a wider avenue, and the afternoon sunlight glinting from *Stormherald*'s burnished iron skin. Valian was immersed, just for a moment, in the wash of exterior imagery fed through the mind-link. Hundreds of pict-takers, each one showing pristine silvery skin, or dense armour – cracked and pitted with its legacy of small arms fire.

Ahead, down the wide avenue, was the enemy engine that blinked like a red-smeared migraine on the cockpit's auspex scanners. Valian shuddered at the sight of it, breathing deeply of the scent-thick cockpit air. As always, living within *Stormherald*'s head smelled of oiled gears, ritual incense and the burning reek of crew members sweating and bleeding, their bodies exerted despite remaining motionless in their thrones.

The enemy scrap-Titan was grotesque – unappealing on a level that went far beyond mere design distaste to Valian. Its junk metal appearance showed no reverence, no respect, no care in its construction. *Stormherald*'s iron bones were thrice-blessed by tech-ministers even before they were brought together as the skeleton of a god-machine. Each of the million cogs, gears, rivets and plates of armour used in the Imperator's birth was honed to perfection and blessed before becoming part of the Titan's body.

This avatar of perfection incarnate faced its hideous opposite, and every crewmember piloting the Titan felt disgust flow through them. The enemy engine was fat, big-bellied to hold troops and ammunition loaders for its random array of torso cannons. Its head, in opposition to the Gothic-style machine skull worn by *Stormherald*, was stunted and flat, with cracked eye lenses and a heavy-jawed underbite. It stared pugnaciously down the street at the larger Imperial walker, its cannons covering its body like spines, and roared a challenge of its own.

It sounded exactly like what it was: an alien warleader within the cockpit head blaring into a vox-caster. *Stormherald* laughed in response, its warning sirens slamming back with a wall of sound.

In her tank of fluids, Zarha raised her arms, her handless stumps facing forward.

In the street, with an immense grinding of gear joints, *Stormherald* mirrored the motion.

It never fired. The trap, as crude and simple as it was, exploded around the great Titan.

* * *

'YOUR REQUEST FOR reinforcement is acknowledged,' the voice crackled.

Ryken lowered the vox-mic, readying his lasrifle again.

'They're coming,' he hissed to Vantine. The other trooper was with him, crouched with her back to the wall, sharing his slice of cover. Her expression was unreadable, masked by her goggles and rebreather, but she gave the major a nod.

'You said that half an hour ago.'

'I know.' Ryken slammed a fresh cell into his lasgun. 'But they're coming.'

The wall behind them buckled as it took the brunt of another shell. Debris from the ceiling clattered down onto their helmets.

Ryken's platoon were up to their necks in trouble, and no amount of hard fighting alone was going to get them out of it. Most of his men, the ones that weren't bleeding to death on the ground, were at the windows on the various floors of this hab-block, pouring their fire into the street outside. The rooms were still full of furniture, left by the families who were taking shelter in local underground bunkers. It was, as last stands went, a pretty terrible place to be holed up in, but their barricade had fallen half an hour before, and it was every squad for themselves until they could regroup at the next junction.

The problem was that Ryken's platoon was cut off much too fast when the last bastion fell. As rearguard covering the other squads' escapes, they'd been encircled and forced to find whatever cover they could.

'They're climbing the damn walls!' someone cried out. Ryken scrambled to the nearest window, keeping low and bracing to fire into the street again. As he rose to fire, he found himself face to face with a green-skinned creature hauling its way through the second-storey window. It reeked of mould and gunsmoke, and its piggish eyes were glazed by whatever alien emotions it felt in the heat of battle.

Ryken bayoneted the beast in the throat, firing three shots even as he stabbed. The alien was hurled back from the window to fall on its companions below.

They were indeed climbing the damn walls.

Ryken ordered three of his men to cover the window, and raced for the stairs leading down to the ground floor. The snapping *crack* of lasrifles firing was even louder from downstairs, where the bulk of the platoon was entrenched.

'Reinforcements are en route!' he called down the stairs.

'You said that half an hour ago!' Sergeant Kalas called back up.

Ryken caught a glimpse of the sergeant, his bolt pistol clutched in a two-handed grip, kneeling at a window and firing booming shots out into the road. He retreated back to a nearby window himself, adding his fire to the onslaught.

In the street, a riot of alien flesh was taking place. Only the most foolish or bloodthirsty orks were seeking to race across the road and scale the building's walls. Most of the xenos – and Ryken thanked the Emperor for small mercies – possessed enough intelligence to remain in cover themselves, behind their own junk-transports or shooting from windows of adjacent habitation blocks. They laughed and jeered as the barrage continued, and great howls of porcine laughter would rise up when another pack of baying aliens would charge across the street only to be cut down by the Steel Legion's defences. Raucous enjoyment of their own kin's death was a barbarous madness Ryken had long come to associate with this accursed xenos breed.

There was no understanding such creatures.

'We can't hold here,' Vantine crouched under cover again, whispering a rapid litany of devotion as she reloaded her rifle. 'You hear those engines? More are coming, major.'

'We're not breaking out anytime soon,' he spoke the words as a bitter curse, setting his rebreather straight. 'So we *will* hold.'

'Or we die.'

'That's not an option, and I'll shoot you the next time you give voice to it.'

She smiled behind her own gas mask, but Ryken saw none of it. He had risen to his feet and was leaning against the wall, his lasgun braced against his chest. He kept close to the wall, risking a look out of the window. What he saw made him curse more colourfully than Vantine had ever heard before.

'So,' she rose close to him, taking position on the other side of the window, 'not good news, then?'

'Tanks. The bastards are rolling armour up the road.'

Vantine chanced a look herself. Three tanks, Imperial Leman Russ chassis looted and 'improved' with crooked armour panels bolted on and painted in mismatched hues. The jagged fronts of the three tanks showed alien glyphs of allegiance that meant nothing to human eyes.

'We're dead,' she shook her head. 'And there's no need to shoot me. They'll shell this block to rubble and do it for you.'

Ryken ignored her. 'Nikov,' he keyed his vox-bead live. 'Nikov, how's the launcher coming?'

Nikov was on the hab-block's top floor, where he'd retreated with his missile launcher ten minutes before. The weapon had taken a beating when the barricade had fallen earlier.

'It's still jammed,' Nikov's reply came over the vox in a crackling hiss. After a pause of several moments, he added, 'Did I hear you shouting about reinforcements again?'

'They're coming! Throne, why is everyone whining about that?'

'I think it's because we'd rather not die, sir.'

The west wall chose that moment to explode. Debris burst into the room, filling it with stone dust. Through his goggles, Ryken stared at a hole the size of three grown men in the hab-block's wall. Most of the soldiers nearby picked themselves up off the floor. Two stayed where they were, mangled and unmoving.

'Get that launcher working,' Ryken said in the moment of eerie calm. Vantine scrambled to her feet and ran from the gaping hole in the wall.

Outside offered alien laughter, the grinding of tank treads and a distant thrum of racing engines.

'More?' Vantine called out.

'That's not the enemy,' Ryken said. 'Those aren't tank engines.'

And they weren't. His vox-bead screeched a distorted chatter of mixed channels, but one voice broke through. 'Your request for reinforcement,' it said, much too deep to be human, 'is acknowledged.'

The room darkened as the gunship rattled past on whining turbines. It swooped low, strafing the street, opening up with its weapons. From its cruising angle, it clearly didn't intend to stay long, but the pilot was inflicting all the punishment he could while the Thunderhawk remained.

Heavy bolters mounted on its wings and cheeks spat a torrent of lethal shells into the visible groups of enemy warriors. Inhuman blood misted the air as packs of the creatures burst under the explosive ammunition. Snarling, the diminishing groups of survivors returned fire – their stubbers chattering, the solid shells raining off the black gunship's hull like harmless hail.

The tanks were another matter. The first shell crashed into the gunship's side with a storm's force, and Ryken flinched back from the detonation. It spun the gunship on its axis, sending burning wind breathing from its boosters as it turned. In reaction to the attack, the avian shape gained altitude in a sudden thrust, banked over the first of the tanks, and at last dropped its cargo.

Dark figures clanged onto the surface of the tanks, as black as beetles crawling on the metal skin.

The first to fall – a figure on the roof of the lead tank – wore a silver-faced helm and wielded a mace with a sparking power field around its eagle-winged head. The weapon descended in a slice to shatter the vehicle's turret. It broke clean off and fell into the horde of aliens that mobbed the tanks from below.

'Good morning, Reclusiarch,' Ryken's voice was breathless with relief.

The knight didn't answer at first. He and his standard bearer were already engaged by the greenskins swarming up over the useless tank's hull, clambering higher in a desperate need to shed the blood of the black knights.

Artarion's bolter emitted its stuttering crash, blowing the aliens back down to the street. With the brilliance of a sunflare, Grimaldus's plasma pistol disintegrated two of the climbing beasts, letting their burning skeletal remains tumble in pieces back into the horde.

The second tank was dead in its tracks, smoke pouring from vents and cracks in its armour. The Templars had dropped grenades into the interior, and Ryken saw two knights leaping clear, ignoring the slain vehicle as they waded into the aliens massing on the street.

'Forgive the delay, major.' The Reclusiarch wasn't even out of breath. 'We were required at the barricade breaches in south section ninety-two.'

'Better late than never,' Ryken replied. 'The last word from central command suggested that Sarren's plan in this sector was working better than almost all hololithic estimations. Are we getting redeployed for a counter-attack?'

On top of the tank, Grimaldus swung his mace in a vicious arc, pummelling an ork into ruined biological matter.

'You are still breathing, major. Let that be enough for now.'

DAWN HAS BROUGHT nothing more than a continuation of the night's bloodshed.

The Helsreach Crusade begins its first bloody day. Across the city, millions of us now fight for our lives.

The noise is like no other sound I have ever heard. In two centuries of life, I have waged war at the heels of god-machines whose weapons were louder than the death-cries of stars. I have stood against armies of thousands, while every soul that stood against us screamed their hatred. I have seen a ship the size of a hive tower crash into the open ocean on a far distant world. The plume of water it threw into the sky and the tidal wave that followed were like some divine judgement come to flood the land and erase all humanity beneath its salt-rich depths.

Yet nothing has matched the sound of Helsreach's defiance.

In every street, humans and aliens clash, with their weapons and voices merging into a gestalt wave of senseless noise. On every rooftop, turrets and multi-barrelled defence cannons bark into the sky, their loaders never ceasing, their rate of fire never slowing. The machine-roars of Titans duelling can be heard from entire districts away.

Never before have I heard an entire city fighting a war.

As we fight to clear the streets of Major Ryken's besiegers – and as the Legionnaires themselves leave their havens and join us in the slaughter – I keep an edge of focus for the general vox-channels.

Ryken was not wrong. While we are locked in our planned fighting withdrawal across the entire hive, precious few sectors are in unplanned retreat.

The wreck-Titans are in the city now. Coldly delivered kill ratios from Invigilata commanders are a recent addition to the chaos of communication traffic, but they are a welcome one. Helsreach stands defiant as the sun rides the sky into noon.

My brothers remain scattered across the city, reinforcing the weakest parts of the Imperial chain, supporting the defences where the orkish tide breaks into the city with overwhelming force. I regret that we did not have the chance to gather together one last time. Such a lost opportunity is another of the failings I must atone for.

The reports of their engagements reach me hourly. As yet, no casualties blacken our record. I cannot help but wonder who the first to fall will be, and how long the hundred of us will last as the hours become days, and the days become weeks.

This city will die. All that remains to be learned is just how long we can defy fate. And above all, I want the weapon buried beneath the wasteland's sands.

I am drawing breath to recall our gunship when the vox

explodes with panic. It is difficult to make any sense from the maelstrom of noise. Key words manage to break through the mess: Titan. Invigilata. *Stormherald.*

And then, a voice so much stronger than all others, speaking a single word. She sounds in pain as she says it.

'Grimaldus.'

CHAPTER XII
IN A PRIMARCH'S SHADOW

THE GUNSHIP BURSTS across the sky, rattling around us in its ferocious race southwards. It is all too easy to imagine the thick Armageddon clouds left in turmoil in our wake.

Wind roars into the crew compartment through the open bulkhead door. As is my right, I am first at the portal, gripping the edge of the airlock with one hand as the wind claws at my tabard and parchment scrolls. Beneath us, the city slides by – towers aiming up, streets laid flat. The former are aflame. The latter are flooded by ash and the enemy.

Already, many of the city's outermost sectors are burning. Helsreach is what it is: an industrial city devoted to the production of fuel. There is much that will burn, here.

The flames choke the sky as the ring of fire swallowing the hive's edges creeps ever inwards. Reports of refugees spilling into the city's core have increased tenfold. Housing them is no longer even the greatest problem; the trouble in the

avenues where the civilians flock is that Sarren's redeployment of his armour divisions suffers crippling congestion.

I do not judge him for this. His mastery of the city after
arriving in the final weeks – only barely before we did – has
been as efficient as could be expected from a human mind
under such duress. I recall the initial briefings, when he was
stifled by large sections of the civilian populace refusing to
abandon their homes even in the face of invasion. In truth,
it is not as if the city was built with an abundance of bunkers
to house refugees anyway. With reluctance, he had allowed
them to remain where they were, knowing the problem was
– in part – a self-correcting one. As districts fell to the invaders, the civilian death toll would be catastrophic.

'Well,' he had said one night to the gathered commanders,
'it will mean fewer refugees in the siege itself.'

I had admired him greatly in that moment. His merciless clarity was most commendable.

With a lurch, the Thunderhawk begins its descent. I brace
myself, whispering words of reverence to the machine-spirit
within the propulsion engines now attached to my armour.
The jump pack is bulky and ancient, the metal pitted and
scarred and in dire need of repainting, but its link to my
armour is without flaw. I blink-clink the activation rune,
and the hum of the backpack's internal systems joins the
growl of my active armour.

I see *Stormherald*.

Over my shoulder, Artarion sees the same. 'Blood of Dorn,'
he says, his voice uncharacteristically soft.

The entire scene is tainted by the grey dust clouds in the
air from fallen buildings. In this cloud of grey, half buried
in the debris of the exploded buildings, the Titan kneels
in the street.

Sixty metres of walking lethality – an unstoppable weapons platform with the ornate cathedral adorning its shoulders – *kneels in the street*, defeated. Around it is the devastation of several fallen habitation towers. The invaders, curse their soulless lives, had set the surrounding hab-blocks to detonate and collapse on the Titan.

'They have brought an Emperor-class Titan to its knees,' Artarion says. 'I never thought I would live to see such a thing.'

Hundreds of them swarm the streets now, climbing onto the defeated god-machine's back with grappling hooks and boosting up there on burning thruster packs. They crawl across its dust-coated armour like insectile vermin.

'**Grimaldus,**' the Titan hails me, and suddenly it is so obvious why the voice is pained. Not from agony. From shame. She has advanced ahead of her skitarii phalanxes, and is undefended against this massed infantry assault.

'I am here, Zarha.'

'**I feel them, like a million spiders across my skin. I… cannot stand. I cannot rise.**'

'Make ready,' I vox to my brothers. Then, to the humbled princeps, 'We are about to engage the enemy.'

'**I feel them,**' she says again, and I cannot tell from her machine-voice if she is bitter, delirious, or both. '**They are killing my people. My prayer-speakers… My faithful adepts…**'

I am not blind to the meaning in her words. To the Machine Cult, each death was more than a mortal tragedy – it was the loss of knowledge and perspective that might never be recovered.

'**They are inside me, Grimaldus. Like parasites. Violating the Cathedral of Sanctuary. Climbing inside my bones. Drilling towards my heart.**'

I do not reply to her as I watch the crumbled cityscape below. Instead, I tense myself for a moment's sensory dislocation, and hurl myself out into the sky.

GRIMALDUS WAS FIRST to leap from the circling Thunderhawk.

Artarion, ever his shadow and still bearing his banner, was only seconds behind. Priamus, his blade in hand, came next. Nerovar and Cador followed, the first of them leaping into a dive, the latter merely stepping out in an uncomplicated plummet. Last of all was Bastilan, the sergeant's insignia on his helm catching the dull evening light. He voxed to the pilot, wishing him well, and drew his weapons before falling into air.

Altitude gauges on retinal displays showed fast-falling numbers, the digital readouts a blur as the knights dropped from the sky. Beneath them, the kneeling god-machine presented a huge target. The multi-levelled cathedral on its shoulders was like a city in miniature – a city of spires – bristling with weapons batteries and crawling with alien vermin.

The knights saw the aliens as they descended: the beasts clambering up on tethered lanyards, or flying up on primitive rocket packs, laying siege to the stricken Titan. *Stormherald* itself was a pathetic statue depicting its own failure. It was driven to one knee, buried to the waist in the debris of six or seven fallen hab-block towers. The avenue was in ruin around it, where the detonated buildings had collapsed and levelled the city flat. The Titan's arm-guns, as large as some habitation towers themselves, were grey-white with dust and resting on the mounds of broken brick, twisted steel supports, and rockcrete stone.

Grimaldus held off firing his boosters to slow his freefall.

'Come down in the courtyard in the centre of the cathedral,' he voxed to the others. Their acknowledgements came immediately. In turn, each of them engaged their jump packs, arresting their dives into more controlled descents.

Grimaldus was the last to fire his boosters, and the first to hit the ground.

His boots thudded onto the paved courtyard, smashing the precious mosaics into gravel beneath his feet. Immediately, he leaned to the side, compensating for the angle of the ground. *Stormherald*'s defeated posture was tilting the entire cathedral forward almost thirty degrees.

The courtyard was modest, ringed by nine plain marble statues that each stood four metres tall. In each of the cardinal directions, a set of open doors led into the cathedral itself. The mosaic tiles on the floor depicted the black and white bisected, cyborged skull of the Machine Cult of Mars. Grimaldus had come down onto the dark eye socket of the skull's human side, crushing the black tiles to powder underfoot.

Nothing moved nearby. The sounds of battle, of looting, of desecration – these all came from within the surrounding building.

Priamus landed with a skid, his armoured boots tearing at the mosaics and shearing them off in a wave of broken pebbles. His blade, chained to his wrist, crackled into life.

Nerovar, Cador and Bastilan were altogether more graceful in their landings. The sergeant came down in the shadow of one of the tilted statues. Its stern face eclipsed the setting sun.

'These are the primarchs,' he said to the others as they readied their weapons.

All heads turned towards Bastilan. He was right.

As representations of the primarchs went, they were plain to the point of almost being crude. The sons of the Emperor were usually depicted in grandeur and glory, rather than by sculptures so subtle and austere.

There was Sanguinius, Lord of the Blood Angels, prominently unwinged, with a childlike face lowered in repose. And there, Guilliman of the Ultramarines, his robed form so much slenderer than any other depiction of him that the knights had seen before. In one hand, he clutched an open tome. The other was raised to the sky, as if he were caught and forever frozen in a moment of great oratory.

Jaghatai Khan was bare-chested, bearing a curved blade in his hands and looking to the left, as if staring at the distant horizon. His hair was shaggy and long, whereas in so many masterpieces it was shaven but for a topknot. Next to him, Corax, the Prince of Ravens, wore a plain mask that was utterly featureless but for the eyes. It was as if he were unwilling to show his face in the company of his brothers, hiding his visage behind an actor's mask.

Ferrus Manus and Vulkan shared a plinth. The brothers were bareheaded, and the only two primarchs sculpted here in armour. Both wore vests of mail, the fine links of chain on Manus's breast a counterpoint to the larger scales adorning Vulkan's. They stood back to back, facing in opposite directions, both carved to bear hammers in each hand.

Leman Russ of the Wolves stood with legs apart, head cast back, facing the sky. Whereas the other sons of the Emperor wore robes or armour, Russ was clad in rags sculpted over his chiselled musculature. He was also the only primarch with tensed fists, as if he stared into the heavens, awaiting some grim arrival.

A robed figure, hooded yet visibly slender to the point

of emaciation, clutched the hilt of a winged blade, its tip between the statue's bare feet. Here was the Lion, depicted as a warrior-monk, eyes closed in silent contemplation.

And, last of all, rising above Bastilan, was Rogal Dorn.

Dorn stood apart from his brothers, neither facing his kin, nor looking into the skies above. His regal visage was aimed at the ground to his left, as if the primarch stared at something vital only he could see. The robe he wore was plainer than those adorning his brothers' icons, though it showed a cross on its breast, sculpted with care. Although he had been the Golden Lord, the commander of the Imperial Fists, his personal heraldry had inspired that of his Templars sons who followed.

His hands were what drew the knights' eyes more than any other aspect in this gathering of demigods. One was held to his chest, the fingertips joined to the cross there, frozen in mid-stroke. The other was held out in the direction Dorn stared, palm up and kindly, as if offering aid to one who would rise from the floor.

It was quite the most humble and exquisite rendition of their gene-father Grimaldus had ever laid eyes on. He fought the sudden burning urge to fall to his knees in reverent prayer.

'This is an omen,' Bastilan continued. Grimaldus could barely believe only a handful of seconds had passed since the sergeant last spoke.

'It is,' the Reclusiarch replied. 'We will purify this temple under the gaze of our forefather. Dorn watches us, brothers. Let us make him proud of the day he sired the first Templar.'

WE MOVE WITHOUT hesitation, and without caution, through the cathedral.

The angled floor is an irritation that I've managed to blank from my mind by the time the third alien is dead. Room by room, we move in unison. The cathedral is divided into a series of chambers ringing the courtyard, each one with its own stained glass windows now shattered and gaping like missing teeth, each room reaching high up with a pointed ceiling ending in the spire above.

The slaughter is easy, almost mindless. Priamus is like a wolf on the leash, eager to run ahead on his own.

My patience is wearing thin with him.

Each chamber also shows its own unique desecration. Tech-adepts and Ecclesiarchy priests lie dead and butchered, their bodies in pieces across the mosaic floors. Unarmed as they were, they offered little resistance to the rampaging invaders. Bookshelves are overturned, ceramic ornaments shattered... I would never put feral destruction past this xenos-breed, but it almost seems as if the greenskins sought something specific in their rabid assault.

'The articulation structures are sealed. My bones are defended by internal forces. My heart-core is cut off from the parasites.'

Ambush or not, it is disgusting that it took them even this long to achieve such basic necessities.

'We are retaking the Cathedral of Sanctuary,' I tell her. 'Resistance is minimal, Zarha. But you must stand. They are still coming. Bring the cathedral out of range of boarders, or we will be overwhelmed.'

'I cannot stand,' she says.

What a sin it is, for such a majestic warrior to speak with such shameful defeat tainting her words. Were she one of my men, I would kill her for such dishonour. Slowly. By strangulation. Cowardice does not deserve the rush of a blade.

'**I have tried**,' she intones.

The emotion colouring her machine-voice brings my bile rising. For all I know, she could be weeping. My disgust is so powerful I must fight the need to vomit.

'*Try harder*,' I breathe into the vox, and sever the link.

We fight our way to the outer battlements at *Stormherald*'s front, where the incline allows for easy boarding. An ork's fat hand slaps on the red metal of the battlement's edge, and the brute hauls itself up. My pistol meets its face, the heat exchanger vanes hissing against its skin. It has a moment to bawl its hatred at me before I pull the trigger. What remains of the alien falls from its handholds, tumbling to the ground, burning briefly on its way down as a living torch of white-hot fire.

The battlements resemble a true siege in all respects. The last remaining tech-adepts and priests defend the cathedral against boarding aliens, though no more than a small cluster remains. Few humans, augmented or otherwise, are a match for one of these beasts.

Priamus slips the leash of discipline. His charge carries him ahead, his sword flaring with light each time its power field saws into alien flesh. My brothers lay into the enemy along the besieged wall with bolter and blade. The few servitor-manned spire turrets that had been spitting solid shots into the mass of orks fall silent, not willing to risk striking any of us.

'You will do penance for this, Priamus.'

He doesn't answer. 'For the Emperor!' he cries into the vox. 'For Dorn!'

In the pockets of battle where none of us stand, the turrets open fire once again. At least their servitors are worth something, then. The orks turn from butchering the few priests still standing. Their bestial faces are afire with brutish, eager emotion as they come for us.

One of them… Throne of the Emperor… One of them dwarfs its piggish brethren. Its armour makes it twice the size of us, looking like scrap metal and primitive, chugging power generators bolted onto an exoskeletal frame. Its hands are industrial claws that look as if they could peel a tank apart without effort. It even kills his own kin as it strides towards us on the inclined floor. Its claws swing, battering its lesser allies aside, hurling them against the cathedral wall or over the battlement's edge.

I raise my crozius in a two-handed grip.

'That one is mine,' I tell my brothers.

Dorn is watching this.

'YOU ASKED TO see me, sir?'

Tomaz didn't bother to straighten his crumpled work overalls as he stood at what could loosely be called attention. Around him, the command chamber was its usual bustling hive of activity. A junior staff officer bumped him as she passed.

Tomaz said nothing. He'd worked fifteen hours straight today, on a dock backed up with dozens and dozens of ships, with almost no room to unload. Fifteen hours of shouting, of broken vox-casters and no techs spare to fix them, of cargo being dumped wherever it could be dumped – which was inevitably the wrong place (and the most inconvenient one for someone else) – necessitating its removal minutes later when another worker's already fouled-up work was fouled-up even further.

Frankly, he didn't much care if he got shoved over onto the ground. Maybe he could curl up and get some damn sleep.

'Sir,' he prompted.

Sarren finally looked up from the hololithic table. The colonel had aged in the last week, Maghernus could see it clearly. He looked as tired and bone-achingly sick of it all as Tomaz felt.

'What?' Sarren asked, narrowing his bloodshot eyes. 'Oh. Yes. Dockmaster.' Sarren looked back down at the hololithic display. 'I need your crews to speed up. Is that understood?'

Maghernus blinked. 'I'm sorry, sir. I didn't quite hear you.'

'I need,' Sarren didn't look up, 'your crews to speed up their work. The reports I'm getting from the docks show they are at a standstill. We are talking about significant portions of the north and east perimeters of the city, dockmaster. I need to move troops. I need to store materiel. I need you to do your job.'

Maghernus looked around the room in disbelief, unsure how to respond.

'What would you have me do, colonel? What is there that I can possibly do?'

'Your *job*, Maghernus.'

'Have you even seen the docks recently, colonel?'

Sarren looked up again, laughing without even a shred of humour. 'Do I look like I have seen anything except casualty reports recently?'

'I can't do anything about the docks,' Maghernus shook his head, a sense of unreality settling over him. 'I'm not a miracle worker.'

'I appreciate you have an... intense... workload.'

'That's not the half of it. We're dealing with a backlog of weeks, months even, and no room to handle anything.'

'Nevertheless, I need more from you and your crews.'

'Of course, sir. I'll be back in a moment, I feel the sudden need to piss expensive white wine and turn everything I touch into gold.'

'This is no laughing matter.'

'And I'm not laughing, you pompous son of a bitch. "Work harder"? "Do more"? Are you insane? There's nothing I can do!'

Nearby officers glanced his way. Sarren sighed and rubbed his closed eyes with the tips of his fingers.

'I respect the difficulties of your position, dockmaster, but this is the first week of the siege. This is only going to get worse. We are all going to sleep much less, and we are all going to work much harder.

'Furthermore, I understand that you are sweating blood in an underappreciated duty, but you are not the only one suffering. You, at least, are guaranteed to live longer than many of us. I have men and women in the streets, fighting and dying for your home, so that you may continue to complain at how I crack the whip over you. I have hundreds of thousands of citizens under arms, facing the greatest alien invasion force the world has ever seen.

'Sir,' Maghernus took a breath. 'I will–'

'You will shut up and let me finish, dockmaster. I have platoons of men and women lost behind the advancing enemy line, no doubt hacked to pieces by the axes of barbarous xenos monsters. I have armour divisions running out of fuel because of resupply difficulties in the embattled sectors. I have an Emperor-class Titan on its knees, because its commander was too angry to think clearly. I have a city with its edges on fire, and its population in rout with nowhere to run to. I have tens of thousands of soldiers dying to prevent the enemy from reaching the Hel's Highway – people dying for a *road*, dockmaster – because once the beasts reach the city's spine, we are all going to die a great deal faster.

'Now, am I making myself perfectly clear when I tell you that while I have sympathy for your difficulties, I also expect you to work through them? We are, just to be sure, no longer speaking past one another? We are, for the record, now on the same page?'

Maghernus swallowed and nodded.

'Good,' Sarren smiled. 'That's good. What can you do for me, dockmaster?'

'I'll… speak to my crews, colonel.'

'My thanks for understanding the situation we are in, Tomaz. You are dismissed. Now, someone raise a reliable vox-signal to the Reclusiarch. I need to know how close he is to getting that Titan walking.'

IN THE COGNITION chamber, Grimaldus stood before the crippled Zarha.

His armour's calm, measured hum was marred by a mechanical ticking sound at random intervals. Something, some internal system linking the power pack to the suit of armour was malfunctioning. His skull helm with its silver faceplate was painted with alien blood. His armour's left knee joint clicked as he moved, the servos inside damaged and in need of reverent maintenance by Chapter artificers. Where scrolls of written oaths had hung from his pauldrons, the armour was burned, the ceramite cracked.

But he was alive.

At his side, Artarion looked similarly battered. The others remained in the cathedral above, maintaining a vigil now the orks were punished and slain for their blasphemy.

'Your Titan,' Grimaldus uttered the words, 'is purged. Now *stand*, princeps.'

Zarha floated in the milky waters, not hearing him, not even moving. She looked as if she had drowned.

'*Stormherald* has taken her,' Moderati Carsomir said, his voice low. 'She was ancient, and had oppressed her will over the Titan's core for many years.'

'She still lives,' the knight noted.

'Only in the flesh, and not for much longer.' Carsomir looked pained even explaining this. His eyes were bloodshot and rimmed by dark circles. 'The machine-spirit of an Imperator is so much stronger than any soul you can imagine, Reclusiarch. These precious engines are born as lesser reflections of the Machine-God Himself. They carry His will and His strength.'

'No machine-spirit is the equal of a living soul,' said Grimaldus. 'She was strong. I sensed it in her.'

'You understand nothing of the metaphysics at work here! Who are you to lecture us in this way? We were linked to the Titan's core at the end. You are nothing, an... an *outsider*.'

Grimaldus turned to the crewmembers in their control seats, his broken armour joints snarling.

'I shed blood in the defence of your engine, as did my brothers. You would be torn from your thrones and buried in the rubble of your own failure, had I not saved your lives. The next time you call a Templar *nothing* is the moment I kill you where you sit, little man. You are nothing without your Titan, and your Titan lives because of me. Remember to whom you speak.'

The crew shared uncomfortable glances.

'He meant no offence,' one of the tech-priests mumbled through a facially-implanted vox-caster.

'I do not care what he intended. I deal in realities. Now. Make this Titan walk.'

'We… can't.'

'Do it anyway. *Stormherald* was supposed to move in synergy with the 199th Steel Legion Armoured Division over an hour ago, and they are in full retreat due to being unsupported. The delay is finished with. Get back in the fight.'

'Without a princeps? How are we to do that?' Carsomir shook his head. 'She is gone from us, Reclusiarch. The shame of it all, the rage of defeat. We all felt the Titan rush into her. Her mind has joined the union of all previous princeps, amalgamated in the Titan's core. Her soul is buried as surely as her body would be in a grave.'

'She lives,' the knight narrowed his eyes.

'For now. But this is how princeps die.'

Grimaldus turned back to the amniotic coffin, and the unmoving woman within. 'That is unacceptable.'

'It is the truth.'

'Then the truth,' the Reclusiarch growled, 'is unacceptable.'

SHE WEPT IN the silence – the way one weeps when truly alone, when there is no shame to be found in being seen by others.

Around her was nothingness absolute. No sound. No movement. No colour. She floated in this nothingness, neither cold nor hot, with no reference of direction or sensation.

And she wept.

Upon opening her eyes moments before, a thrill of fear had sliced up her spine. She did not know who she was, where she was, or why she was here.

Her memories – the fractured, flashing images that were

all that kept her mind from being completely hollow – were of a hundred worlds she could not recall seeing, and a hundred wars she could not remember fighting.

Worse, they were each tainted by an emotion she had never felt – something inhuman, abrasive, sinister… and partway between exultation and terror. She saw these moments of memory, and felt the unnerving presence of another being's emotions instead of her own.

It was like drowning. Drowning in someone else's dreams.

Who had she been before? Did it even matter? She slipped deeper. What remaining sense of self existed began to break away and diminish, sacrificed to buy a peaceful, silent death.

Then the voice came, and it ruined everything.

'Zarha,' it said.

With the word came a weak understanding, an awareness. She had memories of her own – at least, she had once possessed such things. It suddenly seemed wrong to no longer have access to her own recollections.

As she resurfaced slowly, the infiltrating memories returned. The wars. The emotions. The fire and the fury. Instinctively, she pulled away again, preparing to return deeper within the nothingness. Anything to escape the memories belonging to another soul.

'Zarha,' the voice clawed after her. 'You swore to me.'

Another layer of comprehension returned. Within the revelation were her own emotions, waiting for her to reclaim them. The overwhelming sensory storm of the other mind's memories no longer frightened her. They angered her.

She would not be so easily shackled. No false-soul's thoughts would conquer her like this.

'You swore to me,' the voice said, 'that you would walk.'

She smiled in the nothingness, rising through it now like

an ascending angel. *Stormherald*'s memories assailed her with renewed vigour, but she cast them aside like leaves in the wind.

You are right, Grimaldus, she told the voice. *I did swear I would walk.*

'Stand,' he demanded, stern and cold and glowering. 'Zarha. Stand.'

I will.

THE VOICE CAME without warning, emerging from the vox-speakers on the coffin.

'**I will.**'

Crew members flinched back from the sound, their hands white-knuckled as they clutched the backrests of their thrones. Only Grimaldus remained where he was, face to face with the glass sarcophagus, his blood-smeared skull mask glaring into the milky depths.

The old woman's body twitched once, and her head rose. She looked around slowly, her augmetic gaze at last coming to rest on the knight before her.

RUBBLE SCATTERED IN an avalanche, and a dust cloud rose again as the wreckage of fallen buildings went tumbling aside. With a thunderous grinding of gears and the clanging-hammering of a multitude of tank-sized pistons in its iron bones, *Stormherald* raised its immense bulk, metre by painful, machine-squealing metre.

The avenue shuddered as its bastion of a right foot pounded onto the road. The sound was loud enough that the nearby buildings still untouched by orkish demolition charges lost their windows in a blizzard of breaking glass.

As the crystal rain fell to the scarred streets below, the

Imperator raised its weapons, standing – once more – defiant.

'SHIELDS UP,' THE Crone of Invigilata demanded.

'Void shields active, my princeps,' responded Valian Carsomir.

'Make ready the heart.'

'Plasma reactor reports all systems at viable integrity, my princeps.'

'Then we move.'

The chamber shuddered with a familiar rhythm as the god-machine took its first step. Then a second. Then a third. Throughout the metal giant's bones, hundreds of crew members cheered.

'We walk.' The ancient woman turned in her tank, looking at the tall knight once more. 'I heard you,' she told him. 'As I was dying, I heard you calling me.'

Grimaldus removed his filthy helm. Although he didn't look a day over thirty, his eyes told his true age. Like windows into his thoughts, they showed the weight of his wars.

'There is a story of my father,' he said to Zarha.

'Your father?'

'Rogal Dorn, the Emperor's son.'

'The primarch. I see.'

'It is a tale of a once-strong brotherhood, broken by Horus the Betrayer. Rogal Dorn and Horus were close before the Great Heresy. None of the Emperor's sons were bonded as truly in the years before the malignant darkness took hold of Horus and his kin.'

'I am listening,' she smiled, knowing how rare this moment was. To hear a warrior of the Adeptus Astartes speak of their gene-sire's life outside of their Chapter's secret rituals.

'It has always been told among the Black Templars that when the two brothers crusaded together, they would compete for the greater glory. Horus was legendarily hungry for triumph, while my father was – it is told – a more reserved and quiet soul. Each time they made war together, they were said to have made an oath in blood. Clasping hands, they would each swear that they would stand until the final day dawned. "Until the end", they would say.'

'That is a touching legend.'

'More than that, princeps. Tradition. It is our most binding oath, spoken only between brothers who know they will never see another war. When a Templar knows he will die, it is the promise he gives to his brothers that he will stand with honour until he can no longer stand at all.'

She said nothing, but she smiled.

'Yes, I called you back to this war.' He nodded, his gentle eyes fixed upon her bionic replacements. 'Because you made a similar oath to me. Promises like that – they matter more than anything else in life. I could not let you die in shame.'

'Until the end, then.'

'Until the end, Zarha.'

PART TWO

KNIGHTFALL

PART TWO

CHAPTER XIII

THE THIRTY-SIXTH DAY

DARGRAVIAN.
The 5th day. Meritorious defence of the Torshav refuelling complex.
Gene-seed: **Recovered.**

FARUS.
The 7th day. Discovered in the Kurule Junction surrounded by no fewer than twelve of the slain enemy.
Gene-seed: **Recovered.**

THALIAR.
The 10th day. Lost in the petrochemical explosions at White Star Point.
Gene-seed: **Unfound / Unrecovered.**

KORITH.
The 10th day. Lost in the petrochemical explosions at White Star Point.

Gene-seed: **Unfound / Unrecovered.**

TORAVAN.
The 10th day. Lost in the petrochemical explosions at White Star Point.
Gene-seed: **Unfound / Unrecovered.**

AMARDES.
The 11th day. Unable to survive 83 per cent body tissue immolation suffered at White Star Point. Granted the Emperor's Peace.
Gene-seed: **Ruined / Unrecovered.**

HALRIK.
The 13th day. Eyewitness reports from Armageddon 101st Steel Legion relate intense personal courage and heroism in the face of overwhelming odds. Awarded posthumous Crusade Mark of Valiant Conduct for rallying Guard forces at the fall of Cargo Bridge Thirty.
Gene-seed: **Recovered.**

ANGRAD.
The 18th day. Single-handedly destroyed five enemy tanks at the Breach of the Amalas Concourse. Brought down by alien treachery and lost beneath enemy tank treads.
Gene-seed: **Ruined / Unrecovered.**

VORENTHAR.
The 18th day. Fought at the Breach of the Amalas Concourse.
Gene-seed: **Recovered.**

ERIAS.

The 18th day. Fought at the Breach of the Amalas Concourse.

Gene-seed: **Recovered.**

MARKOSIAN.

The 18th day. Fought at the Breach of the Amalas Concourse. Notably slew an enemy warlord in single combat, atop the alien's command tank. Awarded posthumous Crusade Mark of Unbroken Courage. Body was incinerated by the enemy in wrathful response.

Gene-seed: **Ruined / Unrecovered.**

IT WAS ALWAYS going to happen.

That did not make the reality any easier to bear, or the defeat any less bitter. But preparations were in place. When it happened, the Imperials were ready.

It happened first on the eighteenth day, at the Amalas Concourse, Junction Omega-9b-34. That was its assigned identifier according to the Imperial hololithic displays.

Colonel Sarren was watching through heavy, fatigue-dulled eyes as the flickering holo-images moved silently back from the location of their barricade. It was such a small thing – no more than a few marking runes blinking back a few centimetres, moving away from the point of the map marked *Amalas Concourse, Junction Omega-9b-34*.

Behind the flickering holo-runes was an illusory ramp, which in turn threaded into a much, much, much wider road. Sarren watched the runes falling back along this ramp, and tried to breathe in. It took four attempts, his breath catching in his throat on the first three.

'This is Colonel Sarren,' he spoke into his hand-vox. 'All units in Omega Sector, Subsector Nine. All units, prepare to retreat. Cancel assigned fallback locations, repeat: cancel withdrawal to assigned fallback locations. When the order comes, you will retreat, retreat, retreat to contingency positions.'

He ignored the storm of demands for confirmation, letting his vox-officers respond on his behalf.

'We did well,' he said to himself. 'We did damn well to keep the bastards away for this long.' Eighteen days – over half a month of siege warfare. He had every reason to colour his bitterness with that fierce core of pride.

The minutes passed in unblinking slowness. An aide came to his side, and quietly asked for his attention.

'Sir, your Baneblade stands ready.'

'Thank you, sergeant.'

She saluted and moved away. Finally, Sarren reached for his vox-mic again.

'All units in Omega Sector, Subsector Nine. Retreat, retreat, retreat. The enemy has reached Hel's Highway.'

MALATHIR.
The 19th day. Missing in action since the successful enemy siege of the Yangara Installation.
Gene-seed: **Unfound / Unrecovered.**

SITHREN.
The 20th day. Fell in personal combat with an enemy Dreadnought at the Danab Junction, Titan rearming site.
Gene-seed: **Recovered.**

THALHAIDEN.
The 21st day. Fell in personal combat with an enemy Dreadnought at the Danab Junction, Titan rearming site. Survival

depended on extensive and immediate surgical augmentation. Granted the Emperor's Peace.
Gene-seed: **Recovered.**

DARMERE.
The 22nd day. Body discovered with massacred elements of the 68th Steel Legion at the Mu-15 barricades.
Gene-seed: **Recovered.**

IKARION.
The 22nd day. Body discovered with massacred elements of the 68th Steel Legion at the Mu-19 barricades.
Gene-seed: **Recovered.**

DEMES.
The 30th day. Missing in action since the fall of the Prospering Haven habitation sector. Significant civilian casualties recorded.
Gene-seed: **Unfound / Unrecovered.**

GORTHIS.
The 33rd day. Led a counter-attack after the defences at Bastion IV were overrun. Also lost in the engagement were two Warlord-class Titans of the Legio Invigilata.
Gene-seed: **Recovered.**

SULAGON.
The 33rd day. Missing in action since the failed defence of Bastion IV. Last sighting reported his honourable conduct in the face of overwhelming enemy numbers.
Gene-seed: **Unfound / Unrecovered.**

NACLIDES.
The 33rd day. Orchestrated and inspired the last stand defence at Bastion IV, seeking to hold the militia fortress until reinforcements could arrive.
Gene-seed: **Recovered.**

KALEB.
The 33rd day. Part of the counter-attack at Bastion IV. Body suffered extreme mutilation and dismemberment at the hands of the enemy.
Gene-seed: **Ruined / Unrecovered.**

THORIAS.
The 33rd day. Pilot of the Thunderhawk *Avenged* – vehicle destroyed by gargant anti-air fire on routine patrol.
Gene-seed: **Unfound / Unrecovered.**

AVANDAR.
The 33rd day. Co-pilot of the Thunderhawk *Avenged* – vehicle destroyed by gargant anti-air fire on routine patrol.
Gene-seed: **Unfound / Unrecovered.**

VANRICH.
The 35th day. Lost in an action to mine the road before an enemy armour division.
Gene-seed: **Recovered.**

NEROVAR LOWERS HIS arm, his attention drifting from his narthecium bracer-gauntlet.

Cador lies on the cracked road, the old warrior's armour broken and split.

'Brother,' I tell Nero, 'now is not the time to grieve.'

'Yes, Reclusiarch,' he says, though I know he does not hear me. Not really. With mechanical dullness, his movements are leaden as he lowers his hand to Cador's chest.

Around us, the shattered highway is deserted but for the bodies of our latest hunt. The war here is a distant thing, and though the sound of battle in other sectors reaches our ears, this far behind enemy lines, all is quiet and still. The skies are calm and untroubled – unbroken by wrathful turrets.

The sharp *crack!* of the reductor doing its work splits the silence. First once, then again. The meaty, wet sound of flesh being pulled open follows.

Nero lifts his arm, the surgical gauntlet's armour-piercing flesh drills buzzing, spraying dark, rich Adeptus Astartes blood against his armour. In his hand, with great care, he holds the glistening purplish organs that had rested within Cador's chest and throat. They drip and quiver, as if still trying to feed their host with strength. Nero slides them into a cylinder of preserving fluids, which is in turn retracted into his gauntlet's protective housing.

I have seen him perform this ritual too many times in the past month.

'It is done,' he says, dead-voiced, rising to his feet.

He ignores me as I approach the corpse, occupying himself with entering information on his narthecium's screen.

CADOR.
The 36th day. Ambush along enemy-controlled portions of Hel's Highway.
Gene-seed: **Recovered.**

* * *

THE THIRTY-SIXTH DAY.

Thirty-six days of gruelling siege. Thirty-six days of retreat, of falling back, of holding positions for as long as we are able until inevitably overwhelmed by the insane, impossible numbers arrayed against us.

The entire city smells of blood. The coppery, stinging scent of human life, and the sickening fungal reek of the foulness purged from orkish veins. Beneath the blood-scent is the stench of burning wood, melted metal, and blasted stone – a city's death in smells. At the last gathering of commanders in the shadow of Colonel Sarren's Baneblade, the *Grey Warrior*, it was estimated that the foe controlled forty-six per cent of the city. That was four nights ago.

Almost half of Helsreach, gone. Lost to smoke and flame in bitter, galling defeat.

I am told we lack the force to take anything back. Reinforcements are not coming from the other hives, and the majority of the Guard and militia that still fight are exhausted remnants of the regiments, forever falling back, time and again, road by road. Hold a junction for a few nights, then withdraw to the next position when it finally falls.

Truly, we are fated to die in the most uninspired crusade ever to blight the name of the Black Templars.

'Reclusiarch,' the vox calls me.

'Not now.' I kneel by Cador's defiled body, seeing the holes in his armour and flesh – some from alien gunfire, two from the ritual surgery of Nerovar's flesh-boring tools.

'Reclusiarch,' the voice comes again. The rune blinking at the edge of my retinal display signifies it as from the *Grey Warrior*. I suspect I am to be begged, again, to fall back to Imperial lines and help in the defence of some meaningless roadway junction.

'I am administering the rites of the fallen to a slain knight. Now is not the time, colonel.'

At first, the colonel had replied to such words with the worthless, polite insistence that he was sorry for my loss. Sarren no longer says such things. The tens of thousands of lives lost in the last four weeks have utterly numbed him to such personal sentiment. That, too, is almost admirable. I see the strength in the way he has changed.

'Reclusiarch,' Sarren's voice betrays how ruined by exhaustion he is. Were I in the room with him, I know I would feel the weariness in his bones like an aura around where he stands. 'When you return from your scouting run, your presence is required in the Forthright Five district.'

Forthright sector. The southernmost docks.

'Why?'

'We are receiving anomalous reports from the Valdez Oil Platforms. The coastal auspex readers are suffering from offshore storms, but there *are* no storms off the coast. We suspect something is happening at sea.'

'We will be there in an hour,' I tell him. 'What anomalies are we speaking of?'

'If I could give you specifics, Reclusiarch, I would. The auspex readers look to be suffering some kind of directed interference. We believe they're being jammed.'

'One hour, colonel.' Then, 'Mount up,' I say to my brothers. It is not a short ride down the Hel's Highway, especially when it crawls with the enemy. Scouting teams are more often mounted on motorcycles now – the risk of Thunderhawks being shot down in enemy territory is too great.

'It is strange,' Nero says, cradling Cador's helm in his hands, as if the old warrior merely slept. 'I do not wish to leave him.'

'That is not Cador.' I rise from where I have been kneeling next to the body, anointing the tabard with sacred oils, before tearing it from the war-plate. In better times, the tabard would be enshrined on the *Eternal Crusader*. In this time, here and now, I rip it from my brother's body and tie it around my bracer, carrying it with me as a token to honour him. 'Cador is gone. You are leaving nothing behind.'

'You are heartless, brother,' Nero tells me. Standing here, in this annihilated city, with the bodies of so many dead aliens around us, I almost burst out laughing. 'But even for you,' Nero continues, 'even for one who wears the Black, that is a cold thing to say.'

'I loved him as one can love any warrior that fights by your side for two hundred years, boy. The bonds that form from decade upon decade of shared allegiance and united war are not to be ignored. I will miss Cador for the few days that remain to me, before this war kills me, as well. But no, I do not grieve. There is nothing to grieve over when a life has been led in service to the Throne.'

The Apothecary hangs his head. In shame? In thought?

'I see,' he says, apropos of nothing.

'We will speak of this again, Nero. Now mount up, brothers. We ride south.'

HALF OF THE city was a wasteland, one way or the other. Some of it burned, some of it was silent in death now that the xenos had moved on to other sectors, and some of it was simply abandoned. Habitation towers stood under Armageddon's yellow sky, lifeless and deserted. Manufactories no longer churned out weapons of war, or breathed smoke into the heavens.

Packs of orks – the jackal-like stragglers who had fallen

behind the main advance – looted through the empty sectors of the city. While there was little of calculated malice in the beasts' minds, what few human civilian survivors remained were slain without mercy when they were found.

Five armoured bikes growled their way down Hel's Highway. Their sloped armour plating was as black as the war-plate worn by each rider. Their engines emitted healthy, throaty roars that told of a thirst for promethium fuel. The boltguns mounted on the motorcycles were linked to belt-feeding ammunition boxes contained within the vehicles' main bulks.

Priamus throttled back, falling into formation alongside Nerovar. Neither warrior looked at the other as they rode, weaving through a shattered convoy of motionless, burned-out tank hulls spread across the dark rockcrete of the highway.

'His death,' the swordsman began, his vox-voice crackling from the distortion of the engines. 'Does it trouble you?'

'I do not wish to speak of this, Priamus.'

Priamus banked around the charred skeleton of what had once been a Chimera trooper carrier. His sword, chained to his back, rattled against his armour with the bike's vibrations.

'He did not die well.'

'I said I have no desire to speak of this, brother. Leave me be.'

'I only say this because if I were as close to him as you were, it would have grieved me, also. He died badly. An ugly, ugly death.'

'He killed several before he fell.'

'He did,' the swordsman allowed, 'but his death-wound was in the back. That would shame me beyond measure.'

'Priamus,' Nerovar's voice was ice cold and heavy with both emotion and threat. 'Leave me alone.'

'You are impossible, Nero.' Priamus revved his engine and accelerated away. 'I try to sympathise with you. I try to connect, and you rebuke me. I will remember this, brother.'

Nerovar said nothing. He just watched the road.

THE JAHANNAM PLATFORM.

Six hundred and nineteen workers stationed on an off-shore industrial base. Its skyline was a mess of cranes and storage silos. Beneath it, only the deep of the ocean and the richness of the crude oil that could be refined into promethium.

A new shadow entered the depths.

Like a black wave under the water's surface, it drifted closer to the support struts that held the gigantic platform above the water. Lesser shadows, fish-like and sharp, spilled ahead of the main darkness like rainfall falling from a storm cloud.

The platform shuddered at first, as if shivering in the chill winds that always howled this far from shore.

And then, with majestic slowness, it began to fall. A town-sized, multi-layered platform fell into the ocean, crashing down into the water. The ships around it began, one by one, to explode. Each one, once breached, sank alongside the Jahannam Platform.

Six hundred and nineteen workers, and one thousand and twenty-one crewmembers from the ships died in the freezing waters over the course of the following three hours. The few men and women that managed to reach vox-casters shouted into their machines, little realising their voices were carrying no further.

The platform was eventually submerged except for a fleet of floating detritus. The ocean no longer teemed with potential profit, but the scrap metal of destroyed enterprise.

Helsreach heard nothing of this.

THE SHEOL PLATFORM.

In a central spire, nestled between tall, stacked container silos, Technical Officer Nayra Racinov cast an annoyed look at her green screen, and the sudden fuzzy wash of distortion it was displaying for her.

'You're joking,' she said to the screen. It replied with white noise.

She thumped the thick glass with the bottom of her fist. It replied with slightly angrier white noise. Technical Officer Nayra Racinov decided not to try that again.

'My screen's just died,' she called out to the rest of the office. Looking over her shoulder, she saw that the 'rest of the office', which usually consisted of an overweight ex-crane driver called Gruli who monitored the communications system, had gone for a mug of caffeine.

She looked back at her console. Warning lights were flickering cheerily around the confused screen. One moment, the green wash showed a chaotic burst of incoming presences on the sonar. Hundreds of them. The next, it showed a clear ocean. And the next, nothing but distortion again.

The room shuddered. The entire platform shuddered, as if in the grip of an earthquake.

Nayra swallowed, watching the screen again. The presences under the water, hundreds of them, were back once again.

She dived across the shaking room, hammering the vox-station's transmit button with the heel of her hand.

She managed to say 'Helsreach, Helsreach, come in...' before the world dropped out from under her and the second of the Valdez Oil Platforms was brought down, with its steel bones burning, bending and screaming, into the icy sea.

THE LUCIFUS PLATFORM.

The largest of the three offshore installations was manned by a permanent work crew population twice the size of those at Jahannam and Sheol. While they were powerless to prevent their own destruction, they at least saw it coming.

Across the platform, sonar auspex readers were suddenly captured by the storm of distortion that had preceded the deaths of Sheol and Jahannam. Here, a fully-staffed control office reacted quicker, with a low-ranking tech-acolyte managing to restore a semblance of clarity to the screens.

Technical Officer Marvek Kolovas was on the vox-network immediately, his gravelly voice carrying directly to the mainland.

'Helsreach, this is Lucifus.' Massive, repeat, massive incoming enemy fleet. At least three hundred submersibles. We can't raise Sheol or Jahannam. Neither platform is responding. Helsreach? Helsreach, come in.'

'Uh...'

Kolovas blinked at the receiver in his hand. 'Helsreach?' he said again.

'Uh, this is Dock Officer Nylien. You're under attack?'

'Throne, are you deaf, you stupid bastard? There's a fleet of enemy submersibles launching all kinds of hell at our support gantries. We need rescue craft immediately. *Airborne* rescue craft. Lucifus Platform is going down.'

'I... I...'

'Helsreach? Helsreach? Do you hear me?'

A new voice broke over the vox-channel. 'This is Dockmaster Tomaz Maghernus. Helsreach hears and acknowledges.'

Kolovas finally let out the breath he'd been holding. Around him, the world shook as it began to end.

'Good luck, Lucifus,' the dockmaster's voice finished, a moment before the link went dead.

'This is the situation,' Colonel Sarren began.

The Forthright Sector dockmaster's office was, putting it politely, a pit. Maghernus was not a tidy man at the best of times, and a recent divorce wasn't helping his state of cleanliness. The sizeable room was a hovel of old caffeine mugs that were growing furry mould-masses in their depths, and unfiled stacks of papers were scattered everywhere. Here and there were some of Maghernus's cast-off clothing from the nights he'd slept in his office rather than go back to his depressing bachelor hab – and before that, back to the woman he'd taken to calling The Cheating Bitch.

The Cheating Bitch was a memory now, and not a pleasant one. He found himself worrying against his will. Had she already died in the war? He wasn't sure his bitterness stretched quite far enough to wish something like that.

His dawdling thoughts were dragged back in line by the arrival of the Reclusiarch. In battered black war-plate, the knight stalked into the room, sending menials and Guard officers scurrying aside.

'I was summoned.' The words blasted rough from his helm's vox-speakers.

'Reclusiarch,' Sarren nodded. The colonel's bone-tiredness bled from him in a slow drip. In his weary majesty, he moved like he was underwater. The officers gathered around

the room's messy table, poring over a crinkled paper map
of the city and the surrounding coast.

Room was made at the table as Grimaldus approached.

'Speak to me,' he said.

'This is the situation,' Colonel Sarren began again. 'Exactly
fifty-four minutes ago, we received a distress call from the
Lucifus Platform. They reported they were under attack by
an overwhelming submersible fleet numbering at least three
hundred enemy vessels.'

The gathered officers and dock leaders variously swore,
made notes on the map, or looked to Sarren to provide an
answer to this latest development.

'How long until they reach–'

'...must move the reserve garrisons–'

'...storm trooper battalions to assemble–'

Cyria Tyro stood alongside the colonel. 'This is what the
bastards were doing in the southern Dead Lands. It's why
they touched down there. They were taking their landing
ships to pieces and building this fleet.'

'It's worse than that,' Sarren gestured to the portable hololithic table with a control wand, zooming out from the city
and showing a much wider spread of the southern coast of
the Armageddon Secundus landmass.

'Tempestus Hive,' several officers muttered.

Enemy runes flickered as they drew nearer to the other
coastal hive. Almost as many as those bearing down on
Helsreach.

'They're dead,' Tyro said. 'Tempestus will fall, no matter
what we do. A hive half our size, and with half our defences.'

'We're all dead,' a voice spoke out.

'What did you say?' Commissar Falkov sneered.

'We have done all that can be done.' The protests came

from an overweight lieutenant in the uniform of the conscripted militia forces. He was calm, sanguine even, speaking with what he hoped was measured wisdom. 'Throne, three hundred enemy vessels? My men are stationed at the docks, and we know what we can do there. But the defences are as thin as… as… Damn it, there *are* no defences there. We must evacuate the city, surely. We've done all we can.'

Commissar Falkov's dark stormcoat swished as he reached for his sidearm. He never got the chance to execute the lieutenant for cowardice. A snarling, immense blur of blackness sliced across the room. With a crash, the lieutenant was slammed back against the wall, held a metre off the ground, short legs kicking, as the Reclusiarch gripped his throat in one hand.

'Thirty-six days, you wretched worm. Thirty-six days of defiance, and *thousands upon thousands of heroes lie dead.* You dare speak of retreat when the day finally comes for you to spill the enemy's blood?'

The lieutenant gagged as he was strangled. Colonel Sarren, Cyria Tyro and the other officers watched in silence. No one turned away.

'Hnk. Agh. Ss.' He fought for breath that wouldn't come as he stared into the silver replica of the God-Emperor's death mask. Grimaldus leaned closer, his skulled face leering, blocking out all other sight.

'Where would you run, coward? *Where would you hide that the Emperor would not see your shame and spit on your soul when your worthless life is finally at an end?*'

'Pl-Please.'

'Do not shame yourself further by begging for a life you do not deserve.' Grimaldus tensed his hand, his fingers snapping closed with wet snaps. In his grip, the lieutenant

239

went into spasms, then thumped to the floor as the knight released his grip. The Reclusiarch strode back to the table, ignoring the fallen body.

It took several seconds for conversation to resume. When it did, Falkov saluted the Reclusiarch. Grimaldus ignored it.

Maghernus tried to make sense of the lines being drawn across the map showing troop disposition, but it might as well have been in another language to him. He cleared his throat and said, above the din, 'Colonel.'

'Dockmaster.'

'What does this mean? In the simplest terms, please. All of these lines and numbers mean nothing to me.'

It was Grimaldus who answered. The knight spoke low, staring down at the map with his helm's unblinking scarlet eyes.

'Today is the thirty-sixth day of the siege,' the Templar said, 'and unless we defend the docks against the tens of thousands of enemy that will arrive in under two hours, we will lose the city by nightfall.'

Cyria Tyro nodded as she stared at the map. 'We need to evacuate the dockworkers in the most efficient manner possible, allowing for the arrival of troops.'

'No,' Maghernus said, though no one was listening.

'These avenues,' Colonel Sarren pointed out, 'are already clogged by inbound/outbound supply traffic. We will struggle to get all of the dock menials – no offence, Dockmaster – out in time. Let alone get troops in.'

'No,' Maghernus said again, louder this time. Still, no one paid him any attention.

One of the Steel Legion majors present, a storm trooper set apart by his dark uniform and shoulder insignia, traced a finger along a central spine road leading from Hel's Highway.'

'Evacuate the drones down the other paths and leave the highway route clear. That'll be enough to fill the central docks with trained bodies.'

'That still leaves almost two-thirds of the dock districts,' Sarren frowned, 'with no defence except the garrisoned militia. And the militia will suffer from the fleeing dock menials being in their way.'

'Hello?' said Maghernus.

'We can reroute the traffic through to these secondary veins,' Tyro pointed out.

'Troops would trickle in,' Sarren nodded. 'That might not be enough, but it may be the best we can ask for in the situation.'

A sound emerged, machine-like and harsh, like the engine of a Chimera troop transport choking on the wrong fuel. One by one, heads turned to Grimaldus. The sound was emitted from his helm's vocalisers. He was chuckling.

'I believe,' said the knight, 'the dockmaster has something to say.'

All heads turned to Maghernus.

'Arm us,' he said.

Colonel Sarren closed his eyes. The others watched the dockmaster, unsure if they had heard correctly. Maghernus continued, as the silence spread out, 'There are over thirty-nine thousand of us on those docks – and that's just the workers, not including the militia. If you need time, arm us. We'll give you the time.'

The storm trooper major snorted. 'You'll be dead in an hour. All of you.'

'Maybe,' said Maghernus. 'But we were never going to win this war, were we?'

The major wasn't done, and his voice had less of a sneer

now. 'Brave, but insane. If we allow the enemy to butcher the dockworker forces, the city won't be able to function for decades after this war. We're fighting to preserve our way of life, not just survive.'

'Let us focus,' Sarren opened his eyes, 'on surviving first. The fact remains that the majority of the Steel Legion cannot be moved. They are holding the city, and pulling them back from their positions will see the city fall as surely as if we leave the docks undefended. Invigilata and the militia can't hold everything.'

'There's little choice,' said Tyro. 'The dockworkers will die unsupported.'

'Arm them first,' Grimaldus said, his vox-voice heavy with finality. 'Then argue how long they have left to live.'

'Very well. Our course is clear.' Colonel Sarren cleared his throat. 'Dockmaster. I thank you.'

'We'll fight like... like... We'll fight damn hard, colonel. Just don't take too long getting the troops to back us up.'

'We have immense stockpiles of materiel in the dock districts.' The colonel nodded to Cyria Tyro. 'You heard the Reclusiarch. Arm them.'

She saluted with a grim smile, and left the table.

'We can hold,' Sarren told everyone that remained. 'After all we have done, I refuse to believe this will be the treacherous blow that breaks our back. We can hold. Major Krivus, the movement of storm trooper squads to the docks is already under way, but I need you to take personal command of that process immediately. Grav-chute them in if you have to. Drop them from the Valkyries that remain. Every rifle counts.'

The major saluted, and moved out of the office with all the grace and speed his bulky carapace armour allowed.

'The civilians,' Tyro murmured, staring at the hololithic. Almost all of the city's reinforced shelters were situated – and sealed – within and beneath the docks district. Sixty per cent of the hive's population, crowded in civilian shelter bunkers, now no longer away from the front lines. 'We can't have that many people left in the direct line of fire.'

'No? We can't release them onto the streets.' Sarren shook his head. 'There is nowhere for them to run, and the panic would choke the byways, preventing the Steel Legion ever reaching the docks. They are as safe as they can be in their shelters.'

'The beasts will tear down those shelters,' Tyro argued.

'Yes, they will. Nothing can be done now.' Sarren would not be deterred. 'There will be no evacuation. We can't arm them in time, and we can't protect them if they leave the shelters. They will do nothing but die in the streets and clog the veins of reinforcements.'

Tyro didn't raise another objection. She knew he was right.

Sarren continued, 'I need insurgency walkers and light armour battalions riding in from the tertiary arterial roads here, here, here and here. Sentinels, my friends. Hellhounds and Sentinels. Everything we can muster.' More officers left the table.

'Reclusiarch.'

'Colonel.'

'You know what I am going to ask of you. There is only one way we will survive this assault long enough to flood the docks with tried and tested troops. I cannot order you, but I would ask it nevertheless.'

'There is no need to ask. My knights will deploy from our remaining gunships. We will stand with the civilians. We will hold the docks.'

'My thanks, Reclusiarch. Now, we are as ready as it is possible to be, given the nature of this unwelcome surprise. We are, however, placing a great deal of pressure on Invigilata and the bulk of the Imperial Guard. The city will bleed while we divert our elite infantry to the docks, and this fight… It'll take days. At best.'

'Let Invigilata hold the city,' Grimaldus said, gesturing to the map with a black gauntlet. 'Let the Steel Legion stand with them. Focus on what matters in the here and now.'

'No grand speech? I'm almost disappointed.'

'No speech.' The Templar was already stalking from the room. 'Not for you. You won't be dying this day. I save my words for those who will.'

CHAPTER XIV
THE DOCKS

THEY CAME AS the sun began its downward arc in the sky.

The Helsreach docks took up almost a third of the hive's perimeter. Thousands of uninspiring warehouses and harbour office towers stood watch over an expansive bay which featured an endless number of quays and piers that stabbed out into the sloshing, filthy greyish water.

The air across the entire world might have always reeked of something faintly sulphuric, but here – at the heart of Helsreach's industry – the reek bordered on petrochemically unhealthy. It only took an hour for a person's clothes and hair to become saturated with the greasy, heavy stink of spilled oil and ammoniac seawater. Lifers, the dockworkers who spent their entire careers here, hacked up a fair share of blackness when they hawked and spat. Respiratory tumours were the second-largest cause of death among the populace, only behind industrial accidents by a small margin.

The chaos of the docks was a natural deterrent to the

enemy assault, but not a true defence. The first sign of the enemy came as crews leaped from their vessels, risking a kilometre-long swim through pollution-foul waters to reach the docks. On dry land, the defenders of Helsreach watched as the hundreds of undocked tankers, lurking offshore with their volatile manifests, began to explode.

The men and women of Helsreach stood together on cargo crates, on the paved groundways, on steel piers, all eyes turned to the seas and the fleet of enemy vessels breaching the surface of the water, powering closer to the city. A horde of humanity, looking out to sea.

Maghernus was close to the front of one crowd, leading his worker gang in their filthy overalls, clutching a newly-forged lasgun to his chest. They were being handed out by Guard officers from weapon crates stored in warehouses across the dock districts. Every dock gang was treated to a short, simple talk on how a lasrifle was loaded, unloaded, set to safety and fired after aiming. Maghernus had felt his palms sweating as he collected the rifle and extra power cells, which now sat in a small sack hanging from the side of his belt. The hurried Guard sergeant had shouted his way through a quick demonstration, and now here Maghernus was, gun in hand, dry-mouthed.

'Follow your assigned leaders,' the sergeant had yelled above the noise of so many men and women gathered in one place. 'Every dock gang, and every group of fifty people, will have a storm trooper with them. Follow that storm trooper the way you'd follow the Emperor Himself if He descended from the sky and told you what to do with your sorry arses. He will tell you when to fight, when to run, when to hide and when to move. If you do what this trooper tells you to do, you've got a much greater chance of getting through this in one piece, and not messing up another unit's movements. If you don't listen, there's a greater chance you'll be fouling it up for everyone else, and getting your friends killed. Understood?'

General assent answered this.

'For the next few days, you're in the Imperial Guard. First rule of the Guard: Go forward. If you get lost, *you go forward*. You lose your way? *You go forward*. You fall away from your group? *You go towards the enemy*. That's where you'll do the most good, and that's where you'll find your friends. Understood?'

General assent answered this, too. It came with a little more reluctance.

'Right. Next groups!'

With that, Maghernus's gang and several others filed from the warehouse, making room for others to get exactly the same lecture.

Outside, dozens of Steel Legion storm troopers in their ochre jackets and heavy, thrumming power generator backpacks were directing the flow of human traffic. Maghernus led his gang to one that waved him over. The man was slender, unshaven, scratching his forehead under the domed helmet he wore. His goggles were raised up, fastened around the helmet, and his rebreather mask was hanging slack around his neck. He had the look of someone who, if not lost, was at least not entirely sure where he was.

'Hello,' Maghernus swallowed. 'We need an assigned soldier.'

'Ah, I know this already. That is me. I am Andrej.'

'Thank you, sir.'

The storm trooper laughed, slapping the dockmaster on the shoulder. 'That is funny. "Sir". I may keep you after the

war is done, to make me feel good, eh? I am not Sir. I am
Andrej. Perhaps I will be Sir after I make sure none of you
are dead. I would like that. It would be nice.'

'I...'

'Yes, it is a big pressure. I understand this. I would like a
promotion, so you must all stay alive. We play for big stakes
now, no? I thank you for this idea you have given me. You
have made the day more fun.'

'I...'

'Come, come. No time for making friends now. We will
talk much soon. Hey! All of you dock-working people, come
with me, yes?'

Without waiting for an answer, Andrej began to walk
through the crowds, followed by Maghernus's gang. The
storm trooper would occasionally wave at other soldiers,
most of whom offered silent nods or gruff greetings. One
of them, a pale beauty with black hair so thick and rich it
had no business being leashed in a plain ponytail, smiled
and waved back.

'Throne, who was that?' Maghernus asked as he trailed
just behind Andrej. 'Your wife?'

'Ha! I wish. That is Domoska. We are squadmates. She
is nice to look at, no?'

She was. Maghernus watched her leading another group
through the masses. As Domoska was lost in the teeming
crowds, his gaze fell on the men she was leading. Maghernus prayed he didn't look as nervous as they all did.

'It is very funny, I think. Her brother is the ugliest man
I have ever seen, yet the sister is touched by fortune with
great beauty. He must be very bitter, no?'

Maghernus just nodded.

'Come, come. Time is running away from us.'

That had been an hour ago. Now, they stood with Andrej, unfamiliar weapons held to their chests, pressed against quickened heartbeats. Andrej was occupying himself by picking his nose. This was something he struggled to do in gloves of thick, brown leather, but he went about the task with a curiously stately tenacity.

'Sir,' Maghernus started.

'A moment, please. Victory is almost mine.' Andrej flicked something grotesque from his fingertip. 'I can breathe again. Emperor be praised.'

'Sir, shouldn't you say something to us?' He lowered his voice, stepping closer. 'Something to inspire the men?'

Andrej frowned, absently biting his cut lip as he looked around at the other groups spread down the dock lines. 'I do not think so. No other Legionnaire is talking. I was going to wait for the Reclusiarch's speech, you know? Would you prefer me to speak now?'

'The Reclusiarch will speak?'

'Oh, yes. He is good at this. You will like it. It will happen soon, I am thinking.'

A blast of screeching feedback slashed through the air as across the docks – kilometre upon kilometre of them – every vox-tower came alive in a distorted whine.

'See?' Andrej grinned. 'I am always right. It is what I do best.'

For several seconds, the people of Helsreach heard nothing but breathing – low, heavy, threatening – over the vox-speakers.

'*Sons and daughters of Hive Helsreach,*' the voice boomed across the shore districts, too low and resonant to be human, flavoured by the slight crackle of vox-corruption. '*Look to the water. The water from which you draw the wealth of your city. The water that now promises nothing but death.*

'For thirty-six days, the people of your world, the people of your own city, have been selling their lives to defend you. For thirty-six nights, your own mothers and fathers, your own brothers and sisters, your own sons and daughters have been fighting the enemy to ensure that half of the hive remains in human hands. They have battled, road by road, sweating and fighting and dying so you can enjoy a handful of days of freedom.

'You owe them. You owe them for the sacrifices they have made so far. You owe them for the sacrifices they will make in the days and nights yet to come.

'Here and now, you will have the chance you deserve, the chance to repay them all. More than that, you will have the chance to punish the enemy for daring to lay siege to your city, for breaking your families apart and destroying your homes.

'Watch the tides. See the scrap fleet that sails into your port, bearing a horde of howling beasts. When the sun sets at the end of this week, every single invader in those surfacing ships will no longer draw breath from the sacred air of this world. They will fall because of you. You are going to save this city.

'Fear is natural. It is human. Feel no shame for a heart that beats too fast in this moment, or fingers that tremble as you hold a weapon you have never wielded before. The only shame is in cowardice – in running and leaving others to die when everything comes down to your actions.

'You are led by Guard veterans – the best of your Steel Legions – Imperial storm troopers. But they are not alone. The forces of Helsreach are coming. Stand and defy the enemy for long enough, and you will soon see thousands of tanks constructed in this very city grinding the invaders into dust. Help. Is. Coming. Until then, stand proud. Stand resolute.

'Remember these words, brothers and sisters. "When death

comes, the good we have done will mean nothing. We are judged in life for the evil we destroy".

'*That time of judgement is upon you. I know every man and women here feels it in their blood, in their bones.*

'*I am Grimaldus of the Black Templars, and this is my vow to you all. While one of us stands, these docks will never fall. If I have to kill a thousand of the enemy myself, the sun will rise once more over an unconquered city.*

'*Look for the black knights among you. We will be where the fighting is fiercest, at the heart of the storm.*

'*Stand with us, and we will be your salvation.*'

Silence descended once more.

Maghernus sighed, tension ebbing from him as his breath misted in the cool air. Andrej was adjusting the slide rack settings on his modified lasrifle. The weapon emitted a pulsing, charged hum that set the dockmaster's teeth on edge.

'That was a stern talking-to, no? Not many will run now, I am thinking.'

Maghernus nodded. It took him several moments to speak. 'What's that rifle?'

'This?' Andrej finished his ministrations, gesturing to the thick power cables feeding from the rifle's bulky stock to the humming metal power pack he wore between his shoulders. 'We call them hellguns. Like yours, only brighter and louder and hotter and meaner. And no, you cannot have one. This is mine. They are rare, and only given to people who are right all the time.'

'And what's that?'

'This is a det-pack.' He tapped the hand-sized detonator disc hanging from his belt. 'Used for sticking to tanks and making them explode into many pretty pieces. I once had many, now I have only one. When I use it, I will have none, and that will be a sad day.'

Maghernus wanted to ask if Andrej was really a storm trooper. He settled for saying 'You are not exactly what I expected.'

'Life,' the soldier said, looking off to the side in what appeared to be distracted consideration, 'is a series of very wonderful surprises, until a final bad one.' Turning to the entire group, Andrej buckled his helmet's chin strap with a grin.

'My handsome new friends, it is soon to be time for war. So, my beautiful ladies and fine gentlemen, if you want to remain beautiful and fine, keep your heads down and your rifles up. Always aim from the cheek, with your eyes down the barrel. Do not be firing from the hip – that is the best way to feel excellent about yourself and yet hit nothing. Oh, and it will be loud and scary, no? Much panic, I think. Always wait one second before pulling your trigger, to make sure you are aiming at something you should be aiming at. Otherwise you may be shooting other people, and that is bad news for you, and worse news for them.'

The gangs of workers began to disperse across the docks, taking up positions in alleys between warehouses, behind crate stacks, around the edges of buildings and on the various floors of multi-storey hangars and work blocks facing the sea.

'Come, come.' Andrej led his group into the shadows of a loader crane, ordering them to spread out and take cover around the huge metal strut columns and cargo containers close by.

'Sir?' called one of the men.

'My name is Andrej, and I have said this many times. But yes, what is the problem?'

'My gun's jammed. I can't get the power cell back in.'

From where he crouched at the head of the group, Andrej shook his head with a melodramatic sigh. With his goggles over his eyes and the infantile grin plastered across his features, he looked like some breed of gigantic, amused fly.

'One has to wonder why you would be taking it out in the first place.'

'I was just–'

'Yes, yes. Be nice to the weapon's machine-spirit. Ask it nicely.'

The dockworker looked awkward as he turned his gaze down at the rifle. 'Please?' he said, lamely.

'Ha! Such reverence. Now click that lock switch on the other side. That is the release catch, and you need to slide it back to get the cell back in.'

The man dropped the power cell from his shaking hands, but slapped it home on the second try. 'Thank you, sir.'

'Yes, yes, I am a hero. Now, my brave friends, a siren will soon begin to sing. When it does, it means the enemy is within range of our artillery defences, which are sadly too few in number to make me smile. When I say it is time to be ready, you are all to sit up and start looking for huge and ugly beasts to shoot.'

'Yes, sir,' they chorused.

'I could become used to that, oh yes. Now, listen with both ears my wonderful fellows. Aim for the bodies. It is the biggest target, and that is what counts if you are new to this.'

'Yes, sir,' they said again.

'There is a very beautiful woman I would like to marry after this war. She will almost certainly be saying no to my proposal, but hey, we will see. If she says yes, you are all invited to my wedding, which will be in the eastern territories where the weather is much less like being pissed on by the sky every day. Also, the drinks will be free. You have my word on this. I am always truthful, this being one of my many glorious virtues.'

A few of the men smiled, despite themselves.

The siren began to wail. A banshee's keen across kilometres of docks, howling over tens of thousands of frightened Imperial souls. Muffled thumps started up in response as the Sabre-class defence platforms opened fire on the incoming fleet.

'It is time,' Andrej grinned again, 'to earn some very shiny medals.'

'For the Emperor,' one man breathed the words like a mantra, his eyes closed. 'For the Emperor.'

'Oh, no. Not for Him.' Andrej fastened his rebreather mask, but they could still hear the smile in his voice. 'He is happy on His Golden Throne, a long way from here. This is for me, and it is for you, and that is more than enough.'

The sirens began to fade, one by one, until a last lone wail sputtered out.

'Any moment now,' Andrej said, leaning up to aim over the top of the container he'd been kneeling behind. 'We will have company.'

The first vessels crashed into the docks with the noise of a storm wave breaking against the shore. With no finesse, without even slowing down, they crunched into the gangways and loading platforms, ferociously beaching themselves. Doors and portals immediately blasted open, disgorging a tide of foul alien flesh onto the docks.

The very first of the alien beasts to spill from its underwater scrap-pod was a brute, easily half again the size of its lesser brethren, bearing a trophy rack on its hunched shoulders with human skulls and Adeptus Astartes helms from other wars on other worlds. It had been leading its tribe across the edges of the Imperium for decades, and in a fight with all else even, would have been more than a match for a lone Adeptus Astartes.

Its face, shoulder and torso disintegrated in a ruthless volley of las-fire that sent the burning remains spinning off the edge of the docks and into the polluted water below. Less than a hundred metres away, Domoska shouted encouragement to the dockworkers she led, and ordered them to fire again. Many had missed, but more than enough had struck home. It was a pattern being repeated along the Helsreach docks now, as the first wave of xenos creatures howled and laughed their way into the city.

From his makeshift cover within the den of loosely-stacked cargo containers, Maghernus fired shot after shot, feeling the rifle in his hands growing warmer with each *crack* of release. He lowered himself below the lip of the crate he knelt behind, and reloaded his lasgun with inexpert fingers. The bastard thing was stuck.

'Use force,' Andrej said from his place next to the dockmaster. The storm trooper didn't look at him, didn't even glance away from where he was aiming and firing. Another migraine-bright beam of overcharged energy spat from the soldier's hellgun. 'The slides often jam on new rifles. This is a sad truth with the rifles of our home world. Their spirits take time to wake up.'

Maghernus was amazed he could even hear the other man over the din of beaching vessels, alien roars and discharging lasguns filling the air with a scattered chorus of mechanical cracks.

'I fired a Kantrael rifle once,' Andrej was continuing, his

words punctuated by slight shifts in his posture and aim as he tracked target after target, releasing round after round. 'It was a very keen weapon, oh yes. That world forges eager guns.'

Maghernus slotted the fresh power cell home and raised himself back into position. His back already ached from his first two minutes as a soldier. How the Steel Legion crouched like this for days on end and got used to battle was a mystery to him. He fired at distant figures, lumbering alien hulks that ran with almost no sense of direction or purpose, as if hunting for a scent – lost until they found it. Others in the emerging packs would race to the source of the las-fire being thrown at them, and were cut down in their headlong run. A few, clearly cunning by the standards of these creatures, remained back and loaded heavy weapons. These last beasts sent shrieking missiles into the entrenched Imperial lines, exploding stacks of cargo crates or pulverising the sides of warehouses.

Slowly but surely, with an insidious creep, the docks were being enveloped by thick smoke from the destroyed submersibles and burning buildings.

'We will have to move soon,' Andrej called over his shoulder to the others. The words proved prophetic. With a crash of metal on stone and a wave of flooding water, a submersible beached itself on the docks not thirty metres from their position. Saltwater splashed down on the crouching dockworkers. Alien growls came from the wrecked sub as its doors blasted open.

'That is far from good,' the storm trooper scowled behind his rebreather as he slammed back into his firing position, drawing a bead on the first creature to emerge. It dropped like a puppet with its strings cut as the harsh beam lanced through its face and blew out the back of its head.

Maghernus and the others joined their fire to his. Still more beasts came spilling from the submersible. The green-skins were charging now, having sniffed out the nearby cluster of humans behind the barricade, and following the streams of laser fire.

'Sir...' one of the men stammered, his eyes wide and bloodshot. 'Sir, they're coming...'

'That is a fact I am aware of,' Andrej replied, not stopping his stream of fire for a moment.

'Sir–'

'Please *shut up* and *keep firing*, yes?'

The beasts reached the cargo containers. They reeked of blood, smoke, bitter sweat and the alien stench of fungal corruption. Bunched muscles hauled the beasts over the barricades, and the brutes roared down at the humans – no longer in cover, but hemmed in by the cargo pods.

Las-rounds sliced up, punching dozens of the scrambling beasts back. The remnants of the first wave were joined by the second, and the creatures dropped in amongst the dock-workers, scrap-pistols barking and heavy axes swinging.

'Fall back!' Andrej shouted, firing his hellgun at point-blank range, using it to slash a way through the erupting melee. 'Run!'

The dockworkers were already in a panicked flight. 'With me, you idiots!' the storm trooper yelled, and for a wonder, it actually worked. The dockers with enough presence of mind to clutch their lasguns in the chaos moved with Andrej, adding their fire to his again.

He left a third of his team in the shelter of the containers and crane struts. Screaming dockworkers, unable to escape the invaders. Andrej sensed a momentary hesitation in those that remained with him; a handful of seconds where they ceased against all logic, some freezing rather than open fire on their dying friends, and others mesmerised in astonished fear by the sight of such slaughter.

'They're already dead!' Andrej slammed his gloved palm into the side of Maghernus's head, jolting him back into the moment. 'Fire!'

It was enough to break the spell. Las-fire opened up again, streaming into the embattled aliens.

'Fall back only when you must reload! Stand and fire until then!'

Andrej swore under his breath after he gave the order. The orks were already scrambling closer in an avalanche of green flesh, axe blades and ragged armour. Around the retreating team, the docks burned and thundered with the sounds of more submersibles beaching themselves. Andrej caught a momentary glimpse of another team of dock-workers through the smoke some distance away, breaking into flight as they were chopped to pieces by the orks in their midst.

The same was about to happen to his ragtag gang, and he swore again. He hoped Domoska was faring better.

What a stupid place to die.

KILOMETRES AWAY FROM Helsreach, beneath the sands of the wastelands to the north-west, there was a loud and unprecedented *clunk* of heavy machinery.

Jurisian, Forgemaster of the *Eternal Crusader*, rose to his feet with a slowness born of exhaustion. Tears stood in his eyes – a rarity indeed for a being that had not wept in over twenty decades. His mind pulsed with a thundering ache, a dull and thudding heat that had nothing to do with physical weakness.

He could smell his servitors now that his senses were returning from their focusless lock on his primary task. Turning to regard them where they lay, Jurisian could smell the decay setting into their organic parts. They had been dead for weeks, starved of sustenance. He hadn't noticed. They had proven useless after the first few hours, over a month ago, their internal cognitive processors unable to keep up with the ever-evolving code. Jurisian had needed to work alone, cursing Grimaldus all the while.

Another deep clunk of grinding machinery restored his attention to the present. His joints ached – both the mechanical ones and his still-human ones – from such a period of inactivity. He had been a statue in place for four weeks, his mind alive and his body in hunched, tense stasis by the console.

He had not slept. He knew that on several occasions, as his closing, exhausted mind had drifted close to shutting down, he had almost lost grip on the code. With his thoughts moving sluggishly, the code had outpaced him just as it had done to his servitors. In these moments of panicked intensity, he had resisted by silencing sections of his mind with clinical meditation, operating at a lessened capacity, but at least he was still awake.

Jurisian stared ahead at the vast doors.

- OBERON -

That word burned itself into his core, written in towering letters, more a warning than a tomb marker.

A last resonant machine-sound signalled the grinding roll-back of the final interior lock. Pressurised coolant vapour flushed into the corridor as the door's seal systems vented it.

It reeked of chlorine – not poisonous, but stale from being cold-cooked for so many years while the door remained silent and still. In a ballet of rumbling, shuddering technology, the portal began to open.

'Reclusiarch,' Jurisian voxed, horrified at the dull scratchiness of his voice. 'The defences are broken. I am in.'

CHAPTER XV
BALANCE

THE CHAMBER OFFERED nothing at first. Nothing except a powerless darkness that was blacker than black, even to Jurisian's visor lenses. A whispered keyword cycled his vision filters through a thermal-seeking infrared, through to a crude echolocation that falsified an auspex scanner's silent chimes to detect movement. He had made these modifications himself, with the proper respect to the machine-spirit of his wargear.

It was this last sense that produced a response. A vague grey blur passed his vision, and with it, the whirring of internal mechanisms. Hinges. Cogs. Fibre muscles. The sound was as familiar to Jurisian as his own breathing, but brought with it an edge of disconcerting curiosity.

Joints. He was hearing joints.

Something was wrong. The suggestion of static interference at the edges of his vision display told a tale of interference, obfuscation, more than a darkness born from a lack of light. He was being jammed, and the manipulation was insidiously subtle.

Jurisian's bolter came up in steady hands, panning left and right in the darkness as his eye lenses continued to cycle through filters. At last, a targeting monocle slid over his right eye lens – the mechanical echo of a lizard's nictitating membrane.

Better. Not perfect, but better.

'I am Jurisian,' he said to the creature before him, as it resolved into focus. 'Master of the Forge for the *Eternal Crusader*, flagship of the Black Templars.'

The creature didn't answer immediately. The size of a man, it smelled of ancient machinery and sour breath.

It was likely the thing had once been human – or some part of it was organic, even if only the smallest aspect. Hunched, robed in a ruined cloak of woven fabric, misshapen lumps in its surface area suggested additional limbs or advanced modification. It remained faceless, either refusing to look up or unable to do so.

Jurisian lowered his bolter. The servo-arms extending from his back-mounted power generator still clutched a host of weaponry, aiming it at the robed being before him. He voiced his next words through his helm's vox-speakers, letting his armour's spirit twist the human language into a universal, bluntly simple machine code – a basic program for communication which he had acquired during his long years of tuition and training on Mars, home world of the Mechanicus.

'My identity is Jurisian,' the code pulsed, 'of the Adeptus Astartes.'

The reply came in a burst of snarled code, the words and meanings bleeding into each other. It was akin to machineslang, evolved from the viral program that sealed the doors.

This creature, whatever it was, had an accent born of hundreds of years of isolation here.

'Affirmative,' Jurisian responded in the foundation code. 'I can see you. Your interference should be aborted. It is no longer relevant.'

The creature raised itself higher, no longer lurking on all fours. It now reached Jurisian's chestplate, though it came no closer, remaining a dozen metres away. The weapons in the Forgemaster's servo-arms tracked the being's movements.

It pulsed another tangled mess of accented code.

'Affirmative,' Jurisian replied again. 'I destroyed the sealant program.'

This time, the creature's response was rendered through a more simple code. Jurisian narrowed his eyes at this development. Like the chamber's virus lock, the creature was adapting and working with new information at a faster rate than standard Mechanicus constructs.

'This is the sanctuary of *Oberon*.'

'I know.' The Forgemaster risked a panning glance left and right, seeking any resolution in the artificial darkness. His targeting monocle couldn't pierce the gloom more than a few metres ahead. Flickering static was beginning to crawl across his eye lenses. 'Deactivate the interference,' Jurisian raised his bolter again, 'or I will destroy you.'

Against his will, emotion coloured the code-spoken declaration. To be limited like this was an affront to his sense of honourable conduct – there was no glory or prudence in allowing oneself to be kept at an enemy's mercy.

'I am the guardian of *Oberon*. Your presence generates negligible threat to me.'

Jurisian tasted anger on his tongue, bitter and metallic. His finger tensed on the thick trigger of his bolter.

'Deactivate the interference. This is your final warning.'
Static mottled his vision now, like a thousand insects clustering on his eye lenses. He could make out no more than the barest silhouette as the Mechanicus warden moved closer.

'Negative,' it said.

Jurisian's servo-arms, answering his mind's impulses a fraction of a second after his true limbs, had raised his axe and other weapons in a threatening display, almost akin to some feral world arachnid predator increasing its size to warn off prey.

The knight's final threat was spoken with conviction, the machine-cant laced with numerical equations indicating emphasis.

'Then die.'

THEIR SAVIOUR WAS one of the black knights.

He charged the enemy from the sky with a whining howl of protesting thrusters. Fire streaked from his flight pack as he landed in the aliens' midst, a dark blur of movement outlined in flame.

Andrej immediately scrambled back, ordering his gang into the relative cover provided by an overturned cargo loader truck.

'Do not dare cease fire,' he shouted over the sound of alien bellowing and thousands of guns crying out. He doubted any of them heard him, but they went back to firing as soon as they slid into cover.

The Templar cut left and right with his chainsword, ripping stinking green flesh from malformed orkish bones. His bolt pistol sang out in a thudding refrain, embedding fist-sized bolts in alien bodies which detonated a moment later. Andrej, who had seen Adeptus Astartes fight before, did all he could to keep up his rate of fire in support of the suicidal bravery taking place. Several of his dockworker crew lowered their guns in slack-jawed, frightened awe.

Perhaps, Andrej cursed, they believed the Adeptus Astartes would actually survive unaided.

'Keep firing, damn you!' the storm trooper yelled. 'He's dying for us!'

The ferocious advantage of surprise did not last long. The greenskins turned to the deadly threat among them, laying about with their crude axes and firing their clattering pistols at close range. Several of them hit each other in their fury, while stragglers and those on the edges of the melee were punched down by las-fire from Andrej's gang.

The Templar screamed – a vox-distorted cry of wrath that went crawling across the skin of every human in earshot. His chainblade fell from his black hand, hanging loose on the thick chain that bound the blade to his forearm.

Behind the staggering warrior, one of the few remaining greenskins tore a crude spear back out from the knight's lower spine. The beast had no more than a moment to enjoy its victory: a searing lance of headache-bright energy dissolved its face and blew the contents of its skull over the dying knight's armour. Andrej recharged his weapon without even needing to look away from the melee.

The Templar regained his balance, then recovered his grip on the revving chainsword a heartbeat after. He lasted for three more savage cuts, tearing gobbets of flesh and shattered armour from the orks closest to him, before the remnants of the alien pack impaled him on their spears and bore him to the ground. His flight pack crashed to the floor, rent from his body. They aimed with brutal efficiency, ramming blades into his armour joints and using their immense strength to force him to his knees. The Templar's pistol came up one final time to hammer a bolt into the chest of the nearest beast, spraying those nearby with inhuman gore as it primed and exploded.

The last three orks were scythed down by Andrej's dock team, collapsing next to the Adeptus Astartes they had slain. The scene before them was a slice of eerie calm, the heart of a storm, while the rest of the docks burned.

'Throne,' the storm trooper hissed. 'Stay here, yes?'

Maghernus didn't even have time to agree before the soldier was making a break across the rockcrete platform, crouched low, moving to the downed knight's body.

'What's he doing?' asked one of the dockworkers.

Maghernus wanted to know that himself. He moved after the storm trooper, doing his best to mimic the crouching run Andrej had just performed. Something hot and angry buzzed past his ear, like the passage of a poisonous insect. It took several seconds to realise he'd almost had his head taken off by a stray shot.

'What are you doing?' He knelt by the storm trooper.

What he was doing seemed obvious to Andrej. His gloved fingers quested under the chin of the knight's helm, seeking some kind of catch, or lock, or release. Throne, there must be something...

'Seeing if he lives,' the soldier muttered, clearly distracted. 'Ayah! Got you.'

With a muted hiss almost drowned out by nearby gunfire, the helm's seals parted and the expressionless helmet came loose. Andrej pulled it off, handing it to Maghernus. It was about three times as heavy as the dockmaster had been expecting, and he'd been expecting it to weigh a hell of a lot.

The knight wasn't dead. His face was awash in blood, the dark fluid filming over his eyes and darkening his features as it ran from his nose and clenched teeth. Adeptus Astartes blood was supposed to clot within instants, so the tales told. It wasn't happening here, and Andrej doubted that was a positive sign.

'Can't move,' the Templar growled. His voice was wet from a burbling throat. 'Spine. Hearts. Dying.'

'There is something inside you, I know,' Andrej spared a glance around, making sure they weren't in immediate danger. 'Something important inside you, that your brothers must reclaim, yes?'

'Progenoid,' the knight's breathing was as raw as a chainsword's snarl. The warrior's oversized armoured hand gripped the front of Andrej's armour. It was strengthless.

'I do not know what that is, sir knight.'

'*Gene-seed*,' the Templar spat blood as he forced the words through numbing lips. His eyes were lolling now, half closed and rolling back. It was clear he was blind. '*Legacy.*'

Andrej nodded to Maghernus. 'Help me move him. Do not argue. It is important that his brothers find his body. Important for their rituals.'

'*Emperor...*' the knight grunted, '*Emperor protects.*'

With those words, the hand gripping Andrej's chestguard went slack, thumping to rest on the heraldic cross on the warrior's own breastplate.

Their eyes met once, and the dockworker and the career soldier started dragging the dead knight.

WE ARE DYING.

We are dying, scattered across kilometres of docks, mixed in with the humans, torn from the unity of brotherhood.

'Wear your helm,' I say to Nero without looking over my shoulder at him. 'Do not let the humans see you like this.'

With tears in his eyes, our healer does as I order. The list of failing life signs is transferred from his wrist display to his retinal readouts. I hear him draw a shaking breath over the vox.

'Anastus is dead,' he says, adding another name to those that came before.

I lean forward, the racing wind clawing over the surface of my armour, sending my parchment scrolls and tabard streaming in its grip. We are several hundred metres up, making ready to drop on the beasts below. The Thunder-hawk's turbines lower their growl as they throttle down.

The docks below us are already in ruin. They burn – black and grey, amber and orange – making the view from the polluted skies like staring down into the mouth of some mythical dragon. Percussive thumps signal the crash landings of more submersibles, or our own munitions stores going up in flames.

'Helsreach will fall tonight,' Bastilan says, giving voice to something we must all be thinking. I have never, in over a century of waging war at his side, heard him speak such a thing.

'And do not lie to me, Grimaldus,' he says, sharing the bulkhead's space with me. 'Save your words for the others, brother.'

I tolerate such familiarity from him.

But he is wrong.

'Not tonight,' I tell him, and he doesn't look away from the skull I wear as my face. 'I swore to the humans that the sun would rise over an unconquered city. I do not mean to break that vow. And you, brother, will help me keep it.'

Bastilan turns away at last. What closeness had been near to the surface cools fast, leaving us distant again. 'As you command,' he says.

'Make ready to jump,' I vox to the others. 'Nero. Do you stand ready?'

'What?' He lowers his narthecium, retracting surgical saws and cutting blades. I see the empty sockets for gene-seed storage withdraw and lock under smooth armour plating.

'I need you, Nero. Our brothers need you.'

'Do not lecture me, Reclusiarch. I stand ready.'

The others, Priamus especially, are taking note now. 'Cador is dead. Two-thirds of the Helsreach Crusade will not live to see the coming dawn. You will carry their legacy, my brother. Grief has its place – none of us have suffered such losses before – but if you are lost in sorrow then you will be the death of us all.'

'I said I stand ready! Why do you single me out like this? Priamus is likely to see us all dead because he cannot follow orders! Bastilan and Artarion are not half the fighters Cador was. Yet you lecture *me* about being the weak one, the crack in the blade?'

My pistol is aimed at his head, at the faceplate marked white as a symbol of his expertise and valuable skills.

'Bitterness is taking root within you, brother. Much longer, and it will bore through you, hollowing out your heart and soul, leaving naught but empty bones. When I tell you to focus and stand with your brothers, you respond with black words and treacherous thoughts. So I tell you again, one last time, that we need you. And you need us.'

He doesn't stare me down. When he looks away, it's not in defeat or cowardice, but in shame.

'Yes, Reclusiarch. My brothers, forgive me. My humours are unbalanced, and my mind has been adrift.'

'"A mind without purpose will walk in dark places,"' Artarion quotes. A human philosopher; one I don't recognise.

'It is fine, Nero,' Bastilan grunts. 'Cador was one of the Chapter's finest. I miss him, just as you do.'

'I forgive you, Nerovar,' Priamus says, and I thank him on a private vox-channel for not sounding like he is sneering for once.

The Thunderhawk slows, thrusters keeping it aloft as we make ready to jump. In the air around us, snapping explosions decorate the sky.

'Anti-air fire? Already?' Artarion asks.

Whether they've beached several submersibles with surface-to-air weapons or taken control of wall defence cannons is irrelevant. The gunship swings violently, shaking as the armour plating takes its first hit. They're firing up through the smoke, tracking the gunship through primitive methods that are apparently effective enough to work.

'Incoming missiles,' the pilot voxes to us. The Thunderhawk re-engages its forward thrust, boosting forward. 'Dozens, too close to evade. Jump now or die with me.'

Priamus goes. Artarion follows. Nero and Bastilan next, launching out of the airlock.

The pilot, Troven, is not a warrior I know well. I cannot judge his temperament the way I can with my closest brothers, except to say that he is a Templar, with all the courage, pride and resolution that honour entails.

In a human, I'd call such behaviour stubbornness.

'There is no need to die here,' I say as I enter the cockpit. I have no idea if I'm right to say such a thing, but if this hope can be forged into the truth, I will make it happen now.

'Reclusiarch?'

Troven has chosen to wrench the Thunderhawk through evasive manoeuvres, rather than disengage himself from the pilot's throne and try to leap from the gunship. Both choices, such as they are, are likely to fail. I still believe he chose wrong.

'Disengage *now*.' I haul him from the throne, power feeds snapping from connection ports in his armour. He spasms with the electrical feedback of an unsafe and flawed disconnect, half of his perception and consciousness still melded with the gunship's machine-spirit. His protests are reduced to garbled, wordless grunts of pain as his armour's power supply kicks back in and the union with the gunship's systems dims.

The Thunderhawk tilts, diving from the sky on dead engines. Nausea fades as soon as it threatens, balanced by the gene-forged organs replacing my standard human eyes and ears. Troven's genetic compensators take a moment longer to adjust, ruined by the disorientation of the severed connection. I hear him grunting through his helm's vox-speakers, swallowing his bile.

This freefall will delay the missiles' impact. I hope.

In this weakened state, he's easy to drag from the cockpit to the open bulkhead. The visible sky is twisting as the gunship plummets. Mag-locked step by mag-locked step, my boots adhere to the iron floor, preventing the spiralling death-dive from hurling us around the cabin.

As I face the air-rushing portal, my targeting display overlays the spinning sky. I blink at a flashing rune of crossed blades pulsing in the centre. A propulsion gauge spills across my retinas, and the jump pack weighing my shoulders down whines into life.

'You'll kill us both,' Troven almost laughs. I spare no more than a second's thought for the two servitors operating the other flight stations.

'*Brace*,' is all I have time to say. The world around us dissolves into jagged metal and screaming fire.

ONCE THE NOISES had faded and the air reeked of the powdery, familiar scent of bolter fire, Jurisian hauled himself back to his feet.

The immediate area around him was illuminated by flashing sparks and energy flares vented by his broken servo arm and savaged armour. The expulsions of electrical force from wounded metal were bright enough to leave violent smears across his sensitive eye lenses. Jurisian blanked the filters with a command word, restoring standard vision mode.

A moan of pain emerged from his vox-speakers as a harsh crackle. Even with no one nearby, it shamed him to voice his weakness in such a way. He would seek out the Reclusiarch and perform penance when... Well, there would be no *when*. This war would never be won.

Retinal displays showed in grim detail the damage to his internal biological and mechanical components. The Forgemaster spared several seconds to examine the flashing warning runes, indicating leaking vital oxygenated haemoplasma from areas near several organs. Jurisian felt a grin steal over his face as his pain-drunk mind latched on to an altogether more human explanation.

I'm bleeding.

He barely cared. It wasn't terminal damage, neither to his living components nor his augmetic modifications. He stepped forward, crushing underfoot one of the many segmented blade-arms the warden had deployed as it launched at him only minutes before.

It lay in motionless repose, its internal power generators cycling down, descending into silence. In death, the truth was revealed with an almost melancholic clarity. The warden was no more than a shadow of what it had claimed to be.

Certainly, the creature would have been a match for most intruders – be they alien or human. But with its robe parted to show the decrepit truth it had concealed, what was once a stalwart Mechanicus tech-guardian was revealed as little more than an ancient, degrading magos, long-starved of the supplies it needed to maintain itself. Once, it had been human. And in an era after that, it had been a powerful sentinel for the Mechanicus, watching over this most precious of secrets.

Time had robbed it of a great deal.

The ancient warden had leapt at Jurisian, its limb-blades snapping into life, stabbing and cutting as they descended on flailing mechadendrites.

The knight's own servo-arms had hit back, slower, weightier, inflicting pounding and lasting damage in opposition to the scrapes and gouges inflicted by the warden. By the time the sentinel creature had severed one of the knight's machine-limbs, Jurisian's bolter was hammering shot after shot into the guardian's torso, detonating vital systems and rupturing the human organs that yet remained. Suspension fluid and chemical lubricants ran in place of blood that would no longer flow.

Piercing pain signalled the moments that the warden punctured Jurisian's ceramite armour. It still possessed enough of its attack routines to stab for his joints and armour's weak points, but just as often as it struck a gouging hit, its efforts were deflected by the customised, revered war-plate that Jurisian had modified himself so long ago on the surface of Mars.

He rose after it had finally fallen. Damaged, but unashamed. Regretful, but with his conviction burning.

Already, the creature – the sentinel that had come so close to ending his life – was forgotten. The interference had cleared with its destruction.

Jurisian stared into the resolving darkness of the colossal chamber, and became the first living being in over five hundred years to see *Oberon*, the Ordinatus Armageddon.

'Grimaldus,' he whispered into the vox. 'It's true. It's the holy lance of the Machine-God.'

THE THRUSTERS KICKED in with desperate force, arresting their insane descent. The jolt was savage – without his armour's fibre bundle musculature, Grimaldus's neck would have snapped as soon as the boosters fired to bring them both stable.

They were still falling too fast, even with the jump pack's engines howling hot.

'Acknowledged, Jurisian,' the Reclusiarch breathed. *Of all the accursed times…*

Grimaldus grunted at the weight of Troven's armour. His pistol dangled on its wrist-bound chain, while he gripped the other knight's vambrace. Troven, in turn, hung in the air, holding to Grimaldus's own wrist. Their burning tabards slapped against their armour, caught in the wind.

With retinal gauges flashing scarlet, the Reclusiarch and the prone knight descended into the atmosphere of black smoke rising from the docks. Before their vision was blocked entirely, Grimaldus saw Troven reaching with his free hand, drawing the gladius sheathed to his thigh.

Interference crackled thick from the surrounding chaos, but Bastilan's vox-voice made it through the distortion, coloured by brutal eagerness.

'We saw that, Reclusiarch. Dorn's blood, we all saw it.'

'Then you are unfocused on the battle, and will do penance for it'.

He bunched his muscles, negating thrust in the moment before thudding into the ground with bone-shaking force. The two knights skidded across the rockcrete surface of the docks, sparks spraying from their armour.

As they both regained their footing, the hulking silhouettes of alien beasts ambled through the surrounding smoke.

'For Dorn and the Emperor!' Troven cried, and brought his bolter to bear from where it hung at his side, forever bound to his armour by the ritual chains. Grimaldus twinned his cries with Troven's, laying into the enemy.

If these docks could be saved, then by the Throne, they would be.

CHAPTER XVI
A TURNING TIDE

A WING OF fighters bolted overhead, their engines leaving smoke-smears across the darkening sky. In pursuit, alien craft rattled after them, tracer rounds spitting across the clouds in futility as they tried to hunt the Imperial fighters back to one of the city's few remaining airstrips.

Beneath the aerial chase, Helsreach burned. Avenue by avenue, alley by alley, the invaders flooded through the docks district, gaining ground with the death of every defender.

Where the fighting was fiercest, vox-contact was a broken, unreliable mess of lucky signals breaking through the interference. The Imperials fell back through the night, sector by sector, leaving thoroughfares packed with their dead. The city added new scents to its reek of sulphur and saltwater. Now, Helsreach had come to smell of blood and flame, of a hundred thousand lives ending in fire between a single sunrise and sunset. Poets from the impious ages of Old

Terra had written of a punitive afterlife, a hell beneath the world's surface. Had that realm ever existed, it would have smelled like this industrial city, dying in fire on the shores of Armageddon Secundus.

In unconnected catacombs below the ground, the citizens of Helsreach remained shielded from the slaughter above. They clustered together in the darkness, listening to the erratic drumbeat of factories, workshops, tanks and munitions stores exploding. Although the walls of the subterranean shelters shook with tremors that bled down through the ground, the booms and thumps on the surface echoed down like peals of thunder. Many parents told their young children that it was just a violent storm above.

Across the embattled world, the besieged cities were visible from orbit as blackened patches scarring the planet's surface. As the planetary assault entered its second month, Armageddon's atmosphere was turning thick and sour with smoke from the burning hives.

Helsreach itself no longer resembled a city. With the docks under siege, the last pristine sectors of the hive were aflame, wreathing the city in a black pall born of burning oil refineries.

The hive's spine, Hel's Highway, was a wounded serpent winding through the city. Its skin was mottled with patches of light and dark: pale and grey where the fighting had ceased, leaving graveyards of silent tanks, and blackened where conflict still raged, pitting the armoured fist of the Steel Legion against the junk-tanks of the invading beasts.

The city walls were half fallen, resembling some archaeological ruin. Half of the hive was surrendered, abandoned to defeat's lifeless silence. The other half, held by Imperial forces that diminished by the hour, burned in battle.

And so dawned the thirty-seventh day.

'HEY, NO SLEEP for you.'

Andrej kicked at Maghernus's shin, jolting the dockmaster back to the waking world. 'We must move soon, I am thinking. No time for sleeping.'

Tomaz blinked the stickiness of exhaustion from his eyes. He'd not even realised he'd fallen asleep. The two of them were crouched behind a stack of crates in a warehouse with the remaining nine men of Maghernus's dock gang. He met their faces now, each in turn, barely recognising any of them. A day of war had aged them all, gifting them with sunken eyes and soot-blackened skin that brought out the lines in their middle-aged faces.

'Where are we going?' Maghernus whispered back. The storm trooper had removed his goggles to wipe his own aching eyes. They'd not slept – they'd barely even stopped fighting – in over twenty hours.

'My captain wishes us to move west. There are civilian shelters above ground there.'

One of the men hawked and spat on the ground. His eyes were red-rimmed and bloodshot. Andrej didn't think any less of him for the fact he'd been weeping.

'West?' the man asked.

'West,' Andrej said again. 'That is my captain's order, and that is what we will do.'

'But the beasts are already there. We saw them.'

'I did not say the order was what I wished to do with my retirement years. I said it was an order, and obeying orders is what we are going to do.'

'But if the aliens are already there...' another worker piped up, snapping Andrej's patience.

'Then we will be behind enemy lines and see many dead civilians we were too late to save. Throne, you think I have good answers for you all? I do not. I have no good answers, not for you, not for anyone else. But my captain has ordered us to go there, and go there we most certainly shall. Yes? Yes.'

It did the trick. A ghost of focus returned to their slack, weary gazes.

'Let's do it, then,' Maghernus said, his knees clicking as he rose up. He was amazed he could still stand. 'Blood of the Emperor, I've never ached like this.'

'Why are you complaining, I wonder,' the storm trooper refastened his goggles with a grin. 'You worked insane shifts on these docks. This is surely no more tiring, I think.'

'Yeah,' one of the others grunted, 'but we were getting paid then.'

With muted laughter, the team moved back out onto the docks.

COLONEL SARREN'S INJURED arm was securely fastened in a makeshift sling. What annoyed him most was the loss of his right arm to gesture with to the hololithic display, but then, that was the price to pay for foolishly leaving the *Grey Warrior* in hostile territory. Shrapnel in the arm was a lucky break, all things considered. The enemy sniper team had killed four of his Baneblade's command crew as they surfaced from the bowels of their tank for much-needed fresh air after countless hours breathing the rank, recycled fumes of the internal filtration scrubbers.

Another sector cleared, only to be wormed through again by bestial scavengers mere hours later.

In the low-ceilinged confines of the tank's principal command chamber, Sarren sat on his well-worn throne, letting the tension ebb from him and trying to forget the column of pain that had been a perfectly normal arm only an hour before. The sawbones, Jerth, had already recommended amputation, citing the risk of infection from dirty shrapnel and the likelihood the limb would never return to – as he put it – 'full functionality'.

Bloody surgeons. Always so keen to graft on some cheap, jury-rigged bionic that would click every time he moved a muscle and seize up because of low-grade components. Sarren was no stranger to augmetics in the Guard, and they were a far cry from the modifications afforded to the rich and decadent.

He stared at the hololithic table now, watching the docks recede from Imperial control with agonising, desperate slowness. Seeing the flickering regiment runes and location sigils, it was hard to translate the skeletal vision to the fierce fighting that was truly taking place.

More and more Steel Legion infantry units were reaching the docks, but it was like holding the sea back with a bucket. The Guardsmen being sent in did little but bolster the general retreat. Reclaiming ground was a distant fiction.

'Sir?' the vox-officer called out. Sarren looked over to him, drawn from his reverie, not realising the man had been trying to get his attention for almost a minute.

'Yes?'

'Word from orbit. The Imperial fleet is reengaging again.'

Sarren made the sign of the aquila – at least, he tried to, and ended with a grunt of pain as his bound arm flared up in pained protest. One-handed, he made a single wing of the Imperial eagle instead.

'Acknowledged. May the Emperor be with them all.'

This scarce acknowledgement made, he lapsed back into watching the deployment of his forces throughout the city. Around him, the tank's crew worked at their stations.

So the Imperial fleet was reengaging.

Again.

Every few days, the same story played out. The joint Adeptus Astartes and Naval fleet would break from the warp close to the planet, and hurl themselves at the ork vessels ringing the embattled world. The engagement would hold for several hours as both sides inflicted horrendous losses on the other, but the Imperials would inevitably be hurled back into a fighting retreat by the immense opposition.

Once they'd fallen back to the safety of a nearby system, they'd regroup over time, under the command of Admiral Parol and High Marshal Helbrecht, and make ready for another assault. It was blunt, and crudely effective. In a void war of such magnitude, there was little place for finesse. Sarren wasn't blind to the tactics at play – lance strikes into the heart of the enemy fleet, bleed them for all that was possible before a retreat back to safety. It was a necessary grind, a war of attrition.

It was also hardly inspiring. The hive cities were on the edge now. Without reinforcements in the coming weeks, many would fall outright. The infrequent transmissions from Tartarus, Infernus and Acheron were all increasingly grim, as were Sarren's reports of Helsreach to them.

If there was no–

'Sir?'

Sarren glanced to his left, to where the vox-officer sat at his station. The man held his headphone receivers to his ear with one hand. He looked pale.

'Emergency signal from the *Serpentine* in orbit. She requests immediate cessation of all anti-air weaponry in the docks district.'

Sarren sat forward in his chair. There was barely any anti-air firepower left in the docks district, but that wasn't the point.

'What did you say?'

'The *Serpentine*, Adeptus Astartes strike cruiser, sir. She requests–'

'Throne, send the order. Send the order! Deactivate all remaining anti-air turrets in the docks district!'

Around him, the tank's crew was silent. Waiting, watching.

Sarren breathed a single word, almost fearful giving voice to it would shatter the possibility it was true.

'Reinforcements…'

ONE SHIP.

The *Serpentine*.

Sea green and charcoal black, it dived like a dragon of myth through the enemy fleet while the rest of the Imperial warships hammered into the orkish invaders, breaking against the ring of alien cruisers surrounding the planet.

One ship broke through, running a gauntlet of enemy fire, its shields crackling into lifelessness and its hull aflame. The *Serpentine* hadn't come to fight. As the Adeptus Astartes vessel tore through the upper atmosphere, drop pods and Thunderhawks rained from its ironclad belly, streaming down to the world below.

Its duty complete, the *Serpentine* powered its way back into the fight. Its captain gritted his teeth against a screed of damage reports signalling the death of his beloved ship, but there was no shame in dying with such a vital duty done. He had acted under the orders of the highest authority – a warrior on the surface below whose deeds were already inscribed in a hundred annals of Imperial glory. That warrior had demanded this risk be taken, and that reinforcements be hurled down to Armageddon no matter the odds facing them.

His name was Tu'Shan, Lord of the Fire-born, and the *Serpentine* did his will.

The *Serpentine*'s end never came. A black shape eclipsed the fat-hulled orkish destroyers cutting the Adeptus Astartes vessel to pieces. Another ship, a far greater ship, pounded the alien attackers into wreckage with overwhelming broadside fire, buying the *Serpentine* the precious moments it needed to escape the gauntlet it had run a second time.

As they broke clear, the *Serpentine*'s captain breathed out a prayer, and signalled across the bridge to the master of communications.

'Send word to the *Eternal Crusader*,' he said. 'Give them the sincerest thanks of our Chapter.'

The response from the *Eternal Crusader* came back almost immediately. The grim voice of High Marshal Helbrecht echoed across the *Serpentine*'s bridge.

'It is the Black Templars that thank you, Salamander.'

THE BEASTS HAVE cracked open another of the above-ground civilian shelters.

Like blood spilling from a wound, humans flood into the streets through the destroyed wall. When the choices are to die cowering, or die fleeing to a safety that may not even exist, any human can be forgiven for giving in to panic. I tell myself this as I watch them dying, and do all I can not to judge them, to hold them to the exalted standards of honour I would demand of my brothers.

They're just human. My disgust is unfair, unwarranted. And yet it remains.

As they die, families and souls of all ages, they squeal like butchered swine.

This war is poisonous. Trapped here, locked away from my Chapter, my mind echoes with bleak prejudices. It is becoming hard to accept that I must die for these people to live.

'Attack,' I tell my brothers, my voice barely carrying over the ranting of the engine. Together, we run from the moving Rhino transport, smashing into the enemy's rearguard.

My crozius rises and falls, as it has risen and fallen ten thousand times in the last month. The adamantium eagle chimes as it cuts through the air. It flares with unleashed energy as its power field connects with flesh and armour. The brazier orb built into the weapon's pommel breathes sacred incense in a grey mist, like coils of smoke weaving between us all – friend and foe.

The weariness ebbs. The grudges fade. Hatred is the greatest purifier, the truest emotion overriding all others. Blood, stinking and inhuman, rains across my armour in discoloured spurts. As it marks the black cross I wear on my chest, my revulsion flares anew.

Crunch. The crozius maul ends another alien's life. *Crunch.* Another. My mentor, the great Mordred the Black, wielded this weapon in battle against mankind's foes for almost four centuries. It sickens me to know it may never be recovered from Helsreach. Nor our armour. Nor our gene-seed. What legacy will we leave once the last of us falls to the filthy blades of these beasts?

One of them roars into my face, spattering my visor with its unclean saliva. Less than a second later, my crozius annihilates its features, silencing whatever pathetic alien challenge I was supposed to be answering.

My secondary heart has joined the primary. I feel them thudding in concert, but not in unison. My human heart pounds like a tribal drum, fast and hot. Twinned to it in my chest, my gene-grown heart supports it in a slow, heavy thud.

They swarm over each other in their mindless fervour to claw at us. Fistfuls of scrap metal that have no right to function as weapons cough solid rounds that clang off our armour. Each shot tears more of the black paint from our war-plate but sheds none of Dorn's holy blood.

At last, they recognise the threat we represent. The aliens abandon their wanton slaughter of the fleeing civilians that still spill from the shell-broken wall. The mob of beasts, flooding the street, has turned to more tempting prey. Us.

Our banner falls.

Artarion's cry of pain carries across the close-range vox as a roar of distortion, but I hear his voice beneath the interference.

Priamus is with him before the rest of us can react. Throne, he can fight. His blade lunges and cuts, every gesture a killing blow.

'Get up,' he snarls at Artarion without even looking.

I crash the faceplate of my helm into the barking maw of the alien before me, shattering its jaw and the rows of shark-like teeth. As it falls back, my crozius crunches into its throat, hammering its wrecked corpse to the ground.

The banner rises again, though Artarion favours his left leg. The right is mauled, his thigh punctured by an alien spear. Curse the fact these beasts have the strength to violate Adeptus Astartes war-plate.

Another vox-distorted growl signifies Artarion has pulled the lance free from his leg. I have no time to witness his recovery. More beasts shriek before me – a thrashing wall of sick, jade flesh.

'We're losing this road,' Bastilan grunts, his signal marred by the sound of weapons crashing against his armour. 'We are but six, against a legion.'

'Five.' Nerovar's voice is strained as he fights with his chainblade two-handed, hewing down the beasts with none of Priamus's artistry but no less fury. 'Cador is dead.'

'Forgive me, brother,' Bastilan's voice breaks off as he fires a stream of bolter shells at point-blank range. 'A moment's lack of focus.'

Ahead, our targets – three junkyard tanks that have long since ceased to resemble their original Imperial Guard hulls – continue shelling the shelter block. These have none of the security offered by the subterranean shelters, for they are not civilian evacuation shelters at all. Each of these squat domes houses a thousand at capacity, designed to resist violent sandstorms and the tropical cyclones all too common on the equatorial coast – not sustained shelling from enemy armour. They are used now because there is nothing else to use, with the city grown far beyond its capacity to shelter all its citizens beneath the ground.

The beasts know us well. They seek to draw the city's forces into the most fevered fighting, so they hurl themselves at our defenceless civilians with sick cunning, knowing we will do all we can to defend these sites above any others.

How easy it is, to despise them.

'Gnnh,' Nerovar voxes, his voice wet and ruined by pain. I vault the falling corpse of the alien closest to me, and stand by his side – maul swinging with relentless motion – as our Apothecary struggles to rise again.

He fails. The beasts have brought him to his knees.

'Gnnnnnh. Not coming out,' he coughs. His hands clutch weakly at the axe hammered into his stomach. His gauntlets stroke without strength along the haft, gaining no grip. Blood from the sunder in his armour is painting his tabard scarlet. 'Can't do it.'

'In the name of the Emperor,' my chastisement comes forth as no more than a low growl, 'stand and fight, or we all die.'

With Nerovar wounded and prone, he becomes a lodestone for the creatures desperate to deliver the death blow to one of the Emperor's knights. They bellow and charge.

My crozius kills one. A kick to the sternum sends another staggering back long enough for me to bring the maul down on its head. A third is claimed by plasma fire, tumbling back as a blur of white-hot flame. Stinging ash, all that remains of the wretched alien, blasts back into the eyes of its bestial comrades.

Too many.

Even for us, this is too many.

I have a momentary glimpse of human families fleeing in all directions down the burning streets, able to escape while the horde focuses its fury on us. Several of the civilians are cut down by sponson fire from the junk-tanks, but many more survive – even if only to run blind into the unsafe labyrinth of their dying city. Before this war, I would never have counted such a thing to be a victory.

With a cry that mixes anger and pain, Nero tears the axe blade from his abdomen. Any relief I feel is swallowed, for he has no time to rise before the beasts are on us.

* * *

'I SEE SOME knights,' Andrej said. This announcement was followed by a whispered 'Damn it,' and the humming of his hellgun powering up again.

The work gang kept their backs to the rooftop's low wall, with only Andrej peering over the edge to look down into the street. 'Everybody, load rifles and be very ready.'

'How many?' Maghernus asked. 'How many knights?'

'Four. No, five. One is injured. I also see thirty of the enemy, and three tanks that were once our Leman Russes. Now, no more talking. Everybody take aim.'

The dockworkers did as ordered, drawing beads on the melee unfolding below.

'Aim low,' Maghernus told his men, drawing a silent smile from Andrej. 'Aim for legs and torsos.' No one needed to be told to be careful with their fire and not hit the Templars.

The storm trooper fired first, his bright lance of laser the signal for the others to join in. Lasguns bucked in increasingly sure hands, focusing lenses burning as they spat their lethal energy into the street below. The tearing laser fire punched into shoulders, legs, backs and arms, and the Imperials had managed three volleys before the beasts ripped their hungry attention from the knights and returned fire up at the men crouching on the warehouse rooftop.

'Down!' Andrej ordered the others. They obeyed, sinking back into cover. The storm trooper hunched lower, but remained where he was. He risked another shot, and another, splitting two aliens through the skull with pinpoint fire.

Around him, around them all, the low wall edging the roof was shredding under the surviving aliens' fire, but it didn't matter. The knights were free. Andrej crouched at last, after seeing the figure of one Templar, the knight's armour more gunmetal grey than black now from battle damage, hurl aside three attackers and lay waste to them with his monstrous, crackling relic hammer.

His last act before falling back was to untrap his last det-pack, and set the timer for six seconds. With a roar of effort, Andrej hurled it down at street towards the tanks. It exploded a half-second after clanging against the lead tank's turret, decapitating the war machine in a burst of noise and fire.

The Templars could deal with the other two.

'Back!' the storm trooper was laughing. 'Back across the roof!'

'What the hell is so funny?' one of the dockworkers, Jassel, was complaining as they ran in crouches away from the disintegrating roof edge.

'They weren't just knights,' Andrej's voice was coloured by a sincere grin. 'That was the Reclusiarch we just saved. Now, quick quick, down to the street again.'

IN THE CALM that followed, the streets gave birth to an atmosphere that was somewhere between serene and funereal. A very different warrior greeted Maghernus this time. The towering figure was far from the regal, impassive statue that merely acknowledged his existence with a nod.

The Reclusiarch's armour still set his teeth on edge, its active hum making his eyes water if he stood too close. But Maghernus knew machines, even if he didn't know ancient artefacts of war, and he could hear the faults in the war-plate now. Its once-smooth, angry purr had a waspish edge to its tone, and intermittent clicks told of something internal no longer running at full function. The joints of the battered armour no longer snarled with tensing fibre-cable muscles – they growled, as if reluctant to move.

Five weeks. Five weeks of fighting, night and day, in the same suit of armour, with the dock assault rising as the most punishing week yet. It was a miracle the armour still functioned at all.

The tabard was ripped and stained grey-green with alien blood. The scrolls that had adorned the warrior's shoulders were gone, with only snapped chains showing they were ever held there at all. The armour itself was still impressive in its violent potential and faceless inhumanity, but where it had been blacker than black before the war, most of the blackness remaining was from scorch marks and laser burns marking the armour like bruises and claw wounds. Much of the war-plate was revealed in a dull, unpolished grey now that the paint was lost to a thousand weapon chops and glancing gunshots.

Somehow, it had the inelegant presence of a rifle or tank churned out of an Armageddon factory: plain, simple, but utterly brutal.

The other Templars looked no better. The one who bore the Reclusiarch's standard now bore battle damage akin to his leader. The banner itself was a ragged ruin, little more than scraps hanging from the pole. The one with the white helm was barely able to stand, supported by two of the others. The voice that rasped from his mouth grille was a wordless, hacking cough.

And rather than humanise them, rather than reveal the warriors beneath the trappings and the knightly war gear, this damage instead stole what little personality had ever been in evidence to human eyes. How could any men, even ones shaped by genetic forges on a distant world, withstand so much punishment and survive? How could they stand before others of their own species and seem so utterly unlike them?

'Hello, Reclusiarch,' said Andrej. He carried his hellgun, uncharged now, resting on his shoulder. He thought this made him look rakish and casual, and he was right. He looked that way to the dockworkers, at least.

Grimaldus's voice didn't growl or boom – it intoned, a low and bleak and grim drawl. It was all too easy to imagine this man back aboard a great, gothic warship, speaking a sermon to his brothers in the endless cold of void travel.

'You have the thanks of the Black Templars, storm trooper. And you, dockworkers of Helsreach.'

'It was good timing, I think,' Andrej continued, a vague nod and the same smile showing he thought nothing of conversations with badly-wounded towering inhuman warriors surrounded by slaughtered aliens. 'But the docks, they are not looking good. I am hearing no orders any more. So I see you, noble sirs, and I am wondering: perhaps they can give me orders.'

There was a pause, but not a silent one. The city was never silent, offering up a background chorus of gunfire rattles and the *crump* of distant explosions.

'All units are called to the shelter blocks. Guard, militia, Adeptus Astartes. All.'

'Even without my captain's voice, we have followed that path. But there is more, sir.'

'Speak.' Grimaldus looked away now, the silver skull that served as his face glaring in the direction of a burning commerce district several streets away.

'One of your knights fell at the docks. We have hidden his body from the enemy jackals. The etchings on his armour named him as Anastus.'

The white-helmed Adeptus Astartes spoke, his voice emerging like a man speaking through a mouthful of gruel.

'Anastus died... as we deployed... last night. Life signs faded fast. Warrior's death.'

Grimaldus nodded, his attention restored to the humans.

'What is your name?' the Reclusiarch asked the storm trooper.

'Trooper Andrej, 703rd Steel Legion Storm trooper Division, sir.'

'And yours?' he asked the next man in line, taking every name until the last, whom he recognised without needing to ask. 'Dockmaster Tomaz Maghernus,' the knight grunted, finally. 'It is good to see you on the field. Courage such as yours belongs at the vanguard.'

Maghernus's skin crawled, not with distaste but raw awkwardness. How does one reply to such a thing? To say he was honoured? To admit that every muscle in his body ached and he regretted ever volunteering for this madness?

'Thank you, Reclusiarch,' he managed.

'I will remember your names and deeds this day. All of you. Helsreach may burn, but this war is not lost. Every one of your names will be etched into the black stone pillars of the Valiant Hall aboard the *Eternal Crusader*.'

Andrej nodded. 'I am very honoured, Reclusiarch, as are these handsome and fine gentlemen with me. But if you could tell my captain about this, I would be even happier.'

The harsh sound emitted from the Reclusiarch's voxspeakers was somewhere between a bark and a snarl. It took Maghernus several moments to realise it had been a laugh.

'It will be done, Trooper Andrej. You have my word.'

'I am hopeful this will also impress the lady I intend to marry.'

Grimaldus wasn't sure how to reply to that. He settled for, 'Yes. Good.'

'Such optimism! But yes, I must find her first. Where do we move now, sir?'

'West. The shelters in Sulfa Commercia. The alien dogs are taunting us.' The Reclusiarch gestured with his massive hammer, the weapon's power field deactivated for now. Between warehouses and manufactories, distant domes were aflame.

'See them. Already, they burn.'

Priamus didn't look where the others did. His attention was lifted higher, to the smog-thick skies.

'What's that?' He gestured skywards, to a ball of flame trailing down. 'It can't be what it looks like.'

'It is,' Grimaldus replied, unable to look away from the sight.

'Ayah!' Andrej cheered as several similar objects appeared, blazing earthwards, leading fiery contrails like comets.

'What are they?' asked Maghernus, caught off-guard by the storm trooper's capering and the knights' reverence.

'Drop pods,' said the Reclusiarch. His silver skull turned amber with the reflection of the burning tank hulls nearby. 'Adeptus Astartes drop pods.'

CHAPTER XVII
INTO THE FIRES OF BATTLE, UNTO
THE ANVIL OF WAR

THE SULFA COMMERCIA district had been a bastion of militia reserves and a strongpoint for the docks' anti-air defences.

The few turrets that remained atop buildings, both automated and manned, fell silent. Around them, the district burned. Above them, ork fighters and bombers dropped their payloads with abandon, barely held in check even when the defence turrets were operational.

Sulfa Commercia, as a trading hub for the western docks that was always densely populated in times of peace, was home to a particularly large concentration of above-ground storm shelters, most of which were already broken by the besieging orks. The enemy advance was at a standstill in this section of the dockyards, not because of Imperial resistance, but because there was so much blood to shed, and so much to destroy. To leave the area devoid of life and in utter ruin meant the aliens had to linger here, slaying with wild joy in their feral eyes.

When writing of the siege in a personal journal some years after the war, Major Lacus of the 61st Steel Legion lamented the 'unbelievable loss of life' that occurred with the dock breaches, citing the destruction of the Sulfa Commercia as 'among the bloodiest events in the Helsreach siege, which no man, no tank battalion, no legion of Titans could have dreamed of preventing'.

The trading concourse resembled little of its former grandeur. While warehouses were less in evidence here, the houses of the wealthy mercantile families of Helsreach burned just as well, and those citizens that had elected to remain in their homes rather than seek out the subterranean municipal shelters now fell to the same fate as the civilians trapped in the cracked-open storm shelters. The aliens descended without mercy, and no contingent of house guards, no matter how well trained they were, were capable of defending their lords' estates against the xenos tide that swarmed the docks districts.

The most notable defence – one that captured the spirit of defiance surging throughout the hive's stunted propaganda machine – was not, as might be suspected, the one that inflicted greatest harm upon the enemy. The estate defence that did the most damage numerically-speaking was performed by the House Farwellian Constabulary, employed for seven generations by the noble Farwell bloodline. Their extended survival wasn't quite the soul-lifting story that Commissar Falkov and Colonel Sarren were seeking, as the esteemed House Farwell were, in truth, considered decadent pigs in the public eye, and its various scions were no strangers to political scandal, financial investigation, and rumours of trade double-dealing. In short, they performed so well in this district war because they had shrewdly

CELESTIAL LION

Grimaldus's Wargear

Grimaldus's helm is a treasured relic, worn by every High Chaplain in the Chapter's history. When High Chaplain Mordred died fighting the Archenemy, four Sword Brethren sacrificed themselves to allow the helm to be recovered. High Marshal Helbrecht later presented it to Grimaldus upon his ascension to the leadership of the Reclusiam.

This holy weapon was forged for Grimaldus upon his entry into the Reclusiam. It bears symbols of the ideals for which the High Chaplain fights: the aquila, representing mankind's Imperium; the cross, for the Black Templars Chapter; and a skull, for the sacrifice that all sons of Rogal Dorn will ultimately make.

During the Battle of Alfava Metraxis, an Imperial Fists sergeant threw himself on a blade meant for Grimaldus when the dusty atmosphere caused the Chaplain's bolter to jam. Snatching up the sergeant's plasma pistol, Grimaldus killed the chieftain of the world's indigenous two-headed aliens, ending five months of war with a single shot. He kept the pistol in tribute to the bravery of his fellow son of Dorn.

Black Templars Artefacts

Each of the twelve adamantium studs driven into this storm shield represents a valorous deed by its bearer, Brother Kaephon. The most recent stud was awarded during the Bessan uprising, when Kaephon and his squad stood alone against a horde of cultists many thousands strong. Fighting his way through the horde, Kaephon struck the head from their demagogue, ending a ritual that would have drowned nine worlds in Chaos.

This blade, which belongs to Sword Brother Borusa, is both a ceremonial and practical artefact. Before battle, Borusa leads his Crusader squad in prayers, and slices each brother's palm with the sword as they make their oaths of moment, an ancient tradition dating back to the Great Crusade. Once the blade is unsheathed, the Sword Brother is honour-bound not to return it to its scabbard until it has tasted the blood of the enemy.

A Godwyn-pattern boltgun recovered from the fields of Trenzalor. The crusader seal affixed to the casing was added to commemorate three Black Templars Initiates who carried this weapon, each of whom died in the first battle in which they fired it. The Techmarines declared the boltgun's machine-spirit to be malign, and it has since been placed in the deepest stasis-vaults of the Reclusiam in the Chapter Keep on Iphitus.

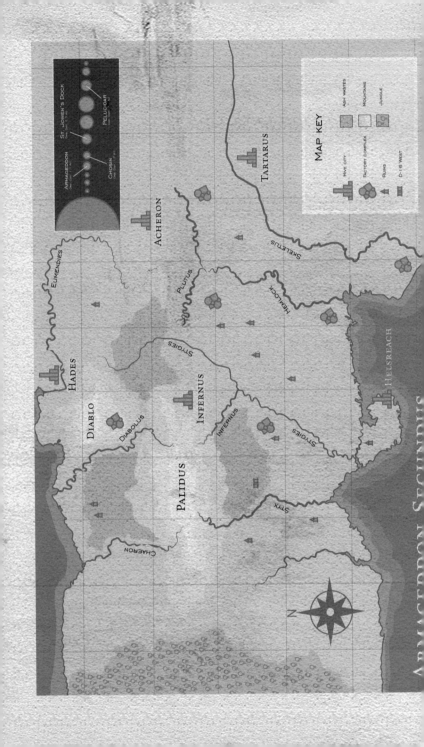

ARMAGEDDON SECUNDUS

cheated their way to immense wealth, and had a standing army of six hundred soldiers at their beck and call.

A standing army that, it was noted in Imperial records, the Farwells refused to lend to the defence of the docks or the city's militia.

This sizeable force was also their bane. As words flashed through the orkish ranks that there was a nexus of defence formed at the House Farwell compound, the aliens stormed it en masse, ending the tenacious resistance – and the bloodline itself.

The most notable defence, as stated, was a far cry from this exercise in doomed selfishness. House Tarracine, with only five off-world mercenaries hired as protection, defended their modest estate through a series of guerrilla strikes and automated security traps for nineteen hours. Although their home was destroyed by the invaders, seven family members emerged unscathed in the days after the dock battle, leaving them in a relatively strong position for the rebuilding of the city, with Lord Helius Tarracine's four daughters suddenly pursued with great vigour by weakened and heirless noble bloodlines.

At shelter CC/46, one of the few shelters still intact as the second day of the dock war stretched on, annihilation was averted at the very last moment.

The first drop pod came down with a thunderbolt's force, striking into the roadway leading to the front doors of the sanctuary dome. The ork rabble that had been clamouring in the street was thrown into disarray, and several of the beasts were incinerated in the pod's retro burst or crushed beneath its hammering weight.

The pod's sides blasted open, slamming down into descent ramps which pulverised the beasts that had recovered enough to start beating their axe blades against the green hull.

Across the docks, several more pods rained down, their arrival mirroring the destruction unleashed by the first.

With bolters raised, crashing out round after round, and flamers breathing dragon's breath in hissing gouts of chemical fire, the Salamanders joined their Templars brothers in defence of Hive Helsreach.

'WE ARE SEVENTY in number,' he says to me. Seven squads.

His name is V'reth, a sergeant of the Salamanders' Sixth Company. Before I speak, he says something both humbling and unexpectedly respectful. 'I am honoured to fight at your side, Reclusiarch Grimaldus.'

This confession throws me, and I am not certain I keep my surprise from my voice when I reply.

'The Templars are in your debt. But tell me, brother, why you have come?'

Around us, my knights and V'reth's warriors stalk among the dead and the dying, slaying wounded orks with sword thrusts to exposed throats. The storm trooper and his dockworkers follow suit, using the bayonets of their rifles.

V'reth disengages his helm's seals and lifts it clear. Even having served with the Salamanders before, it is difficult to look upon one of the sons of Nocturne and feel nothing at all. The gene-seed of their primarch reacts to their home world's viciously radioactive surface. The pigmentation of V'reth's skin is the same charcoal-black as every unhelmeted warrior of the Chapter I've ever seen. His eyes lack pupils and irises. Instead, V'reth stares out at the world around us through orbs of ember red, as if blood has filled his eye sockets and discoloured his eyes in the process.

His true voice is a low, aural embodiment of the igneous rock that leaves the surface of his home world dark, barren and grey. It is all too easy to see how these warriors come from a world of lava rivers and volcanic mountain ranges that turn the sky black.

'We were the last of the Salamanders in orbit. The Lord of the Fire-born called us to him, and we obeyed.'

I am familiar with the title. I have heard their Chapter Master referred to by this name many times before.

'Master Tu'Shan, may the Emperor continue to favour him, fights far from here, brother. The Salamanders bleed the enemy many leagues to the east, and the Hemlock river runs black with alien blood.'

V'reth inclines his head in a solemn nod, and his red-eyed gaze rises to take in the shelter dome at the end of this very street.

'This is so, and it gladdens me to know my brothers fight well enough to earn such words from you, Reclusiarch. The Lord of the Fire-born makes his stand with the war engines of Legios Ignatum and Invigilata.'

'So answer my question, for time is not our ally. Helsreach burns. Will you stay? Will you fight with us?'

'We will not stay. We cannot stay.'

I bite back the wrath that rises from disappointment, and the Salamander continues, 'We are the seventy warriors chosen to make planetfall here and stand with you until the docks are held. My lord and master heard of the assured civilian devastation in the fall of this city's coastal districts.'

'Few messages reach the ears of our allies elsewhere in the world. Few messages from them reach us.'

'The Salamanders were not blind to your plight, honoured Reclusiarch. Master Tu'Shan heard. We are his blade, his will, to ensure the survival of the city's most innocent souls.'

'And then you will leave.'

'And then we will leave. Our fight is along the banks of the Hemlock. Our glory is there.'

This gesture alone is enough to earn my eternal gratitude. For the first time in decades, emotion steals the words I wish to voice. This is all we needed. This is salvation.

We can hurt them now.

I remove my own helm, breathing in the first taste of Helsreach's sulphuric air in... weeks. Months.

V'reth inhales deeply, doing the same.

'This city,' he smiles, teeth white against his onyx features, 'it smells like home.'

The heated wind feels good on my skin. I offer my hand to V'reth, and he grips my wrist – an alliance between warriors.

'Thank you,' I tell him, meeting his inhuman eyes.

'If you are needed elsewhere,' V'reth matches my gaze with his own, 'then go to your duty, honoured Reclusiarch. We stand with you, for now. And together, we will not let these docks fall.'

'First, tell me of the orbital war. What news of the *Crusader*?'

'The deadlock remains. It grieves me to say this, but it is so. We are shattering the enemy, battle by battle, but it is like hurling fire at stone. Little is achieved against such an overwhelming foe. It will take weeks before your High Marshal dares a full assault to reclaim the heavens. He is a shrewd warrior. My brothers and I were honoured to serve with him in the fleet.'

To hear his words is like a lifeline. A connection to

existence beyond the broken walls of this accursed city. I press him for more.

'What of Tempestus Hive? They suffered as we did.'

'Fallen. Lost to the enemy, its forces in retreat. The last word from any remnant of command structure was that the city was being abandoned, and its retreating survivors were making their way overland to connect with the Guard regiments serving alongside my lord and master.'

Scattered defence forces and Guard units, crossing hundreds of kilometres of wasteland. Such tenacity was to be admired.

This world will never recover, that much is clear. Fatalism may not be bred into my bones, but there is no valour in living a lie. What we do here is defiance – the selling of life as dearly as possible. We are not fighting to win, but waging war out of spite.

This Salamander, brother though he may be, has a destiny beyond this city. I relent to it.

'Coordinate the dispersal of squads with Sergeant Bastilan. Focus your efforts on the westernmost districts, where the bulk of storm shelters are to be found. Bastilan will provide you with the required vox frequencies to connect with the storm troopers leading the civilian defences. Do not expect clarity in communications. Many of the city's vox-relay towers have fallen.'

'It will be done, Reclusiarch.'

'For the Emperor.' I release V'reth's wrist. His reply is a curious one, betraying his Chapter's unique focus.

'For the Emperor,' he says, 'and His people.'

Jurisian, Master of the Forge and knight of the Emperor, threw his head back and laughed. He had not laughed in many years, for he was not a soul given to humour. What he was seeing now however struck him as immensely funny. So he laughed, without meaning to.

The sound echoed throughout the immense chamber, resounding off metal-reinforced walls of stone and the hulking adamantium shape that stretched for fifty metres into the darkness.

The Ordinatus Armageddon. *Oberon.*

Jurisian's armour had been the only sound in the chamber for hours, the overlaid ceramite plating clacking and whirring as he moved around the great weapon. He'd circled it several dozen times, staring, scanning, taking in every detail with his own eyes and his war-plate's auspex sensors.

It was, without question, the most beautiful creation he had ever laid his augmetic eyes upon.

In aesthetics, perhaps it would not appeal to a poet or a painter. But that was hardly the point. In power, it would appeal to any general in the Imperium. It was a triumph of design and intent, a glorious success in mankind's quest to master a greater ability to destroy its enemies.

The great construct consisted of a strong, three-sectioned base that held up a weapons platform on gantries and struts. Atop the platform was the weapon itself. Jurisian considered each aspect of the war machine in turn, silent in its deactivation.

From the front, *Oberon* was as wide as two bulky Land Raider battle tanks side by side. Its length was fifty metres in total, giving it the appearance of a land train, long and segmented. Immense to say the least, it was of approximate size to a towering battle Titan lying on its back.

The war machine's base was divided into three sections – a helm segment, the drive module, with a reinforced cockpit chamber; a thorax section next, pinned under the weight of massive metal stanchions; lastly, an abdomen segment, bearing the same weight as the section before. Each of these base sections was bulked up further by side-mounted power generators, shielded behind yet more armour plating. These, Jurisian knew, were the gravitational suspensor generators. Anti-gravitational technology on such a scale was no longer heard of in the Imperium, except for the deployment of war machines of this calibre.

These generators' rarity made them the most precious thing on the entire planet, bar nothing.

The stanchions and gantries supported the colossal weapons platform, which in turn housed dozens of square metres of energy pods, fusion chambers and magnetic field generators. It was as if an industrial manufactorum had been installed on the back of a column of tanks.

These generators would, if active, supply power to the land train's weapon mount: a tower of a cannon forged of heat-shielded ceramite and joined to the forward power generators. Coolant vents ran the length of the cannon like reptilian scales. Like parasitic worms, nests of secondary power feed cables hung from the barrel, while industrial support claws held the weapon in place.

A nova cannon. A weapon used by starships to end one another across the immensity of the void. Here it was, mounted on priceless and infinitely-armoured anti-gravitational technology from a forgotten age.

'Titan-killer,' the Master of the Forge whispered.

Jurisian reverently stroked his gloved fingertips down the drive section's metallic skin, feeling the thick armour plating, the chunky rivets... down to the miniscule differences in the layers of adamantium: the tiniest variations and imperfections from its forging process hundreds of years before.

He'd withdrawn his hand, and that was when he'd laughed.

Oberon, the Death of Titans. It was real. It was here.

And it was his.

He gained access to the forward command module through a ladder leading to a bulkhead that required opening manually. Once inside the powerless cockpit chamber, Jurisian spared a glance for the winches, levers and black, blank screens along the drive console. It was all new, all alien to him, but nothing he considered beyond his intuition and Mechanicus training. Another bulkhead barred his way to the second module. With the Ordinatus powered down, this one also required him to manually turn the iron wheel on its surface.

The door squealed open with the reluctance of an unused airlock. Jurisian's gaze pierced the blackness beyond with aid from his helm's vision filters. It was confined and claustrophobic, despite there being little in the module beyond armoured pods fixed to the walls that housed the power generators for the anti-grav lifters, and crew ladders leading up into the main generatorium on the platform above. Jurisian ascended, opening another two bulkheads as he rose through the support gantries.

The innards of the platform-top generatorium were familiar enough in their cluttered, industrial layout. He stood within the heart of a spaceship's weapon system, condensed to offer less range and power, but on a more manoeuvrable and manageable scale. The projectiles from this sacred cannon didn't, after all, have to travel across thousands of kilometres of open space to strike a target.

It was, bluntly speaking, the sawn-off shotgun of nova cannon technology. The notion brought a smile to Jurisian's mirthless lips.

It took a further three hours of investigation, feed-checks and generator testing to ascertain whether the Ordinatus Armageddon could be reactivated, and how such a feat could be achieved.

The result at the close of the investigations was a bittersweet one.

This weapon of war should have been crewed by dozens of specialist skitarii, magi and tech-adepts, born and raised for this purpose above all others. It should have been ritually blessed by the Lord of the Centurio Ordinatus and its newest duty inscribed upon its hull alongside the ninety-three prayers of reawakening.

Instead of the chanting and worship due to the spirit of such a war engine, the soul of *Oberon* awoke in silence and darkness. Its vague, reforming consciousness did not detect a gestalt host of abased Centurio Ordinatus minds supplicating themselves for its attention, but a single other soul in union with its own.

This soul was strong: ironclad and dominant.

It identified itself as Jurisian.

In the drive module, his brain, spine and body armour linked via telemetry cables to the interface feeds in the princeps throne, the Master of the Forge closed his eyes. Around him, the systems flared into life. Scanners chimed as they began to see again. Overhead lights flickered and held at low illumination settings.

With a great shudder and the accompanying thrumming of power generators coming back to life, all three modules shook once, twice, and jolted hard.

In the drive section, Jurisian lurched in his seat. He hadn't jolted forward, but *up*.

Five metres up.

There the modules remained, cradled on a pulsing anti-grav field that distorted the ground below with something that was, and was not, a heat-shimmer.

'**Activation Phase One,**' the war machine's voice issued from vox-speakers around the command module.

Beneath the mechanical tone seethed a roiling, uncoiling hatred. Jurisian bowed his head in respect, but did not cease his work.

'My brothers call me to Helsreach,' he spoke into the cold control pod, expecting no answer and receiving none. 'And though that may mean nothing, I know that war calls to you.'

Through the interface connection, the spirit of *Oberon* growled, the sound inhuman and untranslatable.

Jurisian nodded. 'I thought so.'

ASAVAN TORTELLIUS LINGERED over a single phrase.

He had no idea how to describe just how cold he was.

Around him, the deserted cathedral still bore more than its share of wall scars and battle damage. On a fallen block of masonry, the acolyte composed his memoirs of the Helsreach war, while the great Titan pitched slowly forward and back in the rough rhythm of walking. Occasionally, air pressure and gravity would exert themselves on his left or right side, as *Stormherald* rounded a corner. As he had done for years, Asavan ignored these things.

The ruined cathedral around him was altogether harder to ignore. It still appeared much as it had over thirty days ago, when the alien brutes had brought the god-machine to its knees. The statues still lay as alabaster corpses in broken, facedown repose, limbs cracked off to lie several metres distant. The walls were still decorated by gunfire holes and ugly cracks that cobwebbed outwards from impact points. The stained glass windows – his only succour from the irritation of the Shield above – were still gaping holes in the war-blackened architecture, as unpleasant to look upon as missing teeth in the smile of a saint.

Day in, day out, Asavan sat in the lonely, contemplative quiet of the cathedral, and composed what he knew full well were poorly-worded poems commemorating the coming victory in Hive Helsreach. He would destroy well over half of what he wrote, sometimes wincing as he reread the words he'd brought into being.

But of course, there was no one else to witness them. Not here.

The cathedral had stood almost empty since it had been besieged. The Templars had come, 'in purity, protecting us, and in wrath, indefatigable,' Asavan had written (before deleting the cringe-worthy words forever), but they had come too late to do much more than preserve the wounded, hollow bones of Stormherald's monastery. Weeks had passed since. Weeks during which nothing had changed, nothing had been repaired.

Asavan was one of the few people still living in the cathedral. His fellows consisted mainly of servitors hardwired into the battlement turrets, slaved to the targeting and reloading systems along the walls. He saw these wretches often, because it had become his duty to keep them alive. The lobotomised, augmented once-humans were little more than limbless and slack-jawed automatons installed in life support cradles next to their turret cannons, and had no means to sustain their own existences. Several had lost their feed/waste bio connection cables with the damage taken in the siege, and even all these weeks later, the remaining magi in *Stormherald*'s main body had not reached repairs so minor on the long list of abuses in need of correcting. Key systems took priority, and few enough Mechanicus adepts remained alive as it was. The fighting had been fierce below, as well.

So it fell to Asavan, as one of the few cathedral survivors, to spoonfeed these mindless creatures with soft protein-rich paste in order to keep them from dying, and flush their waste filters once a week.

He did this not because he was ordered to, or because he particularly cared about the continuing functionality of the handful of battlement cannons that were still unscathed. He did it because he was bored, and because he was lonely. It was the second week when he started talking to the unresponsive servitors. By the fourth, they all had names and backstories.

At first, Asavan had sought to order one of the seven medial servitors still patrolling the cathedral to perform these actions, but their programming was cripplingly limited. One was mono-tasked with walking from room to room, broom in hand, sweeping up any dust from the boots of the faithful.

Well, there were no faithful any more. And the servitor had no broom. Asavan had known the servitor before his augmentation, as a particularly dull-witted acolyte that earned his fate for stealing coins from his lay-brothers. His punishment was to be rendered into a bionic slave, and Asavan had shed no tears at the time. Still, it was no joy to see the simple creature stagger from chamber to chamber, clacking the broken end of a brushless broomstick against the rubble-strewn ground, never getting closer to cleaning up the mess, and unable to rest until its duty was done. It refused orders to cease work, and Asavan suspected what was left of its mind had been broken at some point during the battle. An unnoticed head wound, perhaps.

Six weeks in, the servitor had collapsed in the middle of a row of broken pews, its human parts no longer able to function without rest. Asavan had done with it as he'd done with all of the slain. He and the handful of survivors threw the body overboard. A morbid curiosity (and one that he always regretted afterwards) compelled him to watch as the bodies fell fifty metres to rupture on the ground below. Asavan took no thrill or amusement from such sights, but found he could never look away. In work he quickly erased, he confessed to himself that seeing the bodies fall was a means of reminding himself he was still alive. Whatever the truth of the situation, the sights gave him nightmares. He wondered how soldiers could get used to such things, and why they would ever want to.

His main concern this past week was the cold.

With the Titan committed to battle for this prolonged engagement, the damage it had sustained in the ambush weeks ago was forever being repaired, compensated for, and re-aggravated by new war wounds sustained in the conflict. The command crew (*'blessings be upon them as they lead us to triumph,'* Asavan still whispered) were drawing ever-increasing maintenance attention and power from secondary systems throughout the Titan.

Minor systems went unrepaired by the adept tech-teams that were already spread thin throughout the gigantic construct and dealing with the vital systems. Some systems even went powerless as energy feeds were drained and disconnected, their thrumming fuel flooded to the plasma cells used to power the Shield and the main weapons.

A week ago, the heating systems to the cathedral had been drained to the point of no longer functioning. With typical Mechanicus efficiency, there were secondary and tertiary fallback options in the case of such a development. Unfortunately for Asavan and the few acolytes left alive up there, both the secondary and tertiary contingencies were lost. The secondary fallback had been a smaller, self-sustaining generator that fed itself from a power source reserve that was linked to nothing else, and could therefore never be drained for other purposes. The generator was now no more than scrap metal in the ruined mess that had once been the cathedral's maintenance deck.

The generator's destruction also annihilated the tertiary contingency plan, which was for four mono-tasked servitors – good for nothing else – to be activated and set to turn the generator's manual pumps by hand. Even if the generator had been fully functional, all four of the servitors were killed in the battle five weeks ago.

Asavan had gamely tried to turn the first of the hand-cranks himself, but lacking a servitor's strength meant all he achieved was a sore back. The crank never moved a centimetre.

So now, here he sat on a fallen pillar, trying to compose something to describe how bone-achingly cold he was, and how bone-achingly cold he had been for the last six days.

In place of organs, *Stormherald* possessed a generator core of intensely radioactive and fusion-hot plasma. Asavan found it a curious paradox that the heart of a sun was hermetically sealed and insulated many decks below him, yet here he was, on the edge of freezing to death.

These were the kinds of observations that he would write down, and then destroy in shame at daring to complain while so many innocent Imperial souls were out there in the burning city, dying moment by moment.

It was in that moment Asavan Tortellius decided he would change fate himself. He would not freeze to death on the Titan's back, in this hollow monastery. Nor would he gripe about the cold while thousands of deserving and loyal people died in their droves.

His fellow acolytes had never been kind to him regarding his intelligence, but people could say what they wished about his wits, slow or otherwise – Asavan liked to believe he always arrived at the right answer eventually. And now he had.

Yes. It was time to make a difference to the people of Helsreach.

It was time to leave the Titan.

CHAPTER XVIII

CONSOLIDATION

THREE MORE NIGHTS passed as every day had passed before them. The docks were lost at dawn on the sixth day after the submersible assault.

The defeat was unusual enough to bring the Imperial commanders together again. Around the battle-damaged hull of the *Grey Warrior*, Sarren gathered the leaders. In the dawn gloom, most of the Guard colonels were dead on their feet with fatigue, several showing telltale signs of combat narcotics to keep them going – a twitch here, a shiver there. Overtaxed minds and muscles could only be kept active for so long, even with stimulants.

Sarren wouldn't reprimand them for this. In times of need, men did as they must in order to hold the line.

'We've lost the docks,' he said, and his voice was as tired and scratchy as he felt. This was not news to any of the gathered officers. As the colonel outlined the details of what little remained of the dock districts, a Chimera rumbled up to park in the *Grey Warrior*'s shadow. The crew ramp slammed down, and two people disembarked. The first was Cyria Tyro, her uniform still clean but clearly ruffled from constant wear. The second was dressed in a pilot's grey flightsuit.

'I've found him,' Tyro said, leading the pilot to the gathered commanders.

'Captain Helius reporting,' the pilot saluted Sarren. 'Commander Jenzen died two nights ago, sir.'

Third in line, after Jenzen and Barasath? They were lucky to have any flyers left.

'A pleasure, captain.'

'As you say, sir.'

Sarren nodded, returning the aquila salute with his wounded arm still aching like a jungle wildfire. A morning breeze, chilling and unwelcome, gusted across the stretch of the Hel's Highway. The Baneblade's hull blocked most of the wind, but not enough as far as Sarren was concerned. Throne, he was tired of aching all over.

'Remaining forces?'

'Three airstrips, though it looks like the Gamma Road will fall today; it's been besieged for days now. At last count, we had twenty-six Lightnings remaining. Only seven Thunderbolts. Gamma Road is already being evacuated and the fighters are landing on the Vancia Chi Avenue.'

Sarren made a grumbling noise. He still lamented the loss of Barasath and the majority of his air power, even after all this time.

'Intentions?'

'Currently, no change from Jenzen's orders. Provide air support for embattled Titan forces and armour battalions. The enemy are still showing next to no offensive capacity in the air. It's reasonable to suggest that, this far in, they've simply got nothing left.'

'Was that a barb, captain?'

Helius saluted again. 'By no means, sir.'

Sarren smiled, the indulgent grin ruined by weariness. 'If it was, it's forgiven. Barasath was right, and he sold his life at great cost to give us an edge in the air. The beasts have thrown up nothing but a handful of scrap-fighters since the siege began, and I've already noted on the campaign record – as well as Barsath's personal file – that he made the right call.'

'Yes, sir.'

'I'm sorry to hear about Jenzen. She was an asset we'll greatly miss: solid, reliable, steady.'

And she had been. Commander Carylin Jenzen, for better or worse, had been a by-the-book flyer, dependable and constant, if rather uninspired. Under her, the city's air forces had maintained a campaign of reliable defensive support for over a month. The Crone of Invigilata herself had commended Jenzen's endeavours in recent weeks.

'Sir...' Helius began.

Here it comes... Sarren thought.

'I had hoped to discuss the possibility of a more aggressive tactical pattern.'

Yes. Yes, of course you had hoped to discuss that.

'In good time. For now, the docks.'

Sarren nodded back to the gathered officers. Cyria Tyro and Captain Helius joined them, standing next to one another. Major Ryken scowled at the pilot, and Sarren resisted the urge to roll his eyes. *Bloody Throne, Ryken. Now is hardly the time for schoolyard jealousy.*

'We did not lose the docks,' one of the Adeptus Astartes

argued, his vox-voice laden with resonant calm. Colonel Sarren had not met Sergeant V'reth of the Salamanders before this morning. He knew from vox-traffic that the green-armoured warriors had deployed close to the remaining civilian shelters and their valour was directly responsible for a great many lives spared.

But it seemed his tactical outlook varied wildly from the colonel's.

'I'm not sure I understand, sir,' Sarren offered.

V'reth's armour was dented and scratched, but remained pristine in comparison to the wreckage worn by the Reclusiarch at his side. A golden-eyed helm glared down at the human officers.

'I am merely stating, Colonel Sarren, that we did not lose the docks. The enemy is beaten. The seaborne invasion was denied, for the city still stands. The invaders lie dead at the docks.'

This was and wasn't true, from the way Sarren looked at it. The disparity was the reason the colonel had called this gathering.

'Allow me to amend my appraisal. The docks are gone. As an industrial factor in Armageddon's collective output, Helsreach no longer exists. We're receiving reports now of ninety-one per cent harm to the city's refinery infrastructure, taking into account the loss of the offshore oil platforms.'

The soldiers shared uncomfortable glances. The Imperium demanded heavy tithes of materiel from Armageddon. If the other hive cities suffered as Helsreach had, the grade of Exactis Extremis would be lowered significantly. Certainly to Solutio Tertius, and perhaps to Aptus Non. If Armageddon provided nothing, it would be offered little in return. The Imperium would turn away. Without the support and finances to recover after the war, the world might never recover.

'However, all is not dark. As the noble Sergeant V'reth makes clear, thanks to the tenacity of the dockworker population, our own storm troopers, and our Adeptus Astartes allies, the xenos were repelled.'

At insane cost, he decided not to add. *Tens of thousands dead in four days. The city's industry reduced to a worthless husk.*

'We have received further word from the Crone of Invigilata,' the colonel continued. What he had to say next almost caught in his throat. 'The most honourable Legio Invigilata has been petitioned by outside forces to leave the city.'

'She will stay.' The Reclusiarch's tone was cold even through his helm's vox-speakers. 'She swore to fight.'

'As I understand it, the Imperial advances along the length of the Hemlock River are grinding to a halt. The settlements there, protected by the Salamanders and regiments of the Cadian Shock, are now considered a higher priority than the city.' Sarren let the words resonate for a few moments. 'This is from the Old Man himself. It came over the vox an hour ago.'

Grimaldus snarled as he spoke, 'I do not care. Our mandate is to defend Helsreach.'

'*Our* mandate, yes. But Princeps Zarha's mandate was to deploy where she desired. Most of the Legio Invigilata is already stationed along the Hemlock and across the wastelands, alongside elements from Ignatum and Metalica.'

'She will not leave,' Grimaldus snorted. 'She is here until the end.'

Sarren felt his ire rising at the way the Reclusiarch dismissed his concerns with such blasé finality. On another day, another morning, after any other week of fighting, he would have reined in his emotions better. As it was, he sighed and closed his gritty eyes.

'Enough, *please*, Reclusiarch. *Stormherald* is embattled seven kilometres down the Hel's Highway, with an enemy scrap-Titan battalion in the Rostorik Ironworks. She has given no further word of her decision.'

Grimaldus crossed his arms over his ruined heraldry. 'Tartarus Hive and the battles along the shores of the Hemlock will be won and lost without us. This war has taken everything from the city, and we are reduced to fighting like desert jackals over Helsreach's bones. The only question that matters to us is: What can we still save?'

Ryken removed his rebreather and took a deep breath. 'It may be time to consider the last fallback point.'

Sarren nodded. 'That's why we're here. We stand in the heart of a dying city, and the time has come to decide where we will make our final stand. What of the... weapon, Reclusiarch?'

'A fool's hope. The Master of the Forge is a single soul. Without Mechanicus support, Jurisian has been able to do nothing more than activate *Oberon*'s core systems. He can certainly not crew it alone. As of four nights ago, the Ordinatus has locomotion, and on his own the Forgemaster is able to fire the Oberon Cannon once every twenty-two minutes. But that is all. It cannot be defended by a lone pilot. It is worthless in battle.'

The colonel's ire rose again. 'You waited four days to tell me of this? That the Ordinatus has power once more?'

'I have not waited. I filed coded confirmation across the command network the same night I learned *Oberon* was operational. Yet as I said, it is almost worthless to us.'

'Is your Forgemaster bringing the weapon to the city?'

'Of course.'

'Has the Mechanicus been informed we are defiling their weapon and dragging it into a warzone, almost certain to lose it in its first engagement against the enemy?'

'Of course not. Are you insane, human? The best weapons are those that remain secret until wielded. This truth would force Invigilata to act against us, or to leave the city.'

'You are not the commander of this city. You surrendered that honour to me. This is information I have been eagerly awaiting, only to find it denied to me because of broken vox-traffic?'

The silver skull breathed out a mechanical growl.

'I was knee-deep in alien dead at the docks, Sarren, selling the lives of my brothers to ensure the people of your home world lived to see another sunrise. You are tired. I understand the limitations of the human form, and you have my sympathies for them. But remember to whom you are speaking.'

Sarren bit back his disappointment. It wasn't supposed to be like this, yet with the Adeptus Astartes, it always was. Compliant and valuable one moment, superior and distant the next, shaped as much by their fierce independence as they were by their loyalty to the Imperium.

It felt... petty. That was the only word that encapsulated it in the colonel's mind. An awkward divide between humans fighting for their home, and once-humans fighting for intangible ideals and heroic codes of conduct.

'Well...' Sarren began, but knew he had nowhere to go with the words.

'I am not to blame for your malfunctioning vox. It is a plague upon the city's defence, and a burden we must bear. I was not about to abandon the docks to deliver the news into your ears like some enslaved courier, nor would I entrust such a development to any other soul. If the Mechanicus learns of this, we lose Invigilata.'

'None of us had much hope pinned on the Ordinatus,' Ryken said, seeking to defuse the tension. 'It was the longest of long shots, any way you slice it.'

'Have you tried the Mechanicus forces again?' Cyria Tyro asked. Her tone didn't hide the fact she still pinned a great deal of hope on the weapon, despite what Ryken had just said.

'Of course.' The Reclusiarch gestured west along the Hel's Highway, in the direction of *Stormherald* fighting out of sight in the Ironworks. 'Zarha refused as she refused before. It is blasphemy to do what we have done.'

'Still no word from Mechanicus royalty,' Sarren put in. 'Wherever this arch-priest of theirs is, he's not responding to any of our astropathic pleas.'

He spat onto the broken roadway beneath his feet. Indeed, whoever this Lord of the Centurio Ordinatus was, his arrival in the Armageddon system would be far too late to make a difference to Helsreach.

'At least the weapon may yet be put to use in the defence of other cities,' the colonel forced a chuckle. 'We stand on the very edge now. The fallback plan is, however, not something I wish to consider any more. There are few enough surviving Imperial forces left in the city. Let us not gather together for the last days of our lives and offer an easy target.'

'So it's over,' one of the captains said.

'No,' Grimaldus answered. 'But we must keep the enemy locked in the city as long as we can. Each day we survive increases the chances of reinforcement from the Ash Wastes.

Each day we hold out costs the enemy more blood, and keeps them here in Helsreach, where they cannot add their axes to the beasts besieging the other cities.'

Ryken scratched at his collar, soothing an itching scar he'd earned the week before.

'Uh. Sir?' he said to Sarren.

'Major?'

Ryken let his expression of disbelief do the talking. Sarren rubbed grit from his eyes with dirty fingertips as he answered. 'I have studied the hololithic projections in the wake of the dock siege. I have managed, blessings upon the Emperor, to actually maintain a conversation over the vox with Commissar Yarrick that lasted for more than ten seconds, and offered more productivity than merely listening to the crackle of static for once. We are following a pattern being used in several of the other hive cities. The Steel Legion will disperse throughout the city, centring at population centres that remain untouched.'

'What about the highway?'

'The enemy already claims most of it, Captain Helius. Let them have the rest. As of this morning, we are no longer fighting to preserve the city. We are fighting to save every life that can be saved. The city is dead, but over half of its people are not.'

The captain scowled, rendering his handsome face immediately unattractive. Unreliable friends borrowed a great deal of money with expressions like that.

'None of our remaining airstrips are anywhere near civilian population centres. Forgive me for pointing it out, colonel, but that was the very point of setting them up where we did. To hide them.'

'You did well. And I'm certain you will hold off the enemy

for an admirable space of time before you are overrun. Just like the rest of us.'

'We need to be defended!'

'No. You would *like* to be defended. You do not wish to die. None of us do, captain. But I command the Steel Legion, and the Steel Legion marches in defence of the hive's people now. I cannot spare regiments of men just to continue covering the air squadron's inexorable dance across the city. The plain truth is that there are no longer enough of you to be worth defending. Hide when you must, and fight when you can. If Invigilata stands with us, fly in support of them. If Invigilata leaves, then fly in support of the 121st Armoured Division, who will be based at the Kolav Residentia District, defending the entrances to the subterranean bunkers. Those are your orders.'

The captain's salute was reluctant. 'Understood, sir.'

'The coming weeks will go into Imperial records as the 'hundred bastions of light'. We no longer have the forces required to defend large swathes of territory. So we will fall back to the cores – the most vital points – and die before we ever give another metre of ground. The Jaega District, with its storm shelters. The Temple of the Emperor Ascendant, at the heart of the Ecclesiarchal sector. The Azal Spaceport in the Dis industrial sector. The Purgatori Refinery, that blessedly still stands on the docks. A list of primary and secondary defence points is being circulated over the vox-network and via hundreds of courier teams throughout the city.'

The colonel turned to the hulking figures of the Adeptus Astartes. 'Sergeant V'reth, the people of Helsreach and Armageddon offer their thanks to you and your brothers for the assistance. You'll quit the city today?'

'The Lord of the Fire-born calls.'

'Quite so, quite so. I offer my personal thanks. Without your arrival, many more would have lost their lives.'

V'reth made the sign of the aquila, his green gauntlets forming the familiar shape to mirror the bronze eagle on his chest.

'You are fighting with ferocity unmatched, Steel Legionnaire. The Emperor sees all and knows all. He sees your sacrifices and your courage in this war, and you are earning your place in the Imperium's legends. It was an honour to fight at your side, on the streets of your city.'

Sarren glanced between the two Adeptus Astartes – the warrior and the knight. He could not doubt the valour of the Templars in past weeks, but Throne, if only he'd had the Salamanders here. They were everything the Templars were not: communicative, supportive, *reliable*...

He found himself offering his hand. A moment's tension followed the gesture, as the towering warrior remained unmoving. Then, with care, the Salamander held the colonel's small, human hand in a shake. The joints of the sergeant's power armour hummed with the minor movement.

'The honour was ours, V'reth. Hunt well in the wastelands, and give my thanks to your lord.'

The Reclusiarch watched this in silence. No one knew what expression was masked by his relic helm.

ONCE THE DISCUSSION is done, I walk from the gathered humans. V'reth remains with me, shadowing my movements. Away from the pitted and cracked hull of Sarren's Baneblade, I slow in my stride to allow him to catch up. Does V'reth not have his own orders to obey? Does the Hemlock not call? Curious that he chooses to remain.

'What do you want, Salamander?'

As we walk along the Hel's Highway, I cannot help but stare at the city below. The platformed road rises above the habitation blocks here, once allowing traffic to rattle through the heart of the city between the spires of its tall residential towers. Now it remains aloft – a rockcrete wave riding above urban devastation. The buildings here are flattened, reduced to rubble by the enemy's scrap-Titans and shelling from our own forces.

Across the city, the Highway has come down in several places. Fortunate that it has not done so here, as well.

'To speak, if you are willing, Reclusiarch.'

'I would be honoured,' I tell him, but this is a lie. We have spent a week fighting together, side by side, and although his presence was invaluable, his warriors are not knights. Too often, they fell back to guard civilian shelters rather than press the attack and prevent the enemy from escaping. Too often they withstood repeated assaults rather than strike first and eliminate any need of further retaliation.

Priamus loathes them, but I do not. Their ways are not our ways. It is not cowardice that drives them to these tactics, but rather tradition. Yet still, their valour is as alien to me as the disgusting savagery of the orks.

It is difficult to hold my tongue. I wish him to leave before honesty stains the deeds we have achieved together, and before truth spoken too brutally threatens the alliance between our respective Chapters.

'My brothers and I came to this city without the illuminating guidance of our Chaplain. We would offer reverent thanks if you would lead us in prayer before we quit the city and rejoin our Chapter by the shores of the Hemlock.'

'I know little of your Chapter's cult and creed, Salamander.'

'We know this, Reclusiarch. Still, we would offer sincere thanks.'

It is a magnificent and bold gesture, and I know it honours me far more than it would honour them if I agreed. To lead brothers from another Chapter in prayer is beyond merely rare. It is almost unheard of. In my life, I can recall only one such instance, and that was with our gene-brothers and fellow sons of Dorn, the Crimson Fists, when the Declates system burned.

'Think of the battle last night,' I tell him. 'Think of the rooftop battle in the Nergal district. There was one moment in the chaos that still preys upon my mind. It casts a shadow over us now, like an enemy's spear threatening to fall.'

He hesitates. This is clearly not the way he thought his request would be answered. 'What aspect of the battle troubles you, Reclusiarch?'

A fine question.

The beast falls from my hands, its skull broken, to die at my feet.

I hear the burning hiss of Priamus's blade tearing through alien flesh. I hear the strained snarls of meat-clogged chainblades. I hear the yelling of panicked humans as they cower in the storm shelter, their fear reaching my senses through the armour-plated walls.

Another creature snarls in my face, spitting thick saliva over my faceplate. It dies as Artarion's bolter kicks once from a few metres away, shearing its malformed head off in a burst of gore.

'Focus,' he grunts over the vox.

I return the favour a moment later, my maul pounding into a beast that sought to leap at him from behind.

The battle is close, down to pistols, blades and the crashing beat of fists into faces. In the centre of the expansive plaza, the thickly-armoured storm shelter endures siege from close to two hundred of the enemy.

Footing is treacherous. Our boots are stamping down on pools of cooling blood and the bodies of dead dockworkers. The Salamanders are…

Curse them all…

Priamus blocked a cut from the closest ork, the beast's chopping sword deflected with a shower of sparks from the brief blade contact.

He killed it with the riposte – an ugly strike he felt no pride for, slipping past the creature's non-existent guard and ramming the blade's point into the beast's exposed neck.

The brute's axe slammed with clanging force against the side of his helm. His vision receptors showed angry static for two seconds.

Not deep enough. The swordsman yanked back with the blade, and on the second plunge he hilted it in the ork's collarbone. The beast collapsed in a heap of dead limbs.

Priamus resisted the urge to laugh.

The next ork to leap at him came with two of its brothers. The first fell to Priamus's blade lashing out to carve through its torso, the energised blade going through meat and bone like soft clay. The second and third would have had a fair chance at overpowering him, had they not been battered to the ground by a sweep of the Reclusiarch's maul.

'Where are the Salamanders?' he voxed, his breath coming in ragged gasps.

'They're holding.'

'They're what?'

* * *

Bastilan's fist vibrated with the crashing judder of his bolter. Streaks of alien blood painted his battered armour yet again.

Recriminations spilled out over the vox. The Salamanders weren't advancing with the Templars. The Templars were pushing ahead too far, too fast.

'Follow us, in the name of the Throne!' Bastilan added his voice to the vox-chatter.

'Fall back,' came the staid voice of Sergeant V'reth. 'Fall back to the eastern platform and be ready to engage the second wave.'

'Advance! If we strike now, there will be no second wave. We're at the warlord's throat!'

'Salamanders,' V'reth spoke calmly, 'Hold and be ready. Cut down any stragglers that seek to breach the shelter.'

Bastilan kicked a hunched alien in the chest, breaking whatever passed for its rib structure. In the moment's respite, he ejected his spent bolt magazine and slammed a fresh one home.

They were advancing unsupported, away from the shelter, in pursuit of the fleeing orks. Ahead, through the crowd of panicking beasts, Bastilan could see the armoured warlord of this wretched tribe, its staggering gait made all the more pronounced by the ablative armour plating that seemed surgically bolted to its nerveless flesh.

Bolts slashed after the retreating warleader, roaring from the muzzles of Templars fighting their way through a bestial and ferocious rearguard. Several shells detonated against the creature's armour, while others smacked into the backs and shoulders of fleeing orks around their commander.

'He's getting away,' Bastilan grunted. The words shamed him even to speak them.

'Fall back,' came the Reclusiarch's growl.

'Sir,' Bastilan began, coupled with Priamus's decidedly more annoyed 'No!'

'*Fall back. This is not worth dying over. We do not have the numbers to spill the warlord's blood now.*'

V'RETH, TO HIS credit, nods.

'I see. You consider this a stain on your personal honour.'

He does not see. 'No, brother. I consider it a waste of time, ammunition, and life. Two of your own squad were killed in the successive waves that followed. Brother Kaedus and Brother Madoc from my own force were slain. If we had pursued in unity, we could have broken through to the enemy leader and taken his head. The rest of the beasts would have scattered, and the bulk could easily have been purged by kill-teams in the aftermath.'

'It is tactically unsound, Reclusiarch. Pursuit would have left the shelter undefended and vulnerable to regrouping waves attacking from other sectors. Three thousand lives were saved by our defiance last night.'

'There were no attacks from other sectors.'

'There may have been, had we pursued. And there was still no guarantee we would have overpowered the rearguard quickly enough to reach the warlord.'

'We weathered six further assaults, wasted seven hours, lost four warriors, and expended a hoard of ammunition that my knights can ill-afford to throw away.'

'That is one way of seeing the final cost. I see it more simply: we won.'

'I am finished with this... debate, Salamander.' Again, I recall the grinding cut of Nero's medicae-saw, and the puncturing retrieval of cutting tools extracting glistening gene-seed organs from the chests of the slain.

'It grieves me to hear you speak this way, Reclusiarch.'

Listen to him. So patient. So calm.
So blind.
'Get out of my city.'

CHAPTER XIX

FATE

THE GIANT STOOD above its worshippers in silence.

Its skin and bones were harvested from crashed and salvaged ships, each column, gear, pylon, girder and plate of armour that went into its birth stolen from something else. Although the giant was not alive, living creatures served it in place of blood and organs. They clambered through the god's form, insulated by the armour, hanging from the metal bones, moving like the blood cells in sluggish arteries.

The giant had taken over two thousand labourers over a month to build. It had finally awoken outside the walls of Hive Stygia three days before, to great roars of praise from its devoted faithful.

And then, in its first hours of life, it had wiped the hive city from the face of the planet. Stygia was a modest industrial city, defended by the Steel Legion and its own militia with little in the way of Adeptus Astartes or Mechanicus support. From the moment the giant awoke to the moment the last vestiges of organised Imperial resistance was crushed, the city lasted a total of five hours and thirty-two minutes.

And now, the giant stood silent, idle, making ready for its journey south.

Its face was piggish and round-eyed, all jagged jaw and red-iron tusks. Behind the broken windows that served as its eyes, hunched crewmembers moved in loping gaits, attending to their bestial imitations of Imperial Titan command.

The giant's name, splattered across its ugly, fat-bellied hull in crude alien hieroglyphs, was *Godbreaker*.

With a slow tread that shook the earth around it, *Godbreaker* began to move south, towards the coast.

Towards Helsreach.

If it could remain mobile without breaking down – a difficult feat given the skills of its creators – it would arrive by dawn the following day.

IN A FATEFUL sense of opposed unity with the *Godbreaker*, another powerful war machine drew nearer to Helsreach. Its journey was a far longer one, and its progress was a melancholy fraction of what it might have been in a better age.

Waves of ashy soil blew aside in the land train's wake, as its gravity suppression field exerted its influence on the ground below the rattling, serpentine vehicle. Jurisian felt its resistance in every touch upon its controls. The soul of the machine was rising from its slumber now, finding itself disrespected and on the edge of lashing out at the living being responsible.

'Reclusiarch,' he spoke into the vox again, once more receiving no answer.

Oberon's existence in his mind was akin to a beast alone in the woods. Jurisian could keep it at bay as long as he focused on its presence, just as a traveller could face down a wolf in the wild if he kept watch for the beast and carried a torch of flame to ward it away. It was a game of focus, and despite his weariness, the Master of the Forge possessed focus in abundance. He was a conscientious and patient soul, devoted to each of his tasks like a predator hunting prey. This demeanour and dedication, coupled with his ability and deeds of honour, had seen him promoted to his rank aboard the *Eternal Crusader* nineteen years before.

Jurisian had been present at Grimaldus's induction into the inner circle, and though it shamed him to admit it now – even silently, even only to himself and the lurking soul of the war machine – he had cast his vote against the Chaplain ascending to Mordred's role as Reclusiarch.

'He is not ready,' Jurisian had said, adding his voice to Champion Bayard's. 'He is a master of small engagements, and a warrior beyond peer. But he is not a leader of the Chapter.'

'The Forgemaster speaks the truth, High Marshal,' Bayard had added. 'Grimaldus is flawed by hesitation. A second's delay in all he does, and it is no secret why. He holds himself to his master's standards. Doubt clings to him, darkening his place in the Chapter.'

'He is shaken by Mordred's death,' Jurisian had pressed. 'He seeks his place in the Eternal Crusade.'

Helbrecht had sat musing on his throne, his cold eyes lowering the temperature of the room.

'In the coming war, I will give him the chance to find that place.'

Jurisian had spoken no more, and inclined his head in a bow. The Emperor's Champion was not so subdued, and had put forward his recommendations for warriors other than Grimaldus to succeed Mordred.

The High Marshal had kept his own counsel, but the voices of the Sword Brethren around Helbrecht's dais sounded out in jeers as fists crashed against shields. Grimaldus was the chosen of Mordred the Avenger, and skilled in personal combat beyond question. Two centuries of valour and glory; two hundred years of unrelenting courage and a host of enemy dead across a horde of worlds; his short years as the youngest Sword Brother in the history of the Chapter – there was no arguing with such truths.

Jurisian and Bayard had relented. The following night, they watched Grimaldus accept Mordred's mantle.

Oberon tilted as it rose over an ash dune, the anti-grav field changing its tone to a more strained whine.

On the horizon, a blanket of blackness rose from a burning city.

'Reclusiarch,' he voxed, trying once more to speak with the warrior that did not deserve the title he now carried.

LEAVING THE TITAN had proved less of a trial than Asavan had feared.

He'd managed it two days ago, and had been on the streets of the city ever since. All it had taken was a slow descent through the decks, and what felt like about eight million spiral staircases, each one shaped from dense bronze and riveted heavily to the walls.

Well. Perhaps closer to four staircases. But by the time Asavan was approaching ground level, he was blinking sweat from his eyes and cursing his lack of fitness. On the Titan's lower levels, all was emergency red lighting, narrow corridors, and stuffy air filled with the smell of sacred incense holy to the Machine-God, as well as His disciples chanting blessings in His name. Through their devotion was *Stormherald* empowered. Praise be.

'Halt,' a machine-voice barked, and Asavan did exactly as he was told. He even raised his hands in the air, mimicking some unnecessary surrender. 'What are you doing here?' the voice demanded.

Here was at the base of the Titan's pelvis, in one of the lowest accessible chambers, lit by a flickering yellow siren light. Six augmented skitarii stood stationed around a bulkhead in the floor. The room itself rocked back and forth, tilting with the Titan's tread.

'I'm leaving the Titan,' the priest said.

The skitarii glanced at each other with focus lenses instead of eyes. The air buzzed with inter-vox communication. They were confused. This… this made no sense.

'You are leaving the Titan,' one of them, apparently their leader, said. His eye lenses revolved, scanning the unaugmented human.

'Yes.'

More vox-chatter. The leader, his face noticeably more bionic than the others', emitted a blurt of machine code. Asavan knew an error/abort complaint when he heard one.

'*Stormherald* is engaged in locomotive activity.'

Asavan was aware of this. The entire room was, after all, moving. 'The Titan is walking. I know. I still wish to leave. This service maintenance ladder will take me down the left leg struts to the shin-fortress, will it not?'

'It would,' the skitarii leader allowed.

'Then please excuse me. I must be going.'

'Halt.' Asavan did, again, but he was growing tired of this. 'You wish to leave the Titan,' the skitarii repeated. 'But… why?'

This was hardly the ideal setting for a debate on crises of faith and the sudden revelatory desire to walk among the city's people and help them with one's own hands.

Asavan reached for the medallion around his neck, marking him as an honoured member of the Ecclesiarchy of Terra and a minister ordained to preach the word of the Emperor in His aspect as the Machine-God of Mars.

The skitarii stared at the icon for several moments – the double-headed eagle and the divided skull backing it – and lowered their weapons.

'My thanks,' the sweating priest said. 'Now if it's not too much trouble, could you open that bulkhead for me?'

His stomach lurched at the sight beyond the opened trapdoor. Beneath, the broken rockcrete of Hel's Highway passed by, a good twenty-five metres down. Pudgy hands gripped the black iron service ladder as he descended, rung by rung, through the wind, hanging on to the Titan's thigh. Above him, the bulkhead slammed with a chime of finality.

So be it. Down, he went.

Behind the god-machine's knee, another bulkhead blocked his descent into the bulky lower leg section. Below, Asavan heard the servos of turrets mounted on the shin-walls panning back and forth, seeking targets.

It took almost a full minute to work the bulkhead's wheel lock, but he was energised now, drawing close to his objective. Once more, he descended into red-lit, downward spiralling corridors, avoiding the troop chambers where ranks of skitarii stood in tomb-like silence.

The Titan's movement now was almost unbearable, slamming him to the wall and rocking him from his feet on several occasions. This low, the gravitic stabilisers were little use against the sheer degree of movement necessary for each leg to make. His surroundings rumbled with sickening violence every eleven seconds, as the foot came down on the road below. Asavan vomited against a wall, and tried not to laugh. He was trying to keep his balance while walking through the steel bones in the ankle of a striding machine giant. Perhaps this wasn't such a wonderful idea, after all.

And now came the hardest part.

This last bulkhead opened onto the Titan's tiered claw-toes, which formed steps by which the skitarii battalions in the leg-fortresses could ascend and descend, when *Storm-herald* was at rest.

Disembarking with the Titan in motion was going to be... exciting.

Asavan pulled the door open on squealing hinges, gripping a nearby handrail and watching the ground in bug-eyed horror, waiting for it to level out with the foot touching down. It did, with a bone-jarring rumble of thunder, and the fat priest ran, huffing and puffing, down the tiered stairs.

The other foot came down, shaking the ground and sending Asavan tumbling down the last steps to land in a heap of overweight flesh and filthy robes on the dirty surface of the highway.

A metre away, the stairs rose again as the great war machine lifted its foot to take another step. Squealing without even realising he was doing so, Asavan Tortellius sprinted, with his additional chins shaking, away from the leg's ascent and inevitable descent. He hurled himself the last few metres, landing hard.

As the Titan walked on, monstrous feet still pounding into the ground, the priest lay on his back, breathing in ragged gasps.

And thus was completed the least dignified disembarkation from an Imperator Titan in the history of the Imperium.

That had been two days ago.

Since then, Asavan had not improved his situation by a great deal, but by the Throne, he was doing the Emperor's work. And that was a start.

His journey along the Hel's Highway (which he was resolutely calling his 'pilgrimage') had begun on an uninspiring note. Hauling himself to his unsteady feet and recovering the shoe he had lost in his fall, he began to make his way down the wide road, clutching his bag of dehydrated foodstuffs and electrolyte fluid packs.

Away from the Titan, with *Stormherald* thumping away in the far distance now, he realised how utterly silent a dead city could be. The crashing of weapons and war machines was a muted murmur, seeming a world away. His immediate surroundings were quiet almost to the point of eeriness.

He left the highway to trudge through an abandoned commercia district that had been punished heavily weeks before. Slain tanks littered the central market zone, both Imperial and alien, and each one commanding its own mound of nearby bodies. Red flies – the bloated and oversized tropical vermin that bred like a plague in the jungles to the west – were here in swarms, blanketing the dead and feeding from them.

He'd not been prepared for the smell of a city at war. On the back of a Titan, one strode the battlefield like a colossus, far from what the princeps, blessings upon her, referred to as the 'distasteful biological carnage'.

The smell was somewhere between untreated sewage and spoiled food. He vomited again halfway across the plaza, releasing a stringy ooze that stuck to his teeth. Fluid packs and dehydrated foodstuffs were not wonderful for the digestion.

That night, he'd camped in the broken shell of a Leman Russ. The tank was half buried in a fallen wall, which evidently it had rammed. Whatever had become of its crew was a mystery Asavan didn't feel like looking into. He was glad enough that they weren't there, slouched and rotting in their seats like so many others had been.

When he finally slept, he dreamed of everything he'd seen that day. After three hours of dreaming that every corpse he'd passed was staring at him, he gave up the attempt to find rest and instead pushed on deeper into the city.

On the second day, he had found his first survivors. In the ground floor of a collapsed habitation block, movement drew his eye.

He'd voiced a tremulous 'Hello?' before he'd even realised he might be calling out to one of the invaders. The sound of scampering footsteps emboldened him. Alien beasts would not run from a lone human's cry. 'I've come to help,' he called.

Silence was the only answer.

'I have food,' he tried.

A filthy face rose from behind a pile of rubble. Narrowed eyes never left him – bright and quick like a scavenger's gaze.

'I have food,' Asavan said again, lowering his voice this time. With no sudden movement, he unslung the satchel from his back and held up a dehydrated food pouch in its silver packaging. 'It's dehydrated. Rations. But it's food.'

The face became a person, a middle-aged woman, as she left her hiding place and drew closer. Gaunt and wild-eyed, she moved with the caution of the forever fearful. It took three attempts for her to speak. Before the words left her mouth in a scratchy whisper, she had to clear her throat repeatedly.

'You're a priest?' she asked, still not coming within arm's reach. She pointed at his white and violet robes, her gesture weak and dismissive.

'I am. The God-Emperor sent me to you.'

She had wept in that moment, and soon after, they shared a small meal in the ruins of her hab-chamber. He asked questions of her life, and the losses she'd suffered. Before he left an hour later, he made sure she had several days' worth of food and fluid, and blessed her in the name of the God-Emperor. It was strange to be ministering to the genuinely needy, and the fully-fleshed. So many of his sermons had been to fellow clerics and machine-altered skitarii that a weeping woman praising the Emperor was quite beyond his experience.

It was strange, but it was good. It was worthy.

Asavan Tortellius's first meeting with a survivor had gone well. He walked on, similar encounters repeating themselves over the next day and night. It was only on the third day that he ran into trouble.

A small group of ragged survivors huddled around a trash-fire, warming their hands as night fell over another tank graveyard along the Hel's Highway. Asavan cleared his throat as he approached, raising a hand in greeting.

The survivors whirled, bringing lasguns to bear. Several of the group were in workers' overalls, blood-spattered and dark with grime. One of them was clad in a Guard uniform, a bulky power pack on his back and a cabled lasrifle aimed at Asavan's face.

'No more surprises, please, yes?' The soldier spat onto the ground, his thin face marked with suspicion. 'I am tired and I am cold and I am sick to my core of shooting looters in the skull.'

'I'm not a looter.'

'That is not a surprise to me, given what I have just said I do to looters.'

'I'm a priest.'

'Explains the robes,' one of the workers chuckled. 'I think he's telling the truth, Andrej.'

'A priest,' the storm trooper repeated.

'A priest,' Asavan nodded.

The storm trooper lowered his rifle. 'That is most definitely a surprise. I am Andrej of the Legion. These are my friends, who were unlucky enough to be born in Helsreach instead of a city worth defending.'

The workers snickered.

'I am Asavan Tortellius, of *Stormherald*.'

'The god-machine?' Andrej barked a laugh. 'You are far from your walking throne, fat priest. Did you fall off and fail to catch up?'

Asavan drew nearer to the fire, and the workers made room for him.

'Tomaz Maghernus.' One of them offered his hand for the priest to shake. 'Don't mind Andrej, sir. He's not all there.'

'All of me is exactly where it needs to be.' The storm trooper shook his head, his dark, weasel eyes glinting with the fire's reflection. 'Throne, I have never been so cold. We are all lucky that our balls have not frozen and cracked by now.'

'Good to see you,' one of the other men muttered to the priest.

'Yeah,' another nodded, his voice sincere despite not meeting the newcomer's eyes. Asavan was touched by their almost-shy gratitude to see a priest amongst all this.

'Looters?' Asavan asked. 'Did I hear that correctly?'

'You did,' Maghernus breathed into his hands, before holding them out to the flames. 'Dockworkers. Militia and Guard deserters. It's ugly out here. They're going through the habs, stealing credits and whatever else they can find.'

'May I ask, why are you out here?'

Andrej shook his head as he joined the group. 'Do not sound so suspicious, holy man. We are not hiding from duty. We are merely the Forgotten, lost in the dead city, making our way back to… wherever the closest front line might be.'

'You have no contact with the rest of the Guard?'

'Ha! I like this. I like the way you think. You fell off your Titan, fat man. Do you have a vox-link back to ask your Mechanicus masters for advice? No. Exactly. You were not at the docks, priest. Half the city died last week. The Guard is broken, and the vox is no more than a hundred frequencies of hissing noise. If I am right, and I hope to be wrong, then no Imperial force is able to contact any other in perhaps half of the city.'

'What do you intend to do?'

'We are moving west. The Templars went to the west, and so shall we. Why are *you* here?'

Asavan shrugged. It wasn't something he could explain with any conviction. 'I wanted to walk the streets and help where I could. I was serving no one on the back of a Titan.'

A few of the group made the sign of the aquila and murmured their admiration.

'You wish to come with us, fat priest? You will like what is in the west, I am thinking.'

'What's in the west?' Asavan asked.

'A great number of burning industrial sectors, too many looters for my innocent heart to consider at this moment in time, and of course, the Temple of the Emperor Ascendant.'

'What is this temple you speak of? A monastery? A cathedral?'

Maghernus shook his head. 'Both. Neither. It's a shrine – built by the original colonists who came to Armageddon.'

In his surprise, Asavan almost ordered a servo-skull to take a dictation. 'You are telling me that the first church ever built in Helsreach still stands? It endured the First War against the daemon armies? It remained unbroken through the Second War, when the Great Enemy first came to this world?'

'Well... yeah,' Maghernus replied.

This was providence. This was why he had left the Titan, and this was why the God-Emperor had guided him through the city to these men.

Andrej snorted at his questions. 'It is not simply the first church built in Helsreach, my fat friend. It is the first church ever raised in the whole world. When the first settlers prayed to the Emperor, they prayed in the Temple of the Emperor Ascendant.'

Asavan felt his hands trembling. 'How do we reach it?'

Andrej gestured to the expansive, raised road in the distance. 'We walk the Hel's Highway. How else?'

ARTARION STOOD AWAY from the others.

The building they occupied had once been a small temple, serving as the spiritual heart of this industrial sector. Now it was a tumbledown ruin, no longer fit to house dawn and dusk prayers for the local workers. In the altar room, Artarion had paused his bored exploration, finding bloodstains on some of the fallen rubble that had buried the floor in broken architecture.

The blood-scent was old, the stains themselves flaking.

Whoever was entombed beneath had been dead for days. Artarion breathed in through his helm's filters. Female. Had not bled much after being crushed. Dead for perhaps three days; the delicate scent of decomposition was little more than spice on the air.

He'd removed himself to perform the rites of maintenance on his weapons, as well as to get away from Priamus muttering about the Salamanders.

As he lowered himself to sit on the dead woman's cairn, the knee joint of his armour locked for several seconds. Runic warnings flickered across his visor display. Instead of blanking them, he disengaged his helm's seals, removed it, and breathed in the smell of the fire, ash and brick dust that was all Helsreach had become. The faulty joint crunched back into motion, eliciting a grunt from the knight as he sat.

His bolter, chained to his thigh and mag-locked in place, was starved of ammunition. He had not spoken of this to the others yet, but knew they must surely be approaching similar difficulties. Before the week of bloodshed at the docks, the supplies brought down by the Helsreach Crusade from the *Eternal Crusader* so long ago had been reduced to a Thunderhawk cargo bay half full of bolts and an almost-empty crate of replacement tooth-tracks for chainswords.

The gunship itself sat cold and silent in the courtyard of a factory complex, almost two kilometres to the west, in a sector of the city still securely in Imperial control.

Artarion examined the bolter's fire-blackened muzzle, turning the weapon over in his hands as he followed the path of winding, once-gold inlaid scriptures etched along the gun's sides. A list of enemies slain, battles won, worlds defended…

In wordless silence, he lowered the bolter again.

* * *

'THERE IS NOTHING to like in them,' Priamus spat as he paced the prayer room. 'They wage war to defend, to preserve. Everything in their way is devoted to maintaining what humanity already has.'

Bastilan was sharpening his combat blade, running a whetstone along the gladius's killing edges. The small chamber was filled with Priamus's crunching bootsteps and the *resssh, resssh* of the whetstone scraping.

'It is flawed,' the swordsman added. 'I mean no offence to them as warriors. But drop podding into the city purely to defend civilians? Madness.'

Resssh, resssh.

'Why do you not answer, brother?'

'I have little to say.' *Resssh, resssh.*

'Do you think ill of me for my beliefs? Bastilan, please, you know I am right.'

'I know you are treading on unstable ground. Do not besmirch the honour of our brother Chapter. The Salamanders shed as much blood as we did this week.'

'That is not the point.'

Resssh, resssh. 'That is where you and I disagree, brother. But you are young. You will learn.'

Priamus didn't bother to hide his disgusted sneer from infecting his voice. 'Do not patronise me, old man. You know of what I speak. You are just quietened by the mounting years and too reserved to say it aloud.'

'I am not that old,' Bastilan laughed. The boy was annoying, but he certainly knew how to drag out a smile or two with his misguided fervour.

'Do not laugh at me.'

'Then stop making me laugh. What two Chapters fight the same? What two Chapters wage war according to the same principles? We are all born of different worlds and trained by different masters. Accept the differences and stand with them as allies.'

'But they are *wrong*.' Priamus stared at the older warrior in disbelief. How could he be so obtuse? 'They could have landed anywhere in the city. They could have struck at one of the alien commanders. Instead, they crash down amongst us at the docks to defend the humans.'

'That is why they came. Do not mistake their compassion for tactical idiocy.'

'That is my point.' Priamus resisted the rising urge to draw his blade. There was nothing to cut beyond the air before him, yet he felt a keen need to draw steel. 'They preserve. They defend. We are Adeptus Astartes, not Imperial Guard. We are the spear thrust to the throat, not the blunt anvil. We are all that remains of the Great Crusade, Bastilan. For ten thousand years, we and we alone have crusaded to bring the Emperor's worlds into compliance. We do not fight for the people of the Imperium, we fight for the Imperium itself. We attack. We *attack*.'

Resssh, ressh. 'Not here. Not at Helsreach.'

Priamus lowered his head, unwilling to concede the point, despite the fact he knew he was defeated. That bastard Bastilan always did this to him. A few quiet words and he'd puncture all of what Priamus was trying to say. It was far, far beyond annoying.

'Helsreach is…' the swordsman's voice was lower now – less bitter, and somehow less confident. 'Nothing about this war has felt right.'

NEROVAR HAD ALSO retreated from the others.

But apparently not far enough.

'Brother,' came a voice. Grimaldus had returned. Nero acknowledged him with a nod, and returned to his feigned examination of the blistered and burned mural on the temple wall. Scenes of the Emperor watching over Helsreach: a golden god with His radiant visage regarding scenes of great industry below. With the wall ruined by flame and the artwork charred, it now resembled the city outside more than it ever had.

'How was the command meeting?'

'A tedious discussion of last stands. In that respect, it was no different from any other time. The Salamanders have withdrawn.'

'Then perhaps Priamus will cease his complaints.'

'I doubt that.'

Grimaldus removed his helm. Nerovar watched him as he examined the paintings, seeing the Reclusiarch's scarred features set in a thoughtful frown.

'How is the wound?' Grimaldus asked, his voice both deeper and softer now, unfiltered by helm vox.

'I will live.'

'Pain?'

'Does it matter? I will live.'

The chains binding his weapons to his armour rattled as the Reclusiarch moved across the chamber. Ceramite armour boots thudded on the dusty mosaics, breaking them underfoot. In the centre of the room, Grimaldus looked up at the holed ceiling, where a stained glass dome had once mercifully blocked the view of the polluted sky.

'I was with Cador,' he said, staring up into the heavens. 'I was with him at the end.'

'I know.'

'So you will believe me when I say that you could have

done nothing for him had you been at our side? He was dead the moment the beast struck him.'

'I saw the death wound, did I not? You are telling me nothing I do not already know.'

'Then why do you still mourn his fall? It was a magnificent death, worthy of a vault on board the *Crusader*. He killed nine of the enemy with a broken blade and his bare hands, Nero. Dorn's blood, if only we could all inscribe such deeds on our armour. Humanity would have cleansed the stars by now.'

'He will never rest in that vault, and you know it.'

'That is not worth mourning over. It is just a regrettable truth. Hundreds of our own heroes have fallen and remained unrecovered. You carry Cador's true legacy. Why is that not enough? I wish to help you, brother, but you are not making it easy.'

'He trained me. He taught me the blade and bolter. He was a father in place of the parents I was stolen from.'

Grimaldus had still not looked at the other knight. He watched as an Imperial fighter streaked overhead, and wondered if it was Helius, the heir to Barasath and Jenzen.

'It is the way of the warrior,' he said, 'to outlive the ones that train us. We take their lessons and wield them as weapons against the enemies of Man.'

Nero snorted.

'Did I say something amusing, Apothecary?'

'In a way. Hypocrisy is always amusing.' The Apothecary removed his own helm. As he did so, he could suddenly feel the unwelcome weight of the cryo-sealed gene-seed in his forearm storage pod.

'Hypocrisy?' Grimaldus asked, more curious than annoyed.

'It is not like you to comfort and console, Reclusiarch. Forgive me for saying so.'

'Why would I need to forgive you for speaking the truth?'

'You make it sound so clear and easy. None of us have been truthful with you since… we came here.'

Grimaldus lowered his gaze from the dark skies. He fixed his eyes – eyes that the commander of a god-machine had called kind, of all things – on Nerovar's own.

'You say "Since we came here". I sense another lie.'

'Very well. Since before we came here. Since Mordred died. It is difficult to be near you, Reclusiarch. You are withdrawn when you should be inspiring. You are distant when you would once have been wrathful. I believe you are wrong to lecture me on Cador's death when you have been lost to us since Mordred fell. There are flashes of fire beneath the cold surface, and we have warned you of these changes before. But to no avail.'

Grimaldus chuckled, the sound leaving his lips as a soft exhalation through a reluctant smile.

'I am seeing the world through his eyes,' he said, looking down at the silver skull mask in his hands. 'And I am seeing, night after night, that I am not him. I did not deserve this honour. I am no leader of men, nor am I skilled at dealing with the humans. I should not be wearing the mantle of a Reclusiarch, yet I was certain once the war began, my doubts and discomforts would fade away.'

'But they have not.'

'No. They have not. I will die on this world.' Grimaldus looked at the Apothecary again. 'My master died, and mere days later, I was consigned to die on a world that has no hope of surviving an ugly war, far from my brothers and the Chapter I have served for two centuries. Even if we win, what does victory buy? We will be kings astride a ruined world of dead industry.' He shook his head. 'And this is where we will die. A worthless death.'

'It is glorious, in its own way. The Helsreach Crusade. Our brothers and the people of this world will remember our sacrifice forever. You know this as well as I.'

'Oh, I know it. I cannot escape it. But I do not care for *glory*. Glory is earned through a life lived in service to the Throne. It should not be a consolation gift, or something sought to sate a hunger. I want my life to matter to my brothers, and I want my death to further the cause of the Imperium. Do you not recall Mordred's last words to me? They are written in gold upon the plinth of the statue that honours him.'

'I remember them, Reclusiarch. *"We are judged in life for the evil we destroy"*. And we will be judged well, for a great many have fallen before us already.'

'Our deaths inspire no one. They benefit no one. Do you recall the Shadow Wolves? When we saw the last of that Chapter die, I felt my heart sing. Never before had I craved the taste of alien blood as I did in that moment. Their deaths mattered. Every warrior clad in silver armour died in true glory that day. What of Helsreach? Who will draw courage from a footnote in the archives of a fallen city?'

Grimaldus closed his eyes. He did not open them again, even as he heard Nerovar approaching. The fist crashing against his jaw knocked him to the ground, where he at last looked back at the Apothecary. Grimaldus was smiling, though in truth he had not expected the blow.

'How dare you?' Nero asked, his teeth clenched and his fist still tight. '*How dare you?* You throw filth on our glory here, yet you dare tell me Cador's death means something? It means *nothing*. He died as we will all die: unremembered and unburied. You are my Reclusiarch, Grimaldus. Do not lie to me. If our glory matters to no one, then Cador's death is meaningless and I have every right to mourn him as you mourn for all of us.'

The Chaplain licked his lips, tasting the chemical-rich blood that marked them. In silence, he rose to his feet. Nerovar did not back away. Far from it, he stood his ground, and activated his bracer-mounted storage pod. A plastek vial slid from its secure housing, and Nerovar threw it to Grimaldus.

The Reclusiarch caught it in hands that threatened to shake. NACLIDES, the script on the vial denoted. The gene-seed of a brother fallen days before.

'Nero...'

Nerovar ejected another tube and tossed it to the Reclusiarch. DARGRAVIAN, it read. He had been the first to fall.

'Nerovar...'

The Apothecary ejected a third vial. This one he held in his fist, his gauntlet clutching it just shy of crushing it into shards. CADOR showed between Nero's fingers.

'Answer me,' the Apothecary demanded. 'Is what we do here worthless? Is there nothing to be proud of in our sacrifice?'

Grimaldus didn't answer for several moments. He looked around the modest, broken temple, the light of thought bright in his eyes.

'The city is falling, brother. Sarren and the other humans faced that fact today. The time has come for us to choose where we will die.'

'Then let it be where we will be remembered.' Nerovar reverently handed the vial bearing Cador's cryogenically frozen gene-seed organs to the Chaplain. 'Let it be where our deaths will matter, and give birth to tales worthy of being recorded in humanity's history.'

Grimaldus looked at the three vials resting in his gauntleted palm.

'I know of a place,' he said softly, a dangerous flicker appearing in his eyes as he looked back up at his battle-brother. 'It is far from here, but there is no holier place on this entire world. There, we shall dig our graves, and there, we will ensure the Great Enemy forever remembers the name of the Black Templars.'

'Tell me why you have chosen this place. I must know.'

THE TRUTH IS… surprising, but as I speak the words, there is no doubt within them. This is what we must do, and it is how we must die. Our lives are sacrifice, from implantation of the gene-seed to its extraction from our bodies.

'We will die where our deaths matter. Where we can spite the enemy with our last breaths, and inspire the warriors of this city.'

'Now those,' Nero says, 'are at last the words of a Reclusiarch.'

'I am a slow learner,' I confess. This brings a smile to my brother's lips.

'Mordred is dead,' Nero said, keeping his voice low. 'But he trusted you as his heir above any other for one reason. He believed you were worthy.'

I say nothing.

'Do not die without ever living up to him, Grimaldus.'

CHAPTER XX
GODBREAKER

Maralin moved across the botanical garden, her fingertips trailing along the dewy leaves and petals of the rosebushes.

They were not hers, but that didn't stop her admiring them. Only one of her sisters had the patience and skill to grow roses in the choking air and sickened soil of the city, and that was Alana. All other blooms in the botanical garden were raised by cultivation servitors, and in Maralin's opinion, it showed. Her fingers danced along the wet petals of the soot-darkened roses, amazed as always at how lovelier and fuller Alana's flowers were in comparison to the modest blooms grown by the augmented slave workers.

They lacked inspiration, clearly, and no doubt the severance of their souls had much to do with it.

Passing through the spacious garden, she entered the rectory. The building's air filters were straining, keeping the main chamber cooled. Prioress Sindal was sat, as she almost always was, at her oversized desk of rare stonewood, scribing away in meticulous handwriting.

She looked up as Maralin entered, peering through the corrective eyelenses that had slipped to the end of her nose.

'Prioress, we've received word from Tempestora.'

Sindal's cataracted eyes narrowed, and she gently sprinkled sand across her parchment, drying the fresh ink. She was seventy-one years old, and she didn't just look it – she also sounded it when she spoke.

'What of the Sanctorum?'

'Gone,' Maralin swallowed.

'Survivors?'

'Few, and most are wounded. The hive has fallen, and the Sanctorum of the Order of Our Martyred Lady is overrun by the enemy. We received word now that there aren't enough survivors to retake their Sanctorum as of yet. Our own sisters in the Ash and Fire Wastes are moving to support.'

'So Tempestora is gone. What of Hive Stygia to the north?'

'Still no word, prioress. They are surely enduring the siege as we are.'

The old woman's hands were palsied, though she found that writing always steadied them for reasons beyond her understanding. They shook now as she set the completed parchment aside, on a loose pile of several others.

'Helsreach has weeks left, but little beyond that. The siege is almost at our own gates.'

'That... brings me to the second of the morning's messages, prioress.' Maralin swallowed again. She was clearly uncomfortable, and resented being the one sent to deliver these messages, but she was the youngest, and often relegated to these tasks.

'Speak, sister.'

'We received a message from the Adeptus Astartes commander in the city. The Reclusiarch. He sends word that his knights are en route to stand with us in the defence.'

The prioress removed her eyeglasses and cleaned them with a soft cloth. Then, carefully, she placed them back onto her face and looked directly at the young girl.

'The Reclusiarch is bringing the Black Templars here?'

'Yes, prioress.'

'Hmph. Did he happen to say why he felt the sudden wish to fight alongside the Order of the Argent Shroud?'

He had not, but Maralin had been paying close attention to the scraps of information that made it over the vox with any clarity. This, too, was one of her duties as the youngest, while her sisters were preparing for battle.

'No, prioress. I suspect it ties into Colonel Sarren's decision to break up the remaining defenders into separate bastions. The Reclusiarch has chosen the temple.'

'I see. I doubt he asked permission.'

Maralin smiled. The prioress had fought with the Emperor's Chosen before, and many of her sermons had included irritated mentions of their brash attitudes. 'No, prioress. He didn't.'

'Typical Adeptus Astartes. Hmph. When do they arrive?'

'Before sunset, mistress.'

'Very well. Anything more?'

There was little. The compromised vox-network had offered several suggestions of severe enemy Titan movement to the north, but confirmation wasn't forthcoming. Maralin relayed this, but she could tell the prioress's mind was elsewhere. On the Templars, most certainly.

'Damn it all,' the old woman muttered as she rose from

her chair, placing the quill in the inkpot. 'Well, don't just stand there gawping, girl. Prepare my battle armour.'

Maralin's eyes widened. 'How long has it been since you wore your armour, prioress?'

'How old are you, girl?'

'Fifteen, mistress.'

'Well, then. Let's just say you couldn't wipe your own backside the last time I went to war.' The old woman's forehead barely reached Maralin's chin as she shuffled past. 'But it'll be good to deliver a sermon with a bolter in hand again.'

ELSEWHERE IN THE Temple of the Emperor Ascendant, the sisters were making ready for war. The Order of the Argent Shroud were not in Helsreach in any significant force, their contributions thus far being little more than a series of fighting withdrawals from churches across the city.

Ninety-seven battle-ready sisters manned the temple's walls and halls, standing guard over several thousand menials, servitors, preachers, lay sisters and acolytes. The temple itself was formed of a central basilica, surrounded by high rockcrete walls bedecked in leering angels and hideous gargoyles staring out at the city beyond. Between the walls and the central building, acre upon acre of graveyard reached out from the basilica in every direction. Thousands of years before, they had been lush garden grounds, grown and tended by the first of Armageddon's settlers. Those same settlers were buried here, their bones long turned to dust and their gravestones weathered faceless by time. Interred alongside them were generations of their descendants; holy servants of the Imperium; and the respected dead of Armageddon's Steel Legions.

No one was buried here now; the graveyard was considered

full. Official records numbered the graves around the basilica as nine million, one hundred and eight thousand, four
hundred and sixty. Currently, only two people knew this was
incorrect, and only one of them cared about the discrepancy.

The first was a servitor who had been a gardener in life,
and had devoted several of his living years, before the augmetics had stolen his reason and independence, to counting
the graves as he tended the gardens around them. He'd been
curious, and it had satisfied him to learn the truth. He kept
it to himself, knowing to report it to his superiors might
bring down accusations of laxity in his primary duties. He
was, after all, a garden-tender and not a stock-counter or
cogitator. Three months after he had satisfied himself with
the truth, he was found stealing from the temple's tithe
boxes, and sentenced to augmetic reconfiguration.

The second person who knew the truth was Prioress Sindal. She had also counted them herself, over the course of
three years. To her, it was a form of meditation; of bringing
herself to a state of oneness with the people of Armageddon. She had not been born here, and in her devoted service
to the people of this world, she felt her meditative technique was apt enough.

She had, of course, filed amendments to the records, but
they were still locked in the bureaucratic cycle. The temple's cardinal council were notoriously foul at having their
staff deal with paperwork.

Most gravestones were stacked close together in clusters
of bloodline or fealty, and there was no conformity in the
markers – each was a slightly different size, shape, material or angle to those nearby, even in sections where the
rows were ordered in neat lines. In other parts of the graveyard district, finding one's way along a pathway was akin

to navigating a labyrinth, with weaving a way between the graves taking a great deal of time.

The Temple of the Emperor Ascendant itself was, by Imperial standards, a thing of haunting and gothic beauty. The spires were ringed by stone angels and depictions of the Emperor's primarchs as saints. Stained glass windows displayed a riot of colours, showing scenes of the God-Emperor's Great Crusade to bring the stars into union beneath humanity's vigilant guidance. Lesser depictions were of the first settlers themselves, their deeds of survival and construction exaggerated to deific proportion, showing them as the builders of a glorious, perfect world of golden light and marble cathedrals, rather than the industrial planet they had founded in truth.

The Sisters of the Order of the Argent Shroud had not been idle during the months of warfare that ravaged the rest of the city. Lesser shrines in the graveyard were both heavy weapon outposts and chapels to their founder, Saint Silvana. Angular statues of solid silver – each one of the weeping saint in various poses of grief, triumph and contemplation – stood silent watch over turret pods and barricaded gun-nests.

The walls themselves were reinforced in the same way as the city walls, and bore the same ratio of defence turrets per metre. These remained manned by Helsreach militia.

The temple courtyard's great gates were not closed. Despite the protestations of the cardinal council, Prioress Sindal had demanded the doors be kept open until the last possible moment, allowing more and more refugees to enter over the weeks of siege. The basilica's undercroft housed hundreds of families who hadn't been able to enter the subterranean shelters, for reasons of criminal activity, administrative error, or outright bad luck. Bunched together in the gloom, they came up for morning and evening prayer, adding their voices to the singing pleas that reached up to the immaculately-painted ceiling, where the God-Emperor was depicted staring off into the heavens.

The Temple of the Emperor Ascendant was, in short, a fortress.

A fortress filled with refugees, and surrounded by the largest graveyard in the world.

WE ARE THE last to arrive.

Twenty-nine of my brothers already await my arrival, with our cargo gunship grounded nearby. It brings our total force to thirty-five, if one was to count Jurisian labouring on the forlorn hope, trying to bring the weapon across the Ash Wastes.

Thirty-five of the hundred that landed in Helsreach five weeks before.

One of those awaiting our arrival is the one warrior I have done all I can to avoid for the last five weeks.

He kneels before the open gates of the temple's compound, his black sword plunged into the marble before him, helmed head lowered in reverence. As with the Templars around him, almost all evidence of scripture parchment, wax crusader seals and cloth tabard is gone from his armour. I recognise him because of his ancient armour and the dark blade he prays to.

Jurisian himself has worked on that armour, repairing it with reverence each time he has been honoured with the chance to touch it. Before Jurisian, a host of other Masters of the Forge maintained the relic war-plate through the centuries, back to its original forging as a suit of armour for the Imperial Fists Legion.

While our armour shows dull grey wounds under the stripped paint, this knight's war-plate, forged in a time when primarchs walked the galaxy, shows gold beneath the battle damage. The legacy of Dorn's Legion is still there if one knows where to look; between the cracks, revealed by war.

The knight rises, pulling the sword from the marble with no effort at all. His helm turns to face me, and a faceplate that once stared out onto the battlefields of the Horus Heresy regards me with eye lenses the colour of human blood.

He salutes me, sword sheathed on his back and his gauntlets making the sign of the aquila over his battered breastplate. I return the salute, and rarely in my life has the gesture been so heartfelt. I am finally ready to stand before him, and endure the judging stare of those crimson eyes.

'Hail, Reclusiarch,' he says to me.

'Hail, Bayard,' I say to the Emperor's Champion of the Helsreach Crusade.

He watches me, but I know he is not seeing me. He sees Mordred, the knight whose weapon I bear, and whose face I wear.

'My liege.' Priamus comes forward, kneeling before Bayard.

'Priamus,' Bayard vox-laughs. 'Still breathing, I see.'

'Nothing on this world will change that, my liege.'

'Rise, brother. The day will never come that you must kneel before me.' Priamus rises, inclining his head in respect once more before returning to my side. 'Artarion, Bastilan, it is good to see you both. And you, Nero.'

Nerovar makes the sign of the aquila, but says nothing.

'Cador's fall tore at my heart, brother. He and I served in the Sword Brethren together, did you know that?'

'I knew it, my liege. Cador spoke of it often. He was honoured to serve at your side.'

'The honour was mine. Know that fifty of the enemy died by my blade the day I heard of his passing. Throne, but he was a warrior to quench the fires of the stars themselves. I miss him fiercely, and the Eternal Crusade is poorer without his sword.'

'You... do great honour to his memory,' Nero's voice is choked with emotion.

'Tell me, brother,' Bayard's tone lowers, as if the refugees standing and staring at us outside the great gates have no right to hear of what we speak. 'I heard his death-wound was in the back. Is this so?'

Nero's nod comes with reluctance. 'It is.'

'I also heard he killed nine of the beasts alone, before succumbing to his wounds.'

'He did.'

'Nine. *Nine.* Then he died facing his enemy, as a knight must. Thank you, Nero. You have brought me comfort this day.'

'I... I...'

'Welcome, brothers. It has been too long since we stood united.' There are general murmurs of assent, and Bayard looks to me.

I smile behind my mask.

THEY RODE IN the back compartment of a trundling Chimera armoured personnel transport, their backs thumping against the metal walls with each sharp turn. It had been parked on the highway itself, riddled with bullet holes and las-burns, but still very much fuelled and ready to roll. Andrej and the others had dragged the bodies of dead Legionnaires out onto the road, and the storm trooper had forced the dockers to say a short prayer over the corpses before he would, as he put it, 'steal their ride'.

'Manners cost nothing,' he told them. 'And these men died for your city.'

The troop section in the back of the Chimera was a typical slice of Guard life, smelling of blood, oil and rancid sweat. On creaking benches, Maghernus and his dockers, along with Asavan Tortellius recruited to their cause, sat and waited for Andrej to get them all the way down the Hel's Highway.

He was not a good driver. They had mentioned this to him, and he professed not to know what they were talking about. Besides, he'd added, the left tank tread was damaged. That was why he kept skidding.

Also, he'd amended last of all, they should shut up. So there.

Andrej cycled through vox-channels, still getting no luck on any frequency. Whether every vox-tower in the city was gone or the orks had some intense jamming campaign going on was beside the point at this stage. He couldn't get in touch with his commanders, and that left him to his own devices. As always, he would *go forward*. It was the way of the Legion, and the creed of the Guard.

The way he saw it, the Reclusiarch owed him a favour. In this case, *going forward* meant making a stand with the black knights until he could find someone, anyone, from his command structure.

There'd been a particularly galling moment when he'd managed to contact elements of the 233rd Steel Legion Armoured Division, but they were in the middle of being annihilated by an enemy scrap-Titan formation and had no time for pleasantries. Fate was laughing at him, Andrej was sure of it – the one Imperial force he'd been able to reach were minutes from being wiped out anyway.

This was no way to fight a war. No communication between any forces? Madness!

Smoke and flames were on the horizon ahead, but that indicated next to nothing of any use in determining direction or destination. Smoke and flames were on every horizon. Smoke and flame was all each of the horizons had become.

Andrej was not laughing. This did not amuse him, no sir.

He changed gear with a nauseating grind of metal hating metal. A chorus of complaints jeered from the back as the Chimera juddered in protest and shook his passengers around some more. He heard someone's head clang off the interior wall. He hoped it was the fat priest's.

Andrej sniggered. At least that was funny.

'...ckr... sn... tl...' declared the vox.

Aha! Now this was progress.

'This is Trooper Andrej, of the–'

He closed his mouth as the transmission crackled into a semblance of clarity. The burning district ahead, through which he'd need to pass to reach the distant temple... It was the Rostorik Ironworks. The vox told of a Titan's death-wails.

'Hold on,' he called back, and accelerated the battered transport along the Hel's Highway, towards the emerging shape of *Stormherald* above the surrounding industrial towers.

THE LINK WAS savaged by *Bound in Blood*'s mortis-cry. Zarha twisted in her coffin, trying to filter the empathic pain from the influx of sensory information she needed to focus on.

Her fistless arm pushed forward in the milky fluid, and the Titan obeyed her furious need.

'Firing,' Valian Carsomir confirmed.

In the centre of the industrial sector, ringed by burning towers and crushed manufactories, the Imperator Titan weathered a hail of enemy fire from scrap-walkers that barely reached its waist. Its shields rippled with searing intensity, corona-bright and almost blinding.

The plasma annihilator amassed power, sucking in a storm of air through its coolant vanes and juddering as it made ready to release. Around the god-machine's legs, the waddling ork walkers blared sirens and howling warnings to one another. Burning vapour clouded around the shaking plasma weapon as it vented pressure, and with a roar that shattered every remaining window in a kilometre-wide radius, *Stormherald* fired.

Three of the lesser scrap-Titans were engulfed in the flood of boiling plasma that surged from the weapon, melting to sludge in the white-hot sunfire.

Zarha's arm was aflame with sympathetic agony. She did her best to blank it from her mind, focusing instead on the rattling crawl of insects over her body. Her shields were taking grave damage now. *Stormherald* could not linger here for much longer.

'*Bound in Blood* isn't rising, my princeps.'

Zarha knew this. She'd heard its soul scream across the Legio's princeps-level link.

He is dying.

'**He is dying.**'

'Orders, my princeps?'

Stand. Fight.

'**Stand. Fight.**'

The Titan shuddered as another wreck-walker staggered closer, its shoulder cannons booming. Standing above the downed Reaver-class Titan *Bound in Blood*, *Stormherald* returned fire with its incidental weapon batteries, flash-frying the lesser machine's void shields in a hail of incendiary fire.

Zarha pushed her other arm forward through the ooze, laughing as she moved. *Stormherald*'s other arm, the colossal hellstorm cannon, thrummed as its internal mechanics chambers and drive engines cycled up to firing speed.

'My princeps...' Lonn and Carsomir warned in the same breath. Zarha cackled in her tomb of fluid.

Die!

'Die!'

The enemy scrap-Titan was shredded by five energy lances blasting from *Stormherald*'s hellstorm cannon. In less than three seconds, its plasma core was breached and critically venting, and in less than five it had exploded, taking the bulk of the fat-bodied gargant with it. Shrapnel shards the size of tanks hammered off the Imperator's void shields, leaving distortions of bruising while the generators struggled to compensate.

'Secondary impact from the turbolaser batteries... Cog's teeth, we struck the G-71 orbital landing platform. My princeps, I implore you to use caution...'

Engine kill. She licked her cold, wrinkled lips. *Engine kill.*

'Engine kill.'

Half a kilometre behind the dead enemy walker – its foundation struts destroyed by the laser salvo from *Stormherald*'s hellstorm cannon – a sizeable landing platform crashed down to the ground, sliding on fouled gantries to smash through the roof of a burning tank manufactorum. An avalanche of rockcrete, broken iron and steel was all that remained of both installations, at the heart of a cloud of grey-black smoke and rock dust.

The ironyard had played host to the pitched battle between Titans and infantry for several days. Little was left, yet neither side was giving ground.

'My princeps...'

No more lectures. I do not care.

'No more lectures. I do not care.'

'My princeps,' Valian repeated, 'new contact. Behind us.'

She spun in the fluid, fish-like and alert. *Stormherald* followed with ponderous slowness, its fortress-legs thudding down onto the ground. The cityscape view through the Titan's eyes panned, showing nothing but devastation.

'The scanner blur is either several walkers together, or a single engine of our size.'

The adept hunched by the auspex console turned to regard the pilot crew with three bionic eyes, each with a lens of dark green glass. A blurt of machine-code disagreed with Lonn's appraisal.

[]Negative. Thermal signature registers distinct single pulse.[]

One enemy engine.

That isn't possible, she thought, but never let it reach her vocalisers. An uneasy tremor was running through the Titan's bones, and she felt it as keenly as she'd once felt the wind on her skin in another lifetime.

'My princeps, we must disengage,' Lonn said, staring out into the burning ironyard. 'We need to rearm and cool the plasma core in standard sustained venting procedure.'

I know that better than you, Lonn.

'I know that better than you, Lonn.'

But I am not abandoning a district I have spent four nights fighting to hold.

'But I am not abandoning a district I have spent four nights fighting to hold.'

'My princeps, there's precious little left standing to defend,' Lonn pressed. 'I repeat my recommendation to withdraw and rearm.'

No. I am sending Regal *and* Ivory Fang *north to hunt the inbound enemy engine and confirm with visual scanning.*

'No. I am sending Regal **and** Ivory Fang **north to hunt the inbound enemy engine and confirm with visual scanning.'**

Lonn and Carsomir shared a glance from across the command deck. Both men were restrained in their control thrones, and both men wore the same expression of frustrated doubt.

'My princeps,' Carsomir tried, but he was cut off.

'See? They move.' On the hololithic display screen, the runes denoting the scout Titans *Regal* and *Ivory Fang* broke away from their perimeter-stalking patrol to the west, and strode northwards in search of the incoming thermal pulse.

'My princeps, we do not have the ammunition reserves required to inflict destruction-level damage on an enemy engine of comparable size to us.'

'I am venting the heart-core's excess fusion matter and flushing the heat exchangers.' Even as she vocalised the orders, she was sending empathic pulses through her links to make it so.

'My princeps, that is not enough.'

'He is right, my princeps,' Carsomir had turned in his throne, and was looking back at her fluid tank now. 'You are too close to *Stormherald*'s wrath. Return to us and focus.'

'We are defended by three Reavers and our own scout screen. Be silent.'

'Two Reavers, my princeps.'

Yes. Two. She pulled back from the immersion of rage.

Yes… two. *Bound in Blood* was silent and dead, its power core cooling and its princeps voiceless. In her confused thinking, she did not mean to vocalise her next words.

'We have lost seven engines in one week of battle.'

'Yes, my princeps. Prudence would serve us best now. If the auspex is true, we must withdraw.'

She floated in her coffin, hearing the curious humanity in their voices. Such emotion. Such curious intensity, affecting their speech tones. She recognised it as fear, without truly recalling what the sensation felt like.

'We have killed almost twenty of the foe's engines… but I concede. Sound the withdrawal as soon as the War-hounds have confirmation.'

THE FIRST IMPERIAL engine to bear witness to the *Godbreaker* was *Ivory Fang*. It stalked fast and low on its backwards-jointed legs, the side-to-side pitch of its stomping gait adding a feral, if mechanical, grace to its dawn hunt.

Warhound-class. And it suited the name, lone wolfing its way through the wrecked industrial sector, striding around the shells of tanks destroyed in the week-long struggle for the Rostorik Ironyard. Sometimes, its hooved feet would crunch down on the soft meat of burned bodies and render them into pulped smears along the ground. Dead skitarii, Guardsmen, factorum workers and greenskins littered the district.

Ivory Fang was commanded most ably by a princeps by the name of Haven Havelock. Princeps Havelock dreamed, as did most of his ilk, of one day mastering a great battle-Titan, and perhaps even one of Invigilata's precious few Imperators. His fellow princeps – equals and superiors alike – spoke well of him, and he knew his place in the Legio as a solid, reliable scout-Titan commander was assured, valued, and deserved.

Patience was foremost among his virtues – patience and cunning. That reasoned, meticulous hunting instinct bled through the mind-bond into *Ivory Fang*. Twinned, man and machine were past masters at the kind of deep-urban stalks where Warhound Titans most excelled.

The rough link between Titan commanders maintained throughout the city had suffered just as Imperial vox had suffered, but Havelock was reassured by the fragments of meaning that pulsed through the chaos. If there truly was an enemy scrap-Titan out there, it was nothing the battle group could not deal with. *Stormherald* was no more than two kilometres to the south, and with it were *Danol's Retribution* and *The Ghoul*, both Reavers with victory banners descending from their armour plating that would put mid-range Titan princeps from any other Legio to shame.

Nothing the beasts could hurl at them would break such a formation. Even the largest gargant would fall to *Stormherald*.

I see nothing, came the aggravated spurt of machine code from his fellow princeps, Feerna of *Regal*.

Havelock spent a quarter of a second consulting his internal tracking runes. The link to his Titan's auspex sensors formed a rough, instinctive knowledge of his kin's locations in his mind.

Regal was a half-kilometre to the north-east, moving at speed through a small cluster of iron smelteries. It would have been in visual range, had the space between the two Titans not been obstructed by ruined manufactories.

I see nothing, either.

It's the heat, she complained. *Hunting for thermal signatures*

*in this inferno is like seeking black in the night sky. My aus-
pex readers show nothing but thermal disruption. Horus himself
could be hiding in here, and I would not kn–*

Feerna? Feerna?

'Registering energy discharge of significant size to the
north-east,' Havelock's moderati called out.

'Confirmed,' murmured the tech-adept that hunched in
a station behind the princeps throne.

Feerna? Havelock tried once more. 'Bring us about and
move north-east at aggressive intent speed. Everyone be
ready.' He twitched in his restraint throne as the Titan
obeyed its pilot's urgings. The connection feeds were alive
with subtle static, itching at his nerves. *Ivory Fang* was keen.
It had sensed something.

And then it hit Havelock, too.

'Hnnngh,' he drooled through clenched teeth, shuddering
against the leather bindings that restrained him in place.
'Hnn… Hvv…'

The pain of *Regal's* mortis-cry faded, and Havelock breathed
again. Feerna was gone, as was her Titan. She'd been a Warhound, and her link to the others was tenuous and weak
in comparison to the strength of a bond to the greater god-
machines. The pain bled away fast, bringing relief in its wake.

The Titan clanked its way down a subsidiary alley, its
weapon-arms rising in readiness. Havelock sent several
mental urgings in quick succession, triggering autoloaders,
coolant valves and bracing pistons into activity. *Ivory Fang*
rounded the corner at the alley's end, stalking out into the
main street. As it had been since this morning, this sector was still aflame because of the destroyed refineries and
petrochemical stores, with about half the buildings finally
quieting into smouldering ruins.

But the fighting was done here.

'Where is the bastard?' Havelock whispered.

The auspex chimed – once, weak.

'We have movement,' the tech-adept grumbled, not looking up from his scanner console. 'There is–'

'I see, it, I see it. Back away *now!*'

It came from the black clouds, rumbling forward on a clumsy mess of tank treads and crushing feet. Its body was slanted, tapering to a head that was all brutal jaw and piggish, alien eye-windows. Every metre of its scrap metal torso bristled with tiered weapons platforms.

It was quite the ugliest and most offensive thing Havelock had ever seen, and that was more than simply because it was an affront to the purity of Mechanicus god-machine creation. No, more than that, it offended him because its manifestation before him made no sense. It... dwarfed *Stormherald*.

It seemed impossibility given form, striding, limping from the oily smoke that blanketed the district.

Havelock pulsed a digitally-translated pict of the enemy gargant across the mind-bond to Princeps Zarha and any other Titan commander in range. It was all the warning he would be allowed to send, for *Godbreaker* opened fire the very moment its main armaments cleared the smoke.

Ivory Fang was pulverised beneath enough solid, laser and plasma weapon fire to level a city block. Its demise, and the end of Havelock's mediocre career, was marked by a vast crater that would remain for decades after the war had bled the whole world almost dry.

Godbreaker moved onwards.

CHAPTER XXI
STORMHERALD DOWN

THE TWO ENGINES faced one another across the burning iro-nyard, as alike in power as they were unlike in dignity. Both were ablaze, both bleeding fire and smoke into the clouded air.

The air between them was a blizzard of weapon fire as secondary turrets and battlement guns spat anti-infantry firepower at each other in the hopes of inflicting as much damage as possible. Inside both Titans, it sounded like a flood of pebbles clattering against the armour-plated hulls.

Inside *Stormherald*, the sirens were wailing long and loud.

Zarha writhed in her fluid-filled tomb, her limbs pushing through the blood-pinked water. Psychostigmata was ravaging her, as *Stormherald*'s wounds played out in a map across her naked body. Where the Titan was battered, she was discoloured by bruising or bent by broken bones. Where the god-machine was rent and torn, her flesh smiled and bled in open wounds. Where *Stormherald* burned, she was haemorrhaging internally.

The Titan's command deck smelled of burning oil and rancid sweat.

'Primary shield layer restored,' Carsomir announced, his hands working at his console with a near-furious focus. 'Core containment holding.'

Raise… raise shields…

'Krrrsssshhhhh.'

RAISE THE SHIELDS.

'**Raise the shields.**'

'Already done, my princeps.'

She was slowing down. The pain stole so much of her attention now. With a moan that was swallowed into silence by the water, she pulsed orders to the various decks and pushed both of her arms forward through the pinkish ooze.

Nothing happened.

She tried again, screaming into the oxygen-rich fluid, the stumps of her hands thumping against the front of her coffin.

Nothing.

'Plasma annihilator venting for sixteen more seconds, my princeps. Fourteen. Thirteen. Twelve.'

Fire the… the… other arm. Fire it.

'**Krrrssssssshh.**'

FIRE THE HELLSTORM CANNON. Her stunted right limb thudded over and over against the glass side of her amniotic tank.

'**Fire the hellstorm cannon.**'

'As soon as it has recharged, my princeps,' Lonn replied, half-ignoring her now. She'd given the order to fire at will several minutes before. Drifting in her pain as the Titan fell to pieces, she was barely trustworthy now. Carsomir and Lonn worked almost independently of their princeps's wishes. They only had one more shot at walking away from this – the enemy Titan was already advancing over the mangled body of *The Ghoul*, which had lasted less than a minute beneath the *Godbreaker*'s initial volleys.

The scrap-Titan was capable of a merciless amount of firepower. None of *Stormherald*'s command crew had seen anything like it before, let alone suffered on the receiving end. Only a few minutes into the god-machines' duel, and the Imperator was wreathed in flame, temperature gauges whining and warning lights flashing throughout the confined corridors threading through the giant's steel bones.

The multitude of layered energy screens that served the Titan as void shields had been torn apart with insane, laughable speed by the ork walker.

'I'm ready,' Carsomir announced. 'Firing.'

'Wait for the stabilisers to come back online!' Lonn yelled. 'They only need another minute.'

Carsomir thought his fellow pilot's faith in the tech-crews working in the shoulder joints was admirable, but unbelievably misguided given the circumstances. He blinked once, wasting precious seconds to even think about listening to Lonn's plea.

'The arm isn't badly damaged. I'm taking the shot. I can make it.'

'You'll miss, Val! Give them thirty seconds, just thirty more seconds.'

'Firing.'

'You son of a bitch!'

Stormherald's knees locked in preparation and the plasma

annihilator tower that served as its left arm began its air-sucking inhalation of coolant.

'You've killed us,' Lonn breathed, watching the enemy Titan through the steamed-up view windows. An unremitting torrent of incidental fire rained against *Stormherald's* shields, turning them violet with strain.

'Void shields buckling,' one of the tech-adepts called from a side terminal.

'Enemy engine making ready to fire primary weapons,' another said.

'They'll never get the chance…' Valian Carsomir smiled with a wicked light in his eyes.

Lonn's shouted protest was drowned out in the roar of discharging sunfire. A beam of plasma – roiling, boiling and white-hot – vomited from the cannon's focusing ring, blasting across the four hundred metres separating the two Titans. *Stormherald* stood rigid, defensive, no longer advancing after the first two minutes of punishing exchange. *Godbreaker* had not stopped its thunderous, slow charge.

'You bastard!' Lonn yelled. Carsomir had missed. The jet of plasma blanketed the ground to the left of the closing ork gargant, where it began to dissolve everything it touched in a vast pool of acidic corruption.

Lonn had been right. The arm-weapon had strayed despite targeting locks, as the supreme force of its own firepower sent it veering off-centre.

'I had the shot,' Carsomir shook his head.

'Void shields failing,' the tech-adept announced without any emotion whatsoever.

'I had the shot,' Carsomir repeated, unable to look away from the wreck-Titan bearing down upon them. Behind the moderati thrones, Zarha floated in her suspension tank, slack and unconscious.

'No, no, no…' Lonn worked at his console, his brow furrowed. 'This can't be.'

The Titan began to shudder around them as the void shields died again, the Imperator's dense armour taking the brunt of the alien attack.

Lonn had never worked like this before in his life. It was a flurry of effort, performed half in the flesh and half with the mind. He could feel the Titan falling into slumber, and its dimming consciousness dragged at his thoughts, slowing them to a crawl. Where he met resistance like this in the mind-link, he compensated by overrides on his command console.

The command deck grew dark as he worked. The enemy gargant eclipsed all outside light, looming before the idle *Stormherald*.

'Why hasn't it fired?' Carsomir worked as Lonn did, cooling essential systems, ordering repair teams to afflicted joints, feeding power from the coughing shield generators to the thirsty weapon energy cells.

To Lonn, the reason was obvious. Like the savages that acted as the gargant's puppeteers, the scrap-Titan was built to kill with its hands. Several of the thing's weapon mounts were taken up by crude arms that ended in spears and claws of salvaged metal. It wanted to savour *Stormherald*'s death, like some many-armed daemon from the impure millennia of pre-Imperial Terra.

Zarha's augmetic eyes flicked back to active as the chamber grew dark. She awoke, seeing the doom bearing down on her, feeling secondary fire devastating her armour plating like she was being skinned alive.

Through the bloody fluid and maddening pain, she raised her shivering arms. *Stormherald* mirrored the gesture as it was pummelled under *Godbreaker*'s guns. Jagged metal fell from the Mechanicus giant like rainfall, ripped from its body and crashing to the ground below. Many of the Imperator's crew that had the sense of self-preservation to flee were killed by the falling chunks of armour plating.

Zarha put the last of her strength, and the last of her life, into throwing both her arms forward. The plasma annihilator did not fire. Neither did the hellstorm cannon. Both were locked in the time-consuming process of recharging from depleted power generators.

Both towering weapon-arms speared forward, hammering through the fat hull of *Godbreaker* and impaling it in place. The cry of tearing scrap metal was cacophonous as *Stormherald*'s cannons pushed deeper, stabbing like daggers through meat, seeking to grind and crush the enemy's heart-reactor.

Grimaldus. I stood until the end, as promised. Awaken Oberon. *Awaken it, or die as we have.*

Perhaps her thoughts echoed across the empathic link to her moderati, for one of them voiced something of her sentiments.

'We're dead,' Carsomir murmured. He wanted to rise from his throne, but the restraints and connection cables bound him too completely. He settled for closing his eyes.

Lonn had sensed the Crone's intent. He leaned all his weight on the control levers, adding his demands to Zarha's, plunging the arms deeper into the enemy Titan's chest with scraping, grinding slowness. He felt sick to stare up through the darkened viewports to see the bestial, tusked aliens clambering along the impaling arm-cannons, using them as bridges to board *Stormherald* as they bled from the wounds in their own Titan's body.

With no peaceful fade or foreshadowing, the power died, leaving him in darkness. He eased up on the levers, knowing without needing to look that the Crone was gone.

Stormherald was a statue, joined to the war machine that was slowly carving it to pieces with great chops of its bladed limbs. As endings went, Lonn mused, this was neither grand nor glorious.

As the command deck shook with rhythmic violence from the *pound, pound, pounding* of *Godbreaker*'s many weapon-arms, Lonn drew his laspistol, and watched the sealed doors, ready for the aliens to eventually breach them. His skin crawled at the gentle sound of Zarha's corpse bumping against the glass front of her coffin, in time to the Titan's shaking.

'I... I had the shot,' Carsomir stammered from the adjacent throne as he waited to die in the dark. 'I had the shot...'

The side of his head burst open as a las-beam slashed through his skull.

'You bastard,' Lonn said to the twitching body. Then he lowered his pistol, took a deep breath, and began the laborious process of disengaging himself from the control throne.

THERE WAS SOMETHING human in the way *Stormherald* died. The way it went slack, the way it staggered, the way it crashed to the ground, its heart-core cold, swarming with enemy bodies like insects feeding upon a corpse.

The god-machine shook the earth when it finally toppled. The spined, spiked cathedral tumbled from its back in a spillage of priceless architecture, left as no more than rubble and scraps of armour plating in a mountain of wreckage by the Titan's head. *Stormherald*'s arms were wrenched from the torso, squealing free of the ruptured shoulder joints when the ancient engine hammered into the ground with enough force to send tremors through the entire city.

The head itself was torn free before the main body fell, leaving a socket of trailing power cables and interface feeds, like a nest of a million snakes. Gripped in the lifter-claw at the end of one of *Godbreaker*'s many arms, the Titan's head was clamped and crushed, then hurled aside as a twisted ball of scrap metal. Its landing flattened a small manufactorum, as the armoured command chamber weighing several dozen tonnes blasted through the building's side wall and pulverised several support pillars.

On board *Godbreaker*, the bestial creature in charge ranted at its subordinates for destroying and discarding the Titan's head in such a way. To the beast's mind, it would have made a very impressive trophy to mount on their own god-machine.

The few Legio crew members, skitarii defenders and tech-adepts that survived *Stormherald*'s fall scrabbled from exits and breaks in the behemoth's skin. In the midday light of Armageddon's weak sun, they were cut down by the ork reavers around the dead Titan.

Miraculously, Moderati Secundus Lonn was one of these. He had managed to break free of the bindings and interface cables linking him to the dying god-machine, and make it out of the bridge by the time *Godbreaker* decapitated *Stormherald*. In the following fall, he broke his leg in two places, earned a concussion as the tilting corridor sent him falling down a flight of spiral stairs, and busted several of his teeth clear out of his gums when his head smacked off a handrail.

On hands and knees, dragging his dead leg and half drunk with concussion, Lonn hauled himself out of an emergency bulkhead to lie on the warm armour plating of *Stormherald*'s torso. There he remained, panting and bleeding in the thin sunlight for several seconds, before starting to crawl his slow way down to the ground. He was killed less than a minute later by the marauding greenskins swarming over the downed Titan.

Through the pain, he was laughing as he died.

GRIMALDUS CAME AT last to the inner sanctum.

He was no longer a warrior here, but a pilgrim. Of this he was certain, though in the wake of his words with Nero, he felt certain of little else.

It had taken very little time within the Temple of the Emperor Ascendant to bring about this certainty within him, but the feeling was undeniable. He felt home, on familiar and sacred ground, for the first time since he had left the *Eternal Crusader*.

It was purifying.

The cool air didn't taste of fire and blood on a world he had no wish to walk upon. The silence wasn't broken by the drumbeat of a war he had no stake in.

Augmented infants – the lobotomised bodies of children kept eternally young through gene manipulation and hormone control – were enhanced by simple Mechanicus organs and pressed into service as winged cherub-servitors, hovering on anti-grav fields as they trailed prayer banners through the halls and arched chambers.

In the myriad rooms of the basilica, the devoted and the faithful of Helsreach went about their daily reverence despite the war blackening their city. Grimaldus walked through a chamber of monks offering prayer through inscribing hundreds of saints' names on thin parchments that would hang from the weapons of temple guards. One of the holy men kneeled as the Adeptus Astartes passed, imploring the 'Angel of Death' to wear the parchment on his armour. Touched by the man's devotion, the knight had accepted, and voxed an order to the rest of his men scattered throughout the temple grounds to acquiesce to any similar charity.

Grimaldus let the lay brother tie the scroll to his pauldron with twine. The offered parchment was a modest but appreciated replacement for the iconography, oathpapers and heraldry that had been scoured from his armour in the last five weeks of battle.

The Reclusiarch had ventured alone into the undercroft, wishing to bear witness to the civilians there in his patrol to examine all defences and locations within the basilica. The subterranean expanse might once have been austere and solemn, featuring little more than infrequently-spaced sarcophagi of black stone. To the knight's eyes, it was a refugee bunker, packed tight with humans that smelled both unwashed and afraid as they sat around in family clusters – some asleep; some speaking quietly; some comforting crying babies; some spreading out meagre possessions on dirty blankets, taking stock of everything they now owned in the world, which was all they had managed to carry with them as they'd fled their homes.

Wordlessly, he'd walked among them. Every one of them had moved from his path; every one of them so openly awed by their first sighting of an Adeptus Astartes warrior. Parents whispered to children, and children whispered more questions back.

'Hello,' a voice called from behind him as he was moving

back up the wide marble stairs. The Reclusiarch turned. A girl-child stood at the bottom of the staircase, clad in an oversized shirt that clearly belonged to a parent or older sibling. Her ratty blonde hair was so dirty that it snarled quite naturally into accidental dreadlocks.

Grimaldus descended again, ignoring the girl's parents hissing at her, calling her back. She was no older than seven or eight. She stood up straight, and reached his knee.

'Hail,' he said to her. The crowd flinched back from the vox-voice, and several of those closest gasped in a breath.

The girl blinked. 'Father says you are a hero. Are you a hero?'

Grimaldus's gaze flicked across the crowd. His targeting cursor danced from face to face, seeking her parents.

Nothing in two centuries of war had prepared him to answer this question. The gathered refugees looked on in silence.

'There are many heroes here,' the Chaplain replied.

'You are very loud,' the girl complained.

'I am more used to shouting,' the knight lowered his voice. 'Do you require something from me?'

'Will you save us?'

He looked at the crowd again, and chose his words with great care.

THAT HAD BEEN an hour ago. The Reclusiarch stood with his closest brothers and the Emperor's Champion in the basilica's inner sanctum.

The chamber was expansive, easily able to accommodate a thousand worshippers at once. For now, it stood bare, the hundreds of Steel Legionnaires that were bunking here in recent weeks currently out on their patrols through the graveyard and surrounding temple district.

The few dozen that had been off-duty were ushered out by monks when the Adeptus Astartes had entered. Almost immediately, the knights were joined by a new presence. An irritated presence, at that.

'Well, well, well,' the irritated presence said in her old woman's voice. 'The Emperor's Chosen, come to stand with us at last.'

The knights turned in the sunlit chamber, back to the entrance where a diminutive figure stood in contoured power armour. A bolter, cased in bronze with gold-leaf etchings, was mag-locked between her shoulders. The gun was a smaller calibre than Adeptus Astartes weaponry, but still a rare firearm to see in the possession of a human.

Her white power armour was bedecked in trappings that marked her rank in the Holy Order of the Argent Shroud. The old woman's white hair was cut severely at her chin, framing a wrinkled face with icy eyes.

'Hail, prioress,' Bayard acknowledged her with a bow, as did the others. Grimaldus and Priamus made no obeisance, with the swordsman remaining unmoving and Grimaldus instead making the sign of the aquila.

'I am Prioress Sindal, and in the name of Saint Silvana, I bid you welcome to the Temple of the Emperor Ascendant.'

Grimaldus stepped forward. 'Reclusiarch Grimaldus of the Black Templars. I cannot help but notice that you do not sound welcoming.'

'Should I be? Half of the Temple District has already fallen in the last week. Where were you then, hmm?'

Priamus laughed. 'We were at the docks, you ungrateful little harpy.'

'Be at ease,' Grimaldus warned. Priamus replied with a vox-click of acknowledgement.

'We were, as my brother Priamus explained, engaged in the east of the hive. But we are here now, when the war is at its darkest, as the enemy approach the temple doors.'

'I have fought with Adeptus Astartes before,' the prioress said, her armoured arms crossed over the fleur-de-lys symbol that marked her sculpted breastplate. 'I have fought alongside warriors who would have given their lives for the Imperium's ideals, and warriors that cared only for accruing glory, as if they could wear their honour like armour. Both breeds were Adeptus Astartes.'

'We are not here to be lectured on the state of our souls,' Grimaldus tried to keep the irritation from his voice.

'Whether you are or not doesn't matter, Reclusiarch. Will you dismiss your fellow warriors from the chamber, please? There is much to speak of.'

'We can speak of the temple's defence in front of my brothers.'

'Indeed we can, and when the time comes to speak of such things, they will be present. For now, please dismiss them.'

'Did you cleanse yourself, by the Stoup of Elucidation?'

This is the question she asks in the silence that descends once my brothers are gone, and the doors are closed.

The stoup she speaks of is a huge bowl of black iron, mounted upon a low pedestal of what looks like wrought gold. It stands by the double doors, which are themselves bedecked in imagery of warlike angels with toothed swords, and saints bearing bolters.

I confess to her that I did not.

'Come then.' She beckons me to the bowl. The water within reflects the painted ceiling and the stained glass windows above – a riot of colour in a liquid mirror.

She dips a bare finger into the water after taking the time to detach and remove her gauntlets. 'This water is thrice-blessed,' she says, tracing her dripping fingertip across her forehead in a crescent moon. 'It brings clarity of purpose, when anointed onto the doubting and the lost.'

'I am not lost,' I lie, and she smiles at the words.

'I did not mean to imply that you were, Reclusiarch. But many who come here are.'

'Why did you wish to speak with me alone? Time is short. The war will reach these walls in a matter of days. Preparations must be made.'

She speaks, staring down into the perfect reflection offered by the bowl. 'This basilica is a bastion. A castle. We can defend it for weeks, when the enemy finally gathers courage enough to besiege it.'

'*Answer the question.*' This time, I could not keep the irritation from my voice even if I had wished to.

'Because you are not like your brothers.'

I know that when she looks at my face, she does not see me. She sees the death mask of the Emperor, the skull helm of an Adeptus Astartes Reclusiarch, the crimson eye lenses of humanity's chosen. And yet our gazes meet in the water's reflection, and I cannot completely fight the feeling she is seeing *me*, beneath the mask and the masquerade.

What does she mean by those words? That she senses my doubts? That they drip from me like nervous sweat, visible and stinking to all who stand near me?

'I am no different from them.'

'Of course you are. You are a Chaplain, are you not? A Reclusiarch. A keeper of your Chapter's lore, soul, traditions and purity.'

My heart rate slows again. My rank. That is all she meant.

'I see.'

'I am given to understand Adeptus Astartes Chaplains are invested with their authority by the Ecclesiarchy?'

Ah. She seeks common ground. Good luck to her in this doomed endeavour. She is a warrior of the Imperial Creed, and an officer in the Church of the God-Emperor.

I am not.

'The Ecclesiarchy of Terra supports our ancient rites, and the authority of every Chapter's Reclusiam to train warrior-priests to guide the souls of its battle-brothers. They do not invest us with power. They recognise we already hold it.'

'And you are given a gift by the Ecclesiarchy? A rosarius?'

'Yes.'

'May I see yours?'

The few Adeptus Astartes singled out for ascension into the Reclusiam are gifted with a rosarius medallion upon succeeding in the first trials of Chaplainhood. My talisman was beaten bronze and red iron, shaped into a heraldic cross.

'I no longer carry one.'

She looks up at me, as if the reflection of my skull visage was no longer clear enough for her purposes.

'Why is that?'

'It was lost. Destroyed in battle.'

'Is that not a dark omen?'

'I am still alive three years after its destruction. I still do the Emperor's work, and still follow the word of Dorn even after its loss. The omen cannot be that dark.'

She looks at me for some time. I am used to humans staring at me in awkward silence; used to their attempts to watch without betraying that they are watching. But this direct stare is something else, and it takes a moment to realise why.

'You are judging me.'

'Yes, I am. Remove your helm, please.'

'Tell me why I should.' My voice is not pitched to petulance, merely curiosity. I had not expected her to ask such a thing.

'Because I would like to look upon the face of the man I am speaking with, and because I wish to anoint you with the Waters of Elucidation.'

I could refuse. Of course I could refuse.

But I do not.

'A moment, please.' I disengage my helm's seals, and breathe in my first taste of the crisp, cool air within the temple. The fresh water before me. The sweat of the refugees. The scorched ceramite of my armour.

'You have beautiful eyes,' she tells me. 'Innocent, but cautious. The eyes of a child, or a new father. Seeing the world around you as if for the first time. Kneel, if you would? I cannot reach all the way up there.'

I do not kneel. She is not my liege lord, and to abase myself in such a way would violate all decorum. Instead, I lower my head, bringing my face closer to her. The joints of her pristine armour give the smooth purr of clean mechanics as she reaches up. I feel her fingertip draw a cross upon my forehead in cold water.

'There,' she says, refastening her gauntlets. 'May you find the answers you seek in this house of the God-Emperor. You are blessed, and may tread the sacred floor of the inner sanctum without guilt.'

She is already moving away, her milky eyes squinting. 'Come. I have something to show you.'

The prioress leads me to the centre of the chamber, where a stone table holds an open book. Four columns of polished marble rise at the table's cardinal points, all the way to the ceiling. Upon one of the columns hangs a tattered banner unlike any I have ever seen before.

'Hold.'

'What is it? Ah, the first archive.' She gestures to the sheets of ragged cloth hanging from the war banner poles. Each once-white, now-grey sheet shows a list of names in faded ink.

Names, professions, husbands and wives and children…

'These are the first colonists.'

'Yes, Reclusiarch.'

'The settlers of Helsreach. The founders. This is their charter?'

'It is. From when the great hive was no more than a village by the shore of the Tempest Ocean. These are the men and women that laid the temple's first foundations.'

I let my gloved hand come close to the humming stasis field shielding the ancient cloth document. Parchment would have been a rare luxury to the first colonists, with the jungle and its trees so far from here. It stands to reason they would have recorded their achievements on cloth paper.

Thousands of years ago, Imperial peasants walked the ashen soil here and laid the first stone bones of what would become a great basilica to house the devotions of an entire city. Deeds remembered throughout the millennia, with their evidence for all to see.

'You seem pensive,' she tells me.

'What is the book?'

'The log from a vessel called the *Truth's Tenacity*. It was the colonisation seeding ship that brought the settlers to Helsreach. The four pillars house a void shield generator system, protecting the tome. This is the Major Altar. Sermons are given here, among the city's most precious relics.'

I look at the tome's curled, age-browned pages. Then at the archive banner once more.

Last of all, I replace my helm, coating my senses in the selective vision of targeting sights and filtered sounds.

'You have my thanks, prioress. I appreciate what you have shown me here.'

'Am I to expect any more of your kind arriving to bolster us, Adeptus Astartes?'

I think, for a moment, of Jurisian, bringing the Ordinatus Armageddon overland, uncrewed, at minimal power and of little to no use once it arrives.

'One more. He returns to join us and fight by our sides.'

'Then I bid you welcome to the Temple of the Emperor Ascendant, Reclusiarch. How do you plan to defend this holy place?'

'We are past the point of retreat now, Sindal. No finesse, no tactics, no long speeches to rally the faint of heart and those that fear the end. I plan to kill until I am killed, because that is all that remains for us here.'

BOTH THE RECLUSIARCH and the prioress turned at the pounding upon the door.

Grimaldus blink-clicked the rune to bring his vox channels live again, but it wasn't any of his brothers seeking his attention.

Prioress Sindal waved her hand in a magnanimous gesture, as if there were a crowd to impress. 'Do come in.'

The great metal-wrought doors rumbled open on clean but heavy hinges. Eight men stood framed by the doors and the austere corridor beyond. Each of them bore a filthy share of blood, mud, soot and oil stains. They carried las-guns with the practiced ease of men who had become utterly familiar with the weapons, and all but two of them wore dirty blue dockworkers' overalls. One of those that did not was dressed in the robes of a priest, but not the cream and blue weave of the temple's own residents. He was from off-world.

The leader of the group raised his goggles, letting them clack back on the top of his helmet. He regarded the knight with wide eyes.

'They said you would be here,' the storm trooper said. 'I beg the many forgivings of this holy place for my intrusion, but I bring news, yes? Do not be angry. The vox is still playing many unamusing games and I could not speak with anyone in any other way.'

'Speak, Legionnaire,' said Grimaldus.

'The beasts, they are coming in great force. Many are not far behind us, and I have heard vox-chatter that Invigilata is leaving the city.'

'Why would they leave us?' the prioress asked, horrified.

'They would quit the city at once,' Grimaldus admitted, 'if Princeps Zarha was gone. Mechanicus politics.'

'She is gone, Reclusiarch,' Andrej finished. 'An hour ago, we saw *Stormherald* die.'

Behind the Guardsman, a warrior-maiden in the white power armour of the Order of the Argent Shroud caught her breath, staring at the prioress with her features flushed.

'Prioress!'

'Take a breath, Sister Maralin.'

'We've received word from the 101st Steel Legion! Invigilata's Titans are abandoning Helsreach!'

Andrej looked at the newcomer as if she had announced

that gravity was a myth. He shook his head slowly, a deep and solemn pity written across his face.

'You are late, little girl.'

THE FIRST WAVE to break against the walls was not a horde of the enemy.

Close-range vox detected them first, with reports of elements from three Steel Legion regiments engaged in panicked retreat. Grimaldus responded with the temple's vox-systems, boosted far beyond what the squad-to-squad comms systems were currently capable of.

He gave the order to any Helsreach forces receiving the message to fall back to the Temple of the Emperor Ascendant, abandoning any further struggle to hold the few remaining sectors in the Ecclesiarchy District. Several lieutenants and captains sent affirmative responses in reply, including a captain of the hive militia still leading over a hundred men.

The fleeing Imperials began to arrive less than an hour later.

GRIMALDUS STOOD WITH Bayard at the gates, looking out into the city. A dark-hulled Baneblade command tank rolled past, guided into the graveyard sector by a platoon of Guardsmen waving directions to the driver. Behind it, a cadre of Leman Russ battle tanks with various turret weapons trundled in loose formation. Mingling between the rolling armour and trailing behind were several hundred Legionnaires, ochre-clad and visibly weary. Wounded were being stretchered by their fellows in serious numbers, and there were plenty of wails and moans calling out over the grind of tank engines.

Two soldiers passed by the watching knights, bearing the writhing body of a junior officer on a cloth stretcher. The man had lost an arm and a leg, at the elbow and knee respectively. His face was a contorted mess of whatever he really looked like, his visage ruined by the pain flowing through him.

One of the stretcher-bearers nodded to Grimaldus as he passed, and muttered a respectful 'Reclusiarch.'

The Templar nodded back.

'Fought with them?' Bayard asked over the vox.

'Desert Vultures. I was with them when the first walls fell. Good men, all.'

'Very few left,' Bayard said, a strange edge to his voice.

Grimaldus turned his skulled face to the Champion. 'There will be enough. Have faith in your brothers' blades, Bayard.'

'I have faith. I am sanguine with my fate, Chaplain.'

'My rank is Reclusiarch. Use it.'

'By your will, brother, of course. But we stand vigil over the city's death with a handful of bleeding humans, Reclusiarch. I am sanguine, but I am also a realist.'

Grimaldus's vox-snarl drew stares from the soldiers passing nearby. 'Have faith in the people of this city, Champion. Such condescension is beneath you. We are the last guardians of the relics prized by the first of Armageddon's colonists. These people are fighting for more than their homes and lives. They are fighting for their ancestors' honour, on the holiest ground in the entire world. The survivors of this war across the globe will take heart from sacrifices made by the thousands destined to die here. Blood of Dorn, Bayard... the Imperium was *born* in moments such as this.'

The Emperor's Champion watched him for a long

moment, during which Grimaldus found his heart thumping faster. He was angry, and feeling the anger rise was as purgative as his time within the temple's serene halls. Bayard spoke, his voice sincere despite the crackle of vox-breakage.

'My voice was one of the few that spoke against your ascension to Mordred's rank.'

Grimaldus snorted, returning to watching the arriving forces. 'I would have said the same in your place.'

SEVENTY SOLDIERS OF the Steel Legion 101st came together in a battered convoy of Chimera transports. The ramp slammed down as the lead vehicle pulled up to a halt. A squad of Legionnaires disembarked, not a one of them free of bloodstains or bandaging.

'Leave the Chimeras outside,' Major Ryken ordered the others. Half of his face was wrapped in grubby cloth bandages, and he leaned heavily on an aide's shoulder, limping as he walked.

'Shouldn't we take them inside?' Cyria Tyro asked. She looked back over her shoulder at the tanks being abandoned.

'To hell with them,' Ryken spat blood as she led him to the two knights. 'Not enough ammunition in the turrets to make it worthwhile.'

'Grimaldus,' she said, looking up at the towering warrior.

'Hail, Adjutant Quintus Tyro. Major Ryken.'

'We got cut off from Sarren and the others. The 34th, the 101st, the 51st... They're all in the central manufactory sectors...'

'It does not matter.'

'What?'

'It does not matter,' Grimaldus repeated. 'We are defending

the last points of light in Helsreach. Fate brought you to the temple. Fate sent Sarren elsewhere.'

'Throne, there are still thousands of the bastards out there.' He spat pinkish spit again, and Tyro grunted as she took more of his weight. 'And that's not the worst of it.'

'Explain.'

'Invigilata has gone,' Tyro said. 'They left us to die. The enemy still has Titans – and there's one that you'll never believe until you look upon it with your own eyes. We saw it march from the Rostorik Ironworks, collapsing habitation towers in its wake.'

'The 34th Armoured rolled out to stop it,' Ryken winced as he spoke. His bandages were growing more stained, around what was likely an empty eye socket. 'It flattened most of them in the time it takes a desert jackal to howl at the full moon.'

A curious local expression. Grimaldus nodded, catching the meaning, but Ryken had more to add.

'*Stormherald* is down.' he said.

'I know.'

'This *Godbreaker*… It killed the Crone, and slew *Stormherald*.'

'I know.'

'You know? So where's the damn Ordinatus? We need it! Nothing else will kill that gigantic clanking… thing.'

'It is coming. Move inside and see to your wounds. If the end is coming to these walls, you will need to stand ready.'

'Oh, we'll all be ready. The bastards took my face, and that made it personal.'

As they moved away, Grimaldus heard Tyro gently teasing the major for his bravado. When they were beyond the gates but still in sight, the Reclusiarch saw the general's adjutant kiss the major on his unbandaged cheek.

'Madness,' the knight whispered.

'Reclusiarch?' Bayard asked.

'Humans,' Grimaldus replied, his voice soft. 'They are a mystery to me.'

CHAPTER XXII
EMPEROR ASCENDANT

AT LAST, VOX reports began to trickle through to the defenders gathered in the temple's graveyard district. Across Helsreach, Sarren's plan, the 'one hundred bastions of light', was in effect, with Imperial forces massing in defensive formations around the most vital parts of the city.

Contact was erratic at best, but the fact it even existed was a boost to morale. Every point of focused defence was holding well, with all divisions breaking down between storm troopers, Guard infantry, Steel Legion armour units, militia and armed civilians who chose to take to the streets rather than cower in their shelters.

The city was fighting to keep its heart beating, and the orks no longer found themselves advancing against a mobile wave of human resistance. Now the aliens were breaking against a multitude of last stands, hurling themselves against defenders that had nowhere left to run.

Fortunately for the Imperials, enemy scrap-Titans were

few in number. With recent engagements such as the Battle of the Rostorik Ironworks, the greenskins' complement of god-machines had suffered furious losses in the face of Legio Invigilata's wrath.

Even as Invigilata recalled its last remaining Titans from the city in the wake of *Stormherald*'s death, the Titans were forced to fight their way free of the orks flooding through Helsreach's unprotected streets. Although several Titans escaped through the broken walls and into the Ash Wastes beyond, the Warlord-class engine *Ironsworn* was brought down by a massed infantry assault in an ambush similar to the one that had laid *Stormherald* low all those weeks before.

The last of the Imperial Navy forces in the city had based themselves at the Azal spaceport, where they continued to mount bombing runs and offer limited air support to the tank battalions ringing the Jaega District's surface shelters. The fighting here was among the thickest and fiercest seen in the entire siege to date, and the archives which would catalogue the Third War for Armageddon came to consider many of the glorious propaganda falsehoods born here as cold fact. Many of these heroic twists of the truth were due to the writings of one Commissar Falkov, whose memoir, entitled simply *'I Was There…'*, would become standard reading for all officers of the Steel Legions in the years after the war.

Although there was absolutely no truth in the tale, Imperial records would state that acting-Commander Helius sacrificed his own life by ramming his Lightning into the heart-reactor of the enemy gargant classified as *Blood Defyla*. The truth was rather more mundane – like Barasath before him, Helius was shot down and torn to pieces shortly after disentangling from his grav-chute on the ground.

The presence of *Godbreaker* was a bane to any Imperial resolve nearby. Although the god-machine appeared a shadow of its former self, bearing a legion of wounds and missing limbs from its death-duel with *Stormherald*, with Invigilata marching away across the badlands the defenders of Helsreach had little in the way of firepower capable of retaliating against the gargant.

After laying waste to the Abraxas Foundry Complex, the mighty enemy engine adopted a random patrol of the city, engaging Imperial forces wherever it chanced upon them.

Imperial records would state that while the Siege of the Temple of the Emperor Ascendant was entering its second day, the alien war machine *Godbreaker* was destroyed on its way to finish the temple defenders once and for all.

This, at least, was perfectly true.

JURISIAN WATCHED THE mechanical giants stride from the city, stepping through its sundered walls. There were three – the first escapees of Legio Invigilata – and the Master of the Forge stared from the quiet confines of *Oberon*'s command module as the Titans left the burning city behind.

The first was a Reaver-class, a mid-range battle Titan that appeared to have sustained significant damage if the columns of smoke rising from its back were any indication. Its flanking allies were both Warhounds, their ungainly gait rocking their torsos and arm-cannons side to side, step by step across the sands.

The wastelands outside Helsreach's walls resembled nothing more than a graveyard. Thousands of dead orks lay rotting in the weak sun: killed in Barasath's initial attack runs or slaughtered in the inevitable inter-tribal battles that arose when these bestial aliens gathered.

Ruined tanks were scattered in abundance, as was the wreckage from countless propeller-driven planes, each one made out of scrap and reduced back to it. The orks' landing vessels stood abandoned, with every xenos capable of lifting an axe now waging war inside the city. The primitive creatures were here to fight and destroy, or fight and die. They cared nothing for what fate befell their vessels left in the desert. Such forethought and consideration was beyond the mental capacity of most greenskins.

Jurisian made no attempt to hide his presence. There would be little point in making the attempt, for he knew the approaching Titans would be able to read *Oberon*'s energy shadow on their powerful auspex scanners. So he waited, all systems active, as the Invigilata Titans drew near. The ground began to shiver with their closing tread, which Jurisian noted by the twisted metal and bodies across the desert floor shaking in rhythm with the god-machines.

The wounded Reaver came to a halt, its immense joints protesting that it was still forced to remain standing. It was damaged enough that a second's focus-drift might see the princeps losing control over the engine's stabilisers. It slowly aimed its remaining weapon arm at the command module, and Jurisian looked up into the yawning maw of a gatling blaster cannon.

With *Oberon*'s shields up, the Master of the Forge would have estimated the Ordinatus could tolerate several minutes of sustained assault even from a weapon as destructive as this Reaver's main armament. But *Oberon* had no shields. They were one of many secondary systems that Jurisian had lacked the time, expertise and manpower necessary to reengage.

He knew what a gatling blaster was capable of. He'd seen

them devastate regiments of tanks, and rip the faces and limbs from enemy Titans. *Oberon*'s armour plating would last no more than a handful of seconds.

The Titan stared down at him in silence, no doubt while the princeps decided how to deal with this unbelievable blasphemy. Hunchbacked and striding with arm-cannons raised in threatening salute, the two Warhounds circled the immobile Ordinatus. Their posturing amused the Forge-master. How they played at being wolves.

'Hail,' he said into a broad range of vox-channels. In truth, he was growing bored of the silence. He was far, far from intimidated.

'What blasphemy is this?' crackled the reply through the command module's internal speakers. *'What heretic dares defile* Oberon's *deserved slumber?'*

Jurisian leaned back in the control throne, elbows on the armrests and his gloved fingers steepled before his helmed face.

'I am Jurisian of the Black Templars, Master of the Forge aboard the *Eternal Crusader*, and trained by the Cult Mechanicus for years on the surface of Mars itself. I am also in possession of the Ordinatus Armageddon, after subduing its defences and reawakening its soul, force-binding it to my will. And, lastly, I am summoned to Helsreach to aid wherever I am able. Aid me, or stand aside.'

The delay was significant in duration, and in other circumstances, that would have made it insulting. Jurisian suspected his words were being transmitted to all nearby princeps, almost definitely summoning them to this position.

Half a kilometre away, another Reaver Titan was breaching the city walls, emerging into the Ash Wastes. The knight watched it begin its halting stride in this direction, noting that it was relatively undamaged.

'You are blaspheming against the Machine-God and its servants.'

'I am wielding a weapon of war in defence of an Imperial city. Now aid me, or stand aside.'

'Leave the Ordinatus platform, or be destroyed.'

'You are not about to open fire on this holiest of artefacts, and I am not empowered by my liege lord to comply with your demands. That brings us to a stalemate. Discuss useful terms, or I will take *Oberon* into the city unprotected, surely to be destroyed without significant Mechanicus support.'

'Your corpse will be removed from the sacred innards of the Ordinatus Armageddon, and all remnants of your presence will be eradicated from memory.'

As Jurisian drew breath to offer terms, his vox-link flickered into life. Grimaldus, at last.

'Reclusiarch. I trust the time has finally come?'

'We are embattled at the Temple of the Emperor Ascendant. How soon can you bring the weapon to us?'

The Master of the Forge looked out of the reinforced windows at the patrolling Titans, then at the city beyond, beneath a smoke-blackened sky. He knew the hive's layout from studying the hololithics before his exile into the desert.

'Two hours.'

'Status of the weapon?'

'As before. *Oberon* has no void shields, no secondary weapon systems, and suspensor lift capability is limited, hindering speed to a crawl. Alone, I can fire it no more than once every twenty minutes. I need to recharge the fuel cells manually, and regenerate flow from the plasma containment ch–'

'I will see you in two hours, Jurisian. For Dorn and the Emperor.'

'By your will, Reclusiarch.'

'Heed these last words, Forgemaster. Do not bring the weapon too close. The Temple District is naught but fire and ash, and we are surrounded on all sides. Take the shot and flee the city. Pursue Invigilata's retreating forces, and link up with the Imperial assault along the Hemlock.'

'You wish me to run?'

'I wish you to live rather than die in vain, and save a weapon precious to the Imperium.' Grimaldus broke off for a moment, and the pause was filled with the anger of distant guns. 'We will be buried here, Jurisian. There is no dishonour that your fate is elsewhere.'

'Call the primary target, Reclusiarch.'

'You will see it as you manoeuvre through the Temple District, brother. It is called the *Godbreaker*.'

FOUR TITANS SOON barred his path.

Mightiest among them – and the last to arrive – was a Warlord, its armour plating black from paint, not battle-scarring. Its weapons trained down – immense barrels aimed at the Ordinatus platform. The numerological markings along the engine's carapace marked it out as the *Bane-Sidhe*.

'I am Princeps Amasat of Invigilata, sub-commander of the Crone's forces and heir to her title in the wake of her demise. Explain this madness immediately.'

Jurisian looked at the city, and thought about his offer carefully before making it. He spoke with confidence, because he knew full well the Mechanicus had little other choice. He was going back into the city, and by the Machine-God, they were going to come with him.

THE GRAVEYARD – that immense garden of raised stone and buried bone – played home to the storm of disorder that had until recently been raging its way through the Temple District.

The enemy had breached the temple walls at dawn on the second day, only to find that the graveyard was where the real defences stood in readiness. As tanks pounded the walls down and beasts scrabbled over the rubble, thousands of Helsreach's last defenders waited behind mausoleums, gravestones, ornate tombs of city founders and shrines to treasured saints.

Burning beams of las-fire cobwebbed across the battlefield, slicing the alien beasts down in droves.

At the vanguard, a warrior clad in black and wielding a relic warhammer battled alongside a dwindling handful of his brothers. Every fall of his maul ended with the crunch of another alien life ended. His pistol, long since powered down and empty, dangled from the thick chain binding it to his wrist. Where the fighting was thickest, he wielded it like a flail, lashing it with whip-like force into bestial alien faces to shatter bone.

At his side, two swordsmen moved and spun in lethal unison. Priamus and Bayard, their bladework complementing one another's perfectly, cutting and impaling with the same techniques, the same footwork, and at times, even in the very same moments.

With no banner to raise, not even the barest scraps left, Artarion laid about left and right with two chugging chainblades, their teeth-tracks already blunted and choked with gore. Bastilan supported him, precision bolter rounds punching home in alien flesh.

Nero was always moving, never allowed to rest for even a moment's respite. He vaulted the enemy dead, bolter crashing out round after round as he blasted the beasts away from the body of another fallen brother, buying enough time to extract the gene-seed of the honoured dead.

This he did, time after time, with tears running down his pale face. The deaths did not move him; merely the feeling of dread futility that all his efforts would be in vain. Their genetic legacy might never escape this hive to be used in the creation of more Adeptus Astartes, and no Chapter could afford to bear the loss of a hundred slain warriors with easy dignity.

Around the time Jurisian was entering the city, escorted by five Titans from Legio Invigilata, the Imperial defences were straining to hold the outer limits of the graveyard. Cries of 'Fall back! Fall back to the temple!' started to spread through the scattered lines.

Assigned squads, appointed teams, random groups of men and women – all began to back away from the unending grind of the alien advance.

The Baneblade exploded, sending flaming shrapnel spinning in a hundred directions. The Imperials nearest to the tank – those that weren't thrown from their feet – started to flee in earnest.

BUT THERE IS nowhere to fall back to. Nowhere to run.

Like a lance pushed close to breaking point, our resistance is bending, the flanks being forced back behind the centre.

No. I will not die here, in this graveyard, beaten into darkness because these savages have greater numbers than we do. The enemy does not deserve such a victory.

My boots clang on the sloped armour plating as I leap
and sprint up the roof of the crippled, burning Baneblade.
In the maelstrom around the rocket-struck tank, I see the
101st Steel Legion and a gathering of dockworkers trying
to fall back in a panicked hurry, their forward ranks being
scythed down by bloodstained axes in green-knuckled fists.

Enough of this.

The beast I am seeking seeks me out in turn. Huge, towering above its lesser kin, packed with unnatural muscle
around its malformed bones and reeking of the fungal
blood that fuels its foul heart. It launches itself onto the
tank's hull, perhaps expecting some titanic duel to impress
its tribe. A champion, perhaps. A chieftain. It matters
not. The brutes' leaders rarely resist the chance to engage
Imperial commanders in full view – they are loathsomely
predictable.

There is no time for sport. My first strike is my last, hammering through its guard, shattering its crossed axes and
pounding the aquila head of my crozius into its roaring
face.

It topples from the Baneblade, all loose limbs and worthless armour, as pathetic in death as it had been in life.

I hear Priamus laughing from the tank's side, voxing it
through his helm's speakers, mocking the beasts even as
he slays them. On the other side, Artarion and Bastilan do
the same. The orks redouble their assault with twice the
fury and half the skill, and though I could reprimand my
brothers for this indignity, I do not.

My laughter joins theirs.

ASAVAN TORTELLIUS WAS serene, and that surprised him given
the shaking of the walls and the sounds of war's thunder.

This was no Titan's fortress-cathedral back, where he had learned to worship in safety. This was a temple besieged.

It had not taken long to find work to do within the basilica. He quickly came to realise that he was the only priest with experience of preaching on the battlefield. Most of the lay brothers and low-ranking Ecclesiarchy servants spent their time attending to their daily tasks in hurried nervousness, praying the war would remain outside the walls. Several others cowered in the undercroft with the refugees, doing more harm than good and failing to ease a single soul with their stuttering, sweating sermons.

Asavan descended into the sublevel, immediately marked out from the other preachers by his grimy robes and dishevelled hair. He walked among the people, offering gentle words to families as he passed. He was especially patient with the children, giving them the blessing of the God-Emperor in His aspect as the Machine-God, and saying personal prayers over individual boys and girls that seemed the most weary or withdrawn.

There was a lone guard stationed at the bottom of the stairs. She was slight of frame, both short and slender, wearing a suit of power armour that seemed too bulky to be comfortable. In her hands was a boltgun, the weapon held across her chest as she stood to attention.

Asavan moved over to her, his worn boots whispering across the dusty stone.

'Hello, sister,' he said, keeping his voice low.

She remained unmoving, at perfect attention, though he could see the tremor in her eyes that betrayed how difficult she found it to bear this rigid nothingness.

'My name is Asavan Tortellius,' he told her. 'Will you please lower the weapon?'

She looked at him, her eyes meeting his. She didn't lower the bolter.

'What is your name?' he asked her.

'Sister Maralin of the Holy Order of the Ar–'

'Hello, Maralin. Be at ease, for the enemy is still outside the walls. Might I ask you, please, to lower the weapon?'

'Why?' she leaned closer to whisper.

'Because you are making the people here even more nervous than they already are. By all means, be visible. You are their defender, and they will take comfort in your presence. But walk among them, and offer a few kind words. Do not stand there in grim silence, weapon held tight. You are giving them greater reason to fear, and that is not why you were sent down here, Maralin.'

She nodded. 'Thank you, Father.' The bolter came down. She mag-locked it to her thigh plate.

'Come,' he smiled, 'let me introduce you to some of them.'

THE BANE-SIDHE'S VOID shields rippled and rained sparks, brought into visibility as another layer was stripped by the explosive shells raining against them. A short growl of accumulating power ended in a blasting discharge of energy as the Warlord annihilated the tanks laying claim to the Hel's Highway ahead.

A black, smoking scorch smear was all the evidence that the tanks had ever existed. Behind the striding *Bane-Sidhe*, *Oberon* drifted forward on its gravity suspensors, gently cruising over any obstructions in its path. Bringing up the column's rear were the clanking, ungainly Warhounds that *Bane-Sidhe* had ordered back into the city.

The agreement made was monumentally simple, and that was why Jurisian was certain it would work.

'Defend *Oberon*,' he'd said. 'Defend it for long enough to take a single shot, to down the enemy command gargant. Then the Ordinatus will be surrendered into your control during the retreat towards the Hemlock River.'

What choice did they have? Amasat's voice over the vox was harsh with the promise of recrimination should the plan fail to run smooth. Jurisian, for his part, could not have cared less. He had the support he needed, and he had a primary target to destroy.

Infantry resistance was met with punishing and instant devastation. Armour formations endured no longer. Through the Temple District, they encountered precious little in the way of enemy engines.

'That is because, blasphemer, Invigilata left the enemy Titan contingent in ruins.'

'Except for the *Godbreaker*,' the Forgemaster replied. 'Except for the slayer of *Stormherald*.'

Amasat chose not to retort.

'I have nothing on my auspex,' he said instead.

'Nor I,' reported one of the Warhound princeps.

'I see nothing,' confirmed the other.

'Keep hunting. Draw closer to the Temple of the Emperor Ascendant.'

The Mechanicus convoy traversed the urban ruination in bitter dignity for another eight minutes and twenty-three seconds before Amasat voxed again.

'Almost one quarter of the enemy inside this hive is embattled at the Temple of the Emperor Ascendant. You are threatening Oberon *with destruction as well as desecration? Does your heresy know no end?'*

It was Jurisian's turn to abstain from the argument.

'I have a thermal signature,' he said, studying the dim

auspex console to the left of his control throne. 'It has a plasma shadow, much too hot to be natural flame.'

'I see nothing. Coordinates?'

Jurisian transmitted the location codes. It was on the very edge of scanning range, and still several minutes away.

'It is moving to the temple.'

'Locomotion qualifiers?'

'Faster than us.'

The pause was almost painful, broken by Amasat's sneering tone. *'Then I will give you the victory you require.* Talisman *and* Hallowed Verity – *remain with the blessed weapon.'*

'Yes, princeps,' both Warhounds responded.

Bane-Sidhe leaned forward, its armoured shoulders hunching as it moved into a straining stride. Jurisian listened to the protesting gears, the overworked joints, hearing the engine's machine-spirit cry out in the stress of metal under tension. He said a quiet word of thanks for the sacrifice about to be made.

CHAPTER XXIII
KNIGHTFALL

ANDREJ AND MAGHERNUS skidded into the basilica's first chamber, their bloody boots finding loose purchase on the mosaic-inlaid floor. Dozens of Guardsmen and militia dispersed through the vast hall, catching their breath and taking up defensive points around pillars and behind pews.

The final fallback was beginning in earnest. The grave-yard outside was blanketed in enemy dead, but the last few hundred Imperials could no longer hold any ground with their own numbers depleted.

'This room…' the former dockmaster was breathing heavily, '…doesn't have much cover.'

Andrej was unslinging his back-mounted power pack. 'It is a nave.'

'What?'

'This room. It is called a nave. And you are speaking the truth – there is no defence here.' The storm trooper drew his pistol and started running deeper into the temple.

'Where are you going? What about your rifle?

'It is out of power! Now follow, we must find the priest!'

RYKEN FIRED WITH his autopistol, taking a moment between shots to regain his aim. It was a custom, heavy-duty model that wouldn't have been out of place in an underhive gang-fight, and as he crouched by a black stone shrine to a saint he didn't recognise, the gun barked hot and hard in his fist, ejecting spent cartridges that clattered off nearby gravestones.

'Fall back, sir!' one of his men was yelling. The alien beasts crashed through the graveyard like an apocalyptic flood, a unbreakable tide of noise.

'Not yet...'

'*Now*, you ass, come on!' Tyro dragged at his shoulder. It threw off his aim, but to hell with it – it was like spit-ting into the ocean anyway. He scrambled away from the relative cover of the weeping statue just in time to miss it being shattered into chips and shards by raking fire from a fully-automatic enemy stubber.

'Are they coming?' he shouted to his second officer, limp-ing badly now.

'Who?'

'The bloody Templars!'

THEY WERE NOT coming.

To the retreating human survivors, it seemed as if the black knights had lost all sense, all reason, cutting their way forward while the humans that had supported them broke ranks and fled back.

No one could see why.

No one was getting a clear answer from the vox.

* * *

BAYARD WAS DEAD.

Priamus saw the great champion fall, and all flair in his killing strokes was abandoned in a heartbeat. He slew with all the grace of a peasant chopping lumber upon the face of some backwater rural world, his masterwork sword reduced to a club with a vicious edge and draped in lethal energy.

'Nerovar!' he screamed his brother's name into the vox. *'Nerovar!'*

Other Templars took up the cry, summoning the Apothecary to extract the gene-seed of a Chapter hero.

Bayard stood almost slouched against the wall of an ornate mausoleum shaped from pink-veined white stone. The body had not fallen only because of the crude spear pinning it through the throat. A killing blow, without a shadow of doubt. Priamus spared a moment of desperate blocks and thrusts, taking an axe blow against his pauldron, risking a second's distraction to pull the spear free. The ork's axe threw off sparks as it crashed aside from the ceramite shoulder guard. The corpse of the Emperor's Champion slumped to the ground, freed of its undignified need to stand.

'Nerovar!' Priamus cried again.

It was Bastilan that reached him first. The sergeant's helm was gone, revealing a face so bloody only the whites of his eyeballs revealed him as human any more. Torn flaps of skin hung in wet patches, leaving his head open to the bone beneath.

'The Black Sword!'

Priamus deflected another dozen cuts in four beats of his pounding twin hearts. He had no time to reach for the blessed weapon Bayard had dropped in death.

Bastilan's ruined face vanished in a burst of red mist.

Priamus had already rammed his power sword through the chest of the bolter-wielding ork behind the sergeant by the time Bastilan's headless body crashed to the ground with the dull clang of ceramite on stone.

'Nerovar!'

WITH BASTILAN'S LAST words, something changed within the Templars.

Twelve remained. Of these, only seven would escape what followed.

The knights pulled together, their blades slashing and carving not only to kill their foes, but to defend their brothers alongside them. It was an instinctive savagery born of so many decades fighting at each others' sides, and it spread through their failing ranks now as they stood on the precipice of destruction.

'*Take the sword!*' Grimaldus roared. His charge carried him ahead of the others, hammering his crozius in arhythmic fury, smashing a bloody path through to Priamus. '*Recover the Black Sword!*'

WE CANNOT LEAVE it here. It cannot lie abandoned on a battlefield while one of us yet lives.

Over the vox, the humans are calling us insane and begging us to fall back with them. To them, this bloodshed must seem like madness, but there is no choice. We will not be the only Crusade to violate our most sacred tradition. The Black Sword will remain in black hands until there are none left to bear it.

I have a moment – just a single moment – of reflexive pain when I see Bayard's body next to Bastilan's. Two of the finest Sword Brethren ever to serve the Chapter, now slain in glory. More alien bodies block my view. More xenos bleed as I force my way closer to Priamus.

A sense of bloodthirsty, eerie calm descends between us. The battle rages, weapons clashing against our armour, but I speak in a fierce whisper that I know carries over the vox to him and him alone.

'*Priamus.*'

'Reclusiarch.'

My maul sends two of the beasts flying back, and for a heartbeat's span, there are no alien barbarians separating us. Our eye lenses meet for that precious second, before we are both forced to turn and engage other foes.

'You are the last Emperor's Champion of the Helsreach Crusade,' I tell him. '*Now recover your blade.*'

MAJOR RYKEN SPOKE into his hand-vox, repeating the same words he'd been saying for almost a minute. His voice echoed around the nave in curiously calm counterpoint to the ragged breathing and moans of pain from the wounded.

'Any armour units still outside the basilica, respond. The *Godbreaker* has been sighted due south of the temple walls. Any armour units still outside, engage, engage.'

From his viewpoint by one of the broken stained glass windows, he watched the gargant's torso rising above the broken graveyard walls in the distance.

He didn't recognise the voice that eventually answered. It sounded both bitter and disgusted, but it still made Ryken grin.

'*Engaging.*'

'Hello? Identify yourself!'

'*I am Princeps Amasat of the Warlord Titan* Bane-Sidhe.'

* * *

THE BANE-SIDHE, NAMED for a shrieking monster from ancient Terran mythology, did everything in its power to gain the *Godbreaker*'s attention. Opening salvoes from its arm-cannons and shoulder-mounted weapon batteries lashed against the larger Titan's force fields. Siren horns, used to warn loyal infantry of the Titan's passing close – or even through – their regiments, blared now at the enemy engine. Whatever primitive communications array passed for a vox system on board the *Godbreaker* was scrambled into white noise by a focussed spike of machine-code from *Bane-Sidhe*'s tech-adepts.

All of this was enough to drag the towering beast-machine away from its intent to flatten the Temple of the Emperor Ascendant.

The Warlord, thirty-three metres of armour plating and city-killing weaponry forged into an iconic image of the Machine-God Himself, began its shameful retreat. All guns fired at will as it clanked backwards, drawing the *Godbreaker* away from the last Imperials alive in the hive's most sacred sector.

'MAY I HAVE a weapon, please?'

Andrej shrugged as he cleaned his goggles with a dirty cloth. 'I have no other pistol, fat priest. For this, I apologise.'

Tomaz Maghernus shook his head when Asavan looked his way. 'I don't, either.'

Several maidens of the Order of the Argent Shroud came down the wide stairs into the undercroft. Prioress Sindal led them, carrying her bolter with ease due to the machine-muscles of her power armour.

'It is time to seal the undercroft,' the old woman said, her voice low. She, at least, knew the merits of not panicking the refugees gathered in the sublevel. 'The beasts have reached the inner grounds.'

'May I have a weapon, please?' Asavan asked her.

'Have you ever fired a bolter?'

'Until this month, I had never even seen a bolter. Nevertheless, I would like a weapon with which to defend these people.'

'Father, with the greatest respect, it would do you no good. My thanks for comforting the flock, but it is time to prepare for the end. Everyone who is staying behind, be ready to be sealed down here within the next three minutes. The oxygen should last a month, as long as the xenos do not destroy the air filtration systems above ground.'

Andrej raised a singed eyebrow. 'And if they do?'

'Use your imagination, Guardsman. And return to the surface, quickly. Every able body is needed in defence of the temple.'

'A moment, please.' Andrej turned back to Asavan. 'Fat priest. You are destined to either survive this, or die at least some time later than I.' He handed the holy man a small leather pouch. Asavan took it, clutching it tight in fingers that would have trembled in this moment only weeks before.

'What is this?'

'My mother's wedding ring, and a letter of explanation. Once this is over, if you are still drawing breath, please find Trooper Natalina Domoska of the 91st Steel Elite. You will recognise her – this, I promise to you. She is the most beautiful woman in the world. Every man says so.'

'*Move*, young man,' the prioress insisted.

Andrej snapped a crisp salute to the overweight priest, and made his way back up the stairs, his laspistol held in both hands. Maghernus followed him, casting a lingering look back at Asavan and the refugees. He waved as the underground bulkheads slammed closed. Asavan didn't seem to see, preoccupied with the refugees who were rising to their feet in panic and protest.

Several of the battle-sisters remained at the base of the stairs, entering codes to seal the doors and imprison the civilians away from harm. The prioress managed to keep up with Andrej and Maghernus. The dockmaster smiled at her, knowing the gesture was meaningless and filled with melancholy. She returned the smile, her expression carrying the same emotions as his. The temple was shaking as the orks battered at its walls.

The next time Maghernus would see Prioress Sindal of the Order of the Argent Shroud, she would be a mangled corpse in three pieces, spread across the floor of the inner sanctum.

That would be in less than one hour's time, and her body would be one of the last things he saw before he was killed by a bolt-round in the back.

BANE-SIDHE TORE CLEAN through the Hel's Highway when it fell.

The Warlord had made it half a kilometre before its void shields burst out of existence and its front-facing armour began to suffer the assault from the *Godbreaker*'s guns. No matter how thick the ceramite and adamantium plating covering the Warlord's vital systems, the sheer level of firepower hurled at *Bane-Sidhe* meant that once its shields died, its existence was measured in minutes.

It was perhaps unfair that such a noble example of the Invigilata's god-machines met its end as a sacrificial lure, but within the Legio's archives, both *Bane-Sidhe* and her command crew were given the highest honours. The wreckage of the Titan would come to be salvaged by the Mechanicus in the following weeks, and restored to working order fourteen months later. Its destruction at Helsreach was marked upon its carapace with a six-metre square engraved image upon its right shin, depicting a weeping angel over a burning, metallic skeleton.

Unable to withstand any more punishment, with flames pouring from its bridge, the great Warlord fell backwards on howling joints. Its immense weight was enough to break the rockcrete columns holding up the Hel's Highway, sending the *Bane-Sidhe* and a significant section of the main road crashing down to land in a mountain of rubble.

The *Godbreaker* stood over the crater of broken road, as if staring down at the body of its latest kill.

Fourteen seconds after the Warlord's shattered remains came to a rest, a flare of sun-bright and fusion-hot energy screamed across the Hel's Highway. It was the shape of a newborn star, flaring with arcing coils of plasma light and surrounded by a blinding corona.

The *Godbreaker*'s shields disintegrated at the sunfire's touch. Its armour disintegrated mere seconds later, as did its crew, skeletal structure, and all evidence that it had ever existed.

Jurisian drooled through clenched teeth, feeling the untamed machine-spirit's quivering rage at being used without being ritually blessed and activated via the correct rituals. As the knifing pain in his skull faded to tolerable levels, he opened a vox-link to Grimaldus, and breathed two words.

They were laden with both agony and meaning – symbolising the completion of his duty, and a final farewell.

'Engine kill,' he said.

'The Godbreaker is dead,' Grimaldus voxed to anyone still listening to the comms channels. The news brought no relief to him, and no joy, even for thought of Jurisian's glory. There was nothing now beyond the next second of battle. Step by step, the Reclusiarch and his last brothers were pushed backwards through the basilica, room by room, hall by hall.

The air reeked of alien breath, spilled innards and the sharp overcooked ozone scent of las-fire.

The walls still shook as xenos tanks shelled the holy temple even while their own forces stormed through it.

A young girl in Argent Shroud battle armour was cut down, wailing as she was disembowelled by the horde. Artarion's two blades, both inactive from meat-clogging and no more use than jagged clubs, ripped across the face and throat of the girl's killer. Then he too was beaten back by the four beasts that took the dead brute's place.

A voice rose above the carnage – harsh and enraged.

'Kill them all! Let none survive! Never has an alien defiled this holiest of places!'

Grimaldus dragged the closest ork against him, gripping its throat and thudding his skulled helm against its face to shatter its hideous bone structure. The voice was the prioress's, and he realised now where he was.

No.

No, how could it all be over already?

We have been beaten back to the inner sanctum in mere hours. Sindal's cries of defiance have the worst effect: they awaken everyone from the mindless heat of battle and bloodshed, dragging us back to face the truth.

The inner sanctum is a gore-slick mess of heaving, slashing, shooting humans and orks. We are beaten. No one in this room is going to survive more than a few more minutes. Already, others have sensed this and I see them through the crowd, trying to run from the room, seeking a way past the orks rather than lay down their lives at the last stand.

Militia. Civilians. Guard. Even several storm troopers. Half of our pathetic remaining force is breaking from the battle and trying to run.

With my hand still at the ork's throat, I drag the kicking beast up with me, standing atop the Major Altar. The beast struggles, but its clawing is weak with its skull broken and its senses disoriented by pain.

My plasma pistol is long gone, torn from me at some point in the last two days of battle. The chain remains. I wrap it around the beast's throat, and roar my words to the painted ceiling as I strangle the creature in full view of everyone in the room.

'Take heart, brothers! Fight in the Emperor's name!' The beast thrashes as it dies, claws scraping in futility at my ruined armour. I tense my grip, feeling the creature's thick spinal bones begin to click and break. Its piggish eyes are wide with terror, and this… this makes me laugh.

'I have dug my grave in this place…' An explosive round detonates on my shoulder, blasting shards of armour free. I see Priamus kill the shooter with the Black Sword in a one-handed grip.

'I have dug my grave in this place, and I will either triumph or I will die!'

Five knights still live, and they roar as I roar.

'*No pity! No remorse! No fear!*'

The walls shudder as if kicked by a Titan. For a moment, still laughing, I wonder if the *Godbreaker* has returned.

'*Until the end, brothers!*'

The cry is taken up by those of us that yet draw breath, and we fight on.

'They're bringing the temple down!' Priamus calls, and there is something wrong with his voice. I realise what it is when I see my brother is missing an arm and his leg armour is pierced in three places.

I have never heard him in pain before.

'Nero!' he screams. 'Nerovar!'

The beasts are primitive, but they are not devoid of intelligence and cunning. Nero's white markings signal him as an Apothecary, and they know of his value to humanity. Priamus sees him first, two dozen metres away through the melee. An alien spear has punched its way through his stomach, and several of the beasts are lifting him from the ground, raising him like a war banner above the carnage.

Nerovar dies like no warrior I have ever seen before. Even as I try to kill my way closer to him, I see him gripping the spear in his fists, hauling himself down the weapon, impaling himself deeper on it in an attempt to reach the aliens below.

He has no bolter, no chainblade. His last act in life is to draw his gladius from its sheath at his thigh and hurl it down with a Templar's vengeance at the ork with the best grip on the spear. He'd dragged himself down to get close enough to ensure he wouldn't miss. The short sword bit true, sinking into the beast's gaping maw and rewarding the xenos with an agonising death, choking on a sword blade that had ravaged its throat, tongue and lungs. With the beast unable to keep hold, the spear falls and Nero plunges into a seething mass of greenskins.

I never see him again.

Priamus, one-armed and faltering now, staggers ahead of me. A detonating round crashes against his helm, spinning him back to face me.

'Grimaldus,' he says, before falling to his knees. 'Brother…'

Flames engulf him from the side – clinging chemical fire that washes over his armour, eating into the soft joints and dissolving the flesh beneath. The ork with the flamer pans the weapon left and right, dousing Priamus in corrosive fire.

I am hammering my way with painful slowness to avenge him when Artarion's blade bursts from the ork's chest. He kicks the dying ork from his broken chainsword. With vengeance taken, my standard bearer turns with as much grace as can be salvaged in this butchery, and his back slams against mine.

'Goodbye, brother.' He's laughing as he says the words, and I do not know why, but it brings out my own laughter.

Blocks of the ceiling are falling now, crushing those beneath. The orks in here with us, paying for every human life with five of their own, pay no heed to their kin outside damning them by destroying the temple with them still inside.

Not far from the altar, I catch a final glimpse of the storm trooper and the dockmaster. The former stands above the dying latter, Andrej defending the gut-shot Maghernus while he tries to comprehend what to do with his bowels looping across his lap and the floor nearby.

'Artarion,' I call to him, to return the farewell, but there is no answer. The presence against my back is not my brother.

I turn, laughing at the madness before me. Artarion is dead at my feet, headless, defiled. The enemy drive me to my knees, but even this is no more than a bad joke. They are doomed as surely as I am.

I am still laughing when the temple finally falls.

EPILOGUE
ASHES

THEY CALL IT the Season of Fire.

The Ash Wastes are choking with dust from roaring volcanoes. Planet-wide, the picts show the same images, over and over. Our vessels in orbit watch Armageddon breathe fire, and send the images back to the surface, so that those there might witness the world's anger in its entirety.

Fighting across most of the world is ceasing, not because of victory or defeat, but because there can be no arguing with Armageddon itself. The ash deserts are already turning dark. In a handful of days, no man or xenos beast will be able to breathe in the wastelands. Their lungs would fill with ashes and embers; their war machines would grind to a halt, fouled beyond use.

So the war ceases for now. It does not end. There is no tale of triumph and victory to tell.

The beasts stagger and crawl back to cities they have

managed to hold, there to hide away from the Season of Fire. Imperial forces consolidate the territories to which they still lay claim, and drive the invaders out from those where the orks have managed to grasp no more than a weak hold.

Helsreach is one of these places. That necropolis, in which one hundred of my brothers lie dead alongside hundreds of thousands of loyal souls...

That tomb-city, so much of which is flattened by the devastation of two months' road-by-road warfare, with no industrial output left at all...

Imperial tacticians are hailing it as a *victory*.

I will never again understand the humanity I left behind when I ascended to the ranks of the Templars. The perceptions of humans remain alien to me since the moment I swore my first oaths to Dorn.

But I will let the people of this blighted world claim their triumph. I will let the survivors of Helsreach cheer and celebrate a drawn-out defeat that masquerades as victory.

And, as they have requested, I will return to the surface once more.

I have something of theirs in my possession.

THEY CHEER IN the streets, and line Hel's Highway as if in anticipation of a parade. Several hundred civilians, and an equal number of off-duty Guard. They stand in crowds, clustered either side of the *Grey Warrior*.

My helm's aural receptors filter the noise of their cheering to less irritating levels, the way it would do if an artillery battery was shelling the ground around me.

I try not to stare at them, at their flushed faces, at their bright and joyous eyes. The war is over to them. They care nothing for the orbital images that show entire ork armies taking root in other hives. For the people of Helsreach, the war is over. They are alive, so they have won.

It is hard not to admire such simple purity. Blessed is the mind too small for doubt. And in truth, I have never seen a city resist invasion so fiercely. The people here have earned the lives they still have.

This part of the city, not far from the accursed docks, is relatively unscathed. It remained a stronghold firmly in Imperial control. I am given to understand that Sarren and his 101st fought here to the last day.

A gathering of figures clusters by the *Grey Warrior*. Most wear the ochre uniforms of the Steel Legion. One of them, a man known to me, beckons me over.

I walk to him, and the crowd erupts into more cheers. It is the first time I have moved in almost an hour.

An hour of listening to tedious speeches transmitted from the gathered group, over to a vox-tower nearby that blares the words across the sector.

'Grimaldus, Reclusiarch of the Black Templars,' the vox-voice booms. More cheers as I draw close. The soldier that beckoned to me offers quiet greetings.

Major, or rather, *Colonel* Ryken has regained much of his face since I last saw him. Burn scars spread across much of the remaining skin, but over half of his features are dull-metalled augmetics, including significant reconstruction to his skull. He makes the sign of the aquila, and only one of his hands is his own. The other is a skeletal bionic, not yet sheathed in synthetic skin.

I return the salute. The vox-speech – the speaker is a member of General Kurov's staff I have never met before – drones on about my own heroism alongside the Steel Legion. As my name is shouted by thousands of humans, I raise my fist in salute to them all.

And all the while, I am thinking how my brothers died here.

Died for them.

'Did Adjutant Quintus Tyro survive?' I ask.

He nods, his ruined face trying to make a smile. 'Cyria made it.'

Good. I am pleased for him, and for her.

'Hello, sir,' another of the Legionnaires says. I glance behind Ryken, to a man several places down the line. My targeting reticule locks on him – onto his grinning face. He is unscarred, and despite his youth, has laugh lines at the corner of his eyes.

So. He's not dead, either.

This does not surprise me. Some men are born with luck in their blood.

I nod to him, and he walks over, seemingly as bored with proceedings as I am. The orator is declaring how I 'smote the blaspheming aliens as they dared defile the temple's inner sanctum'. His words border on a sermon. He would have made a fine ecclesiarch, or a preacher in the Imperial Guard.

The ochre-clad soldier offers his hand for me to shake. I humour him by doing the same.

'Hello, hero,' he grins up at me.

'Greetings, Andrej.'

'I like your armour. It is much nicer now. Did you repaint it yourself, or is that the duty of slaves?'

I cannot tell if this is a joke or not.

'Myself.'

'Good! Good. Perhaps you should salute me now, though,

yes?' He taps his epaulettes, where a captain's badges now show, freshly issued and polished silver.

'I am not beholden to a Guard captain,' I tell him. 'But congratulations.'

'Yes, I know, I know. But I must be offering many thanks for you keeping your word and telling my captain of my deeds.'

'An oath is an oath.' I have no idea what to say to the little man. 'Your friend. Your love. Did you find her?'

I am no judge of human emotion, but I see his smile turn fragile and false. 'Yes,' he says. 'I did find her.'

I think of the last time I saw the little storm trooper, standing over the dockmaster's bloody corpse, bayoneting an alien in the throat, only moments before the basilica fell.

I find myself curiously glad that he is alive, but expressing that notion is not something I can easily forge into words. He has no such difficulty.

'I am glad you made it,' he uses my own unspoken words. 'I heard you were very injured, yes?'

'Not enough to kill me.'

But so close. I quickly grew bored of the Apothecaries on board the *Crusader* telling me that it was a miracle I clawed my way from the rubble.

He laughs, but there is little joy in it. His eyes are like glass since he mentioned finding his friend.

'You are a very literal man, Reclusiarch. Some of us were in lazy moods that day. I waited for the digging crews, yes, I admit it. I did not have Adeptus Astartes armour to push the rocks off myself and get back to fighting the very next day.'

'The reports I have heard indicated no one else survived the fall of the basilica,' I tell him.

He laughs. 'Yes, that would make for a wonderful story,

no? The last black knight, the only survivor of the greatest battle in Helsreach. I apologise for surviving and breaking the flow of your legend, Reclusiarch. I promise most faithfully that I and the six or seven others will be very quiet and let you have all the thunder.'

He has made a joke. I recognise it, and try to think of something humorous with which to reply. Nothing surfaces in my mind.

'Were you not injured at all?'

He shrugs. 'I had a headache. But then it went away.'

This makes me smile.

'Did you meet the fat priest?' he asks. 'Did you know him?'

'I confess, I do not recall anyone by that name or description.'

'He was a good man. You would have liked him. Very brave. He did not die in the battle. He was with the civilians. But he died two weeks after, from a problem with his heart. Ayah, that is unfair, I think. To live through the end and die at the new beginning? Not so fair, I am thinking.'

There is a twisted poetry to that.

I would like to speak words that comfort him. I would like to tell him I admire his courage, and that his world will survive this war. I want to speak with the ease Artarion would have done, and thank this soldier for standing with us when so many others ran. He honoured us all in that moment, as did the dying dockmaster, the prioress, and every other soul that faded from life on the night only I survived.

But I say nothing. Further conversation is broken by people chanting my name. How alien it sounds, voiced by human throats.

The orator whips the crowd up, speaking – of course – of the relics. They want to see them, and that is why I am here. To display them.

I signal the cenobyte servitors forward. Augmetic servants, vat-grown by the Chapter's Apothecaries and augmented by Jurisian to haul the temple's artefacts. None of the mindless wretches bear a name; just a relic that represents all I could do to ease my guilt at such a shameful defeat.

The crowd cheers again as the servitors move from the vulture shadow of my Thunderhawk, each of the three carrying one of the artefacts. The ragged scraps of the banner. The cracked stone pillar, topped by the shattered aquila. The sacred bronze globe, sloshing with its precious holy water.

My voice carries with ease, amplified by my helm. The crowd quietens, and Hel's Highway falls silent. I am reminded, against my will, of the impenetrable silence beneath the mountain of marble and rockcrete when the temple came down upon us all.

'We are judged in life,' I tell them, 'for the evil we destroy'.

Never my words. Always Mordred's.

For the first time, I have an answer to them. A greater understanding. And my mentor… You were wrong. Forgive me, that it took so long to leave your shadow and realise it. Forgive me, that it took the deaths of my brothers to learn the lesson they each tried to teach me while they yet drew breath.

Artarion. Priamus. Bastilan. Cador. Nero.

Forgive me for living, while you all lie cold and still.

'We are judged in life for the evil we destroy. It is a bleak truth, that there is nothing but blood awaiting us in the spaces between the stars. But the Emperor sees all that transpires in His domain. And we are judged equally for the illumination we bring to the blackest nights. We are judged in life for those moments we spill light into the darkest reaches of His Imperium.

'Your world taught me this. Your world, and the war that brought me here.

'These are your relics. The last treasures of the first men and women ever to set foot upon your world. They are the most precious treasures of your ancestors, and they are yours by right of legacy and blood.

'I return them to you from the edge of destruction. And I thank you not only for the honour of standing by the people of this city, but for the lessons I have learned. My brothers in orbit have asked me why I dragged these relics from beneath the fallen temple. But you have no need to ask, for you each already know the answer. They are *yours*, and no alien beast will deny the people of this world the inheritance they deserve.

'I dragged these relics back into the sunlight for you – to honour you, and to thank you all. And in humility now, I return them to you.'

This time, when the cheers come, they are shaped by the orator. He uses the title I swore to High Marshal Helbrecht, standing before Mordred's statue, that I would not refuse when it was formally awarded to me.

'*I am told,*' *the High Marshal had said afterwards, '*that Yarrick and Kurov have spoken with the Ecclesiarchy. You are being given the relics, to carry Helsreach's memory and honour with you, in the Eternal Crusade.*'

'*When I return to the surface, I will offer the icons back to the people.*'

'*Mordred would not have done so,*' *Helbrecht said, masking any emotion, any judgement, from me.*

'I am not Mordred,' I told my liege. 'And the people deserve the choice. It is for them that we waged that war, for them and their world. Not purely for the holy reaping of inhuman life.'

And I wonder now, as they chant my new title, what they will decide to do with the relics.

Hero of Helsreach, the crowd cheers.

As if there is only one.

BLOOD
AND FIRE

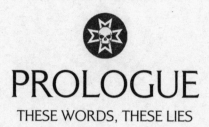

PROLOGUE
THESE WORDS, THESE LIES

Grimaldus. They lied to us about the Mannheim Gap. They sent us there to die.

You know of whom I speak. We cannot outrun the echoes of Khattar. We pay the price now for our virtue in the past.

We are sons of Dorn and we know nothing of surrender, even when victory is out of reach. What concerns us is injustice. Ignominy. If we could be said to fear anything, it is the shame of our legacy being fouled by lies.

And if the Imperium remembers us at all, it will be as one of mankind's most grievous failures. But we have not failed mankind; mankind has failed itself. The bitter hearts and closed minds of weak men and women will see us dead before dawn.

So be it.

Our enemies do not move in the light, where they run the risk of facing our blades. Nor are they truly in the shadows, but they occupy positions of power so far above us in the hierarchy of man that exact identities become meaningless. They have the power and influence to deceive us, and deceive us they did.

The Celestial Lions will never leave this world. A handful of us remain, but we know the truth. We died at the Mannheim Gap. We died the day the sun rose over the scrap-iron bodies of alien gods.

I

SEASON OF FIRE

WE WERE WARNED, as if we needed warning, not to go out into the storm. The air was already severe enough to scald unprotected flesh, and while our armour offered a shield against the elements, it wouldn't protect us for long. All trace of our sacred colours was already flayed away by the gritty wind, leaving us clad in gunmetal grey, stripped of paint and heraldry. I wondered, just briefly, if there was a metaphor in that moment. If so, it remained for one of keener humour to uncover.

The downed gunship was a beached, smashed memory of a thing, all lethality stolen by the savagery of its crash landing. In contrast, the Valkyrie we had acquired from the 101st Steel Legion sat hunched on the sands, a bored crow with its curved wings spread wide. I'd had cause to use this vehicle many times in the past month, and I could not dissuade myself of the notion that its machine-spirit despised me. If gunships could scowl, that one most certainly did.

I looked back at it, its turbine engines still howling impatiently, its grey-green hull being abraded to dull silver by the desert wind. I could hear just how little the engines enjoyed eating this dust.

The pilot was a uniformed blur behind the scratched windshield. He had volunteered for this mission, despite its risks. I admired him for it.

The weeks since my convalescence had passed slowly. I was coming to believe I would never be wholly comfortable with the humans' regard. The people of Helsreach looked upon me as some kind of icon, purely for the virtue of doing my duty. Why did it make me uncomfortable? There are a hundred difficult answers to that. We of the Adeptus Astartes are a breed apart from the humans we might have been. Let that be enough of an explanation.

I turned back to the downed Storm Eagle. Whatever colours it had borne into battle were long gone, stolen by the storm. Its symbols of allegiance were similarly eroded by the ash and dirt in the turbulent air.

Cyneric ducked under the slanted wing, one side of his armour still black in patches where it hadn't yet faced the storm. In his left hand, an auspex scanner sputtered and clicked, murdered by the storm's interference. He said nothing, which was answer enough.

I climbed the rolled hull, braced against the wind by the magnetic locks on the bottom of my boots. The last oath-scroll on my armour was ripped away. I let the wind steal it, to take my inscribed Litanies of Hate into the storm. It felt curiously apt.

The bulkhead was sealed from within. I drew my crozius maul, and heard its energy field buzzing against the grit in the air. It took a single blow, with the sound of a muted belltower, and the bulkhead was gone. I hauled the mangled door free with one hand, and cast it down to the ground. Cyneric still said nothing. It was a habit I liked to encourage.

The interior of the crashed Storm Eagle was set at a stark angle, with equipment crates and loose weapons scattered across the confined crew bay. The cockpit was no better, but what the reinforced visor screen hid from the outside was revealed at once: a lone Space Marine, clad in burnished gold, lying in ungainly repose where the deck met the weapon-racked walls. I knew those colours. I knew the Chapter's heraldry.

What I didn't know was what this gunship was doing all the way out here, so far from Hive Volcanus.

Cyneric dropped down behind me, the chains binding his weapons to his armour rattling in sympathy to his movements. I heard his breathing over the squad's vox link, then came the curse, as he saw what I saw.

'It is the Lions,' he said.

It was just one Lion. The pilot. And from the faint signs of darkening decay in evidence once I removed his azure helm, he was several days dead. None of this made sense.

Before I rose, I pressed my rosarius amulet to the dead warrior's forehead. Cyneric questioned this. Why offer the Lion these last rites? Was he not of another Chapter?

It was not disrespectful to question my actions. It was his duty. He must learn what I do and why I did it.

As I stood again, I asked Cyneric why he objected to this salute of a fallen warrior's soul.

'Because he is not a knight,' he told me. 'The Lion was not one of us.'

I had used the very same reasons myself, often enough.

Even with the noble Salamanders, not so long ago. Yet there were exceptions.

'He does not wear the cross of our calling,' I admitted, 'but he was Dorn's son, as surely as we are. Bloodlines reach beyond Chapter heraldry, Cyneric.'

'Forgive me, master.'

'Forgiveness is irrelevant. There is nothing to forgive.'

Cyneric had only served at my side for three weeks, and still felt the weight of tradition and expectation that comes with the chance of bearing a skull helm. It would be my choice whether to admit him into the sacred mysteries of the Chapter cult; he would be a Chaplain at my command, or he would return to the rank and file.

Cyneric was my Lord Helbrecht's idea. Conversely, going out to the gunship was my decision. I could never abide mysteries.

Mag-locked to the dead warrior's belt was a hololithic imagifier the size of a human fist. Once freed and activated, it gave rise to a flickering blue image – the ghost of another warrior in another city – wearing the heraldry of the Celestial Lions and carrying a skull-faced helm beneath one arm. Despite the wraithly image, I could see that the warrior's face was black, the black of birth on a distant jungle world. By contrast, my flesh was as white as veined marble. I had no clear memory of childhood. All I recalled of my pre-initiation infancy was howling white wind and the bite of frost on the fingers.

'Julkhara,' I greeted the hololithic ghost.

'*Grimaldus*,' it said, and its voice wavered the same way as the image itself. '*They lied to us about the Mannheim Gap. They sent us there to die.*'

* * *

442

As THE RECORDING finished in a spurt of flawed electrics, I heard the storm waiting for us outside. It was getting harder, heavier, surely more abrasive. The Imperial Guard gunship we had acquired would never make it back to the city if the weather worsened any further. This venture had already been delayed by several days, until an adequate break in the storm front.

'Master,' Cyneric said.

I sensed the questions coming and warded them away with a shake of my head. None of this made sense. I needed time to think.

Without a word, we emerged back into the fiercening wind, moving to the Valkyrie. Its troop bay was an orderly mess of untouched crew seats, too small for either Cyneric or myself in our armour.

'Orders, Reclusiarch?' came the pilot's voice from the cockpit. The gunship jolted beneath our boots, already rising into the sky. The wind was merciless, it would be a turbulent ride home.

'Back to the city.'

The city. *My* city. Helsreach, the hive that claimed me as its champion; the city that changed how I see my own oath of service. We are Templars, and we attack, we advance, as the last proud knights of the Great Crusade. But we were crusading for the right of mankind to exist. Our wrath must be pure, else it is worthless and futile. We are judged in life for more than the evil we destroy. We are judged for what virtues we represent, for the ideals that lie behind our blades.

I had thought I would die on this world. I was certain of it, until the very moment death came for me. The enemy entombed me beneath the fallen Temple of the Emperor Ascendant, doing me the honour of a cairn while I still drew breath. Weeks after my recovery, I thought of it in the quiet hours of each day: the privilege of such a sacred tombstone. It was almost a shame to survive.

But Armageddon didn't kill me. We would leave the world soon – in three days I would sail with the High Marshal aboard the *Eternal Crusader*, back to war. The wounded hive I was sworn to defend had granted me its relics, and I would take them with me as we waged war across the stars.

Caution brought us in low over Helsreach. Several of the city's districts were still in the hands of the mongrel invaders, and although the Season of Fire had forced an unwelcome cessation of hostilities, there were nonetheless forces from both sides willing to risk the breaks between dust monsoons in the hopes of bleeding their entrenched foes. Anti-air rockets were a cursed hope in the wind, but they still spat skywards at our gunships and supply landers with irritating frequency.

I heard the city-wide sirens even before we were over the fallen outer walls – another storm warning, wailing of worse to come.

Helsreach itself no longer existed as anything more than a battlefield. We had killed the city while fighting to save it. Its skyline was an amputated thing of cleaved towers and – in the rare hours the wind died down – pillars of black smoke. The central spire – modest by the standards of many hives – still stood despite extensive shelling from both sides, now home to huddled masses of stinking alien invaders taking shelter from the storms.

The true city that spread around the spire's foundations was a flattened ruin. Of the millions that had lived there a year before, perhaps a quarter yet drew breath. Most were holed up in underground bunkers, or in what precious few intact districts were still warded by the steel ring of Guard armour battalions. The city had been reinforced by huge numbers of fresh Guard soldiers, just in time to linger in a seasonal deadlock. Tens of thousands of rifles going unfired.

The pilot took us through the stumps of shattered buildings, veering between fallen habitation blocks to minimise the risk of enemy sky-fire. It also shielded us from the worst of the wind, calming the Valkyrie's judders.

Soon enough, we cut over the corpse of Stormherald, reduced to a collapsed castle of scrap and slag, spread across two city blocks. The wind had scored away all sign of Imperial loyalty upon its armour plating, and the wrecked spires of its shoulder battlements were too ruined to speak of any gothic majesty. Salvaged metal alien effigies resisted the storm – iron war banners erected by whatever foul clan flooded aboard the downed Titan at the end of its proud life.

We passed overhead, over this monument to defiance in the face of failure, and I thought of Zarha, the Crone of Invigilata, whose mangled remains lay there still. She would be rotting in the cold fluid of her life support cradle, unburied and unblessed. That injustice grieved me. Would that I could have done something to change it, but Stormherald's corpse lay deep in enemy-held territory.

Cyneric stood with me in the troop bay, watching the city roll below from the open bay door.

'By forcing the gunship out into these storms, do we abuse its machine-spirit?'

The philosophy of biomechanical life was not beyond me, but I needed Cyneric's mind on more relevant matters.

'Focus,' I told him, and his reply was a curt nod. He was learning.

We touched down on the Kruja-17-SEC landing platform – a barricaded and bunkered landing pad built over the broken straits of Hel's Highway's westernmost run. Baneblades and multiple patterns of Leman Russ front-line tanks sat in the storm, scratched bare by the wind. As the ramp slammed down, Cyneric walked away first, out into the wind and towards the closest entrance to the flakboarded forward command bunker.

The sky was black with ash and the promise of a vicious night at the mercy of the coming storm. I hesitated, looking back to the pilot, but he was already unbuckled and throwing on his environment suit for the short run to the bunker. Three months before, instinct wouldn't have told me to look back. If nothing else, I thank this world for the lessons I have learned while walking its surface.

Organised chaos reigned in the command bunker. Against the walls, cogitators, auspex relays and vox-engines clicked, ticked and pulsed. Humans scattered before us in the screen-lit darkness. Several saluted, not yet shaken from the habit; their signs of formality and respect were meaningless to me.

'I require a clean vox link to the *Eternal Crusader.*'

Officers and technicians scurried to obey. Contact with the ships in orbit was sporadic at best, and contact with the other cities was relayed through the fleet in the rare hours it functioned at all. The planetary satellite network, and the convenience of communication it brought, was naught but a memory.

One of the tech officers saluted as she came before me. 'We have a link, Reclusiarch. It should hold until the storm breaks.'

'My thanks.' A moment's attention activated my helm's own vox-reader, scanning for uncorrupted local channels.

Icons flashed and chimed on the left edge of my retinal display. Three of them flickered red, then settled green.

'Reclusiarch,' came a voice half-killed by vox crackle – one of the countless Chapter serf bridge crew aboard the flagship. 'I live to serve.'

'I require four tasks completed within the hour. First, you are to make contact with every vessel of the Celestial Lions Chapter still in orbit – I need a full accounting of their war fleet. Second, contact whatever command structure remains in place at Hive Volcanus and acquire a detailed report of every Adeptus Astartes casualty in that region since the war's commencement. Third, Cyneric and I need a gunship to return us to the *Eternal Crusader*. If the storm hits before you are able to arrange it, we will risk teleportation.'

'Your will be done, Reclusiarch. And the fourth order?'

I had to be careful.

'Make contact with the ranking officer of the Celestial Lions, garrisoned at Hive Volcanus. The transmission will be monitored, no matter what encryption processes we run. Record the following message, deliver it, and say nothing more.'

'As you command. The message, Reclusiarch?'

'Only six words. *"No pity. No remorse. No fear".'*

II

HIGH MARSHAL

Ten thousand years ago.

So many of our stories begin with those words. Ten thousand years ago, when the Chapters were Legions. Ten thousand years ago, when the Emperor's sons walked the stars. Ten thousand years ago when the galaxy caught fire, as though it hadn't been burning ever since.

The Adeptus Astartes are the keepers of the oldest lore, and even among our archives so much has been lost. Truth twists and warps over time, as the stories change to reflect the reader's vision. Whole swathes of the galaxy know nothing of the Heresy and the Crusade before it. Thousands of worlds pray to the Emperor not as a man, but as a god or a spirit; a warrior-avatar; a benevolent entity beyond the grave; a seasonal avatar that brings annual floods and commands the sun to rise each dawn.

Each time I return to the flagship, I find myself dwelling on the nature of truth. Our archives are among the

449

purest in the Imperium, but even they are little more than fragments of what happened. Our reverence isn't reserved for scripture and story. When the words *ten thousand years ago* stir the blood of any Templar, it is not because of the scrolls and holorecords we have preserved through the generations. It is because of vessels like the *Eternal Crusader*.

She sailed the stars ten thousand years ago, fighting in the wars that forged our species. We walk in the footsteps of those ancient knights of the Great Crusade. We command the same vessel, train in the same chambers and bring the same wrath. When so many words have been lost, this is a truth we can cling to.

I thought all of this again that day, as Cyneric followed me from the landing bay. I could sense his uneasiness at the respect we were both shown, as well. When I had been a Chaplain, Chapter serfs would salute me. As Reclusiarch, they showed much greater reverence. We allowed our serfs to carry ceremonial weapons of their own – usually unpowered blades and daggers. They drew their swords and knelt, head down against the reversed hilt. When we passed other Templars in the dim corridors, they did not make the sign of the aquila. They crossed forearms, banging their fists to their breastplates, forming the crusader's cross.

Cyneric was still silent when we walked alone. He wasn't used to his equals showing him such elevated respect.

'The discomfort passes,' I told him. This was both true and untrue. My liege Helbrecht had told me it passed, and he was a warrior who would die before speaking a lie. The discomfort had not yet passed for me, but I trusted my lord's assurance.

The *Eternal Crusader* is a fortress in the void; it would take months to traverse if one walked every hallway and chamber. I led Cyneric through the corridors, taking the grinding elevators between decks, heedless of whether we moved through populated areas or not. My targeting reticule leapt from door to door, figure to figure, scrolling with biometric data and basic scanning lore. As we stood on one of the ascension platforms, rising up through the decks, I turned to regard Cyneric's plain, scarred features and a thought occurred to me. To my shame, it was one that should have occurred to me much earlier.

'Put your helmet back on.'

He hesitated before obeying, from surprise rather than disobedience. As it clicked into place at his collar seals, he looked back at me through the red eye-lenses of a stylised, riveted Mark VI Corvus helm. The question was within the gaze. I offered him the answer.

'You may remove it with the Chapter's lord-commanders, but never with your other brethren. You are no longer you, Cyneric. A Chaplain is the Chapter's history and its future, manifest in one man. Your features must be the deathmask of the Emperor.' I tapped the gaunt cheekbones of my helm's silver skull faceplate. 'Your brothers must forget your face, as they have forgotten mine.'

Cyneric nodded, though I sensed he was not convinced. He knew he must use these months to prove he deserved a skull helm, but the logic of my order escaped him. After all, his helm's faceplate was not the visage of immortal death I wear. Not yet, at least.

I could have replied to his doubt by reciting a cold truth: that he still wore the helm of an Adeptus Astartes warrior, one of the Emperor's genetic descendants, and the galaxy was conquered by millions of those emotionless, impersonal masks in the era we sought to embody. If he lacked a skull helm, his warrior's visage was almost as appropriate.

But there was a time to preach, and a time to teach.

'Cyneric,' I replied. 'Behave as if you already carry the responsibilities you seek to earn.'

Another nod, less hesitant and more satisfied.

As we walked down a thoroughfare hallway, doing our mutual best to ignore the obeisance we were both shown by the human thralls, I added another warning over a shared vox channel.

'When we stand before the High Marshal, do not meet his eyes.'

More confusion. 'Master?' Cyneric voxed back.

'Just trust me.'

HE WAITED FOR us in the Chamber of the First Proclamation, more often known as Sigismund's Hall. Legend tells us it was there that the first High Marshal of the Black Templars stood with the brothers who would become the first Chapter lords, looking out over the battlefield known as the Iron Cage, and swore that the Great Crusade would go on, no matter what wounds the Imperium still bore. The other Legions were free to protect mankind's domain, bearing no shame for their decision. But Sigismund's Imperial Fists would darken their armour for the battles to come, and continue their charge to carry the Emperor's message out into the void. They would not defend. They would attack. And so were born the Black Templars, the only warriors for whom the Great Crusade never ended.

Alien worlds and long-dead warriors were portrayed in paintings – each one a masterpiece rendered by a different hand – lining the dark iron walls. The statue of Sigismund himself stood as eternal guardian, flanked by sculptures of our Chapter's original marshals and castellans. Each of these bronze warriors was stained green with the patina of time, but lifted a defiant blade to the age-greyed banners hanging from the arched, gothic ceiling.

Their armour was archaic: rough, overlapping plates in a style rarely seen even among the true successors to the Legion: those noble Chapters of the Second Founding. Outdated helmet crests marked these legendary warriors apart from those of us who had taken their place ten millennia later. One could not help but feel judged, and to wonder if we bore their legacy with the same honour they displayed in life.

The entire hall smelled of dust and the stately, stale parchment scent of old memory. At the far end awaited Helbrecht.

My liege is a man of great resolve, but equally great sorrows. His humours have ever tended towards the melancholic – not from introspection or emotion, but from ambition and devotion. His duty is never done. He cares nothing for personal glory, displays no overt offering of emotion, and spends every second of his life upon the Eternal Crusade. I have never once seen him display any emotion beyond the faintest smile, during the decades of calculated planning; the acid anger of the battlefield; and the cold rage that always follows a fight. He does not feel emotion as other sentient beings. He has mastered it.

His face is a cartographic map of wars won and scars suffered in the name of humanity's dead messiah-king. His voice is unspeakably controlled, impossibly soulful. He has seen more blood, fire, iron and hatred in life than almost any man or woman still drawing breath.

That day, he greeted me by name; one of the few among the Chapter with the rank to do so. Cyneric, he called 'Brother-Initiate', and offered a nod in the younger warrior's direction. Both of us knelt before our lord, as tradition states when first entering his presence. I prayed Cyneric had heeded my words and avoided our liege lord's eyes.

I remember thinking, so clearly, *He is warfare given human form*. No other words could describe him so completely. Armour of black and gold marked him out from the rank and file, not for exaltation but so he drew the enemy's eyes and ire. When Helbrecht pulled steel, he wanted to be seen. My lord was always the first in the fight, at the centre of the front line.

His red cloak was a brown rag, scarcely clinging to his battered, cracked war-plate. Blood had dried across his armour in rainspray flecks, doubtless in patterns of mystical relevance to the alien soothsayers and shamans among the tribes we were butchering on the surface. His bionic arm was bared, the mechanical servos and clicking pistons doing their visible work through damaged portions of his armour. No desire had ever driven him to sheathe the limb in synthetic skin. Such meaningless cosmetic detail would never enter his mind.

'Sire,' I greeted him. Reaching up, I disengaged my helmet's seals, pulling it free to fully taste the antique air of the chamber. The Sword of the High Marshals descended to aim at my throat. My lips brushed the proffered blade in knightly obeisance, the traditional kiss to confirm one's loyalty to the Chapter and its lord-commander.

Next to me, a moment later, Cyneric did the same.

'Rise,' Helbrecht told us. He sheathed the blade at his hip – the blade that, if legend is true, was reforged from shards of our primarch's own sword. We rose as bid.

'Speak, Merek,' said my lord.

Cyneric tensed at the use of my first name.

Instead of speaking, I produced a handheld holorecorder. It projected a life-size avatar of light, an Adeptus Astartes warrior addressing all three of us.

'Grimaldus,' it said. *'They lied to us about the Mannheim Gap. They sent us there to die.'*

H ELBRECHT WAS SILENT after the message ran its course. He looked into the space where Julkhara's image had stood moments before and spoken of the basest treachery.

'Could this recording have been manipulated or falsified?' He didn't mean doctored by the enemy. The greenskin xenos were far too crude for such subtle measures.

I shook my head. 'The traitors Julkhara spoke of would profit nothing by such a message. I believe it to be true.'

'As do I.' Helbrecht turned back to me. 'What is it you wish, Grimaldus?'

'I am still seeking to establish contact with the Celestial Lions and take stock of their losses.'

'And you intend to destroy those who have betrayed them.'

'I doubt that will be possible, sire. No matter how much it appeals to me.'

Helbrecht looked to the statue of Sigismund, resting his hand on the pommel of his sheathed sword. The bronze replica of the First High Marshal carried the same sword, rendered there in the same bronze as the statue itself. Sigismund stood with the blade drawn, aiming it at the wide windows, at the world that turned and burned below.

'You risk dragging the Chapter into direct conflict with the Inquisition.'

There was no denying it. 'Yes, sire.'

'I do not fear that conflict, Grimaldus. Injustice must be opposed. Impurity must be purged. But the *Eternal Crusader* sets sail in three days, my brother. The warlord has fled from Armageddon and our first duty must be to hunt him down.'

I had expected that. 'Then leave me behind.'

For the first time I could recall, surprise crossed my liege lord's scarred features. 'You, who were so reluctant to fight on this world, now plead to stay?'

The irony was not lost on me. 'I can leave on another ship, sire. The *Virtue of Kings* will remain with the remnants of Amalrich's fighting company. If I survive, I will travel with them.'

'I lose my Reclusiarch, either way.'

'Then promote another. The Eternal Crusade will continue without me, Helbrecht.'

It was strange to see him like that, caught between the purity of a war against external enemies, and a just war against an internal foe. He would fight both, if he could. The alien king's death, however, took priority over all else.

'You have been up here,' I said, as he still looked above at the towering statue, 'fighting the xenos in orbit. You have seen the void war with your own eyes. Tell me the reports of Celestial Lions fleet losses are wrong, sire.'

Helbrecht turned, regarding me with eyes far too old for even his war-weathered, time-cracked face.

'The reports are true.'

It was my turn to look through the great window, at the

world slowly rolling below, as Helbrecht continued. 'They have been with us, side by side, in almost every engagement. As we speak, they have but three vessels remaining.'

'That cannot be.'

My voice was cold, but my blood ran hot enough to boil. We were speaking of the death of an entire Chapter. 'How can they have sustained such losses?'

My liege has never been a man prone to even flashes of humour. He took a breath that could not quite be called a sigh. This war had enraged and wearied him in equal measure, and now the final blow was ready to fall; I brought him the threat of another delay.

'Their devastation is the principal reason I believe your concerns are valid,' he said. 'You know the ebb and flow of void war: the endless relay of orders; the voices in the murk; the shouting above cannonfire and the thundering flames of structural damage. Hundreds and hundreds of ships moving in every imaginable angle – firing, ramming, crashing, dying. Facts and fiction twine together.'

But Helbrecht was a void commander without parallel. That was why he had been chosen to oversee the Imperium's forces in orbit. I knew his words were not an excuse for a personal failing. Unfortunately, neither were they an apology for him consigning me to Helsreach with the wider war taking place up here. I was no longer bitter about it, merely regretful at the moments of brotherhood I missed.

'I know,' I nodded.

'The Lions have fought well,' he allowed. 'I would never cast aspersions on their fighting character. Their straits have arisen from apparent ill fortune: orders given but never received, or too slowly answered. We have had many reports of vox breakage and orders never reaching their warship's captains. Much of it reeks of enemy guile.'

I had to hear this. 'Tell me.'

'The battle-barge *Serenkai* was boarded and overwhelmed when it pulled free of our spearhead, failing to heed orders to maintain formation. The cruiser *Lavi* took four hours to die from structural haemorrhage when it collided with the wounded Flesh Tearers flagship *Victus*. The *Nubica* destroyed itself when it was boarded, choosing sacrifice over capture.'

He listed another dozen ships, another dozen deaths. My teeth clenched harder with each name.

'It is difficult,' he finished, 'to know what events were born of sabotage or treachery, rather than honest battle. It has been eventful in Armageddon's skies, brother. And those who might have borne closer witness are in their graves. If the Inquisition moves against the Lions, it is doing so with a tenacity and subtlety I have rarely seen from its agents.'

'Nevertheless, we are left with a Chapter devoid of its fleet, with its remnants annihilated on the surface.'

Helbrecht closed his eyes, musing in solemn silence for several beats of my heart. When they opened again, all doubt was banished. This was how he always acted, and I admired him greatly for it. A man of action, not reaction. He attacked, always attacked.

'Justice calls to us,' he said.

A Chaplain should not smile, for we are avatars of morbid rituals and righteous death in battle. I could not help it. My blood caught fire with his words, the way it does in those holiest of moments: when he declares a Crusade.

'At the very least, we must learn the truth of this matter,' he said, and both Cyneric and I were already making the crusader's cross over our breastplates.

'As you say, sire.'

'Go to Hive Volcanus,' he told us. 'The bulk of the Chapter must sail in three days, Grimaldus. The Old Man requires it, and the arch-warlord responsible for Armageddon cannot be allowed to flee from our grasp, for retribution calls as loud as justice. We cannot commit the Templars to the field again and endure another week or more of recovery, rearming and resupply. But make planetfall and learn the truth of what happened down there. If the Lions are destined to die, I would hear the truth of their tale before it is too late.'

'It will be done.'

'I have no doubt.'

He did not ask me if three days would be enough. There was no choice: it *had* to be enough. 'Do you require more knights?'

I glanced to Cyneric. 'No, my liege. Not yet.'

'Good, for we have few to spare. Three days,' he said again. 'Go. Cut to the truth and cry it to the sky.'

CYNERIC WAS SILENT as we left. His quiet was actually a disquiet: a silence born of words unspoken, rather than a need to say nothing at all. Few human serfs walked those austere decks, but both of our helmets clicked back into place. My vision was washed with red-tinted target locks and streaming bio-data.

'You looked into his eyes.' It was not a question.

Cyneric nodded. 'I did.'

'I warned you not to.'

He nodded again. 'You did.'

I knew what he was feeling. He felt as I always did before the statues of our Chapter's legendary forefathers. He had passed beneath Judgement Incarnate. How best to explain this to him?

'Our liege has seen everything the galaxy can offer, on both sides of reality's veil. He has killed every enemy imaginable and has stood in the ranks of countless Crusades. And he is not a subtle man. He wears his victories and defeats as plainly displayed as any scar. You feel as if your worth was being weighed, and that is only right. He was measuring you, as he measures everything and everyone that falls beneath his gaze. Helbrecht has old, keen eyes that see right into a warrior's heart. I do not know him well, for no one outside his Sword Brethren can claim to know our lord well, but trust me when I say he did not find you wanting, Cyneric.'

Cyneric mused on this as we walked through the dark halls. 'Never have I felt more judged than when my eyes met his.'

'He is the heir of Sigismund and the avatar of the Eternal Crusade. It is right to doubt you will ever live up to his life's legacy, just as it is right to be inspired by him in the same breath. High Marshal Helbrecht finds you worthy. You are with me now on our lord's wishes. He asked that I judge you for initiation into the Chaplain Brotherhood.'

I heard the servos purr in Cyneric's neck as he turned to regard me. 'You did not request me yourself?'

The very idea.

'No, Cyneric. I did not.'

'It was spoken among the brethren that you were seeking to rebuild your command squad.'

Artarion. Priamus. Cador. Nerovar. Bastilan.

'Then it was spoken wrong,' I replied. 'Let that be the end of it, Cyneric.'

III

THE LAST OFFICER

THE CODEX ASTARTES – at least, the *Eternal Crusader's* incomplete copy of that ancient text – detailed several thousand logistical concerns in the preparation, establishment and fortification of an Adeptus Astartes firebase. Humanity did not invest so much into us in order that we should grind frontline to frontline in protracted theatres of war – that is the purview of the Imperial Guard. The Adeptus Astartes are the falling hammer, the spear to the vitals, striking and withdrawing with the force of a killing thrust to the heart.

But no plan survives contact with the enemy. Fortification and digging in during extensive worldwide Crusades are a necessity of the wars we fight. While the Templars may not cling to the Codex Astartes with a tenacity bordering on worship of holy scripture, it is still the most comprehensive treatise on Space Marine warfare ever written, penned by the hand of the Emperor's own son, Lord Guilliman of

Macragge. Its value is immeasurable to any commander, no matter what divergences are found in a Chapter's culture.

It is said that no complete copies still exist in the Dark Millennium. Even the original document's origins are shrouded in more myth than truth. No records even exist as to whether Lord Guilliman wrote the Codex by hand across several dozen tomes, dictated it to nuncio-processors and servitor scribes, or compiled it himself into a hololithic library.

There it is again, of course. *Ten thousand years ago*, when we were not forced to rely on flawed records and fractured accounts.

The Season of Fire raged hottest and hardest on Armageddon Secundus, the easternmost landmass, where Hive Helsreach and its sister cities drowned in the storms of dust. On the west coast of the continent Armageddon Prime, Hive Volcanus was still besieged by the enemy and the winds were more often free of the burning sand and ash that so blighted the other side of the world.

The Celestial Lions firebase was atop a natural rise in the landscape, supremely defensible, with great battlements and sacred statuary of fallen heroes staring down at any who would dare bring the fight to those dark walls. Turret-defended bunkers within the compound sat beneath barricaded landing pads, which in turn stood above repair foundries, vehicle garages and arming barracks.

The whole site was already in ruin. We heard Volcanus on the wind, as the wind brought the faint sounds of battle from kilometres away.

Walking through the ruined structures, I almost expected to see corpses. The attackers were long gone, and those that died here had been given over to funeral pyres outside the walls weeks ago. Three Thunderhawks, sandblasted but still golden, rested on the northern landing platforms. Along the edge of my retinal display, an open vox link cycled through channels, seeking a connection.

'Reclusiarch Grimaldus,' spoke a voice over the vox. 'You honour us with your presence.'

We walked on, drawing near to the stilted platforms, ascending to the launch deck on crew ladders. Using elevators and servitors piloting lifter-Sentinels, twenty Celestial Lions were plundering their own firebase's supplies, loading up their Thunderhawks with brutal efficiency. The warriors themselves hauled crates of ammunition between them, every one of them keeping at least one hand free to reach for a bolter at a second's notice. It was a clean, impressive resupply, even if it bore a few furtive resemblances to a less-noble looting.

One of the Space Marines came forward, bearing the black helm of a Pride Leader. He knelt, though he had no true reason to do so, and removed the dark helmet. The face beneath was the warm, rich brown of humans born to equatorial climes, with cultures dependent on the teeming jungle and expansive savannah. I had never been to the Lions home world of Elysium IX, but I had met many of its dark-skinned sons. A culture of hunters: proud people from birth to death.

This warrior's face was lined with the faint cracks of age. A Chapter veteran, no doubt. His lack of mutilating scars did him great credit.

'I do not know you,' I prompted.

'Pride Leader Ekene Dubaku.' He rose to his feet, the unnecessary honour complete. 'I lead those of us who remain.'

Pride Leader. A squad sergeant. This did not bode well.

'Grimaldus,' I replied. 'Reclusiarch of the Eternal Crusade. Cousin, when you say you lead those who remain...'

Ekene took my prompt again. 'There are ninety-six Lions still drawing breath upon this world, Reclusiarch. I inherited command from Warleader Vakembei, he of the Spear That Hunts Hearts. He walked into the Emperor's embrace eighteen days ago.'

'I knew Captain Vakembei. The Imperium will miss his blade, and his wisdom. What of Brother-Chaplain Julkhara?'

'Deathspeaker Julkhara is dead to the kine, slain twenty-four days past.'

'The kine,' I said, without inflection.

'The greenskins, Reclusiarch. Cattle. Beasts. *Kine.*'

Disrespect of the enemy should be punished, but it was not my place to chastise them for their hatreds, nor would it be wise to annihilate morale by passing judgement against them for such petty transgressions.

The Lions kept working, alongside the trundling stomp of Sentinel loaders. At my gesture, Cyneric joined them, assisting with their loading.

'This looks more like looting than resupply, Dubaku.'

He replaced his helm, speaking through the vox-grille. 'We have little choice, since it was overrun. Our fallback stronghold is within Volcanus itself, but we risk raids out here every three days. Ammunition is low – production and resupply from our fleet has dropped to almost nothing.'

For a moment, I wondered why they had not requested aid from the other Chapters, but Dorn's blood runs thick in the veins of his descendants. It was difficult to lay pride aside, even in the face of devastation. Especially then, for when else was a warrior truly tested? What other time could be finer for proving that a man is strong enough to stand alone?

Dubaku continued. 'We have swallowed our pride long enough to request aid from the Flesh Tearers and the Black Templars, but the former are as depleted as we are, and the latter are preparing to set sail. Your brothers are taking the fight out into the stars, Reclusiarch. We have no right to beg for scraps while being left behind. So we exist by plundering our fallen fortress and looting our own dead.'

So Julkhara's summons had been a personal one. It had still cost him dearly to send it, I was certain.

We moved aside as another three modified Sentinel walkers clanked past, bearing aquila-marked crates in their industrial claws.

I was struck by one thing above all: the Celestial Lions were dead. While a hundred yet remained, they operated now without a single voice from their Chapter's high command, and their ranking veteran officer was a squad sergeant. I had hoped to find Julkhara. I had hoped to find *hope*.

'Finish your loading,' I told Dubaku. 'Once we are aboard the gunship, speak to me of everything that happened since you first made planetfall. Then I will judge how best to answer Julkhara's last words.'

Dubaku saluted, making the sign of the aquila over the winged Imperialis on his breastplate.

'The Deathspeaker vowed that you would come.'

I did not reply. I merely gestured for him to get back to work. It remained to be seen just what Julkhara truly expected of me, or what I could actually achieve here. It already felt less like I was summoned to save the Lions, and more like I was called to hold a vigil, watching over them as they died.

NINE HUNDRED AND eighty-three warriors. They had brought nine hundred and eighty-three warriors to this world, and ninety-six remained.

We rode in restraint thrones in the gunship's dimly lit crew bay. The Celestial Lions had removed their helms, though Cyneric and I left ours in place.

Ekene's tale was a grim one.

Their entire Chapter had landed here, but for the most remote uninitiated training forces, spread across the segmentum.

Before dawn over the Mannheim Gap, they had been on the surface for three months and sixteen days, defending Hive Volcanus on the west coast of Armageddon Prime.

In that span of time, all of which was spent bolter-to-blade in the city's burning streets, they suffered casualties far, far in advance of any other Chapter. Everywhere they fought, the enemy struck back in overwhelming numbers. Countless times they were deployed to reinforce elements of the Imperial Guard that were already long dead by the time the Lions arrived, leaving the Space Marines deep in enemy territory without easy withdrawal.

On at least fifteen catalogued occasions, they were ordered to advance on specific critical objectives, only to find themselves alone without the planned support forces or the promised reinforcements.

Casualties mounted, operation after operation, day by day. Ambushes were common, even on routine patrols through pacified territory. The Lions were assigned to hold

crucial districts and sectors, and accordingly moved in force
to cover all necessary ground. Yet they found their patrols
being hit harder than any orbital intelligence had predicted
possible. The enemy would appear in numbers undreamed,
rising from ambushes in sectors that were recorded as being
most viciously cleansed beforehand.

They were granted orbital picts and auspex-scrye readouts from Hive Command, only to find their intelligence
scarcely matched the embattled realities of their deployment zones. Time and again, the Lions jumped into the
fire. What choice was there? They would not allow the city
to fall. They could not allow the enemy to live.

It did not take long for them to rely first and foremost
on their own scanners and Scouts, but their equipment
suffered unexpected deteriorations and frequent jamming;
their Scouts often fell silent while out in the city alone.
Sometimes, the Lions would find their Scouts' bodies. Usually, they would not.

Pict-feeds from their vessels in orbit were distorted from
the void war playing out above, but those rare, wrecked
visual clues were the most reliable intelligence they could
muster. The Lions swore by them, thanking the thrall-
captains of their warships for any and all devoted efforts.
But these also grew more infrequent as their fleet was massacred in the sky. Less than a month into the campaign,
rearming runs from orbit began to grow as rare as reliable intelligence. Celestial Lions drop-ships were destroyed
high in the atmosphere on two occasions, and on another,
Volcanus's own wall-guns malfunctioned and destroyed an
incoming shipment, blowing seven loaded Thunderhawks
out of the sky.

Never once did Ekene's voice crack as he told me of these

misfortunes; never once did he sigh, or glance away, or lament at what had come to be. Contained within him was a deep, nourishing well of resolve that did credit to any son of Dorn.

It only made my blood run colder with each revealed betrayal, that such a fate had befallen my cousins.

My hands must have been clenched for some time, for Ekene hesitated in his retelling, gesturing to where I gripped the arms of the restraint throne.

'Reclusiarch?'

I forced my muscles to unlock. 'Continue.'

And continue he did.

Mere weeks into the war, half the Chapter lay dead, the names of the slain added each dawn to the rolls of honour. The survivors fought on.

Decades ago, in the Last War, Hive Volcanus fell quickly to the greenskin horde. Like carrion crows, the enemy picked over the city's bones and went to war with the looted spoils of Imperial manufactories. There would be no repeat of such shameful history this time. The city's lords and leaders made that clear at each command briefing, leaving the Lions to make their demands into defiant reality. All the while, the city burned. It burned but did not fall.

Then came Mannheim.

The Mannheim Gap was a canyon running through the mountains north of Hive Volcanus. A rent in this planet's priceless earth, torn open by the slow, active dance of the world's tectonics. Any who dwell here for more than a handful of weeks know that Armageddon is not a world that sleeps easy, whether due to groundquakes, dust storms, or yet another war.

The Lions were told the canyon had to be assaulted, for there lay a nest of mechanical heresy, where the aliens were forgebreeding their scrap iron god-machines. Volcanus's forces had to strike before the alien Titans became active, or the tide would forever turn against the city's defenders. The Guard could not be trusted to deal such a surgical strike, nor could the city organise a mass withdrawal and redeployment of its deeply entrenched Guard elements to make it a plausible option. It had to be Space Marines. It had to be the Lions.

Primitive void shielding protected the site from orbital bombardment. The Lions had to strike overland, without drop pods, marching into the ravine alongside their tanks, attacking in battalion regiments like some echo of the Heresy and the millennia of crude warfare before it.

The Lions reconnoitred, of course. They scouted and watched, deeming Imperial intelligence reliable. None of the alien god-walkers were infused with life.

But time was not on their side. Every hour they spent behind their fortress walls was another hour that brought the Gargant machines closer to awakening.

Five hundred Lions attacked. The last half of the Chapter went to war, knowing that the enemy numbers were beyond the capability of the Guard to confront. They chose to bring overwhelming force, to strike fast and hard, countering their crippling inability to strike from the skies.

Five hundred Space Marines. I have taken whole worlds with a quarter of that number. Even though human resistance and greenskin forces are impossible to compare, five hundred Adeptus Astartes warriors is an overwhelming weapon in any imaginable reckoning. The Lions commanders were right to commit their full fury. Any

Chapter Master would do the same. There was no possible way the enemy could have known such a force was coming to destroy them, and there is simply no way to prepare for *five hundred* Space Marine warriors.

Strike with choking ferocity. Destroy the enemy. Fall back before getting entrenched in a full-scale battle. It should have worked.

The Season of Fire was still weeks away when they charged, but dragon's breath in the air already heralded the storms to come. Gritty, stinking air howled down the canyon as the Lions advanced behind their Warleaders and Deathspeakers. I could picture it so clearly, down to their banners tearing in the wind.

Along the canyon's walls, huge industrial rigging rose against the rock: great construction yard platforms, as the greenskin beasts built their iron avatars higher and higher. Hundreds of them, never of uniform size, each one a bloated, scrap-fleshed icon to foul gods, crawling with screaming aliens.

Still. Five hundred Space Marines...

'When did you realise you had been betrayed?' I asked.

Ekene took a breath before replying. 'It did not take long.'

'The Gargants,' Cyneric interjected. 'They were active.'

Ekene gave a bitter laugh, sharp as a gunshot. 'If that was all we had to deal with, we might still have fought our way clear without being slaughtered. We might even have won, despite dying to the last man.'

He was more solemn as he continued, letting the tale reach its inevitable conclusion. The Gargants were not sleeping, they were waiting. Searing heat spread through the canyon from the solid fuel burners deep in the alien Titans' bellies – beneath the crash of bolters and the cracking rattle of alien rifles, came the clank of gears, with the landslide grind of coal and scrap being fed into the Gargants' heart-fires. Great guns whined downward on protesting joints, while the ground shook with each newborn Gargant's first steps.

The Lions gold battle tanks raged skywards, streams of las-cannon fire bursting thin shields and scoring holes in the hulls of towering enemy war machines. Warleaders shouted orders, in control of their warriors even in the heat of the battle, establishing where to strike, where to push through the orks' lines, where to move in defence of tank battalions threatened by enemy infantry.

My heart soared at his words. Even when the Gargants awoke, Ekene and his brothers – the last half of a noble Chapter – were still fighting to win. They would purge the canyon at the cost of their own lives. Dorn himself would have stood with them that day.

But the tide truly turned. As Ekene described this latest twist of fate, Cyneric leaned forward in his restraint throne, scarcely believing what he was hearing.

The enemy ambush unfolded further. Greenskins spilled from the earth, pouring in hordes from warrens within the canyon sides and the rocky ground. Thousands of them, roaring beneath fanged war banners and standards made from crucified Lions taken in other battles. This fresh army surged into the ravine, filling it like sand in an hourglass, blocking all hope of withdrawal and eliminating any chance of victory.

'They knew we were coming,' said Ekene. 'What other reason could there be to bury whole war-clans under the rock, waiting for such an assault? They knew we were coming. Their overlord was a beast clad in scrapwork armour

– the biggest greenskin we had ever seen. He ate the dead: his own, and ours. Captain Vularakh buried the war-sword Je'hara in the beast's belly and carved three metres of stinking alien guts free. It did nothing. We fought as we fell back, but we knew we were betrayed.'

I could not argue with that. A traitor, somewhere, had fed word to the enemy, and the orks made the most of their ambush. Five hundred Space Marines could take a star system. At Mannheim, they had barely been able to escape alive. It was difficult to imagine the sea of alien flesh necessary to butcher so many of mankind's finest, but having seen the ocean of greenskins spilling over the plains towards the walls of Helsreach only months before, I had a fairly clear frame of reference.

'That is not all.' Ekene gave a grim smile. 'Sniper fire, brutally accurate, rained down from the canyon walls. I am not speaking of the solid shell rattle of greenskin projectile throwers. I know how these aliens fight, Reclusiarch. This was viciously precise laser weaponry, knifing through our officers' helms from above. Warleader Dakembe, shot through the throat. Spiritwalker Azadah, taken before he could unleash his powers, his skull blown open by two crossing las-shots an arm's length away from me. Deathspeakers, Warleaders, Spiritwalkers... even Pride Leaders, cut down with fire too precise, too clinical, to be the enemy.'

He paused, and I could see in his eyes that he was no longer seeing the gunship bay around us. He was seeing his brothers die at Mannheim – some to crude iron blades rending through ceramite, others to spikes of white-hot lasfire lancing down into the ravine.

'It took four hours to fight free. We carved our way back

the way we came, abandoning a sea of dead tanks, slain brothers and butchered enemy bodies. The gene-seed of half our Chapter lies rotting at the bottom of that canyon, unharvested by our Apothecaries and defiled by the thousands of foes we left alive. We *fled*,' he made the word into a spat curse, 'from the field, and the most valiant battle the Celestial Lions ever fought was in that retreat. Never had we faced such odds. The last of us cut our way free, pulled our brothers from the storm of blades and fell back to our fortress with the enemy at our heels.'

'The fortress fell,' I said quietly.

'That implies we even had a chance to defend it.' Ekene shook his head. 'The xenos flooded it before most of our survivors had even arrived. We had to fight just to escape our own falling fortress. Even then, for every gunship that raced free, another two were shot down in flames.'

'Throne of the Emperor,' Cyneric swore softly.

Ekene nodded. 'Our survivors returned to Volcanus. We had three officers left at dusk of that day, three officers above the rank of Pride Leader. Deathspeaker Julkhara, who called you a brother, Reclusiarch; Warleader Vakembei, the last captain; and Lifebinder Kei-Tukh, our last Apothecary. The Chapter's future rested on his skills. And can you guess the final insult, Reclusiarch? The last gasp in this drama of shame and treachery?'

I wanted facts, not my own speculation. 'Say it,' I said.

Ekene smiled. 'Our territory inside the city walls was a cold foundry, nearly lightless, with a perimeter of rockcrete patrolled by our remaining warriors. Kei-Tukh did not survive the first night. We found him at dawn, slouched against our last Land Raider, shot through the eye-lens. The gene-seed he had carried was gone, and he would harvest no more. So now you see the depths of our plight, Reclusiarch. We have lost our fleet, our armoury, our officers and almost all hope of rebuilding our Chapter. We cannot even cling to pride, after the shame of retreat. All that remains to us is the truth. We must survive long enough to speak it. The Imperium must know what happened here.'

I wanted to tell him the Imperium would know. I wanted to reassure him that his entire bloodline had not died in vain. I meant to say it, yet the words that left my lips were more instinctive, and somehow more honest.

'You mean to die on this world.'

Ekene's dark lips curved into another sickle-smile. 'Of course. We will die alongside our brothers, as it should be. Deathspeaker Julkhara wished you to know the truth behind our coming last stand, and ensure those that share our primarch's blood never speak ill of our fall.'

I said nothing. They had asked me to come, but I would decide just what my involvement would be.

Cyneric leaned forward, and his helm's vox-speakers couldn't quite steal the passion from his voice. 'You have to return to Elysium. Endure the shame if you must, as the Crimson Fists endured their shame. You have to rebuild your Chapter – the galaxy must not lose the Lions forever.'

'Elysium? Brother-knight, the Chapter is savaged beyond resurrection. Men, materiel, knowledge… All of it is gone. We have nothing to hand down to any generation that would follow us. You advocate cowardice to fuel false hope?'

'I advocate *survival*.' Cyneric snarled the words. 'Survival to preserve precious blood, and to rise again to fight another day. I hope to die in glory, as any son of Rogal Dorn. But even in our legends of the primarch, when he bled his warriors to purify them, he never let them taste annihilation. Sometimes, the more virtuous path is to carry the shame and survive.'

I looked between them both. The truth was that there was no wrong answer here. No right answer, either. A glorious last stand was no more or less respectable than preserving the infinite value of a Space Marine Chapter. One would earn more glory, no doubt. The other would better serve mankind. I appreciated Ekene's zeal to finish what he began, and die with unbroken loyalty alongside his brothers.

But I also appreciated Cyneric's surprising wisdom, to preserve the Chapter's soul at the cost of carrying personal shame. Few Templars would commit to such a burden. It spoke well of him that he had the insight to consider both paths, but I wondered if he would advocate shame if he were the one facing the prospect of so glorious a last stand. Easier to speak of shame than to survive it.

In the minutes of silence that followed, we touched down in Hive Volcanus. Whatever solution arose from all this had to appease the Lions' hot-blooded need for vengeance at Mannheim, as well as their cold-blooded need to be vindicated by spreading word of their betrayal. Both were essential, and both would see the Celestial Lions wiped clear from the ranks of the Adeptus Astartes.

And yet, the Chapter also had to survive.

As we disembarked, Cyneric opened a vox channel, speaking so the Lions would not hear.

'One question plagues me, Reclusiarch.'

I could guess. 'You would ask how this all began – what the Lions did in the past to earn this fate.'

'Every vendetta has a source, does it not?'

'True. And the truth here is a bleak one, dating back decades. The Lions are being punished now for trying to tell the truth fifty years ago.'

'I do not understand.'

We made our way across the landing pad, and how glorious it was to see a city skyline that was still intact. Volcanus had endured a lesser siege than Helsreach, with many more defenders manning its walls. The central spire was an ugly monolith that lived up to the name *hive*, with anaemic industrial sectors and transit stations spread around its wide foundations. Most of the city's manufactories were protected in the hive tower's shell, making life wretched for its citizens who were forced to live shut inside with the fumes of their own forge fires eternally tainting the ventilation. It meant, however, that the city was monumentally harder to take than Helsreach, and with no central highway, the enemy could not simply run free through the city's core.

'Every Chapter carries a thousand secrets of past wars, unabsolved shames and slights against its honour. This is not the first time that the Lions have dealt with the Inquisition.'

'Julkhara's recording,' Cyneric replied. 'He spoke of the "echoes of Khattar".'

'Khattar is the world where this pathetic grudge began. It is where the Inquisition first betrayed the Celestial Lions.' I finally turned from the Volcanus skyline, watching the Lions unloading their gunships. 'You could argue, as other Chapters have argued upon hearing this rumour, that it was also where the Lions damned themselves by their own naivety.'

That gave Cyneric pause. 'You admire them, but consider them naive?'

'Anyone who trusts an agent of the Inquisition has earned

the right to be named naive, Cyneric. There is a reason the Adeptus Astartes stand apart from the Imperium – autonomous; loyal to the empire's ideals, but rarely its function. The Lions' most grievous error was forgetting that.'

IV

STORIES AT THE FIRE

THE INQUISITION DOES not exist.

It does not exist in the sense many Imperial citizens believe – as a cohesive, interlinked cobweb of organised power. Individual men and women are granted immunity from all persecution and autonomy from all law. They are granted that most nebulous of virtues: *authority*. Everything else comes down to what they achieve, and what personal power they amass. When an inquisitor calls upon Imperial resources, he or she relies on the threat of authority, rather than any real organisation lending support to their needs. Their power is both utterly real and a cunning illusion, all at once.

Men and women with wildly differing ideologies, tactics and goals do exist, and they are invested with ultimate authority, but that is not a collective enemy we could face and fight. Inquisitors will often ally together, but rarely permanently. Even their precious ordos are lines of alignment, philosophies of specialisation and intent, not armies of organised allegiance.

They are, in all ways, the exact opposite of the Adeptus Astartes. Our temporal authority has been stripped back since the Heresy, yet we are essential to the Imperium and need no illusions of commanding great power. Our war fleets and brotherhoods speak for themselves.

Given the nature of the war, Armageddon's cities were fairly thick with warbands of Ordo Xenos agents and their militant ilk, but to move against the Inquisition was to move against a colony of vermin. Trap one rat and it may still mean nothing to the nest. Any number of the inquisitors involved in the war would have nothing to do with the Lions' persecution, and care little if they even knew what was being done to the Chapter. I could not simply approach the closest Inquisitorial representative and demand he reveal what he knew, for the chances were that he would know nothing.

Time was my worst enemy, for it was not on our side. I needed to cut right to the heart of the matter, but the Inquisition was not a beast with one heart. Every Inquisitorial warband was its own sovereign entity.

Few Chapters knew of what happened at Khattar, and even fewer ever spoke of it. Of those that were aware of the planet's annihilation, I would wager that most did not regard it as a true threat to the autonomy of the Adeptus Astartes, preferring to focus on their own concerns and their own wars. As for the others, I can only speak of the Black Templars with any conviction, and even our Chapter is more akin to several dozen individual Crusade fleets with their own goals and traditions, united in lineage rather than united side by side.

What little I knew of Khattar came down to a conflict of pride and duty between the Lions and their Inquisitorial allies – the kind of conflict that takes place a thousand times each year across the Imperium's vast spread of worlds. Many of these disagreements turn to bloodshed; what made the Lions' situation so galling was that they had reacted with a measure of composure and reason, when they had every right to draw their bolters and finish it in a blunter, more efficient manner.

The Lions are a Chapter of storytellers and saga-singers. As the sun set over the besieged city walls, we remained in the outlying industrial sector, circled by tanks in the Lions' makeshift armoury at the heart of a powered-down foundry. Beneath the rumble of growling, idling engines, I could almost hear the ghosts whispering among the bare bolter racks and empty ammunition crates.

We had agreed to speak of Khattar. I had the story of how my cousins had paid a butcher's bill since coming to Armageddon. Now I wished to know what had happened before.

Seven Lions had gathered – the survivors of Ekene's own squad – while the others prepared for the final assault to come, or patrolled on sentry duty. Cyneric was aiding them; I thought the experience of living among another Chapter would aid his perspective.

The air was charged with the expectation of attack, even this deep in an Imperial-held city. It left a foul taste in my mouth.

So I sat around a wreckage-fire with Ekene and his proud Lions, the firelight sending amber shadows dancing across our armour. This was how they had told tales on Elysium, though their savannah campfires would be set out under the stars, not beneath the arched ceiling of an abandoned manufactory.

'You first,' Ekene prompted me.

I did not understand, and said as much.

'You first,' he repeated. 'You have come to our hearth and home. Tradition states the first tale must be yours.'

'Outsiders always speak first,' one of the other warriors said. 'It is how they pay for their food and rest at a tribe's camp.'

'I have no stories.'

The Lions chuckled.

'Everyone has stories,' one of them said.

'Tell us of Helsreach,' said Ekene.

'No.' The word came out as sharp as a bolt shot, and they tensed at the suddenness of my reply. I had no desire to speak of Helsreach. The lessons I had learned were still scoring themselves on my soul.

They accepted my refusal with shared glances and murmured agreement, but a warrior with the name Jaur-Kem etched on his breastplate cleared his throat in almost amusing human politeness.

'Reclusiarch,' he said. 'Tell us the tale of how you earned a Deathspeaker's grin.'

I felt a strange discomfort creeping down my backbone. 'The events of the Pelegeron Cluster are recorded in any number of accessible archives.'

The Lions laughed again, though there was no mockery in it. They were far too wise to insult a Chaplain, even one of other allegiance. Their laughter was for the many difficulties in two Chapters trying to share time in companionship, and the endless differences Space Marines of divergent bloodlines always faced in such moments.

'Official records are dry and lifeless things, Reclusiarch.' Ekene gestured in encouragement. 'Tell us what happened through your eyes. You would do us great honour.'

I looked between them, from one face to the next, gun-sight reticules chiming and unfocusing as they identified null targets.

'Very well.' I took a calming breath. 'There is an ancient saying, a sentiment wedded to humanity's bones, I think, for it emerges from countless cultures with slightly different phrasing each time. My mentor, Reclusiarch Mordred, despised it, saying its very core ran counter to the precepts of the Eternal Crusade, but I always enjoyed its funereal poetry. *"There will never be a war to end all wars".*'

The Lions spoke in agreement. They had a similar sentiment on their home world.

'On the fourth world of the Pelegeron system,' I said, 'they believed the opposite was true. Their sedition became secession, and their rebellion became war. "The Last War", they called it. The "war to end all wars". If they could throw the Imperium back with enough defiance, then mankind's empire would let them drift away in peace, to live as they wished in the filth of their heresy. They truly believed this.'

Strange, how fierce the memories felt as they came back. There is always such bestial comfort in sweat and screaming rage.

'Imagine a fortress formed from a most diseased mind,' I said. 'The capital of a world at the whim of tectonic rage, on one of the few landmasses stable enough to inhabit. Imagine this world's priceless rock made living among lava rivers a necessity for hundreds of thousands of mining settlers, but the planet itself still cringes back from all human touch. That is Pelegeron IV, cousins. That is what it was like. A world only half-formed, still writhing in protracted birth throes, with magma for blood and smoke for air.'

Ekene was smiling. 'You are a better tale-teller than you give yourself credit for, Deathspeaker Grimaldus.'

I was warming to the idea, myself. It was not so different from giving declarations of judgement, or reciting the Litanies of Hate.

'This final fortress was called Apex, as was the volcano within which it was built. Few geological archives have ever chronicled a volcano to match the scale of Apex, for the mountain eclipsed even the Olympus forge-peak on Sacred Mars. Apex was a boil on Pelegeron's crust, the size of lesser continents on saner worlds, with its infected roots digging all the way to the world's core. In times of peace, the Imperium hollowed it out, and drilled ever deeper. When war came, it became the enemy cult's final fortress. We had to strike at their last bastion before they could seal themselves inside.'

'You said the foe called it the Last War,' one of the Lions interrupted. 'What did your black knights call it?'

'The Vinculus Crusade,' I replied. 'And it ended at the Battle of Fire and Blood. Many archives record the final duel between Vinculus himself and the arch-heretic atop the cathedral.' I shook my head. 'It never happened. But when has the truth ever mattered to Imperial chroniclers?'

That earned a few grim laughs. I barely acknowledged them. I could feel the heat again. The insane heat of those final hours under the mountain.

'Though the volcano had great transit vents wide enough for tankers and cargo haulers to drift in and out of the mountain's industrial chambers, they had been sealed and shielded from aerial attack for weeks. It left us facing an assault on the main thoroughfare gate, despite the impossibility of landing an army there.'

I looked to each of the warriors with me, unsure if I was doing justice to the day itself. They listened, paying full heed to my words.

'I stood among the Sword Brethren of High Marshal Ludoldus at the assault's vanguard. We had to hold the fortress gate while the rest of the army marched up the mountainside. With no room to deploy in force at the gate, the Sisters of the Bloody Rose Order and our own brothers landed at stable plateaux and struggled up the rockslides from there. The vanguard deployed by drop pod, through atmosphere thick enough to choke a man without a rebreather. Thirty of us. Thirty knights – the High Marshal's chosen.'

I met the Lions' eyes, though they saw nothing but my eye-lenses. 'That was how it began. *Hold the gate,* our liege lord demanded of us. *Hold until the others reach us.* Nothing more.'

He wants to vent his anger, but lacks even the breath to shout. Weary rage pulls at his limbs, miring him with its sluggish caress. Never has he felt so drained, so leeched of all vitality. War has become work – an exhausting slaughterhouse chore, reduced to the rise and fall of blades, with the push and pull of burning muscles.

Slain foes blanket the rocky ground in every direction. His brothers, those still standing, fight behind a barricade of armoured enemy dead. The shrieking madmen that come against the knights know nothing of fear. They spend their lives like copper coins, charging in a screaming horde.

'Ai-ai-aiiiiiii,' the bastards keep shrieking as they run to the butchers' blades. 'Ai-ai-aiiiiii.'

The knight hears his liege lord above the chaos. Not shouting orders, for no orders are needed when there's nothing to do but fight or die. Neither is he crying defiance, for the knights' refusal to run is defiance enough. No, he hears his lord – that golden warrior – laughing.

It is Ludoldus's way. The High Marshal stands with one boot on the barricade of bodies, his ancestral sword swinging and spearing down in a ceaseless blur of charged steel. Laughing in the heat of battle-fever.

By contrast, Grimaldus barely has the breath to curse. The knight's chainsword sings for him, its snarls switching between the roar of whirring teeth and the meat-muted growl of carving through human flesh.

Down the mountainside, the Imperial army hauls itself higher. At the main gate, the cultist-soldiers of Pelegeron, faced with their rebellion's collapse, are no longer fighting for their twisted truth. They are fighting to survive, and they are losing. Their cities are in dust. Their stronghold endures siege.

Then it comes. That moment, disgustingly sharp and impossible to predict, when the defenders are no longer defending at all, but fighting a retreat. It's a change in the toxic air, a divergence from the angry cries that rise from any army like an aural tide. Everything is different without any real warning, but it spreads the way fire devours a bracken forest. It is no longer a fighting retreat, but a rout. The defenders are broken, and the slaughter begins as they turn and flee. Soldiers who had faced the invaders with fanatical pride only moments before now die with their wounds on their backs. To the knight's eyes, there is no surer testament to a coward's death.

Grimaldus fights at his lord's side, beneath the gaze of towering stone angels that beckon the faithful into the subterranean stronghold. His helm is gone, torn away almost an hour before, and his enhanced respiration labours in the thick air. But he stands, and he fights, and his sword never falls still.

The enemy flood around him, sacrificing their lives for the chance to pull at his limbs, seeking to drag him down. He kills them with blade, with boot, with fist. They are only human, he tells himself. Only human. *Their bones break. Their blood stains his tabard a sick pink. He kills most of them fast enough that they can scarcely cry out. As for the others, without their insect-faced oxygen masks, they strangle and die without the need for a death earned by the blade. Smashing their respirator tanks is enough to leave them dead.*

The great gates cannot close. Even if the black knights had not destroyed the mechanics with melta detonations upon arrival, the number of corpses spread across the avenue now defies any chance of the portals sealing shut. With animal desperation, the blasphemous faithful try to save their temple-city from defilement. Teams of sweating soldiers work to haul the immense stone gates shut as their brethren die on the black knights' blades.

The first Imperial soldier to reach the knights is Vinculus himself, a lord of the Inquisition and temporary commander of the Adepta Sororitas forces. He, like the army behind him, has had to climb the barricade of bodies.

High Marshal Ludoldus of the Black Templars is waiting for him, with the remaining nine knights of his Sword Brethren. Grimaldus is one of them. Exhausted, his breath saws in and out.

There is no shame in kneeling. They have been fighting for almost three hours, alone and without even the whisper of reinforcement. The dead lie broken in their hundreds. Amongst them, the Sword Brethren kneel on weary limbs, catching precious respite. Some are too weary to even lift their heads. As Space Marines, they will recover within minutes where mere men would need days of rest. Yet, as mortal warriors, their flesh has been pushed through torment, and even bionic limbs have malfunctioned with overworked joints.

One still stands. He will not kneel. He will not kneel.

'You fought well,' his liege lord tells him. 'I am beginning to believe you were born lucky, Merek.'

Grimaldus pulls a bayonet knife from the armpit joint of his scratched armour, and casts the blade aside without wiping his blood from it. He makes the crusader's cross to his commander, letting the wound seal itself.

Ludoldus has fought unhelmed, letting his three lungs filter the filth in the breath-starved air. Grimaldus sees his commander's eyes flick to the left, and turns to follow the High Marshal's gaze.

Mordred, Reclusiarch of the Eternal Crusade, stands among the dead. He watches the newest of Ludoldus's Sword Brethren, saying nothing, staring with red eye-lenses and a grinning silver skull for a face.

Within the Temple City.

The streets are vast tunnels worming through the rock. Homes and shrines are hollowed-out caverns, forced into stability by great stone pillars, defended by shrieking, chanting, cowering families.

The war has ended, and the massacre has begun. Gouts of chemical fire spray forth in hissing rushes from the charred muzzles of sacred flamers, while the crashing bang of bolters plays in relentless percussion. Flailing, burning bodies line the ground. Despite the ingenuity of the subterranean city's ventilation engines, filtration systems are failing under the strain of cleansing the oxygen supply. Fire eats the air before the Space Marines and Sisters of Battle can breathe it. After needing rebreathers for the march up the mountainside, Imperial forces find themselves needing to don them again to prevent suffocation underground.

The mines run deep in the volcano, but the habitable sectors of the great city sit much closer to the surface. It takes less than an hour to reach the heart of the heresy, and Grimaldus – a warrior incapable of admiring allies and enemies alike – is awed by the cathedral hewn from the burning rock. Here, great landing platforms of magma-scarred metal sit beneath the sealed sky-tunnels, where once pilgrim shuttles and mining haulers came to refuel before journeying deeper into the volcano's innards.

A geological monument to a whole world's power takes up kilometre after kilometre of space in the great cavern. The cathedral itself is born right from the rock, its pillars and battlements moulded from the cave walls, suspended above a molten river. The running lake of magma puts him in mind, just for a moment, of the underworld rivers flowing through so many human myths.

The last survivors still flee before the advancing Imperials, spilling in a tide across the earthen bridges leading into the temple. They die with their wounds in their backs.

High Marshal Ludoldus leads them to the rock avenue over the molten chasm. He levels his blade at the angel-adorned walls of the heretic cathedral, and sends the black knights forward in a shouting tide.

'Destroy the power generators,' Inquisitor Vinculus's orders crackle over the vox. 'I want the sky shafts open before the sun rises over this worthless world.'

His voice is joined by the High Marshal's. 'And kill every living soul within that temple.'

Swords cut deep and blood runs cold. After the executions, they find the arch-heretic alone, unarmed, and weeping. He wears no flowing robes of priestly office, and he sits upon no ornate throne of gold and volcanic glass. What they find is a man in miners' overalls kneeling in meditative prayer, his cheeks silvered by the slow flow of tears. He wears a breathing mask as he prays on the battlements of his cathedral, but doesn't even open his eyes as his killers approach from behind.

Grimaldus is among them, at the shoulder of his liege lord.
He is the first to tense, to move forward in an eager rush. Ludoldus restrains him with a gesture.

'No,' the High Marshal says to the black knight. 'Not you.'
Grimaldus's chainsword sputters to stillness, idling in the burning air.

It is Vinculus – too human and so very frail – who steps forward. His frame is weak next to the knights at his side, but his voice is cold iron.

'In the name of the God-Emperor of Mankind,' he says to the kneeling heretic, 'I do judge thee diabolus extremis, unfit for existence within His Holy Majesty's galaxy.'

'You do not understand,' the kneeling, weeping man replies. He makes no move to defend himself as Vinculus closes from behind, bearing doom in the form of a short, energised blade. 'I am a vessel. Just a vessel.'

The tip of the sacred sword rests against his spine. Vinculus braces for the push that will finish the traitor's life, and end the war.

The heretic's watering eyes turn to the knights. 'Forgive me.'

'Wait.' Grimaldus steps forward, a hand raised in warning. 'Wait!' Reclusiarch Mordred is at his side, saying the same words, giving the same order.

The sword lances home, biting deep into the man's body. The self-proclaimed vessel falls to the stone, dying, breaking apart to free the thing within. Cancer spills from the wound, a ghost of oily smoke, leaping in a spreading cloud and clinging to the inquisitor's wide eyes and open mouth. He damns himself to death the moment he breathes it in.

Mordred is the first to move, his crozius maul raised high. Sword Brother Grimaldus is a heartbeat behind him, chainsword revving. Vinculus falls back, screaming, tearing at his eyes, *dragging them from his face with curled fingers. They come free, strings of viscera behind, and he holds them out, seemingly offering them to the two charging knights.*

Vinculus falls, howling, vomiting wet blackness that has no place in a human body. Mordred and Grimaldus take him to pieces with their weapons, as if they can carve the corruption from its new host.

The inquisitor laughs through the excreted filth. Pressure builds in the air around them, as though heralding a peal of thunder. Just as it strikes, the inquisitor's body bursts open.

Sourceless, directionless darkness falls, with the finality of a hammer blow.

The first thing he feels is the familiar pain of a broken body. Life is war, and war is pain: this is a truth he has survived a thousand times. There is no great secret to pain; he sees it no differently to the biorhythmic signs playing out on his retinal display. Pain is nothing more than a sign he is still alive.

Grimaldus drags himself to his feet, boots thudding on the scorched rock bridge above the chasm of liquid fire. His armour is halfway to annihilation, burned and scraped and chipped, bleeding sparks from severed power cables. The cathedral is a detonated ruin, and its besiegers have been cast across the cavern. Huge chunks of masonry still rain down on the cavern, plunging into the fire chasm.

Bodies lie everywhere. Dead knights, dead Sisters, dead heretics in their hundreds. Among the corpses, survivors begin to stir. But not enough. Some are already standing, weapons in their hands. But not enough.

Three minutes. According to his retinal display, he has been unconscious for three whole minutes. He will do penance for his weakness, if he survives this night. No matter that almost *every soul in the cavern has suffered the same way – he sees it as a weakness that deserves punishment. Dorn's martyring blood burns hot in his veins.*

The daemon walks through the dead, hunting the living, smashing aside the few swords that rise to bar its way. It is a seething mass of deep-sea nightmare fears given form, that underwater sensation of looking into the endless black of the open ocean, never knowing what lies beyond the mist of human vision. No longer the size of the man inside which it hosted, the poisonous creature has swollen to a riper, truer scale, crushing bodies beneath its cartilaginous claws. It dances at the edge of Grimaldus's focus, a thing of two worlds and at home in neither. The knight's eyes water through the chiming pulses of target locks, his mind aching from the sin of witnessing the thing's existence.

Ludoldus, High Marshal of the Black Templars, faces the beast on the black stone bridge. At his feet are the armoured forms of Jasmine, Caroness of the Bloody Rose, and Ulricus, Emperor's Champion of the Vinculus Crusade. Two great heroes, champions of humanity in their own right, slain while Grimaldus surrendered to unconsciousness. He will ensure the penance for somnolence lasts a long, long time.

On a whim, he looks up, seeking any damage to the cavern's expansive ceiling. He has no wish to be buried here, dead or alive. A moment later, he's reactivating his vox link.

'This is Sword Brother Grimaldus to the Eternal Crusader. Eternal Crusader, *respond.*'

'Sword Brother.'

'The power generators are down and the sky thoroughfares are open.'

'Understood, Sword Brother. Gunships en route.'

The black knight reaches for a sword that isn't there. In the absence of his own blade, he takes a weapon from the dead.

The chain that had bound it to its former owner's armour hangs loose and broken.

Ludoldus is forced onto the defensive, parrying rather than cutting, each lift of his relic blade warding away another sweep of fanged tentacles and fleshy claws. Soon enough, he's stepping backwards, giving ground with silent curses.

He aches as never before. No single creature can be so strong. No beast of the warp has ever tested his warriors in this way. Ulricus, a warrior without compare, traded a mere seven blows with the creature before it gutted him with its talons. Jasmine lasted no longer – the two pieces of her body lie shrouded by the fall of her scarlet banner.

They cannot kill this thing. They cannot overwhelm it with numbers. Skill is meaningless against its speed. The beast's blows weigh on him, numbing his muscles. Each of its breaths comes with a mucosal spray of rancid air, clouding the knight-lord's sight.

The Sisters and knights fighting with him are smashed away, broken and cracked-open things tossed into the chasm of fire. Another knight reaches his side; slain in a heartbeat. And another, bashed aside by a flailing claw, knocked from the stone bridge to plummet into the magma river. Next, a Sister dies, melting and shrieking in the backwash of her own flame weapon as the beast roars the fire back against her. In a queasy blur, it looms back over Ludoldus.

He risks reaching for the grenade at his belt, but the creature's assault batters at his blade. He needs both hands to ward the thing's attacks away. He's down on one knee now, kneeling among the beast's kills, parrying above him. He needs a second – just a single second – to reach for...

The daemon pushes down against his blade. Ludoldus pours his strength into the parry, feeling his muscles crackle with tightening sinew. As the talon draws back, the High Marshal is already bringing his blade up again to block the claw's next descent.

It never comes. The falling claw is blocked by a war maul. The weapon's energy field crackles and strains, failing under the beast's strength.

'Mordred.' Ludoldus is laughing.

It isn't Mordred. Another warrior carries Mordred's crozius arcanum.

Sword Brother Grimaldus's red cloak is aflame. His armour is an ornate ruin of dented plate and blackened chains.

'Sire,' he breathes over the vox. An acknowledgement of fate.

The High Marshal frees one hand from his sword long enough to clutch at the holy incendiary buckled to his belt. The grenade comes free. Ludoldus thumbs the activation rune, hard enough to crack the orb's armoured shell. He raises it, a holy icon, shouting defiance as the daemon bellows downward.

Ludoldus hurls it, not at the beast, but at the creature's feet.

An Antioch orb is among the rarest weapons sacred to the Chapter. First created several thousand years before by Techmarine Antioch of the Black Templars, they are – by any measure – many magnitudes more lethal than the standard grenades available to other Chapters among the Adeptus Astartes. Consecrated oils and sacred acids are blended with compacted explosives, making each incendiary a personal masterpiece, inscribed with its own damnations, blessings and High Gothic mandalas. A grenade will kill the righteous and unrighteous alike, but an Antioch orb will ensure the blasphemous burn in agony as they meet their end.

The sacred sphere detonates as it crashes against the bridge. Ludoldus and Grimaldus are already retreating, refusing to show their backs to the foe, accepting flash blindness as the price of *witnessing their enemy's end. The explosion comes in a sunflare of white light, bathing the daemon in holy fire and blasting rock in every direction. The bridge starts to fall, crumbling, dragging many of the cavern's support pillars down with it.*

The beast is falling, aflame. Its shrieks don't end even when it plunges into the magma. Grimaldus falls back from the shattered bridge, staring in disgusted disbelief as the creature thrashes in the molten rock, its flesh igniting further, spraying liquid rock from its flailing limbs. New arms form as others melt away. New mouths tear open in its grey-squid flesh, sealing closed after they've jettisoned their screams. Some swallow the lava, while others vomit it back out.

Ludoldus stumbles as gravity eats the ground from under him; Grimaldus's gauntlet slams into the collar of his golden armour, dragging him back from the precipice.

'Gunships inbound,' the Sword Brother grunts as he pulls his lord to safety.

'It isn't dead,' Ludoldus warns him.

Grimaldus can see that himself. 'Not yet.'

They open fire. The crashing of bolters echoes from the walls as they fire down into the molten muck – remnants of the Sisters and the black knight squads, gathered in their bleeding dozens and standing among the hundreds of dead.

The dying beast has abandoned all pretensions of humanity. With thrashing, coiling limbs too numerous to count, the sub-aqueous, cephalopodic thing is revealed as an avatar of pain, manifest as spraying magma and steaming screams. It defies size, for it defies mortal sight. It is the size of a man's trapped soul; it is the size of a monster from myth, swelling and pulsating, abused by the thousands of explosive shells raining against its form.

Bolts burst inside its body, sending lava spraying in place of blood and flesh. Still it climbs. Metre by agonising metre, the thing of rock and molten sludge hauls itself up the cavern walls, seeking the lives of the insects that still volley their pinprick torment. They can feel its hate like a wind against their faces. It despises them for the sin of living. That hatred is enough to fuel its manifestation past the point of destruction.

It doesn't reach for them. It reaches for the cavern's support pillars. Wrapping round them. Gripping them. Cracking them.

Breaking them. One after the other, the monstrous soul claws its way from pillar to pillar, bringing down the cavern in its rage.

Nothing in the material realm can ignore its wounds forever. As the rocks begin to fall, the creature's howls turn to whines. The sacred orb, and the bursting wounds of so many bolt shells, rip free the last of its strength. It flails at another pillar, its winding limbs failing to latch on, leaving it thrashing and tumbling to the ground among the rain of rock. Boulders shatter on the cavern floor and the ruined bridge, filling the air with dust.

The knights and Sisters ring the fallen horror, executing it with blade and flame. Feeble struggles claim no more human lives. The thing collapses in on itself, dissolving, tainting the air with clouds of stinking vapour from its scabrous wounds.

There is no silence after any victory. A battlefield will still clamour with the cries of the dying and the growling flames of burning tanks. Here, beneath the earth, any silence is slain by the thunder of falling rock and the guttural rumble of the shaking ground.

The first gunships stream in through the sky vents. On the ground, knights and war-maidens look to the vaulted cavern ceiling, praying for each Thunderhawk that weaves between the plummeting debris. Stalactites drop in a torrent of earthward spears. The burning, rolling hulks of destroyed gunships smash across the ground alongside the monsoon of lethal stone.

A blow crashes into Grimaldus, the sudden crash staggering him. It was no rockfall: Reclusiarch Mordred looms above him, coldness staring out from the red eye-lenses of his silver skull facade.

'It is a sin most foul,' the warrior-priest growls, 'to steal a Chaplain's weapon.'

Grimaldus stares up at the Reclusiarch from the ground. Instinct almost has him launch back to his feet and throw himself at his attacker, but temperance prevails at the heart of the rock storm.

'I thought you were dead.'

Mordred doesn't reply. He holds out his hand, waiting with insane, silent patience as the world falls down around them.

'THAT IS ALL?' asked Ekene. The Lions were all watching me.

'That was how the battle ended.'

'So you earned the skull-smile through valour.'

I did not know the answer, myself. Mordred had always ignored the question when I had asked it, considering it meaningless. *The result matters,* he always replied, *not the decisions made to reach it.*

'I was one of the last still standing at the gate. I was the first to sense the change within Vinculus, and act with Mordred. I guarded my liege lord's life with the Chaplain's weapon, and pulled Ludoldus back from the chasm's edge.'

'Those acts look fine on a roll of honour,' Ekene said. The Pride Leader was no fool. He could tell I was holding something back. 'But I sense there is more.'

'There is,' I admitted. 'Nothing of drama and heroism. Just a moment of curiosity I have never been able to set aside.'

* * *

Only two gunships remain.

The first rises on protesting engines, whining for altitude as the boulders fall. One moment it lifts from the crumbling ground, landing gear folding closed in a clanking chorus of technology – the next it detonates in a heartsick flash of promethium fuel. Its wreckage, crushed beneath a toppled pillar, gives an animal-corpse twitch as its engines die.

The last gunship breathes lung-burning jet wash as it begins its own rise. The last knights run and leap for the gangramp, hauled up by their waiting brothers.

'The void,' orders Ludoldus, breathing heavily with his back to the cargo bay wall. 'Get us into the void, Artarion.' The pilot voxes acknowledgement as the Thunderhawk climbs higher.

'Grimaldus.' The High Marshal rests back next to Mordred, his weathered features in stark contrast to the Chaplain's cadaverous faceplate.

'Sire?' Grimaldus replies.

'You are the last of my knights still wearing a red cloak.'

For a moment, the knight hesitates, almost arguing that it cannot be true. But he stood with the High Marshal watching the survivors evacuate, unwilling to leave the field of battle before his men and their allies. He saw no other Sword Brothers among the living.

'That may be true, sire.'

'It is true.' Ludoldus turns to Mordred. 'I told you fate favoured him, did I not?'

Mordred says nothing, just staring with that skullish grin.

THE LIONS NODDED among themselves, sharing smiles.

'Not just valour, then,' Ekene ventured. 'Luck, as well. You were marked out from your brothers by fortune as well as ferocity.'

'It is a possibility,' I confessed. 'Mordred was a mercurial soul. I have never known why he chose me.'

'Or why he was told to choose you.'

'Or… what?' In all my life, I was so rarely speechless. That night, I felt my words and breath both catch in my throat.

Why he was told to choose you. As I was told to choose Cyneric.

'I meant no offence,' Ekene replied.

'None offered, and none taken.' I almost smiled, though they would never have seen it even if I had. My faceplate – Mordred's faceplate before it was mine – revealed nothing of emotion. 'My tale is told, cousins.'

'Not enough blood,' one of them said, earning agreement from his brothers.

'And yet another reason never to trust the weak little souls claiming inquisitor rank,' said Ekene. That earned another few chuckles. 'I would, however, have engaged the beast myself. Blade to claw.'

'Of course,' the other Lions join in, with good-natured growls.

I was starting to realise the informality in their ranks was not one of ill-discipline, but unreserved brotherhood. Curious, how two Chapters from the same gene-stock can be so different. Birth world meant everything to these warriors. To the Templars, almost nothing.

'So, cousins,' I said. 'I have paid your toll. Tell me what I wish to know. Speak of Khattar.'

V

DEATH SENTENCE

'Khattar.' Ekene made a curse of the name.

'Khattar,' several of the others echoed. They were unhelmed, their dark faces bronzed by the flames. As rank and file troopers, they seemed reluctant to look at me for long. I caught them making occasional glances in my direction, at my tabard, heraldry, or the polished silver of my skull faceplate.

'That was no war,' one of them said.

'Nothing but a slaughter,' chimed another, from the other side of the fire. Their way of retelling tales seemed be almost ritualistic. Every voice was equal. Everyone's story mattered.

Ekene was leading the storytelling gathering. 'I was never present at meetings of Chapter command,' he said. 'But I was there. I was on Khattar.'

'I was there,' the others chorused, in their low voices.

Around us, Lions patrolled between the hulls of the few remaining tanks left to the Chapter. The vehicles were worn down by gunfire, with smoke taint darkening their cerulean paintwork. Ekene and his brothers could have been spirits themselves, drifting among the memories of their dead Chapter.

'Khattar was a world of priests and preachers,' he began. 'Of followers and the faithful.'

'An Ecclesiarchy world,' I said. They did not regard it as interruption. Most of them nodded, and Ekene smiled.

'As you say, Reclusiarch. A world in thrall to the ivory tower priests of the Imperial Creed.'

'But it soured,' one of the others added. From the scrollwork on his shoulderguard, the warrior's name was Jehanu. He looked young, scarcely out of his Scout trials. Space Marines show their age in their scars.

'Their faith rotted on the vine,' Jehanu said. 'And they called for us.'

'The priesthood fell into deviancy,' Ekene took over, 'as so many do, in so many of our tales in this Final Age of Man. They prayed to the Gods behind the Veil, and their dark untruths carried the faithful masses away from the Emperor's light, spreading to the highest echelons and furthest reaches.'

Jehanu interjected again. 'You ask what could those priests have chanted to poison the souls of a whole world?'

Were the Lions mission briefings relayed in the same warrior-by-warrior retelling of facts? A curious custom.

'Blasphemy,' said another Lion with an amused snort. 'Blasphemy and lies, compelling enough to sound like truth to a society weary of their prayers going unanswered.'

The Lions nodded. I wondered how true that was, across the galaxy. The Emperor was immortal and mighty beyond reckoning. But he was no god. Mankind – in its blessed ignorance – worshipped him as one.

Yet false gods cannot answer prayers. How tempting it must seem to those sects and societies far from Terra to seek other answers when pleading with the Emperor brings only silence.

'Where were the world's defenders, I hear you ask?' Ekene showed his teeth in a feral shadow of a smile. 'The planetary defence forces did not rise up to purge the revolt. They joined it. And more were still to come: Imperial Guard regiments in nearby systems did the same – such was the ferocity of Khattar's blasphemy.'

'Apollyon,' Jehanu spoke up again. 'Apollyon was the inquisitor who pleaded for our support, for his efforts to crush the faithless lies had met with failure after failure.'

Ekene stared into the fire as he agreed. I could see the sparks of memories in his eyes. 'He had a Naval blockade, but nothing in the way of surface troops. So in the wake of his failure, we made planetfall in full force. Hundreds of us, Reclusiarch. We rained holy fire, sacred iron and true faith on a world that had forgotten the taste of all three.'

'Slaughter followed,' said Jehanu.

'What chance did they have?' another Lion, Ashaki, put forth. 'They were mere men, following the lies of false prophets. We destroyed them.'

'All of them,' Jehanu grinned. 'Every man and woman with a weapon in their hands.'

Ekene took over once more. 'We quenched the rebellion in a matter of weeks. No armies existed once we were finished with Khattar, not even a town militia. Nowhere on that world did a single priest still draw breath. With the armed resistance annihilated, we returned to our ships. Whatever heresy lingered among the defenceless population was under the eyes of others now – no longer a matter for bolters and blades.'

Jehanu barked a nasty laugh. 'Such faith in our allies, we had that day.'

'As with any cleansing,' Ekene continued, 'we expected preachers of the Creed to take over, shepherding the lost populace back to enlightenment.'

Ekene had been cleaning his bolter. Now he lay it aside, looking back into the fire. 'It took several days to recover our materiel, honour our dead, and prepare to leave. Apollyon's underlings worked on the world below, assessing the population of eight billion for signs of further deviancy. We were scarcely out of orbit when Apollyon's warship opened fire on the world below. The rest of the Imperial Navy blockade fired with him, targeting cities and population centres.'

'We watched them,' said Ashaki, 'spitting fire onto the world we had just bled to cleanse of corruption. Our honour burned with those cities. Every shot we had fired, betrayed as a waste.'

I remained silent, waiting for the rest.

'Our lords demanded the blockade cease fire and answer for its actions,' Ashaki spat into the fire. 'Apollyon claimed he had determined the entire population tainted beyond salvation. He even thanked us for our "worthy efforts, though they were in vain".'

'An hour later,' said Jehanu, 'Khattar's cities were dust.'

I took a slow breath, shaping the words to suit my reply. 'It is possible that he was astute in his observations. Heresy had clearly taken root through Khattar's society. Perhaps it had wormed as deep as Apollyon claimed.'

The Lions bristled. I could tell they ached to show their anger, but the skull helm I wore stayed their hands. That,

and the fact I could kill any one of them without breathing hard.

Ashaki was the one to speak. 'Are you saying he was capable of determining the taint running through several billion
souls in a handful of days?'

'No. I am saying nothing more than the fact it has taken
me a single heartbeat to see corruption in the minds of
men before, and a man in Apollyon's position can afford
no chances.'

'You stand with him?' Ekene was growling now.

Words came to me in that moment, Mordred's words. I
could have merely opened my mouth and spoken them for
him, as surely as if he were still alive, still telling me what
to think and who to kill.

*The innocent will always die when the guilty are punished. Is
that wrong? By what scale of virtue do we judge morality? This
is life. This is duty. This is necessity. We mourn the innocents
lying in mass graves with the guilty, and we move on. The blood
of martyrs is the seed of the Imperium.*

I said none of this, though it was as true as anything else.
Ekene took my silence as disregard.

'You believe he was justified?' the Lion almost snarled the
words. 'That he slaughtered billions of men, women and
children on the chance they were all tainted, and it is our
place to *ignore it?*'

Before Helsreach, yes, I would have said exactly that. But
no longer. *Balance,* I thought. *Balance between wrath and
wisdom.* I looked at him, still saying nothing. He seemed
to recall to whom he was speaking, and nodded a subtle
apology.

'Calm your spite, Ekene, for it is meaningless here. Apollyon acted within the rights granted by his rank; he did as

many of his Inquisitorial kindred would do. He also did as many Chapter Masters would have done. That does not make it wise, or right, or virtuous. It merely makes it real.'

'It makes it an effort to hide some filthy secret,' Jehanu insisted, and his brothers nodded. 'The tale reeks of a man seeking to hide some grievous error, does it not?'

'Perhaps. But if he had so much to hide, why summon a Space Marine Chapter? Perhaps Apollyon was merely a hasty fool to whom life meant little, and that mournful truth is one we have to live with. He is hardly the first man of exalted rank to decay in a position of power.'

'You are as cold as any Deathspeaker,' Ekene said, but the anger was bleeding from his words.

Cold-blooded off the battlefield, hot-blooded upon it. This is your place. More of Mordred's words.

'I will not pass judgement on a moment I never saw, between men I do not know. That is not my place. I judge my brothers – their actions and their souls – not the pathetic intricacies of Imperial Law. Tell me what came next. Did you fire on his fleet?'

Ekene shook his head. 'No, never. Chapter Command sent word throughout the subsector, warning all Imperial outposts and regional governors what had occurred and decrying the actions of the Inquisition. Word was also sent directly to Terra – a delegation of Deathspeakers and Warleaders chosen for the task, to show the gravity of the situation.'

'They never reached Terra.' I did not need to guess the fate of those well-intentioned souls. They would never set foot on the Throneworld. 'They were never seen again.'

'Oh, we saw them again,' Jehanu said, quietly.

'We found their vessel two years later,' Ekene admitted.

'Dead in the void, deep in greenskin space. All damage was indicative of a ruinous warp flight. No signs of weapons fire on the hull.'

I had seen the interior of several vessels gutted by warp storms. All life torn into genetic scrap; all metal mutated and poisoned beyond salvage.

'And then?'

'We kept demanding an investigation into the Khattar Massacre. We sent word to any Imperial officials who would listen, from planetary regents to the priest-kings of Ecclesiarchy worlds. If any such investigation took place, it remained a mystery to us. Armageddon called, and we answered. Which brings us... here.'

Jehanu gestured at the hollow armoury as Ekene finished. 'They want to silence us.'

'No,' I replied. 'Far from it.'

The Lions looked at me, seemingly unsure if I were making some dark jest. But I was not; the Inquisition were not acting to silence the Lions, and I was certain Julkhara had known that when he reached out to me.

'Then what?'

'They are using you,' I told the survivors around the scrap-fire. 'They are using you to make an example. The Lions are the most recent casualty in the institution's campaign to rein in the autonomy of the Adeptus Astartes. The Inquisition tolerates no attacks on its sovereign rights – yet you challenged them. And now all will bear witness to the price of your rebellion. The sabotages, the conflicting orders, the ambushes. A Chapter will not just suffer for defying the Inquisition and slandering its virtue. A Chapter will die in shame for it. Millions will hear of how you were killed on Armageddon. A mere handful will know the truth behind your deaths, and each of those will be Adeptus Astartes officers who will tread with much more caution when they deal with the Inquisition in the future. The lesson will be learned, just as Apollyon's cronies wish.'

The Lions digested this in silence. Eventually, Ekene spoke, looking into my eye-lenses.

'We are going back to Mannheim,' he said.

I had been waiting for those words.

'I know.'

'Many of the Gargants are gone, but it is still a well-defended stronghold. It remains a cancer of enemy presence in Volcanus's territory, and it must fall.'

That seemed idealistic, at best. 'It will not fall, Ekene. Not to a handful of Lions, no matter how noble and proud.'

He spread his hands in calm acceptance. 'Then we will die trying.'

Akashi leaned forward, adding his voice to his sergeant's. 'That is where we have chosen to die. It has to be there. Our bones shall lie alongside our brothers".

Jehanu nodded. 'Remember us, Reclusiarch.' His voice was low, and his tone plaintive. 'Take the truth with you when you leave this world. Spread it among the Chapters that share Dorn's bloodline.'

They were asking a great deal of me. If I did as they asked, it could all too easily draw the Inquisition's ire upon the Black Templars. Even so, they should have known they had no need to ask. Of course I would do it. It was the valorous truth. I could no more hide that than I could forsake the Eternal Crusade and retire to a life of ignorant peace.

'The truth will sail with me,' I vowed. 'And you are fools for believing it might not.' They shared smiles again; that curious tribal brotherhood. 'You mean to fight alone?' I asked.

'We must,' replied Ekene. 'Volcanus cannot spare its Guard regiments. Even with Mannheim emptied of Gargants in the weeks since the massacre – a fact we still cannot be certain is true – it is still a brutal target, rich with enemy presence. Five of our battle companies failed to take it. A few thousand Guardsmen will be nothing more than spitting into the wind.'

Ashaki snorted in derision. 'And we can trust none of them, anyway. The Inquisition's talons are everywhere.'

Ekene growled, little different from the beast that gave his Chapter its name. 'I just want one chance to kill the warlord that devoured our dead. I will die content if I drag him to the grave with me.'

I breathed the stale, recycled air of my suit's internal oxygen supply. It tasted of sweat.

'Mankind's galaxy will mourn the loss of the Celestial Lions.'

'Let them mourn.' Ekene's lip curled in disgust. 'If this is our reward for loyal service, they are welcome to their grief.'

Something in my demeanour must have warned him, for he continued more cautiously. 'This is how it has to end, Deathspeaker. Let it finish in fire, not in centuries of painstaking laboratory work to preserve our bloodline. We will die as warriors.'

Yes, they would. A hundred warriors, dying in glory... and denying the possibility of thousands of warriors who might be needed in a darker future.

As the stories and oaths came to a close, the unwelcome truth was that I heard nothing but empty promise in their words. Was there worth in glory, even if defeat was the only legacy? I had watched the Shadow Wolves die, and been inspired by their sacrifice. Now the Lions threatened to make the same journey, down the same path. But my blood ran cold, beating from a calmer heart.

A Chaplain is the future of his Chapter. He must guard its rituals and traditions and histories, as well as his battle-brothers' souls. It was not senseless violence that shaped our worth, but focused ferocity. Ferocity in war, when we killed our foes. Ferocity in peace, when we shepherded our kindred's souls. Our place was to make the decisions others could not be trusted to make. Ferocity was our weapon against ignorance or blind faith, the same as it was our weapon against humanity's enemies.

It was Dorn's way to fight no matter the odds. Death against overwhelming odds was no shame to us, or to any warrior of Imperial Fists gene-seed. Yet, those were lessons first taught ten thousand years ago – *those words again* – when the Imperium was so, so much stronger. The last centuries of this Dark Millennium had all but bled man's empire dry.

So I admired Ekene for his hunger to taste a glorious death, even if it was in a last charge few would remember.

But viciousness and glory were no longer enough. Killing enemies in battle was no longer enough. I wanted to fight the Eternal Crusade. I wanted to win the war.

Cyneric was right. The Lions' deaths now would be a disservice to the Imperium, no matter the greatness of their glorious last stand; no matter the heroism of individual warriors as they spent their life's blood.

Ekene was not finished. He cleared his throat, sensing the dissipation of my thoughts.

'One more thing, Reclusiarch. Would you perform the Heart's Thunder Dirge for us?'

The Heart's Thunder Dirge. I did not know the words, but I could guess their meaning. Among my Chapter, we called it the Rite of the Forlorn Knight, in honour of a warrior's last battle. A prayer for the dying. I felt my skin crawl, and my teeth close together.

'I said I would speak of your death. That I understand it. Now you wish me to bless your damnation? To give your extinction my personal blessing?'

The Lions were all looking at me, but now none sought to meet my eyes. 'We have no Deathspeakers,' said Ekene. He recoiled, slowly but surely, the way the Salamanders had recoiled from me months before in the ruins of Helsreach.

I was merciless, for I wanted to be absolutely clear. 'You wish me to give my blessing to warriors of another Chapter, sharing the Templars sacred rituals, and vowing before the Emperor and Dorn that your death is a noble testament to the Imperial Fists bloodline. You wish me to endorse your deaths. That is what you ask?'

'Yes, Reclusiarch.' Several nodded at Ekene's affirmation. 'It is a curse to die unblessed.'

'When do you intend to make this last stand?'

'What benefit is there in delaying the inevitable?' he replied. 'We will gather our resources tomorrow at our forward base, and make one last scouting run for supplies and survivors. The Lions charge to war at dawn the day after.'

The *Eternal Crusader* would break orbit the same day, in pursuit of Armageddon's arch-warlord. I would have to time this very well.

'Will you bless our last hours, Reclusiarch, and consecrate our final deeds?'

I looked across the foundry's junkyard, where Cyneric patrolled with another Lion, bolters in their hands. I rose

to my feet amidst their desperate, respectful silence. Ekene
started to object, to ask me to stay, but my mind was ironclad. The decision had been made.

'No.'

VI

CHOICES

WE COULD NOT return to Helsreach. The Season of Fire played its tempestuous games around my city, harsh enough to kill sky traffic but not quite violent enough to slay vox signals. The storm was predicted to last between three and nine hours. The former would be an acceptable flaw in the plan; the latter would leave precious little time to do anything at all. If the storm died down at all.

Aboard the *Eternal Crusader*, I walked the cold halls of the Temple of Dorn. Relics of war and glory rested behind shimmering auras, atop marble plinths housing rattling, grinding stasis field generators. War banners hung proud from the vaulted gothic ceiling. There was always something skeletal about the temple, and it derived from more than the arched architecture. I always believed it reminiscent of some sepulchral afterlife, where warriors walk after their deaths in battle. Legacies go there to die.

Cyneric walked with me, astute enough to know that

515

when I was silent, I was silent for a reason. He did not push me to talk. I would not say that I liked him then, but I was finding it easier to tolerate him.

In truth, I had not gone there to be alone with the Chapter's revered treasures. I had gone there to put plans in motion. From the great bay window, I looked down on the embattled, scarred globe of Armageddon. Its cities were smoking scabs. Its canyons were dirty scars. Its oil-rich oceans were graveyards for dead greenskin ships.

A lesser man might see a world at war, and feel sorrow for the loss of life. All I could feel was hate. I hated the greenskins for defiling our territory. I hated the planet itself for defying our attempts to save it.

A lesser man. There is the lack of humility that so coloured Mordred's thoughts. *An unchanged man,* then. A true human, one not altered by the Emperor's genetic designs, would feel sorrow.

The fleet was at anchor, relishing a respite from the near-constant void warfare that still broke out in the skies. No new alien reinforcements had translated in-system for almost a week – the longest ceasefire yet. Shuttles, gunships and cargo haulers drifted between our vessels – the final refuelling and rearming taking place before we left in pursuit of the alien warchief.

It felt as though I waited an age for my handheld hololithic transmitter to give a signal pulse. Cyneric kept his distance, paying reverence to the weapons and suits of armour on display, each one waiting to be claimed by a worthy warrior from our generation, or the generations that would follow.

'Vox link established,' came the bridge servitor's voice. Using the *Eternal Crusader's* communications array had been the only way to amplify my transmitter's signal. A holo-lithic avatar started to form, ghostly blue, above my palm.

'Colonel Ryken,' I greeted the flickering image.

'That is not the case,' the hololithic ghost replied, in a voice husky with flawed vox. Details of the soldier started to drift into resolution. It was not Colonel Ryken – as if the man's reply had not revealed that already. 'This link is not so good, eh? I have no visual feed. Also, forgiveness please, but Colonel Ryken is away doing other soldierly things. He is not here. He is gone.'

I took a breath, inwardly counselling myself to be patient.

'I need to speak with him at once.'

'As do I, I assure you, for the colonel owes me money. A serious matter, yes? If he dies before paying me back, my temper will be terrible to behold. I am Captain Andrej Val-atok of the Legion. How may I be of serving use to you?'

'Have your adepts relay this signal to–'

'What is wrong with this vox link? Mountain bears growl less than you, I am thinking. You sound like a Space Marine.'

'I *am* a Space Marine.'

'Aha! I am, if not good friends, then at least well acquainted with Reclusiarch Grimaldus of the Black Tem-plars. The Hero of Helsreach, you know? I saved his life one time. He even thanked me.'

'Andrej,' I replied, making every letter a slow threat. 'This *is* Reclusiarch Grimaldus.'

'Hail, Reclusiarch! You sound angry.'

'*Listen to me.* I need to speak with Colonel Ryken, Adju-tant Tyro or General Kurov.'

'They are all gone from Forward Command, yes? But I am here. I am overseeing the storm trooper divisions in the northern and western engagement zones.'

Cyneric approached, gesturing to the hololithic image in its trenchcoat and steel helmet.

'He is not what I expected in a storm trooper.'

I let that pass unanswered, but Andrej did not. 'Technically, no, we are grenadiers. Yes. But it is slang. Also, it is for reference. The paperwork is a bitch. You know how it is, eh? The only easy day was yesterday. But I sense trouble. That is why you summoned me, no?'

'Hear me well, Andrej. This is important.'

The conversation that followed took longer than was entirely necessary. Andrej, I gathered, was bored. Soldiers do not deal well with tedium, especially soldiers left in a command bunker with nothing to do and no one to shoot.

When Andrej disconnected the link, he had a wealth of orders to obey, and I was braced for several hours of coordinating Helsreach's defences from high orbit. A great many Guard officers were going to vox skyward for confirmation in the hours to come.

Time passed, in the voices of eighty-one Imperial Guard officers and eleven Naval captains. Images were inloaded and exloaded from my data-slate in a constant stream of encrypted information. My clearance was Rubicon-grade. No one hid their answers from me. No one in Helsreach denied me the lore I sought. No one refused what I asked of them.

'Is this not exceeding your authority?' Cyneric asked me at one point.

I was still unused to being questioned, and swallowed the rising bile of my temper.

'Elaborate,' I said instead of snarling at him. It took some effort.

Cyneric had removed his helm, and was unhealthily pale beneath the blue-gleam illumination globes mounted in the walls. His expression was not challenging; rather, it was subtly keen.

'May I?' he asked, nodding to my handheld auspex. I handed it to him, and he cycled through orbital images of Helsreach suffering another storm. The wounded central spire remained constantly in sight, but the rest of the city swirled in frequent dustcloud obscurity.

'Speak,' I bade him.

He kept cycling through the images. 'I was given to understand you surrendered active command over the hive city's forces when you left the field after the Battle of the Temple of the Emperor Ascendant. General Kurov is listed as active commander in the Helsreach region.'

And he had heard General Kurov two hours ago, one of the many voices heeding my requests.

'If you object to my actions,' I said, 'then say so without fear of retribution.'

'It is not an objection, sire.'

I felt my blood run cold at his passivity. 'If you are to be inducted into the secrets of the Reclusiam, I will need you to speak your thoughts.'

'The Lions will march to their deaths tomorrow while the *Eternal Crusader*'s engines are priming to fire. We will be gone from Armageddon in pursuit of the alien warlord, and whatever transpires at the Mannheim Gap will take place without us. But you mean to save the Lions, do you not? To force them to preserve their Chapter.'

I looked at him, and at the streams of bio-data scrolling next to his austere features.

'I do. You made it clear you believe their duty is to survive and rebuild their Chapter, as well. If you cling to that belief, how do you find flaw in my plans?'

'Their survival would be for the best,' he allowed. 'It is the path of the greatest good. But you do so by deceiving them. There is the question of honour.'

Honour is life. More ancient words.

'Nothing so crude,' I replied. 'My last words to Pride Leader Ekene were to refuse his request to perform a ritual, and to bid him die well among the bones of his brothers. There is no deception at work, here, Cyneric.'

Cyneric was relentless. 'But if you deplete Helsreach's defences to march alongside them at Mannheim...'

'The city is vastly overdefended now, with entire battalions sitting idle and awaiting redeployment.' An irritating truth; would that we had such a problem when the real war was being fought.

'And are you not playing on the people's regard for you? The Hero of Helsreach calls them to war. Of course they will follow. But is this their war?'

'They are soldiers on an embattled world.' I snarled the words at him, and forced myself to hold a facade of calm. He deserved commending for thinking of so many facets in this matter, not enduring my anger for daring to question me. Apprentices were a chore, and I wondered how often Mordred had struggled with me over the years.

'It is their world, Cyneric. And it is the only chance the Lions have.' I rested a hand on his shoulderguard, as Mordred had done with me in moments of quiet instruction. His eyes locked to mine, just as mine had locked to my mentor's so often, through so many years. 'The Lions' unseen enemies may well allow them to die in the glory they deserve. But you were right to argue with Ekene. They must survive. Their deaths serve nothing but to ease the soreness of wounded pride. They must not die on Armageddon. Without help, the Lions are doomed. But if I can take Mannheim…'

Cyneric was immediately on edge. 'If *you* can take Mannheim?'

I nodded, and handed him a sealed scroll case of black iron. 'Bear this to the High Marshal. I have always despised farewells.'

He tensed, jaw clenched tight. 'If you fight with the Lions, I will fight with you.'

'That is your choice.' I admired him for that decision, though it did not surprise me at all. Helbrecht had chosen this one well. 'But you will take this to him now.'

He made the crusader's cross, and went to do as I had asked.

Alone once more, I turned back to my plans. Everything centred on just how fast my former forces at Helsreach could break out from the storm, and redeploy halfway across the world.

VII

INK

Helbrecht,

I am remaining on the war-world. Someone must fight alongside the Lions, saving them from futile glory and the worst
excesses of their otherwise pure blood. I will rejoin you when I
am able. We both know it is likely to be several years, given the
whims of the warp, just as we both know my first prophecies may
prove right after all, and I will die on this world.

Forgive these words reaching you in ink on parchment, but
I have little time and even less inclination to hear you remark
how Mordred would let the Lions meet the end they believe they
have earned. I will not argue with you about which war matters
more. I see no degrees of import in this. The alien king must
pay for his transgressions on Armageddon, and it is the Templars' glory to be chosen for the chase. But these are warriors of
our blood. To abandon them is to betray Rogal Dorn, and the
Imperium he fought to forge.

Both battles matter, so we will fight both battles.

Months ago, I cursed you for leaving me on the surface while you earned all the glory in the skies. How times change.

Hunt well in the stars. I will do the same on this world's cursed soil.

If you cannot condone my decision, then remember this. The Lions have no Chaplains remaining, and they are our cousins. Honour and brotherhood demand this of me.

Honour is more than glory. If Helsreach taught me nothing else, it taught me that. Honour is loyalty. Honour is control over our baser instincts, mastering rage into the most potent weapon it can be, not spending it purely to earn a saga around the camp-fire, or an annotation in a roll of victory.

Honour is not bowing to the whims and schemes of fearful weaklings. The Inquisition has already claimed its pound of flesh. I will not let a proud bloodline fall into shadow to sate the end-less hunger of starving fools.

The Lions cannot call upon the resources of their hive city, but they will not fight alone. Let Volcanus hide behind its walls. Helsreach is going to war.

VIII
GATHERING

Planning with Helsreach's command teams took all night. I had wondered if the Lions would have already left their fallen fortress by the time we arrived, marching towards their last stand.

Dawn was less than an hour away as we broke the cloud cover. The Lions had not left us behind. The opposite was true – half of Helsreach's army had already arrived before us.

Unwilling to secure one of our own Thunderhawks, Cyneric had arranged for a Navy shuttle to carry us down to the surface. We descended through a sky cut apart by the contrails of Lightning fighters, with hunched gunships alighting on the landing pads of the Lions' ruined fortress stronghold.

One building – the crenellated central enclave – was plainly serving as the central hive of activity. Almost every other building was abandoned. Battlemented bunkers with anti-aircraft cannons stood in silence. The fortress's walls were pulled down, bent beneath the aliens' rage when they had first swept through the Lions defences in the hours after the massacre at Mannheim. But the final enclave still held firm. Four dust-blasted and paint-stripped Thunderhawks were nesting on the wide rooftop landing platform, marking where the Lions had touched down hours before. Dozens of inelegant, blocky troop landers were joining them there, as well as dusting off outside the enclave's tumbled walls.

Cyneric looked through the shuttle bay window, down at the organised carnage of an Imperial army making ready for war.

'I see a Baneblade,' he said, gesturing to a bulk lander – beetle-ish in its densely armoured shape – releasing a gigantic tank from its payload claws.

'The *Grey Warrior*,' I replied, feeling my voice thicken in gratitude. 'General Kurov is taking to the field.' The tank's storm-flayed hull was pockmarked and proud, so it had not been idle in the weeks since the war began to ease.

We wished to land at the central enclave, but the pilot struggled to locate an unmarked, untaken patch of ground, let alone a free few metres on a landing pad.

'Break off the descent,' I voxed to him. 'Get back into orbit. Be ready to compensate for the bay doors opening in ten seconds.'

Cut off from our brothers in the void, we were ready for any eventuality. The shuttle's confines were a testament to the fact it had been built to ferry a dozen humans in restraint thrones – not two warriors of the Adeptus Astartes in full battle armour. Our jump packs threatened to clang against the walls each time we moved, and we would have to abandon the additional ammunition crates at our boots, but no matter.

Cyneric struck the bay release plate with a fist, admitting the roaring wind. We stepped out to meet it, falling through the sky.

As far as I am aware, I do not dream. If I do, perhaps I simply never recall what takes place in the theatre of my subconscious, but the result is the same. Many medical records cite humans referring to nightmares of falling, ending abruptly the moment before impact. I have always found that curious. Humanity is such a fragile condition, fearing every imaginable loss of control. Nightmares of falling makes even gravity a psychological enemy to them.

Fear. The rancid piss-stink of it. I cannot envision a more disgusting emotion.

High altitude insertions are no rarity among the Adeptus Astartes, even without drop pods. We leaned forward, diving hard, plunging through the gold spit of tracer fire that had no hope of ever hitting us. Cyneric fired his back-mounted boosters once, to veer clear of an Imperial Guard hulk rising from the fortress.

Altitude runes chimed and flared as the ground rose. My engines whined into life a moment later, slowing the descent enough that it wouldn't be terminal. We landed with twin thuds, denting the landing platform and spreading a cobweb of cracks from each of our boots. The sky above us was alight with the whirring, revolving anti-air turrets automatically and harmlessly tracking the inbound gunships and troop landers.

With portentous timing, a communication rune chimed on my retinal display the same moment my boots ground into the deck.

'Reclusiarch? My lord... I demand an explanation for this.'
'So ungrateful, Ekene.' I found myself laughing for the first

time since the cathedral came down upon me. 'We thought you might appreciate the extra bodies.'

That day marked the first time I have ever been embraced by a human. Less than an hour after we landed, Cyneric and I walked outside the fortress walls, surveying the gathering battalions. Vulture gunships rattled overhead. The very air breathed with engine smoke from the idling tanks. Entire regiments of Steel Legion soldiers were packing munitions, and themselves, into Chimera transports and six-wheeled Shedu-class overlanders.

The man to embrace me was not, as one might have guessed, Captain Andrej of the Steel Legion. It was General Kurov – an otherwise distinguished and greying gentleman officer, who greeted me with a sabre at his hip and tears in his eyes.

'Reclusiarch,' he said by way of greeting. The embrace was swift, and surprising enough that I had no reaction to it. His head scarcely reached the heraldry on my chest before he stepped back, looking up at me. 'The Hero of Helsreach calls, and his city answers.'

My skin still crawled in the aftermath of his nearness. His affection made sense, in that he was born, raised and trained in Helsreach; the War for Armageddon represented a bitter homecoming for him, and he held me in a paragon's regard. Amazing, however, the difference in this meeting, and our very first. The levels of warmth in the latter, and coldness in the former, were difficult to align.

'It is good you are here, general,' I replied, trusting he would not be offended by my absolute neutrality.

Cyneric, sensing my unease, stepped to my side. 'I am

Cyneric,' he greeted the general, looking down at the man, and I heard my brother's dark little chuckle at the way Kurov performed the crusader's cross rather than the Imperial aquila.

'Such an effect you had on these men, sire,' he voxed to me.

The war council that day was a blunt and brutal thing, as our plans were ordained before a battalion of revving tanks. Guard officers crowded around Cyneric and myself, several of them touching my armour for good fortune in the coming fight. These I ignored, as I had ignored the embrace. Let them keep their strange superstitions if it would work to the betterment of morale.

'Did you bring what I left in Helsreach?' I asked Kurov, during a pause in proceedings.

He nodded in the affirmative, smiling to himself.

The plan was simple. We would march into the Mannheim Gap, and we would destroy anything that moved or breathed.

'I like this plan.' Andrej was sitting on the dozer blade of a gunmetal grey Chimera, thumping his ankles on the hazard-striped metal. His opinion was met with nods and murmurs of agreement from the gathered Legion officers, who stood at ease in their trenchcoats, helmets and gasmasks not yet fixed in place.

Ekene stood with me at the heart of the impromptu conclave, silent all the while. His anger was a palpable thing, an aura he bled in my direction. Only at the end did he speak, as if almost a hundred human officers were not nearby, and as if they had not just dedicated their lives to aiding his last charge.

'You overstep your authority,' he said to me. His helm's

vox speaker made the words a growl, though I suspected they needed little assistance in that regard.

'I do as my duty bids. Nothing more, nothing less.'

He aimed a chainsword to the horizon, where the mountains rose and his brothers' bodies rotted.

'This is *our* fight.'

I could have struck him, knocking him to the ground for addressing me in such a tone. The temptation was there, and I certainly had the authority to do so. I refrained partly because I did not wish the Guardsmen to witness division in the ranks of the Adeptus Astartes, and partly because I understood Ekene's rage; even sympathised with it. It simply needed redirecting. Now was a time for me to be cold-blooded, not hot. He needed guiding, not beating and shaming.

'It is still your fight,' I told him. I doubted he had missed the way many of the Guard officers had clutches rifles tighter or rested their hands on their holstered pistols, when Ekene had addressed me with such aggression. 'The difference is, cousin, now it is a fight you can win.'

He turned – ever so subtly – to regard the crozius maul I had over one shoulder. I perceived the true nature of his complaint in that moment. It was not that I had summoned thousands of Guardsmen to aid his assault. The humans had nothing to do with it.

It was me. I was the source of his unease.

'If we face the warlord...' Ekene began, and I silenced him with a gentle gesture.

'Vengeance will be yours, Lion. My duty is to get you to your prey. Honour demands you kill him yourself.'

'That is all I ask, Reclusiarch. He must die to a Lion's blade.'

'Then see that he does.'

I turned back to the Guard officers, tasting the charcoal and promethium stink of so many idling engines, seeing the ochre-on-grey tide of their trenchcoats and battle tanks.

'Speech!' Andrej called. Laughter followed this demand. I waited until it subsided.

'Not this time. This time, we go to war for honour and revenge, over survival. Such virtues need no speeches to enhance them, for they are inherently righteous. But I will say this.'

I hefted my war maul, sweeping it in a slow arc across the front line, encompassing every soldier, every vehicle, every supply crate.

'You have all heard that almost five hundred Space Marines died in the canyon I have asked you to conquer today. The number is staggering, it defies belief. Why then do I request that you spend your blood and sweat in a battle that has already cost so many of my cousins their lives?

'The answer, warriors of Helsreach, is not because I value your souls less than those of the Adeptus Astartes. It is not that I would waste your blood like coins of copper in a futile gamble. It is because you taught me the tenacious strength of the human spirit when my brothers bled for your city, and I can trust no other men and women to stand with us now. We answered you in your hour of need, and you have answered us in ours. For that, I thank you. We all thank you, Lion and Knight alike.

'As for whether you will live to fight another day, I will speak the words of a much wiser man. My gene-sire, the Lord Rogal Dorn, primarch and son of the Emperor, said these words: *Give me a hundred Space Marines. Or failing that, give me a thousand other troops.*'

I paused to take in the sight of the gathered masses again. This was a poor portion of Helsreach's full garrison, but given the complexities of orbital redeployment and transcontinental passage, it was a blessing to see so much flesh and iron under aquila banners.

'Look at your own numbers. By the war poetry of the Emperor's own blood-son, you are worth three times the number of Lions that fell at Mannheim. Cling to courage, no matter what madness awaits us in that canyon. You are here because I intend to win. And you are here because you *should* be here – you deserve, more than any others, to be on the battlefield the first time these relics go to war.'

General Kurov signalled to a Valkyrie gunship waiting nearby. The rear gangramp lowered on squealing hydraulics thirsting for oil, and three servitors lurched forward, bearing the relics of the Temple of the Emperor Ascendant in their cyborged grip. The first bore the great aquila statue on his shoulders, heaving it like a man condemned to carry his own crucifix. The second bore the tattered scraps of the city's founding charter high, the way a herald brings forth a war banner. The last carried a bronze globe of the fallen temple's blessed holy water. Mindless they marched, slaved to my will. How glad I was that I had left them in Helsreach rather than sending them up to the *Eternal Crusader*.

The humans cheered loud and long, raising rifles and bayonets to the cloudy sky. I was almost – almost – transported back on the city walls, as the green tide surged towards the city. *Our city. Our world. Our city. Our world.*

Grimaldus. Grimaldus. Grimaldus.

Cyneric's voice broke through the uproar of several thousand men and women chanting my name.

'I thought you said you would give no speech.'

'You have a great deal to learn about being a Chaplain,' I replied, 'if you consider that a speech.'

IX

MANNHEIM

ANY PARSING OF the archives on the *Eternal Crusader* will offer no shortage of detail on the events of the Second Mannheim Siege. It is fair to say, with the result so easily accessible, what matters most in this personal archive are the moments of heroism and humanity that led to the endgame. They are what I was asked to record, and I will endeavour to do so as my chronicle moves towards its conclusion.

What then, is thus far not recorded in the archives? All reports indicate the vast force and the exact regimental strength we hurled into that lethal ravine. Similarly, every report cites the immense force we encountered upon laying siege. Every hope we had possessed that Mannheim would be near devoid of enemy Titans was crushed before the first Steel Legion soldier had set foot on the loose rock slopes leading down into the canyon. Each prayer that the orks' infesting numbers would be culled by battles elsewhere were likewise shown to be wasted breath.

The enemy was present, and present in grotesque force. Great sockets in the rigging and stanchions along the canyon walls marked the absence of several Gargants, but many more were undergoing repair or reawakening after fighting in recent battles. The ravine was choked by living aliens going about their work, and thousands of mouldering corpses piled up into a sea of decaying organic matter. What foulness inspired them to leave their dead unburied? Was there no end to their pestilential influence?

Gold armour, darkened and soiled by waste, showed among the barricades of the looted dead. The dead Lions had been heaped in undignified repose with their xenos murderers, and their ceramite plate – useless to the junk-yard heresy that constituted greenskin technology – was left to encase the rotting warriors amidst their flesh cairns.

We advanced over this sea of the disrespected dead. Tearing the barricades down was not an option, leaving us to climb and wade and ride on the hulls of our tanks. *Grey Warrior* was the first to reach the mounds of the slain, its treads hauling its immense bulk up the corpse piles and grinding them into compacted meat beneath its weight. Lesser vehicles struggled manfully; others blasted holes in the dead-wall with their turret weapons; still others followed *Grey Warrior* and the super-heavies that led the way.

Above the advance rode the gunship fleet – Valkyries, Vultures and Vendettas, all flanking the four remaining Thunderhawks in the Lions' arsenal. The moment they streaked through the ravine's trench, cannonfire began to bring them down in tumbling fireballs.

Official chronometers cite the joining of battle with the first shot fired in anger at exactly five hours, thirty-one minutes and twelve seconds after dawn. That shot was a blast from the main armament of General Kurov's own *Grey Warrior.* From the Thunderhawk above, I saw that shot impact against the distended belly armour of an enemy Gargant, showering the nearby alien technicians with blazing wreckage.

Chronometers also cite that the engagement lasted a few minutes short of three hours. As one of the only Space Marines to survive the Second Mannheim Siege, I can confirm this is true: my helm's auto-senses recorded the same figure.

The Legion did not baulk at the sight of such a vast enemy horde. They ploughed into the enemy's disarrayed ranks, slaughtering them to make room on fields of their bodies for the gunships to land.

The first hours of that battle were remarkable only for their ferocity. There is nothing unique or worthy of remembrance in two armies grinding in a deadlock over their own dead. The Imperial Guard's massed cannonades devastated the greenskin war machines. In reply, the aliens butchered the Guard at every point along the advance where it fell to men and women with bayonets to hold the line. As is so often the way with the Guard, they had the stronger steel, but the enemy had the stronger flesh.

The orks fought for their mad religion and their even madder joy at butchery. The Guard fought because this was their world, and because they believed it was a battle worth fighting.

When human and ork blood runs together, the result is something as black and viscous as refined, thinned oil. By the third hour, each step through the canyon splashed in a river of mixed blood that had nowhere to run. The earth was too rocky to drink it, and the ravine itself was a natural basin. The land itself made a bowl for the blood we spilled in offering.

I saw Andrej, black to the knees, bayonetting an ork in the throat with two of his Legionaries. The corpse of their slain foe drifted away once they pulled their blades from its body – taken by the liquid muck. The smell of it, the sheer reek of the mixed-blood lake we were wading through, penetrated even Guard rebreathers. Soldiers constantly fell back to throw up when they could, or vomit where they stood and fought.

In such a grinding lock of armies, winning and losing is relative. We were pushing deep into the canyon, no different from a needle pushing into a boil and expelling the corruption within. But at what cost? Hundreds of men and women were falling face down into the dirt. Every second brought another crunching pop of a tank's engine catching fire and bursting its hull apart.

Andrej and his squad reached my side, using me as cover to reload their weapons. I killed the orks that reached for them, crushing the aliens' fungal bones with swing after swing.

My cenobyte servitors struggled at my side, too mind-locked to realise the efforts they were putting their muscles through. The artefacts of Helsreach were as filthy as its army, but time and again they rallied the Steel Legion to where I stood... whether I willed it or not. The orks seemed blind to the significance of my cyborged slaves, hunting only those of us who carried guns and blades.

Ekene reached us in the same time, and he turned his defence into a crude art of spinning and hacking with knife and chainsword, more like dancing than duelling. The Lion's armour was black with ooze. Breathlessness savaged his voice as he spoke through his helm's mouth grille.

'Do you still feel fortunate, Deathspeaker?'

'We still live, Ekene.' The chain binding my weapon to my armour was severed by a greenskin's axe, but I still held the maul in my hands. 'There is your answer.'

'And do you yet regret not sailing with your brothers?'

I executed an alien at my boots, caving in its chest with my maul. 'I *am* with my brothers,' I told the Lion. My voice was as rasping as his.

Andrej crouched in the slop, firing down the canyon at the aliens vaulting the next barricade.

'The Reclusiarch is the luckiest man I know,' he said with curious calm, not bothering to look away from the orks he was killing with beams of laser light from his hellgun. 'A cathedral fell on him once, and still he is here, to ask me to run into a canyon full of monsters with him.'

None of us could say more. We were separated again by the charging enemy tide. I saw Andrej sprint for a passing Chimera, hauling himself up the side. Then he was gone.

War is psychology and momentum, more than fire and blood. The press of regiments and hordes against one another; the ebb and flow of advance and fall back. Every battle between mortal beings comes down to a fulcrum moment, when the balance threatens to shift irrevocably. It is the moment the warriors of one side see enough of the wider scheme to realise they are losing. Or, rather, that they believe they see enough – they bind themselves to the belief that their side will be defeated, or has achieved an unbreakable advantage.

This can come at any moment, striking at any soul upon the battlefield. A moment of imbalance only occurs when the individual's actions inspire and influence those nearby.

It might be the front rank of soldiers fleeing an enemy

they fear to attack, or charging headlong in pursuit of their foes' broken ranks, against all mandate and wisdom. It could be the rearmost soldiers believing their lives will be wasted if they suffer the same fate as their kindred ahead, or pushing forward too fast and too far to reach the battle, preventing their fellows from attaining an otherwise sound tactical retreat. It could just as easily be a general viewing a rout from behind the lines, who waits a handful of seconds too long to assign orders of redeployment and counterattack. Or it could be one warrior, a champion, falling to enemy blades in view of his or her brothers and sisters; thus the champion's death becomes the fulcrum on which the battle turns. In another life, on another world, a champion's defiance turns a retreat into a killing charge; whether by deeds or by words he rallies his flagging kin.

I have seen every stripe of victory and defeat, always rising from this simple truth: war is psychology. This is the primary strength of the Space Marine Chapters that serve mankind. That they 'know no fear' is merely the truth's shadow. They devote their lives in absolution to training, training, training – forsaking all else in the quest for purity of purpose, in a life of war.

A front-line soldier sees nothing, *nothing*, of the wider battlefield. What he experiences around him is the entire reality in which he lives, and that is a flickering moment-by-moment assault of blades, shouting enemies and bleeding kindred. He makes judgements based upon these stimuli, and lives or dies by how he deals with them. This is why planning, communication, and trust change everything in war. With planning, you know where your brother-warriors should be elsewhere in the fight. With communication, you know how they fare as they fight away from you. With trust, you rely on them to survive and succeed, as they rely on you. Most important of all, you have eyes elsewhere in the dust, the chaos, the storm of blades and bolter shells. You know where your leaders wish you to be.

This is where Space Marines excel above all other mortal warriors. They live their lives in perfect trust of their battle-brothers. They possess more accurate and damage-resistant communication than any other human soldiers, down to the individual level. They are scourged of all emotion in battle, and trained to fight without concept of retreat until at last told to lower their weapons above the corpse of their slain foes.

This evolution is as much denial of flaw as addition of merit. Take a child, allow it to develop without ever under-standing the frailties of human weakness, and force it to grow through ingesting nothing but the virtues of obedi-ence, loyalty, and combat prowess. Surround it in ceramite. Arm it with fire. Tell it that it answers to no authority beyond its equally powerful, equally unrestrained brothers.

That is a Space Marine. Not a human trained to be a weapon, but a weapon with a human soul.

When the humans look upon us and cannot tell us apart but for the markings on our armour, this is why. We are hollow men by comparison to their brief, ignited lives of high passion and the weak, vulnerable frenzy of emotion.

It is not mockery of Guardsmen to acknowledge these fundamental truths of the Adeptus Astartes. It does the human men and women of our Imperium no disservice, nor does it exalt the warriors of the One Thousand Chap-ters to undeserved heights. We are the chosen, the Emperor's Finest. Those words have meaning, and these are the rea-sons why.

During the Helsreach Crusade, the fulcrum moment of so many battles rested on my shoulders. My knights would look to me for the word to charge or fall back; they would rally behind my cries, or withdraw at my silence. The human officers were reluctant to push too far ahead without my promise the Templars would join them; and most obvious of all, wherever I stood, the fighting was always at its thickest, whether I willed it or not. I hunted the enemy champions. I stood to stem the tide. But my heraldry drew alien commanders to me as often as I fought my way to them, and they would bellow their own inhuman names into my faceplate as we battled, so their brethren – and presumably, I – would know which alien champion was risking his life to slay me.

It happened again at Mannheim, though I did all I could to avoid it. Yet the fulcrum moment once more came down to me. The largest of the beasts, doubtless hunting me by heraldry, launched itself at me from the back of a bouncing, crashing truck of scrap iron.

How many tattooed, roaring warlords did we slay that day? An eidetic memory only allows perfect recall of the foes you face yourself. I cannot speak for the Steel Legion, or the Lions that fell in what may have been the longest three hours of my life.

Behind us lay a graveyard of tanks – practically all our own, all lost to enemy cannonfire. Lining the canyon's walls were the burning metal corpses of towering god-constructs, holed by missiles and tank shells, melting to slag in the flames of the Imperial Guard bombardment. Stubber fire rattled against our ceramite in a teeth-grinding drizzle, but scythed Guardsmen down in droves. Still we advanced, sloshing through the rising blood. It was knee-deep to most of the humans, turning all advancement into a sweating wade through filth. I wanted more of it. I wanted it to rise high enough to fill the ravine, and flood down into the cavern mouths, drowning any of the alien beasts that still hid below ground. I wanted to choke every living ork with lungfuls of this unholy fusion of blood from the just and unjust alike. Even the smell of it was wrong, like something alchemical and profane.

Before the warlord attacked, Cyneric carved his way to stand with me. His chainsword was a toothless ruin, welded into his fist by alien blood. His other arm ended at the elbow, severed in a ragged mess of cauterised meat and sparking armour cables.

'I do not know when it happened,' he confessed, utterly unfazed.

'Brother.' I wanted to thank him for standing with me in this day of darkness, though it seemed a war without end, perhaps even fought for unsalvageable pride. 'Brother.'

The alien overlord hit me from the side. I heard Cyneric's warning scarcely a heartbeat before the thing struck, and then we went down together, rolling through the oily blood. It was a thing of blunt fangs, sinewy muscle and hammering limbs – larger than me, stronger than me, faster than me. Even confessing that gives me shame, but there are beasts and daemons in this galaxy more than a match for a single Adeptus Astartes warrior. Just as I accept my gifts, I must accept my limits.

I made it to my feet first, the maul still in my hand, and laid into the beast as it rose from the muck. Armour bent and wrenched aside. Dark blood made a mist in the stinking air, but it was far too late to worsen the smell of what we were all breathing in. The thing moved as if immune to everything I inflicted, reaching for me with its great iron claw.

'Reclusiarch!' I heard a Lion call from nearby. 'He is Ekene's kill!'

From striking in anger, I turned my blows to guard myself. The thing was wounded, but what are bruises and broken skin to a thing that size? Kurov – of all the soldiers who could ever have been so foolish – joined me with a useless slash of his sabre. The brute beast aimed a dismissive swipe at the general, blocked only by my maul less than a hand's breadth from Kurov's face. Sparks rained onto the general's face, forming a cosmos of falling stars in his eyes.

'Back away,' I breathed, my arms trembling. 'It's not your fight.'

The general obeyed, thank the Emperor.

The next strike smashed me from my feet, for the beast launched himself at me a second time. Again, I was up first, casting about in the slime for my fallen crozius. Sure enough, when the overlord rose, he held my mentor's war maul in his grip. It was a cudgel to him, a pathetic club with its length of severed chain. I backed away, shame burning with every retreating step.

Las-fire lanced into the creature, going ignored against its armour, and equally ignored as the volleys scored fingertip holes in its flesh. One of the Lions threw himself at the ork, only to be caught in his leap and compacted in the monster's mangling claw. The warping of ceramite was the same plaintive abuse of metal that sounds out as tanks melt in chemical fire.

The corpse was hurled aside. I had my pistol, drained of all power an hour before, and a metre of severed chain forming a useless whip. The thing, in its hulking iron plate armour, stalked forward through the marsh made by the blood of our companions.

Steel Legionaries were charging in, shouting wild cries, firing uselessly at close range. I ordered them back, both because they could do nothing to this beast, and because it would be disaster if, somehow, they did.

Cyneric threw himself onto the ork's back, slapping down with his fangless chainblade. Each blow shed sparks, but no blood. The warlord gave a carnosaur's bellow and threw my brother away into yet another mound of the sodden dead. I heard something give with a wet crunch over the vox, and I prayed – out loud and with no shame – it was not Cyneric's spine.

'Emperor's ghost.'

Throne of Mankind's Master, the thing spoke Gothic. Not well, not with any grace, but enough to convey meaning. Because of their mangled jaws, I understood precious few of the greenskin breed. This one was levelling my own mace at me, aiming at my face, and speaking my lord's name.

No, not at my face. At my faceplate. The Emperor's skull-ish, eternal visage. 'Emperor's ghost,' it said. '*Emperor's ghost.*' It had the tones of a Dreadnought, freshly woken from stasis frost. I had no conception, then or now, of how a living thing could speak with a volcano's voice.

'I am the living will of the Immortal Emperor,' I spoke through teeth as clenched as those of my avataric face mask. 'And you will pay for your transgressions against the armies of humanity.'

It came for me in a lumbering run. I moved aside, ducking and weaving, giving up yet more shameful ground. Lashing back with my chain-whip was loud but fruitless, as was the gunfire poured on in spurts by the Steel Legion.

The las-fire became more sporadic; this close, they risked hitting me.

'Ekene...' I voxed, but managed nothing more. I caught the maul on the ninth swing, clutching its haft with every iota of energy I could burn from my aching flesh. The alien drove me to the ground, down to my knees, but to release my grip was to die by my own weapon.

The beast swung its other hand with a driving whine of overworked servos. No dodging the claw – it crashed into the side of my armour, breeding the same wet crunches I'd heard from Cyneric – and hurling me aside into the muck. My retinal display told me the same as the pulses of pain dancing along my left side. Broken bones. Pain nullifying adrenaline injections. Warning runes chiming of biological trauma and armour damage. I ignored all of it. Ekene's kill or not, I would not tolerate this vile slug to wield my crozius.

Ekene came between us with a leap and a roar, neither of which would have shamed the great cat his bloodline was named for. He held a hand back, bidding me remain away, and forcing myself to obey was a yield I could never countenance in any other circumstance. But we had fought this battle for a bloodline's pride, and here was the moment of reckoning.

Ekene beat his blade against his chestplate, staring at the greenskin lord in its powered suit of tank armour scrap. Despite the sound of the battle above and around us, I heard his words as clearly as if they left my mouth instead of his.

'In whatever underworld your foul breed believes, you shall tell your pig-blooded ancestors that you died to the blade of Ekene of Elysium, Lion of the Emperor.'

I did not know, not then, that Ekene was the last Lion still standing.

Would it have changed anything, had I known? I cannot say.

Ekene attacked. His chainsword was worthless against the beast's claw; he had just as little hope of parrying my war maul with his combat knife. So what he lacked in strength, he poured into speed – never blocking, always dodging.

The battle did not pause around us. General Kurov, half of his face missing from the descent of some nameless, artless junkyard blade, blinked away blood as he sought to reload his pistol. His bodyguard of storm troopers fought around him, spearing out with bayonets and firing in closed ranks.

I saw no other Lions nearby. I heard none on the vox. None responded to my hails.

Cyneric, with bloody slime running in rivulets from his war-plate, tore his stained tabard free with his remaining hand, moving to my side. Together we slammed through the greenskins threatening to overwhelm Andrej and Kurov. I beat one to death with my fists, and strangled a second, feeling sick, primal joy at the life dying in its porcine eyes. Gasping, scrabbling with its weakening talons against my faceplate, it died in my grip.

A hole flash-burned in the thing's forehead after I dropped it into the slime. Andrej, who had no hope of seeing my instinctive snarl behind my faceplate, raised his rifle in salute from a few metres away.

'Just in case,' he said.

'Do not do that again,' I growled.

Cyneric lifted his boot from the throat of another greenskin, a final stamp enough to crush whatever alien equivalent of a trachea it had possessed.

He chuckled as he watched it die. I have recorded elsewhere that what earned Cyneric his commendations to the

Chaplaincy were his other numerous virtues and fervent insights, but in this personal accounting I can confess it was then, in that moment, as he laughed at the asphyxiating alien's pain, that I made my decision.

His hatred was pure – what lesser warriors might call cruel or gratuitous, a Chaplain considers holy. Cyneric belonged behind a skull helm.

'Where is the *Grey Warrior?*' I called to the general. He was up to his thighs in filth.

'Dead.' He turned his ruined face to me. I could see bone beneath the flesh wreckage, yet he was still grinning. 'We'll mourn her later, Reclusiarch. Captain! How long now?'

Andrej wrestled with an incendiary control pack over a comrade's shoulder, thumping it with a fist to straighten its readings.

'One minute. One hour. This is broken, okay, general? That is the truth, I–'

A Vulture gunship laboured above us, its central turbine coughing as it chewed ork bullets instead of breathing air. The thing fell, flames already breaking out across its steel skin, and I pulled the closest two soldiers with me as I threw myself to the side.

As they picked themselves up, one thanked me profusely. The other was Andrej, who did no such thing.

'That was a dramatic reaction, I am thinking. Yes. Yes, indeed.' He shook blood from his hellgun, and prayed to its machine-spirit that it would still fire after being submerged in the muck. The scattered squad came together again, around the gunship's wreckage.

More greenskins were barrelling their way closer. 'Kill them,' I ordered the Guardsmen, and turned to run back towards Ekene.

A burning Gargant close to the canyon's entrance broke from its gantries, setting the ravine quaking as it crashed earthward. I felt the same bitter amusement that had gripped me as the Temple of the Emperor Ascendant came down in a hailstorm of marble and stained glass, but no laughter followed this time. The shaking earth bubbled the blood at our boots, and threw hundreds of soldiers from their feet. I kept running, Cyneric at my side.

Ekene and the warlord were still engaged, both bleeding from scores of wounds. The chainsword had licked out at armour joints and plunged into soft tissue; the power claw had mangled my cousin's armour each time it fell. He was backing away now, just as I had. Fighting such a beast was no task for one warrior alone, no matter the pleasure of pride.

Then came the electrical burst – a thunderclap like nothing else – turning the air to charged static. Orks and men in their droves cried out in pain at the sonic boom.

My helm protected me, though it chimed with alert runes at the sudden atmospheric instability. Serpents of lightning danced between my fingertips. The parchments on my shoulderguards caught fire. The air itself was alive with dispersing force. It felt as though I was inhaling the breath of another living being.

'The shield,' Cyneric cried, gripping my pauldron with his remaining hand. 'The orbital shield!'

I looked up, no longer seeing the mother-of-pearl distortion of the kinetic barrier energised in place above the canyon. At some point in the hours of melee, while I fought with the Lions, the Steel Legion had laid explosives at the void shield reactor. The Emperor alone knew when, where, and how. I had abandoned my delusions – and desires – of general command upon leaving the Helsreach in the hands of its Guard leaders.

No sooner had the shield imploded, spitting its static charges in all directions, than a powerful and priority channel vox-rune chimed loud on my retinal display.

I activated it, watching Ekene and the ork lord stagger around each other, wounded animals too proud to die.

'Brother,' came the voice, lifting my heart.

'You are still there.'

'For now. Not for much longer. Give the word if you require it, Merek. Just give the word.'

Helbrecht's name-rune pulsed, red, gold, fierce. I broke into a run towards Ekene, replying as I moved.

'Do it,' I ordered my liege lord. 'Blacken the sky.'

Ekene was down before I reached him. The beast clutched his arm in its mangling claw, crushing it at the bicep before ripping it free. He retaliated by ramming his chainsword in an awkward thrust into the creature's throat. Deflected by armour, it barely bit. His assault came at the cost of his left leg, as the iron claw scissored through the limb at the knee, dropping him on his back into the slime.

I was on the beast's back a heartbeat later, secure where one-armed Cyneric had been easily thrown, digging into the creature's armour with my boots as I wrapped my weapon chain around its bleeding, sweating throat. The chain garrotted taut, and my broken bones throbbed in narcotic-dulled sympathy with the creaking, cracking sinew in the beast's throat. The iron claw battered at me, shearing chunks of ceramite away. It staggered without toppling, gasped without truly suffocating. Even this – even strangling it with my last remaining weapon – could not kill it. All I could do was buy Ekene the moments he needed to crawl free.

He did. And Cyneric was waiting, a bolter in his remaining hand. The mutilated Lion reached up for it, clutching it one-handed in a pistol grip, and aimed it up as he lay back in the sludge.

I dropped back. Not completely, but enough to pull the chain tighter, adding my weight to my strength, and wrenching the beast's head back to bare its throat.

I heard the bolter sing once, and the kick of something heavy striking near the chain. With a muffled burst, the head came free, tumbling back over its shoulders and landing with me in the filth. The armoured body stood there without anything existing above its neck – still too stubborn, too strong, to fall.

First I reclaimed my maul from its fingers. Then I tossed the thing's slack-jawed head to Ekene where he lay.

The battle continued to rage, as the men and women I had led here fought their way further down the canyon.

With ideal atmospheric conditions, it takes less than two minutes between a drop pod's launch and the impact of planetfall. Ekene was looking up at the darkening sky. I did not need to, nor did Cyneric. The Lion's only reaction was to rise as best he could, and pull his helmet clear.

'Help me stand. I cannot meet the High Marshal on my back.'

Cyneric and I hauled Ekene up between us. While we did so, the vox link I shared with the Imperial Guard erupted in cheers, as Lord Helbrecht blackened the sky with Templar drop pods.

EPILOGUE
FAREWELLS

THREE EVENTS REMAIN to account in this personal chronicle, away from the battlefield. These were my last acts before leaving Armageddon.

The first, such as it was, took three entire days and nights. I memorised the names and regiments of every Steel Legion soldier lost at the Mannheim Gap, and etched them myself onto a pillar of black marble, erected in the courtyard of the foundations that would become – in the years after we departed – a new Temple of the Emperor Ascendant.

I wrote each of the six thousand, eight hundred and eleven names myself, etching them in gold leaf script onto the black stone.

The inscription above the names read, in simple Low Gothic:

> 'Their names and deeds will be remembered,
> always, by the Emperor's own sons,

And by the city they saved.
Honoured for their sacrifice,
And respected for their courage.
These words are carved by Merek Grimaldus,
Reclusiarch of the Eternal Crusade, Son of Dorn,
Hero of Helsreach.'

Among the inscribed names of the fallen were General Arvaley Kurov and Captain Andrej Valatok.

THE SECOND WAS the farewell offered to Chapter Master Ekene Dubaku of the Celestial Lions, escorted with his surviving few warriors onto the Black Templars strike cruiser *Blade of the Seventh Son*, with its course plotted for the distant world Elysium.

His bionic leg clanked on the deck, and he still bore a limp, his physiology not entirely adjusted to the augmetic replacement yet. His armour was the gold war-plate of an ancient Imperial Fists champion, granted as a gift from the *Eternal Crusader*'s halls of memory. His cloak was that of Helbrecht's own Sword Brethren, red on black, elegantly cast over one shoulder. I had worn one of those cloaks once, in a luckier life. For all I knew, it had been the very one Helbrecht had granted to Ekene when he forced him to take the oath of lordship over his depleted Chapter.

The honour guard ready to bid him good journey consisted of myself, Cyneric, and the High Marshal's household knights, clad in ceremonial colours.

'Chapter Master.' I inclined my head in farewell. Cyneric did the same.

At Ekene's hip, bound by a chain of black iron, was the flayed, polished skull of the greenskin warlord we had killed together. My name rune was etched into the bone, as was Cyneric's, alongside Ekene's own mark. An honour indeed, to be named on a Chapter Master's prime trophy.

'It should feel petty,' he remarked, his dark face showing a smile, 'to take such overwhelming vengeance on the site that killed my brothers. But it does not. Thank you, both of you.'

Cyneric's skull helm dipped in further acknowledgement, but he said nothing. I could not resist a last lecture.

'Vengeance is never petty, Chapter Master. It does, however, sometimes serve better to strike with the aid of trusted brothers.'

He made the crusader's cross. 'I will remember that.'

I hope most fervently, as time passes, that his efforts in reconstructing the Celestial Lions and training the generation to follow him are going well.

We will never meet again. Ekene is sworn to a life of defending what he can hold, and the Black Templars always sail forth to attack.

THE THIRD AND final event worthy of chronicling came in the very last hour before the *Eternal Crusader* departed Armageddon's orbit. I was alone in the Chamber of the First Proclamation, leaning on the guardrail before the great window overlooking the burning, wretched, priceless world beneath.

Bootsteps from behind did not draw my attention. Not until I realised there were two sets of them, and only one was twinned with the whirr of active battle armour.

I turned, to see Cyneric escorting a human, who walked with his hands in his pockets. Humans did not come here. I could not recall the last time one had walked this hall.

This one, however, seemed absolutely unimpressed, staring not at the relics, but only at me.

'Hey. Yes, you. I am not dead, eh? You can see this, so very plainly. Go back down there and scratch out my name, yes? I demand satisfaction in this.'

Cyneric turned to leave, abandoning me to this moment of acute discomfort now his escorting duties were done. Because of his helm, I could not tell his humour in this matter, but I suspected he was enjoying it.

I was not.

'You were listed in the rolls of the dead,' I said, which was perfectly true.

The slender Steel Legionary raked his fingers back through his hair, one eye narrowed in… I could not tell exactly what emotion or expression it was meant to convey. He seemed angry, or distressed, or perhaps amazed.

'Must I sing a song or perform a dance in this museum here to convince you I am not dead?'

'Please do not do either of those things.'

'No? Very well. I shall scratch out my name myself. Then perhaps I can collect my pay again, eh? They cease monthly credit wages once you are registered deceased, you know? Now I have a heroic name and no money. Your brother Cyneric brought me to you. He tells me you will fix this.'

The ship shivered underneath us.

Andrej's eyes went wide.

'No,' he said, as if one man could simply speak a single word and shift the tide of inevitability. 'No, no, no. The ship moves. This is unacceptable. If I fly away from the war, I will be shot as a deserter, and then I shall truly be dead. And,' he added, looking past me at the globe below, 'continue going unpaid.'

How could he be shot as a deserter if he was nowhere near his regiment? I did not understand the workings of his mind, and I was not sure what to say. So I said nothing.

'Stop this ship, okay?' He reached to adjust his goggles where they sat back on his helmet. 'Yes. Do that, please. I am apologetic for my angry words.'

The *Crusader* gave another shudder. Dozens of decks away, thousands of slaves were feeding the furnaces, igniting the great power drives. We were already moving from high anchor. The stars began to drift.

'If you run,' I suggested, 'you may reach a shuttle bay in time. I will vox clearance ahead of you.'

He nodded, a gleam in his eyes, beginning to back away towards the door. 'Yes. Clearance. That will be good, eh? Where is the closest shuttle bay?'

'Approximately two kilometres away, if you move straight down the ship's central spinal thoroughfare.'

He hesitated, and went bloodlessly white. 'Please be joking.'

'You may wish to start running, captain.'

He looked at me, shook his head in some subtle human dismissal I could not entirely gauge, and started running.

ABOUT THE AUTHOR

Aaron Dembski-Bowden is the author of the
Horus Heresy novels *Betrayer* and *The First
Heretic*, as well as the novella *Aurelian* and the
audio drama *Butcher's Nails*, for the same series.
He also wrote *The Talon of Horus*, the popular
Night Lords series, the Space Marine Battles
book *Helsreach*, the Grey Knights novel *The
Emperor's Gift* and numerous short stories. He
lives and works in Northern Ireland.